MARSHALL'S GUARD

ISABO KELLY

T&D PUBLISHING

MARSHALL'S GUARD

Published 2019 by T&D Publishing
Cover design: © 2019 EJR Digital Art
Interior book design © 2019 T&D Publishing
ISBN-13: 978-1-944600-21-1 (Trade Paperback Edition)

First printing T&D Publishing edition: April 2019
For information, contact T&D Publishing www.tanddpublishing.com

For my beloved hero and heroes-in-training.

1

———————

Why, oh why, had she taken this assignment?

Lieutenant Leia Ballore sat with her legs up on the security desk, leaning back in her seat, tempting fate with the sharp angle. She stared at the internal vid-screens without seeing them, her mind wandering. Again.

Not a great habit for a bodyguard to the Executive Family of Nas. But the compound's security system was the best on the market. Her charges were as safe as technology and human skill could make them inside this great steel castle. Her job did notch up a level if they left the castle. But lately, the Executives left the security of their home as infrequently as possible.

Inside, sitting in this dim room, with only the light from the screens and computer console and a blue overhead light to see by, she was free to let her mind wander. It kept wandering to the same topic, like a broken disk on perpetual replay.

Why in the name of the saints had she taken this assignment?

She was bored. She hated being bored. She never used to get bored. Then she'd accepted what was supposed to be a promotion. Now here she was, sitting in the virtual dark, staring blindly at the vid-screens and wondering just exactly how she'd gotten to this point in her life.

She shifted and adjusted a knob to her right so one of the hundreds of cameras in the place scanned a new pattern. She ran through another set of checks without conscious thought, then went back to brooding.

Her captain, Jolene, thought she was lonely. Leia supposed there was a bit of that. She was the only Belaxi for light years, and sometimes she did miss her own people. But she could date a Nasen if she wanted to. Maybe. If she ever found one who interested her.

She chewed on an already nonexistent fingernail. Lonely? Maybe. But probably just bored.

She'd traveled to Nas specifically to join the elite security force here. Belax didn't allow women of her…physical attributes the opportunity to join the military or any other police force. It wasn't exactly illegal, just highly discouraged.

As far as Belaxi were concerned, anyone who looked like Leia was too valuable, the type of woman men fought wars over. Why would she waste her life, possibly get herself killed, when she could have any man on the planet, more than one if she really wanted them?

That was easy to answer, though her family and friends hadn't understood. She didn't want to play on her looks for her lifestyle. She wanted to earn it. As old-fashioned as her dream sounded to her mother, it's what she wanted from life. A life!

She hadn't counted on becoming a hero and ending up with the dullest assignment on Nas.

The door to her left cracked open, spilling in more dim blue light from the corridor outside. She didn't look up, just kept gnawing at her nail, wondering what bothered her more. Boredom, loneliness, or homesickness. She did miss her mother's cooking.

Maybe what she needed was a trip home. A reality check. Time to remind herself that not all beautiful women were made of nothing but bones and skin.

She glanced at the box of chocolate on the panel next to her arm, sent at no small expense from her parents. She could hear her mother now. "You're too skinny. Eat, eat! You don't have anything left to hold on to. If you don't eat more, you'll be shaped like a boy before the end of the month!" Leia almost grinned.

The door closed with a snap, disrupting her reverie.

"You can't possibly know what's going on in this house," Jolene said, her voice sharp but quiet.

It was nearly three in the morning. For some reason Leia had never understood, everyone whispered hrough this shift despite the sound-proofed walls.

Without turning her head, she pointed to the screens one at a time. "Malia is sound asleep and Jax has crawled into bed with her. Pan is still working on that mathematical puzzle Ruana gave her. And Dev is having sex with her latest paramour which is why her screen is blacked out."

Jolene glared at the black screen. "Why the hell did you let her do that? Anything could be going on in that room. Our job is to…"

Leia raised a hand to stop Jolene's tirade. With the opposite hand, she tweaked a dial, turning up the volume on the sound monitors in Dev's bedroom. The small ops room filled with the grunting, panting, skin-slapping noises hard to mistake for anything but sex.

Jolene smiled.

Leia suspected her captain was blushing but couldn't tell in the blue light.

"However, with the volume down…" Jolene started, but her voice trailed off as Dev's raised in demand and ecstasy.

Leia lowered the volume back to its original setting and said, "I can hear what's going on just fine from where I'm sitting, Captain. I know exactly what's happening in that room at all times. I just prefer not to have to listen too closely. I've been listening to Dev's sex life long enough to know if anything unusual happened." With a grin that edged toward wicked she said, "Like Dev actually having an authentic orgasm."

"Lieutenant," Jolene scolded, but not before a grin quickened her stern expression.

"All is well in the castle, Captain. Nothing ever happens here. No one ever gets through the net. Nothing much to check on," she said, matter-of-factly.

"Nothing much to do but brood."

"I wasn't brooding." Her protest sounded weak, even to her.

"I'm telling you, Leia, you need a date. Now you're a celebrity, your looks won't matter so much. You can have your pick of men."

Leia shook her head. Jolene never had understood that Leia didn't care about being considered beautiful. Mostly. That was the *reason* she'd moved here. On Nas, her dark hair and golden skin tone were considered bland, her dark eyes too ordinary. On Nas, she didn't have to worry about the stares and attention she got just walking down the street at home. She was fat here. She was short. Her boobs were too big, her hips too wide, her waist too distinct, her muscles too dense, her bones too thick. On Nas, she didn't have to live up to anyone's idea of what she should be or how she should act because she looked a certain way. Here she was free to just be herself.

And for the most part, she loved it. Though, after three years of being considered ugly… Well, she didn't *really* mind. She'd expected it.

She shook her head. "I'm not looking to date, Jolene. I don't need a man hanging over me. And I certainly don't want an emotional attachment while I'm doing a job that could get me killed."

The minute the words left her mouth, she bit her tongue. Jolene was married and had kids. And Jolene still did a job that could get her killed. Her husband watched her go out every day to risk her life without complaint, because it was who Jolene was. But that didn't mean he wasn't scared a lot.

In her quieter, more honest moments, Leia had to admit Nex's attitude to Jolene, his faith in her and his ability to give her freedom to do her job, was one of the few things she envied about Jolene's life.

"Sorry," she offered, knowing the apology was lame at best.

"I just prove my point. If I can have a happy marriage, a family life, and still do this job, then anyone can."

"There are very few men in the galaxy like Nex, Captain, and we both know it."

"True. But then, there are very few women like us."

Leia smiled. "True, Captain. Very true." With the pleasantries and nagging aside and the checks finished, Leia assumed Jolene would leave. But her captain still hovered in the door, frowning slightly. "What's wrong?"

"You're being reassigned," Jolene said.

Leia's legs dropped off the console and her front chair legs hit the floor with a clank. "Reassigned? Where? Why?"

"You're being wasted here, and we all know it. The only reason you were assigned this detail was your media status. It was a coup for the Executives to get you as a personal bodyguard. But you're trained to do more than watch security screens all night."

Since she couldn't disagree, she kept her mouth shut and waited. With a deep breath, the captain settled her hip against the console desk and folded muscled arms over her flat chest. Like other Nasen women, Jolene was over six feet tall and so fine boned and thin she would have reminded Leia of a skeleton if not for the physical training she'd gone through to build up a strong layer of muscle.

"There's been a recovery," Jolene said after a moment. "Off Narik Moon."

Leia leaned forward. "Who?"

"The pirates got away. Again. The Recoveries were taken into custody. They're talking two thousand to two thousand five."

"They think it was Grettel's gang?"

"Who else? She's the only one with the means. No other group has access to a Kyzit family."

"Are they finally sending us after her?" Leia's adrenaline kicked once in anticipation.

"No. You're to lead a small security force to collect the cargo and return them here."

"Why not send them back from Narik?"

"The pirates sabotaged the bracers before getting away, so they can't be sent back without the help of an entire Kyzit family. The cub living in the Narik sector won't be enough."

Damn. Damaged bracers complicated the mission and made sending the cargo back more difficult. "How many were recovered?"

Jolene dropped her arms and rested her hands on the edge of the console. "Small cargo. Two."

Could have been worse, Leia thought. "And the Guain will be able to send them back?" Standard procedure was to clean away as much of the experience from the cargo's memories as they could then return them to the exact moment from which they were stolen.

"Maybe," Jolene said. "Depends."

Leia exhaled a soft whistle. "What happens if they can't?"

"There's not much we can do. Hope the cargo doesn't represent a major disruption to the timeline."

"Have the Guain given a timeline report?"

"They won't until you've returned. They usually don't unless there's a problem anyway." Jolene's voice was impassive. "Wouldn't want us to know too much."

If the captain had an opinion on the fact that the Kyzits kept so much of their knowledge to themselves, she didn't let it show. Leia leaned back in her chair again, her enthusiasm for this new assignment tempered. "Am I just switching bodyguard detail, Captain?"

Jolene looked away, her full lips pursed. "Yes. And no." She pushed off from the panel. "You leave at end of shift, back to HQ for a briefing, documentation and your detail. Vanian will be your second. You're on a transport by tomorrow night." She walked toward the door but kept her back to Leia when she said, "Good luck, Lieutenant. Safe journey."

The door closed with a click. Leia sat in the small blue-lit room, trying to decide if her life had just gotten better or worse.

Jake Marshall's life had definitely gotten worse.

The last thing he remembered, he and Matt had arrived at the station. He could remember climbing out of the beat-up police issue car he drove, discussing the case he and Matt were working on—they finally had a new angle to bring in Patterson for questioning about his wife's murder, the first break they'd had in three weeks. Both he and Matt were anxious to close the brutal case. It had been one of those cases, the ones that really got to you. And he wanted Patterson brought to justice.

The next thing Jake knew, he was here. He didn't remember getting inside the police station, he didn't remember being knocked out. One minute he was walking toward the building, the next he was crammed onto a narrow bunk, staring up at an orange light encased in steel mesh.

He blinked against the orange glow from overhead, trying to focus on something. His vision had been blurry since he'd regained consciousness. He couldn't decide if that was a bad thing or not, given what he'd seen of the place so far.

The room he and Matt were in seemed more like a rusted-out prison cell than a hospital room. They had small, painful cots to lie on, steel floors beneath their bare feet, a musty smell permeating the room, and a locked door keeping them "safe".

He sat next to Matt on one of the cots, too uncomfortable and disoriented to sleep. They'd been dressed in rough-cut pajamas made of some scratchy cloth, and around each wrist, they both wore wide, leather cuffs decorated with metal twisted into abstract and intricate designs. The cuffs reminded him of what an ancient gladiator would wear. They covered his wrists and the lower part of his forearm. While not exactly uncomfortable, he rarely wore a watch so anything covering his wrists was annoying.

The medic tending them insisted the "bracers" had to stay on. If they were caught trying to remove them, he and Matt would be medicated.

At least, he thought that's what the medic had said. The man's accent was heavy and unfamiliar, his English strained. Since the medic was the only person they'd seen so far, Jake couldn't tell where they were. Some Third World country in the middle of a godforsaken desert probably. Even the walls seemed to be sweating in the heat.

He couldn't think why anyone would want to kidnap him and Matt. They hadn't really pissed anyone off in more than a month. At least, not anyone who wasn't currently sitting behind bars. The only high-profile case they were working on was the Patterson murder, but

Patterson's funds were all tied up in legal knots so Jake didn't think the man could fund something this…elaborate.

"You think they're going to feed us soon?" Matt asked, not for the first time in the last ten minutes. "I could use a place to piss, too."

"Go in the corner if you have to go so bad."

"I'll wait."

Jake almost grinned at the disgust in Matt's voice. Not that he disagreed. He didn't particularly want to add to the stench in this stuffy, sweaty room by peeing in the corner. But if he got desperate, he was willing to take the option. He wasn't sure his pretty-boy partner could face it.

Of the two, Jake was the "camping, outdoorsy, only shaved every other day if he had to" type. He wore a suit to work when necessary, but wrinkles were a constant companion and the suit went into the closet in favor of jeans and a t-shirt the minute he was off duty. Matt, on the other hand, was always spotlessly dressed, immaculately groomed, and meticulous in his manner. He would no sooner forget to shave in the morning than he would think to piss on a stranger's front porch.

Matt was also the big ladies' man. Women loved him and he loved women. Most women were afraid of Jake. Could be the scar running down one side of his face, or his scruffy appearance in a town that idealized youth and beauty. Then again, it could be his manners. Matt insisted it was this last defect that really handicapped Jake.

Jake had had his share of affairs, but he didn't draw women the way Matt did. Not that it mattered. The women Matt liked weren't usually Jake's type anyway. Matt went for supermodels—and got them. Jake liked women who could take care of themselves and weren't always dipping into his pockets to enhance their own lifestyles.

He rubbed at the heavy growth on his chin, scratching thoughtfully. He had more stubble than usual. He'd shaved that morning—or at least he'd shaved the morning he and Matt were kidnapped. From the rugged scruff on Matt's face, he figured they'd been unconscious for at least a couple of days. They'd been awake and sweltering in this rusted prison for what he guessed to be about a half a day, given the pains in his stomach and bladder.

More than two and a half days. Was anyone looking for them? Had a ransom been asked for? What now?

The door opened suddenly, breaking into his thoughts, revealing a blinding circle of white light. Jake squinted, holding up a hand to shade his eyes against the glare.

A dark shape moved from the glare into the room. At first, he assumed it was the medic. But as his eyes adjusted to the light, even blurry he could tell the shape standing in front of him was not the male medic. A soft whistle of appreciation nearly escaped. Since he didn't know what the hell country he was in, he decided it best to avoid potential insults. But the woman standing just inside their dingy cell of a room was as perfect a display of feminine curves as he'd ever seen.

She wore a formfitting green uniform, decorated with gold lapels and a rack of ribbons across her ample chest. Her hair was pulled up in a high tail on top of her head and cascaded in soft dark waves down past her shoulders. Her face was shadowed and indistinct. He found himself hoping for a closer look, to see if her face lived up to her body.

She raised a hand to her jaw, setting two fingers to a spot just below her ear then said, "Gentlemen."

Her voice was husky and sultry. Despite his sorry state, the sound of her voice brought Jake to attention.

"I am Lieutenant Leia Ballore," she continued. "I am here to escort you to a holding facility where you will await return to your...homes. I trust you will find the new facilities more to your liking."

The note of disgust in her voice wasn't lost on Jake. So...their surroundings were distasteful to her, too. Good. That gave him hope for their new prison.

Her English was good, better than the medic's, but still accented. What country were they in? The lieutenant's accent was different from the medic's and still not anything he could recognize. "Where are we? How long before we're released?" He kept his voice calm and even, hoping his reasonable behavior would get more answers than Matt's earlier rantings at the medic.

"You will be released when it is safe to do so." She paused and turned to talk with someone just outside the door in a language he'd never heard before.

When she turned to face him again, his gaze narrowed. Something in her stance told him he wasn't going to like what she had to say.

She touched her jaw. "The medic has informed us that, due to your condition, it will be necessary to medicate you for the journey to the next facility. If you would please cooperate, it will make the journey easier."

The way she said, "please cooperate" left little doubt that they'd have an option to do otherwise. He snarled, against his better judgment, and said, "I'd prefer not to be medicated. I'm not worried about the journey being easy."

"I agree, ma'am," Matt said, his voice curling on the words. "We'll take a little discomfort. If you please."

Her shoulders straightened, a gesture that sent the high tail of her hair bouncing back over her shoulders. She motioned sharply with her right hand and a line of soldiers spilled into the room.

Jake sat straighter on the cot.

A low whistle escaped Matt.

The soldiers were all well over six feet tall, some had to duck to get into the room. As they stood, even in the dim light, it was obvious they were all women—gorgeous, thin, leggy women, with big round eyes and the most colorful array of hair shades he'd ever seen.

"I think I'm in love," Matt muttered.

"With which one?" Jake said, still slack-jawed at the sight. It was like being confronted by a row of Amazon warrior women, mixing excitement and a touch of fear in a man's blood.

"All of them," Matt said.

Jake looked away from the women long enough to catch Matt's expression. The open-mouthed, bug-eyed look on the other man's face would have made Jake laugh if he wasn't sure his own expression matched. Well, if they had to be taken prisoners…

When he faced Lieutenant Ballore again, she was tapping her foot, arms crossed over her curvy chest. Though her expression was difficult to see in the shadowed lighting, he'd swear a look of disgust twisted her generous lips. This time, his grin slipped through. She must get this reaction to her soldiers a lot. In fact, he'd bet money that's why they were used. Most men wouldn't refuse a guard that gorgeous, no matter what warnings their self-preservation instincts screamed.

Narrow eyes flashed in the dim light.

He raised an eyebrow. What did she expect?

He swallowed his grin, slowly realizing that despite the look of the soldiers, they were all well armed and competent looking. And he and Matt were their prisoners—even if Matt didn't mind so much anymore.

Ballore touched her jaw. "On your feet," she ordered, her voice losing the covering politeness. "As you refuse benefit of medication, you will be escorted under heavy guard. If at any moment I feel you are a danger to my Guards, the members of the crew or the locals of any area we pass through, you will be medicated. Do you understand?"

Matt nodded, not paying much attention to the lieutenant now. Jake grunted.

"If at any time, you attempt to escape or in any way endanger the lives of my Guards, you will be restrained and sedated. If you engage in any action I deem violent or motivated by intent to harm any person or persons you encounter, I will have you thrown into a cell to await your return. Do you understand?"

"What if we have to defend ourselves?" Jake said before Matt could absently agree to her conditions. They were in a strange land, being held prisoner for an undetermined length of time, by a group of foreigners he couldn't identify. While he didn't think they were in any immediate danger from Ballore and her soldiers, he didn't trust them. For all he knew, they would kill him and Matt as soon as look at them. He refused to agree to rules he might have to break.

She remained quiet for a long moment, staring steadily at him. Finally she said, "We are here to ensure your safety and well-being. You will not need to defend yourselves."

He opened his mouth to object.

But she raised a hand to stop him. "I will not hold you responsible," she said, "if the unlikely event arises that we are unable to protect you from deadly threat and you are forced to defend yourselves. However, such an event will not arise."

She spoke with such assurance, he almost believed her. He suspected Lieutenant Ballore was not a woman to mess with. And despite their supermodel looks, he was sure her soldiers were as competent—and dangerous—as she implied.

He got to his feet, nearly groaning at the stiffness in the muscles of his back and legs. He straightened his shoulders, rolled his neck until it cracked with a satisfyingly loud snap, and faced his captors. Beside him, Matt stood tall and composed. Even dirty, unshaven and wearing gray pajamas, Matt looked slick and handsome.

Jake didn't want to think about how rough he must look in comparison. He had an irrational urge to straighten his hair and tuck in his shirt. Not to impress the models. He couldn't care less about them. They were gorgeous, but they all looked alike. Matt's type of women.

Lieutenant Ballore, on the other hand, made Jake feel like a peasant. For some reason he wouldn't try to explain, even to himself, he wanted Ballore's respect. He wanted her to see him as the proud man he was, not this dirty prisoner he'd been made into by circumstance. He'd never wanted a shave and a wash so badly in his life.

"Gentlemen," Ballore said, the earlier politeness coming back to her voice. She motioned them forward, toward the door.

As soon as they moved, the Guards formed up around him and Matt. Matt was tall at six one, Jake even taller at six three. But the women circling them were taller still, enough so that when they emerged into the corridor, Jake caught only glimpses of his surroundings.

The Guards formed a tight circle, blocking everything but views of the floor and ceiling. What he could see was made of metal and looked rusted and poorly kept. The boot-clad feet of the Guards echoed in the narrow space.

His bare feet protested the hard decking made of lined strips of metal, the type that would allow garbage or water to drop down through the cracks, but he kept the discomfort to himself. From the corner of his eye, he noticed Matt wincing with each step.

They were marched down several empty corridors, past closed round doors similar to the one in their former room. No other person appeared. He frowned, wondering at the quiet. Were there people behind those doors? Was this really a medical facility with such unsanitary conditions and no medical personnel in sight?

As if reading his thoughts, Lieutenant Ballore glanced back over her shoulder, giving him a tantalizing glimpse of her profile, and said, "This facility is nearly empty at present. For your safety, we have cleared a path to our transport."

"Why our safety? Everyone keeps talking about our safety. But aren't we the prisoners?"

She turned back to watch the corridor as they walked, remained silent for long enough he was sure she wouldn't answer. When she did, her voice was quiet.

"You are not my prisoner, Jake Marshall. But there are those who would make you prisoner. You will have to rely on me to prevent that."

She didn't turn to look at him as she spoke, but there was a conviction in her voice, a note of honor he recognized. If she'd been an American, she would probably be a police officer or in the military. Maybe she and her squadron had been sent by the American diplomats to take them home. Maybe she was the friend she claimed to be.

So many questions. He could use some straightforward answers about now. For the moment, he had to rely on the lieutenant's claim she and her Guards were here to protect him and Matt. He had no doubt they'd been kidnapped. And this could still be some sort of ruse. But he was willing to take the situation a step at a time, to watch and wait. The best he could do now was collect information and hope he could find a way home soon.

Both he and Matt were limping by the time they passed through a low, round door into a room that looked much cleaner and better kept than any place they'd seen yet. The metal walls were white-silver and gleamed in the softly muted white light. The floor was smooth, covered with a thin purple carpet that led to another door. Two more doors led out of the room, one to the right and one to the left.

The door behind them sealed shut with a hiss of air. He turned in time to see it locking into place. All of the soldiers, except for the lieutenant and two Guards, dispersed through the two side doors. The remaining three escorted him and Matt along the purple carpet through the opposite door.

They turned left into a narrow, tall corridor, which necessitated walking single file. The space was too narrow though, forcing him to hunch his shoulders as he walked. Matt fared better with his narrow build. And the two Guards seemed to have plenty of room. Jake noted with interest, though, the way Lieutenant Ballore also sucked in her shoulders as they walked. His gaze dropped to the sway of her hips, the movement probably exaggerated so she could better walk down the narrow corridor, but the sight brought an appreciative rush to his blood.

Since seducing his captor was out of the question, he went back to studying his surroundings. The metallic walls and floor were a pale peach color, the carpet underfoot now a soothing pale green. The ceiling glowed with a soft white light that dispensed with shadows but didn't hurt his weak eyes. He realized for the first time, blinking in that soft lighting that his vision was clearing. The edges of the Guards were distinct now. And he could see more detail than he'd been able to in the cell.

Panels along the corridor flashed with multicolored lights and were marked with what looked like some sort of picture language—not Arabic, not hieroglyphics, probably not Chinese or Japanese. He couldn't place it, but since he wasn't a linguist that wasn't surprising. He'd ask Matt later if he could tell what type of writing it was. At regular intervals, they passed long, narrow doors, all closed.

They stopped once when another tall, slim woman intercepted them. This woman wore a black and red uniform. She spoke briefly with Ballore and handed her a small electronic pad.

Ballore stood silent for a moment, then nodded and gave a low response.

The woman flicked a look at him and Matt. Her pale face flushed pink. She turned and all but ran away down the corridor.

They must look really grungy, Jake thought as Ballore started walking again. The poor woman had looked terrified, despite having three or four inches on him.

A deep rumbling vibrated up through his bare feet, like the sound of engines coming to life. After a moment, the rumbling increased to a higher pitch, then dropped away to a background murmur. If he'd had on boots, he was sure he wouldn't even notice the noise. His stomach lifted, like the sensation when a plane took off, but gentler. He didn't feel pressed back by g-forces or even the sharp jolt of sudden assent. But they were moving.

"This is your transport?" He continued studying the corridor, not expecting an answer.

The lieutenant surprised him with one. "This is the *Persephone*. She is the lead ship in House Devonian's fleet. This ship is sent only for the most highly ranked dignitaries and visitors."

"I'm flattered." He wondered briefly if she understood sarcasm.

She flashed him a slit-eyed look over her shoulder, telling him clearly she did. But that flash, his first clear look at her face even in profile, stopped him in his tracks. Wow. Her eyes were a dark brown, fringed by thick lashes. Her cheekbones were high and sharp, her mouth generously heart-shaped. Her tan skin was smooth with just a hint of pink in her cheeks, probably from her annoyance with him.

She was as beautiful as any woman he'd ever seen. And for a beat, all he could do was stare at the back of her head, at the sassy swing of her hair and the generous curves of her hips.

This woman could make him completely forget his situation.

2

———————————

Jake blinked when their escort stopped outside a door, feeling like he'd come out of a trance. Ballore swiped her palm over a blue panel next to the door. The panel turned green and she stood back to allow them entrance.

The full impact of her took his breath.

She stood maybe five foot eight or nine, short compared to the others but still a tall woman. Her figure, now that he could see more clearly, was as curvy and generous as it had looked in the dim orange light of his cell. The contrast between soft golden skin and her dark dark eyes left him speechless, his mouth dry.

Matt pushed past him into the room, accompanied by the other two Guards.

Jake didn't follow. He couldn't look away from the stunning woman before him. A part of him heard Matt say, "So, ladies, how long have you been in this line of work?" He recognized the tone. Matt was turning on his charm. Jake couldn't care less because Lieutenant Leia Ballore was staring back at him.

For a heartbeat, he couldn't think beyond the temptation of her full lips, the promise of her soft body. He swallowed hard. Opened his mouth to speak. Swallowed again. This was ridiculous. He wasn't a teenager. She wasn't the first beautiful woman he'd ever met. Hell, so far every woman on this ship was gorgeous. And Matt introduced him to a string of gorgeous women on a regular basis.

But something about Leia Ballore hit him right between the eyes, interesting a lower part of him, as well. When he realized his lungs were burning, he sucked in a deep breath. To his surprise, she dropped her gaze and a light pink tinted her cheeks. He hid a smile by rubbing a hand over his stubble-roughened jaw.

The scratchy texture reminded him of how he must look. The scar running across his left cheek no doubt stood out in sharp relief against the black of his beard. He didn't want to think what he must smell like. No wonder she was staring—probably shocked by what a dirty animal she'd let walk into her pristine world.

"Don't suppose there's a place in there where I can wash up?" he said, refusing to look away when her gaze jumped back to his. "I could use a shave."

"Why?" she asked in a tone of wonder. Then she blinked, frowning and looking surprised by her own comment. She murmured something under her breath in the language she used with the soldiers.

The confusion creasing her brow relaxed him. His stink didn't seem to offend her. Maybe she didn't have a sense of smell. He grinned, a little self-conscious as she stared at him.

She tapped her jaw, a gesture that looked nervous, and said, "Sorry. Yes, there is a place to wash inside. You will be provided with fresh clothing as well."

"And a razor?"

Her eyes widened, then her gaze turned inward. After a moment, she took a deep breath and said, "Ah, yes, there will be an…electric razor in the…bathroom." She grinned, as if proud of herself. Maybe her English wasn't as good as he thought.

"Thanks." Reluctantly, he turned to inspect the room he and Matt had been given.

He stepped into a large room, the ceilings higher than the corridor, the metal walls the same shade of pale peach. The floor was a darker shade of pink, covered by patterned rugs in blue, white, pink, orange and green. A huge purple cushioned couch took up one whole wall. Above the wall hung a painting designed to look like a window opening out to the stars. He stared for a minute. The painting was stunningly realistic. He could almost imagine he was moving through space.

As he studied the painting, he wondered what kind of vessel they were on. The space felt huge for an airplane. Ballore had called it a ship. But if it was a ship or yacht of some kind, why couldn't he feel the roll of water? Maybe a very large ship. Hell, for all he knew they were on a submarine, though the cleanest, most pastel submarine he'd ever seen. And despite the narrow corridors, the room was so large and had such a high ceiling they'd have to be on one of the biggest subs he'd ever heard of. He'd yet to get a look outside. He wondered what time it was. The star painting made him assume it was the middle of the night.

"Is it night or day?" he asked Ballore. She'd followed him into the room and hung just behind his right shoulder as he inspected the plush surroundings.

"We're in the evening quarter. The shifts change and an evening meal will be served in…one hour."

His stomach grumbled loudly at the mention of food. He half turned, cast her a wry grin. "Will we be able to leave the room to eat or will something be brought here?" He hoped to god they'd be fed soon no matter what way they planned on serving them. He was starving.

She flashed him a dazzling, genuine grin. "We'll have food brought up right away. Tagh was afraid to feed you until after the…drugs you were given wore off. Now, you should be able to keep your dinner where it belongs."

Tagh must have been the medic. Jake nodded his thanks and turned back to inspecting the room. A minute passed before he realized she hadn't answered his question exactly, but she planned on feeding them. At the moment, that was all he cared about.

The rest of the room was sparsely furnished—a small white table fixed to the pink tiled floor, a long vine of some sort of blue-leaved plant crawled across the ceiling, giving the room's light a faintly bluish cast, what looked to be a computer console against the wall to his right next to a sealed door, two more doors to his left. He heard Matt's voice from behind one of the closed doors and assumed it was a bedroom. Matt sounded at his charming best if the feminine laughter was any indication. Jake shook his head and turned back to the lieutenant.

"Does it meet with your satisfaction, Jake Marshall?" Her hand hovered below her ear, at her jaw again.

He wondered if she even realized she made the nervous gesture whenever she spoke. "This is great. Lots better than the hospital room."

"The washing facilities are to the right. I will have to ask that you please do not try to remove the bracers." She nodded to his wrists. "I understand Tagh emphasized their importance. I must echo his warning. Do not attempt to remove them. Do not..." She frowned. "Mess? Do not mess with them. Please."

He couldn't help fingering the bracers, tracing the line of decorative metal. "What are they?"

"They are..." She paused. Her brow creased, her lips pursed. Then her eyes widened. "They are medical devices," she said firmly, bobbing her head. "They will prevent you from contracting any foreign viruses. The drug weakened your system."

She was lying. That suspicious pause, her inability to make eye contact, the way she tried not to fidget but still fisted and relax her hand in a nervous tick gave her away. He'd done too many interviews to be fooled by her story. She wanted him to keep the leather bracelets on badly enough to lie about their purpose. So what were they really? Both she and the medic warned him against tampering with them. A tracking device maybe?

He wouldn't have been able to resist investigating the bracers, if Leia hadn't picked that moment to step closer, look him right in the eyes and say, "Please. Please, do not tamper with them. It could cost you your life."

How was he supposed to resist the plea in her voice, the concern in her eyes? In that moment, if it meant making Leia Ballore happy, he'd wear the blasted bracers for the rest of his life. "I won't mess with them. But will it hurt to get them wet in the shower? I'm not going to electrocute myself or anything?"

She puffed out a loud breath and smiled. "No, they will not react with water."

He had the most irrational urge to touch her cheek. To run his fingers over skin that looked unbelievably soft. He'd never reacted this way to a woman before. Instant fascination. A need to touch that nearly overrode his need for food and a bath. He wanted to cause many more smiles like the one she gave him now. His expression must have given something away because she dropped her gaze and took a step back.

She raised her voice, calling to the other two guards. They came into the main room quickly, standing at attention before the lieutenant. She spoke in her own language, and they left without a backward glance.

Matt sauntered out of the room, a satisfied smirk on his face. When he laid eyes on Leia, he stopped in his tracks. "Well, Lieutenant. It's a pleasure to finally see you face-to-face."

Ballore raised a brow, her expression bemused as she touched her jaw. "As you say, Matthew Donnelly." Her lips quirked in a little half smile. "Dinner will arrive shortly. When you have rested and washed, send for me and I will arrange for a...debriefing? Debriefing session. Gentlemen."

She turned and followed her soldiers from the room.

Matt whistled long and low. "I think I'm in heaven. Even the least attractive woman here is gorgeous."

"They're all too skinny," Jake said without thinking. He was still watching the door through which Leia Ballore had left.

"The lieutenant isn't too skinny."

Jake rounded on the sly note in Matt's voice. He glared at his partner's grin. "And your point?"

"No point. I just think the lieutenant has a nice set of curves. Maybe too curvy for my taste, but that face more than makes up for a little fat, don't you think?"

"She's not fat." Jake scowled at the floor and wondered what was worse, feeling like he needed to defend Leia, or jealousy that she might fall for his partner's renowned charms. Ignoring Matt's smirk, he turned toward the bathroom door. "I'm taking a shower. Call me when the food arrives." He ground his teeth as Matt's chuckle followed him through the door.

Leia detoured to her quarters to catch her breath and regain her balance. She needed time alone to slow her heartbeat. Her pulse beat against her temples like she'd run a ten-kilometer race in heavy gravity. There was no way she could face her squadron or the *Persephone* crew in her current state.

Saints but Jake Marshall was handsome. She hadn't seen a man so absolutely gorgeous in years. And that scar on his cheek! It gave him the perfect balance of warrior menace and rugged competence. A man with a face scar had lived life well and survived to recount the battles. He was, in her opinion, an ideal man.

Part of her planet's culture dictated a boy wasn't considered a man until he had some sort of battle scar. Her people considered facial scars the most attractive, masculine of scars. And Jake Marshall oozed masculinity.

She pressed her hands to her flushed cheeks as she moved down the cool corridor. If she could just reach her cabin before she passed anyone, she'd be able to compose herself.

Marshall had seemed handsome even in the ugly orange light of the cell. But then they always were. Grettel only snatched the best. His friend, Matthew Donnelly, had the pretty look that would sell well on Hrokwall or to clients with more...peculiar tastes. But Jake Marshall was another kind of man. Even slouching on that filthy cot in the rusted, sweltering cell of a room, he had the sort of primitive male aura that would bring a small fortune on any of a dozen planets, outposts and deep space stations.

She hadn't gotten a really good look at him, though, until they finally boarded the ship and she faced him fully in the well-lit corridor outside his quarters. That first look nearly knocked the breath from her.

Hard blue eyes and thick black hair, a strong jaw and firm mouth.

The rough beard stubble on his face just menacing enough to send a tremor through her. He was pure, unadulterated male. Dangerous and beautiful.

And he was cargo she had to return.

She pressed her palm to the lock screen at the door to her small cabin, waited for the air seal to release before pulling back her hand. The door slid upward into the ceiling, letting her pass into the well-lit single room that was hers for the journey. She sealed the door behind her and leaned against the cool metal, taking a deep breath.

She'd been sent to protect Jake Marshall, keep him as isolated as possible, and send him back to his own time. Hopefully with little memory of this place. Sampling the merchandise was not allowed. She suspected if Jolene had known the cargo involved a man like Marshall, she'd have made sure a Nasen commanded this recovery. Nasen women didn't find men like Marshall quite as irresistible as Belaxi women. To Leia, he was perfect.

Unfortunately.

She tapped her head against the door in a steady, chiding rhythm. This wasn't good. She couldn't fall for someone like Jake Marshall. Even if it wasn't taboo, even if it wasn't immoral and unethical, she knew nothing could come of an affair. He'd be gone as soon as they could send him back. So seducing him would not only be a direct violation of her oaths as a Guard, it would be supremely stupid.

And Leia Ballore was not a stupid woman.

She hoped he wouldn't look too clean-cut once he shaved. Maybe he'd leave some of the stubble. Just the thought of the abrasive rub of his face against her skin made her shiver.

She groaned. She'd been on Nas with its thin, smooth-skinned men far too long. Too few had facial scars or beard stubble. They didn't have that edge of menace Belaxi women really loved.

Still, maybe Jolene had been right. Leia should have dated more. Three years of celibacy, three years of not even spending social time with a man, what did she expect? She was bound to react strongly to the first really handsome man she'd seen in ages.

But she couldn't touch. Not Marshall. Seducing him went against every rule, every code of conduct drilled into her for the last three years. She endangered her commission, her reputation with the Nas Guard, her honor if she tampered with one of the cargo.

Time-theft men were kidnapped from their own eras, sold into slavery—sexual or otherwise—for the profit of pirates and the amusement of the callous and sadistic. Those kidnapped rarely survived the experience for more than a year. And even if they did survive, the danger of the bracers being removed either by accident or design increased exponentially. Removing the bracers created a number of very unpleasant reactions for those displaced in time. The best a man could hope for was to be sucked back into his time with some shred of sanity left. The worst... She shivered. She didn't like to think of the worst.

These men were human beings. So few came out of both the shock of truth and the rigors of slavery with much spirit or sanity left. The ones who could be rescued deserved to be treated with respect.

And it was her job to give them that respect.

If she seduced Jake Marshall, she would be admitting on some level she approved of time-theft slavery. She couldn't allow herself to give in to the allure of a primitive male. As much for her sake as his. She'd worked too hard, sacrificed her home planet, her family, her people to become a Nas Guard. She refused to throw it all away for a brief fling with a man who wouldn't even remember her after he returned to his own time.

There were plenty of handsome men in the universe. She would just have to forget that Jake Marshall was by far the sexiest and most appealing man she'd ever seen. She had to remain in control of her desires. No matter how hard that might seem.

She pushed away from her cabin door. They'd received a distress message from a Nas freighter before making the jump to hyperspace. The *Persephone* was the only ship close enough to help so they were detouring to aid the freighter, despite Leia's misgivings. The *Persephone* captain refused to leave the freighter floundering longer than necessary. So Leia and her squad had to secure Jake and Matthew, keeping them isolated from the new people about to be brought aboard.

Preparations were needed, security measures had to be heightened. She couldn't afford to hide in her room and hope the trip went well.

She made a quick detour to the washroom to splash cold water on her face. When she felt in full control, she straightened the tunic of her uniform, studied her face in the mirror. She looked solid and in command. With a sharp nod at her reflection, she left the small room.

She had cargo to deliver.

JAKE STARED FOR A LONG TIME AT WHAT HE ASSUMED TO BE THE shower. How the hell did the thing work? He'd found an electric razor on a shelf beneath a mirror to one side of the washroom. Given the length of his beard, he would have preferred a wet shave, but anything was better than letting the scruff get thicker and itchier. When he'd finished, his skin felt dry but cleansed.

Now he needed a shower to finish the job. The question was, how to get the damned thing to work. He couldn't see taps or temperature controls, and what he took to be the nozzle looked more like an ornamental hanger. There didn't even look to be a drain in the floor. He had a vision of flooding the place and would have laughed if he had the energy.

Since he'd already stripped off the scratchy gray pajamas, and had no intention of putting them on again, he took a chance. Maybe the shower was one of those sensor-activated thingies and he just had to step under the hanger. He held his breath against the potential of a flood of cold water and stepped up onto the raised platform under the nozzle.

For the space of a heartbeat, nothing happened. He let his breath out in a whoosh of frustration. And then the water started to flow.

The deluge was warm and strong, massaging as it cleaned. He groaned and let his head fall forward as the stream beat down his back. He didn't find any soap so he settled for rubbing his hands over his skin. The water running onto the platform turned brown from the dirt. The platform itself seemed to soak up the water like a sponge. And despite the lack of a shower curtain to keep the spray in, the area outside the raised platform remained dry.

Nice, he thought. But he could use some soap. He'd have to stand here for hours to get the grime off this way.

As if in answer to his thought, the color and texture of the water changed. The room filled with a musky, clean scent and a rich lather built up where he rubbed his skin. The soap spray was a pearly green color and felt slippery like the soap pressed out of a hand dispenser at a public toilet. Except this had a slightly abrasive quality, reminding him of some of the strange face-scrubbing gunk—exfoliating scrub?—an ex-girlfriend had clogged up his bathroom cabinets with. But this soap didn't smell remotely feminine, thank god. Although at this point, he'd be willing to smell like a woman if it meant being clean.

He scrubbed until his skin felt raw and fresh and the water-soap soaking into the platform ran clean. He wondered how on earth he was going to wash the stuff off but simply being clean was a step up. He let the soap fall over him, washing him in green. A moment later, clean, warm water replaced the soap. The spray nearly scalded his skin but still felt wonderful. He stood under the stream for as long as he could stand to, until the water finally got too hot. Then he stepped off the platform.

The shower shut off. A slurping sound came from the platform. When he touched the edge of it with his toe, it was dry. Very nice. He plucked a towel off the same shelf that had held the electric razor and dried his reddened skin. He couldn't remember ever enjoying a shower so much. Strange as it was. He wondered at the secrecy of Ballore's country to have developed a technology like this and then kept it to themselves. They could make a fortune selling this shower in the States.

He wrapped the towel around his hips and sauntered back into the main room, yawning. He could use a nap. And food, his stomach reminded him. He could really use a meal.

Matt lurched off the purple couch as soon as he heard Jake. "Did you leave me any hot water?" He started walking toward the bathroom without waiting for an answer.

"I don't think you can run out of hot water in that shower," Jake told him. "Step under the hanger thing to get it started. You'll love it."

"I'll love anything that washes away this grime."

Jake chuckled, then remembered. "Wait," he called, stopping Matt, already half undressed, at the bathroom door. "Don't mess with the bracelets. They'll be okay in the shower. Lieutenant Ballore was pretty adamant we didn't tamper with them."

"Little suspicious. She tell you why?"

"She said they were medical devices, to prevent us getting sick. I think they're something worse."

"Worse?"

Jake shrugged. "Only a guess, but maybe some sort of bomb. Maybe a tracking device. The lieutenant looked scared. I figure it won't hurt to be careful."

"Yeah. Careful." Matt stared at the bracers on his forearms. They looked more awkward on him than they did on Jake. Too big and gangly. "Shit," Matt said. "I'd really hate for these to be bombs."

"Yeah, me too."

Matt disappeared into the bathroom, shaking his head and glaring at his wrists.

Jake collapsed onto the couch. Now what? Ballore said food would be brought up soon. He rubbed a hand over his grumbling stomach and wondered if he could ring someone to speed up the process. He stared up at the ceiling, let his eyes drift shut. He couldn't feel the vibrations in the ship anymore, almost as if they'd stopped moving. He listened to the quiet hum of distant machinery, what was probably the central air system, and the very faint sounds of water coming from the washroom. His breathing slowed. He sank into the clean scent of the room, spiced with some fragrance he couldn't place, the quiet sounds, the soothing lights.

A bell chimed gently, startling him awake. He rubbed a hand over his eyes, surprised he'd actually drifted off. Before he could figure out the source of the noise that had snapped him awake, the outer door slid upward.

Jake jumped to his feet instinctively, tensed for a fight. He relaxed when three very tall women walked in carrying trays. As delicious scents filled the room, his stomach rumbled loudly. A part of him noticed how stunning all three women were, but the bigger part of him lusted after those trays of food. None of the women were as sexy as Lieutenant Ballore anyway.

He was leaning over the trays, lifting heavy silver lids as soon as the women set them down on the room's single table. He didn't recognize anything, but he didn't particularly care. Everything smelled good. Probably leave him sick as a dog but even that didn't deter his demanding stomach. He plucked what looked to be a cracker off one tray and popped it into his mouth. Whatever it was melted on his tongue, the flavor unusual, spicy and delicious. He'd never tasted anything like it. To hell with caution. The food could be drugged, poisoned for all he cared. If the rest tasted as good as that one little cracker, he'd found heaven.

He tried several more odd looking bits of food, had just begun to sate his hunger, when he realized the three women were still in the room. He looked up sheepishly, prepared to apologize and thank them, but stopped with the words on the tip of his tongue. All three women were staring at him with such intensity his muscles flexed, preparing for a fight again. A moment passed before he realized they were staring at his body.

He glanced down at the loosely wrapped towel, the only thing between him and being naked. Then he caught sight of the two jagged knife scars running across his pectoral muscles, white against the tan of his skin and dark hair covering his chest. He touched the scars and glanced up at the women. Past experience told him curiosity motivated their stares.

"I got them taking down a gang thug four years ago," he said, hoping the simple explanation would be enough to satisfy their interest. Thanks to the towel, the scar on his left thigh remained hidden. He hated having to explain the bullet hole scar since he'd received that in his youth when he'd been too stupid to avoid flying bullets.

The women continued to stare, silent and intense. His gaze narrowed. He finally recognized the look in their eyes and it wasn't simple curiosity about his scars. They stared at him like he was their next best meal. Women like this looked at Matt with that intense hunger. Not him.

He raised an eyebrow, waved a hand in front of their faces to bring their attention back to his face. Only one looked up. She smiled, a slow, sexy, dangerous grin that promised long hours tangled in sweaty sheets. Hmmm... Something definitely wrong with this situation.

The smiling woman was as gorgeous as any of the other women they'd seen so far—nearly six and a half feet tall, with long shapely legs and a mound of red-tinted hair, huge blue eyes, and full lips. She didn't have much of a bust line, or very feminine hips, especially compared to Lieutenant Ballore's generous curves, but other than that she was very nearly a perfect woman. The other two were similarly gorgeous. All wore formfitting jumpsuits that left nothing to his imagination. They could have easily competed with any of the models and starlets that populated L.A.

But women like this went for men like Matt. Women like this never gave Jake a second glance except to grimace.

So something was definitely wrong. Some sort of trap maybe? Lull him with food, a shower and the promise of sex most men could only dream of, then hit him with... Well, the punch line. The reason for his kidnapping. Maybe he and Matt were to be tortured, killed. He didn't have any idea what sort of information they'd expect from him. He was a homicide cop from Los Angeles. Maybe this really did have something to do with a former case?

And maybe he was on one of those hidden camera shows.

He put his hands on his hips and studied the three women. No way was he getting sucked into whatever game they were playing. If he were to be tortured, he'd take it up front. And if he was on a TV show, he'd prefer not to make any more of a fool of himself than he already had.

As the silence stretched taut, one of the women, the one with the red hair, seemed to come to a decision. Her smile widened and she sauntered closer.

He shook a head and held up a hand. "I don't think so, sweetheart," he said. "I don't know what you're playing at, but all I want right now is more of this food and a soft bed to sleep in."

She tilted her head, her huge eyes narrowing, her smooth brow creased. She shook her head, lifting her hands in the universal gesture that meant, I have no idea what you're saying.

He groaned. He'd forgotten about the language difference. Both the lieutenant and the medic spoke English so he'd assumed anyone dealing with him and Matt would know the language. Now what?

As he contemplated the problem, the door slid up again. He turned to see Lieutenant Ballore framed in the doorway, a very unfriendly glare on her gorgeous face. Her hands fisted on her hips, her legs planted wide, her jaw clenched. She looked really ticked off. And unbelievably sexy.

He couldn't help smiling. "Hello, Lieutenant."

She flicked at glance at him, did a double take and stared, her hands dropping to her sides. The shock in her eyes turned to heat. Instantly, Jake felt his body respond. He forgot for a minute they weren't alone and took a single step toward her.

She blinked and turned away, shaking her head. She glared at the three women again and her hands moved back to her hips. Rapidly in her own language, she barked out what he assumed was a reprimand from her jerky hand gestures.

He sucked in a deep breath, surprised at his reaction. He hadn't felt the need to jump the other three women, even after they'd made it obvious they'd welcome him. In fact, he'd wanted the other three to leave. But one double take from the delectable lieutenant and he was ready to forget his surroundings and answer the heat in her eyes. He had to stare at the food trays just to keep his body from betraying his physical response. Even growling out orders, Leia Ballore was the sexiest thing he'd ever seen.

He looked up when the three women marched from the room, backs straight against Leia's glare. When the door closed behind them, Leia faced him with a wry shrug. She tapped her jaw and said, "I apologize for their behavior, Jake Marshall. Very inappropriate. I might ask..." She paused, her brow creasing. A faint pink tinted her cheeks.

Fascinated, he moved a step closer, grinning at her blush despite himself.

She cleared her throat, frowned down at the floor. "Might I ask that you do not greet members of my squadron without…" She made a vague gesture with her hand toward him, her cheeks turning pinker.

He glanced down at the towel hanging loosely around his hips. He raised an eyebrow, looking a question at her, but he couldn't keep his grin from widening.

She rolled her eyes. "When my soldiers enter this room, could you please ensure you are fully clothed?" she finally said. She wouldn't look directly at him for more than a darting second.

He chuckled. "As you please, Lieutenant. I apologize for my undress."

Her mouth quirked up at one corner, a rueful smile she wiped away an instant later. She hesitated near the door. "Is the food to your satisfaction?" she said finally.

"It's great, what I've tried so far. No idea what any of it is, but it's good."

She moved toward him. "What isn't familiar?" She frowned, glancing between him and the tray.

"Any of it," he said with a shrug.

Her eyes widened. "None of it?" She switched to her own language, mumbling as she approached the table. She picked up a round, orange ball of something that looked like a cross between bread and melon. She sniffed it and tasted it. "*Mashna* fruit. You don't have *mashna* fruit in your…country?"

"Nope. Is it good? I haven't tried it yet." He plucked the fruit from her fingers, bit into the remains of the ball. A trickle of juice ran down his fingers. The fruit tasted sweet but had the texture of some sort of squash. "Good." He laughed, licking the line of juice off the side of his hand. "Then again, everything tastes good at the moment. I'm starving. Feels like I haven't eaten in days."

She started, looked away from where she'd been staring at his hand. "You should try some of this," she said, picking a flat square of brown and pink something from the tray. "I thought this would be familiar. It's *golbi* beef." She handed him the square.

Beef? Okay. He took a tentative bite. "Oh that's good." He devoured the square and picked up a second. "Any other recommendations. Meat is good."

She smiled, turned back to the tray. "I understand these are good." She picked up a thin blue sheet that looked like pastry.

"You understand they're good? Haven't you tried them before?"

"No." She handed him the sheet. "It's called *yahir* paste."

He shook his head, grinning around another bite of the *golbi* beef. "You first."

Her eyebrows lifted, she licked her lips and looked at the sheet. She took a deep breath that drew his gaze away from her mouth to the movement of her breasts against her uniform, his appetite for food instantly distracted by his appetite for getting Lieutenant Ballore naked.

Get a grip, Jake. He suppressed a groan, clenched his fists to keep his hands off her. She's your guard not your date. No kissing the warden. Even if she did look tastier than anything on the platters.

He dragged his gaze back up to her face just as she lifted the thin sheet of *yahir* paste and took a tentative bite. Her eyes widened. To his surprised amusement, she spit the blue goop back out into her palm.

He laughed. "Not so good, eh?"

She frowned. "Perhaps you will think so. I do not find it appetizing."

"Well if you don't like it, I'm not gonna eat it." He looked around the tray for a napkin but couldn't see anything to hand her. "Sorry. Matt's in the bathroom or I'd get you a towel." He nodded to her closed fist.

She waved him away. "I'll take care of it in a minute." She glared down at the tray, mumbled something.

"What was that?"

Her head jerked up. She tapped her jaw. "Pardon?"

"You just mumbled something."

"Oh. I was just... I gave orders that you were to be fed dishes appropriate to your pl...country. Obviously, the cook didn't do his research properly. I will have it taken care of."

He stopped her with a hand on her shoulder when she would have turned to leave. The contact sent a shiver of awareness over his skin, raising goose bumps. This close, she had to look up to meet his gaze. He didn't consider her short for a woman but compared to the other women he'd seen so far, she was small. Curvier though. His gaze dropped to the swell of those curves. His pulse kicked.

All he'd meant to do was tell her not to go to too much trouble. The food was good enough. Now, he couldn't think beyond wanting to taste her. Her lips were full and lush, slightly parted. Her face tilted up toward his at an angle that would make kissing that generous mouth of hers easy. He moved closer, until her breasts just touched his bare chest. He slid his hand down her arm in a long caress that made her shiver. The primitive male in him growled in satisfaction, savoring her reaction.

Her eyes were wide and so dark they were almost black. She smelled of some exotic spice. He circled her waist with his free hand, pressed against her lower back, and urged her closer until her breasts flattened against his chest and their thighs touched. His erection pressed against her lower stomach, drawing a groan from deep in his throat.

A voice at the back of his mind warned him to stop. This woman was a soldier, not some L.A. starlet he could tumble and toss away. He was a prisoner here, had been drugged and kidnapped. Until they handed him over to an American embassy or returned him to his own country, he knew trusting her was folly. For all he knew, this ploy would earn him a knife between the ribs.

But his body didn't care—not about his need for food, for safety, for caution. All his body cared about was pressing her closer, claiming her lips, getting her out of that damned uniform so he could feel her skin against his. He lowered his mouth to hers and felt her tremble. Her hand came up to his waist. At first, he thought she'd push him away. But her fingers flexed, squeezing him closer.

His lips brushed hers, softly, tentatively, giving her a chance to pull back. He didn't think he could stop on his own, but if she turned away, even now, he'd be able to regain some control. To his surprise, and pleasure, she lifted her mouth and captured his lips in a hard kiss. The thrill of her lips against his pulsed through him. Hunger and need ran fast and hot through his blood. She wanted his touch, his kiss, and he was happy to oblige her.

He tilted his head to deepen the kiss, his arms flexed around her waist. He felt an instant of disorientation, as if the ground had suddenly shifted beneath him then stopped abruptly while he and Leia continued to move.

Then a jolt rocked him backward and his stomach dropped. For a split second, he thought she really had stabbed or shot him. But he heard her gasp, and a stream of what he guessed to be curses tumbled from her as she jerked out of his arms.

Matt ran out into the main room. "What the hell was that?" He wore a pair of loose trousers, but his skin was still wet from his shower. "What happened?" His right hand flexed against his leg, an instinctive gesture Jake understood. He felt the same itch to reach for a weapon that wasn't there. He couldn't guess why he felt the need for his gun.

But one look at Lieutenant Ballore's snapping gaze and Jake didn't care what instinct motivated him. He just knew he needed a weapon.

3

____

L eia frowned at the two men as she took a communicator from her belt. She shouldn't use the device in front of them, but she didn't want to waste precious time trying to contact the bridge using the wall communicator out in the corridor. "Captain Gehalli? Ballore here. What was that jolt after we came out of hyperspace? Has something happened to the freighter?"

She didn't activate the translator, but she watched the two men, trying to judge if they understood her words. To her relief, they looked confused and impatient. The last thing she wanted was for them to realize they were in a spaceship and not on an airplane or some similar vessel.

She pressed her lips together. They still burned from the heat of Jake Marshall's kiss. Saints, but the man tasted good. All hot male and *mashna* fruit. He tasted better than Belaxian wine. Despite the abrupt disruption to their inappropriate kiss, she found it hard to concentrate on anything but kissing him again.

Get your head straight, Ballore, she thought as she tried to focus on Captain Gehalli's explanation of what had rocked the ship. With her head full of Jake Marshall's scent and taste and feel, listening was hard. But two words punched through her daze, shocking enough to snap her mind onto the current situation. "What?"

"We're under attack, Lieutenant." The captain's voice sounded strained as she shouted down the comm. "Pirates. Don't know how but they must have gotten a Nasen distress code. There's no Nas freighter here, not even the debris of one. As soon as we dropped out of hyperspace the pirates fired on us."

"How in the twelve hells did they…? Never mind. I'll need some room to get the cargo to a safe distance. Can you give me cover, Captain?"

"We'll do our best. Gehalli, out."

Cursing under her breath, Leia called her second. "Vanian, I need you at the holding room. Pirates are attacking the ship." She touched the translator chip in her jaw and faced Jake and Matt, wondering how the hell she was going to explain this away. "We need to evacuate. Now. There are clothes in your room." She nodded at Jake and pointed over her shoulder to the room allocated for his use. "Hurry. We don't have much time."

He didn't waste words trying to grill her for more information, for which she was grateful. He and Matt finished dressing with a speed and efficiency she appreciated. They returned to the main room in no more than a minute and waited for further instructions.

She went to the door, pulling her military issue, small arms DEG from her belt and holding it ready as she opened the door and swept the corridor. When she was sure the way was clear, she motioned the men forward. "Stay behind me," she ordered.

She glanced at them long enough to see both men tense, but they didn't object out loud. Moving into the corridor, the men on her heels, she headed toward the emergency shuttle. Vanian and two more Guards met her on the way.

Leia recognized the two women and decided Vanian had chosen well. Bythan, with her silver and black hair and silver-tinted skin, was relatively new to Nas Guard. But she'd been given a high commendation from her former commander and so ended up on this mission. Moyra had been a Guard for longer and had earned a reputation for unshakeable ethics. Her pale face was set in serious lines that seemed a strange contrast to the vibrant, fun cut of her spiky red hair. Her liquid silver eyes scanned the area vigilantly.

The four of them formed up around the two men without a word, providing a shield as they continued toward the rear of the ship.

From a distance, she heard the shouts of the crew, the high whine of weapons charging. While the cruiser had defense capabilities, their weapons weren't up to the strength of most pirate ships.

She had no doubt the attack was instigated by pirates attempting to steal, or steal back, the two Earthmen. How they discovered the cruiser's route, or gained access to a Nasen distress code were questions she'd have to ask later. Now, her job was to get Jake and Matt to a safe location. She had no illusions that the cruiser would be able to keep the pirates at bay for long. She didn't want to be forced into hand-to-hand combat in the close confines of the ship. Especially when the nearest spacesuits hung in the hold. If the pirates were dumb or desperate enough to actually fire a weapon stronger than a stunner in here, when cruiser emergency shields were notoriously bad, they'd all likely get sucked out into the icy vacuum of space. She did not want to die that way.

She pushed the small group faster, hoping they could get off the cruiser before the pirates boarded. The sound of the ship's weapons discharging vibrated through the hull. A second later, the cruiser jumped beneath them, throwing Leia against the wall. Her head bounced against the unforgiving metal, stunning her and dotting her vision with bright sparks. She blinked and shook her head to clear her vision.

When she tried to push away from the wall, she found herself in Jake Marshall's arms.

"Are you okay?" he asked. "How hard did you hit? Spots?"

For an astonished moment, she couldn't answer. She couldn't remember the last time a man had showed that kind of concern for her. Shaking her head again, she tapped the translation chip in her jaw and said, "I'm fine. Let's move. They've broken though the hull."

"They?" Despite the suspicious in his question, the hard edge now in his eyes, he moved.

They broke into a full run, in a race now to see if they could reach the shuttle before the pirates found them.

The escape shuttle docked on the engineering level, which meant getting down two decks without getting caught. Leia had no idea where the pirates had penetrated the hull and boarded the ship. She couldn't risk further communication for fear of giving away their position. Her only hope was that she knew this ship and its specifications better than the pirates—a slim hope at best.

She led her small party to a lift near the stern of the ship, hoping the pirates had attacked from the front. Her stomach clenched tight as they waited, weapons trained, for the lift to reach them. She and Vanian stood to either side of the lift door as it slid up. They swung around, pointing weapons inside simultaneously. Happy the lift was empty, she motioned the others inside, following just before the lift door slid down.

She watched the lights above the door tick from blue to yellow. When they turned red, she raised her DEG and motioned Jake and Matt back against the wall. She and Vanian took lead again, sweeping out into the corridor the minute the door slid up. Empty. She let out a breath.

They had to go forward again to reach the shuttle. She gave Vanian the lead and took up the rear, guarding their backs as they trotted through the darker, more humid corridors of the lower level.

Tempted to hold her breath, she had to remind herself to breathe slow and even as they moved. When she'd saved the life of the Nas Governor General, there had been no buildup, no tense uncertainty. She'd assessed the situation and stepped in to do what was necessary. The whole process took seconds, with little time to think or consider. This was different. She couldn't see her enemy here. She didn't know where they were, how many there were, how much deadly force they were prepared to use. Had the pirates already reached the escape shuttle? Were they lying in wait to ambush her small group? Would she lose Jake Marshall so soon?

She cringed when she realized her biggest concern wasn't so much to save his life but to save his life for her. She'd never felt so selfish. He didn't belong to her. She had to send him home. She would lose him no matter what happened with the pirates. She'd been trained to save lives for the sake of the life, not her own sake. But she wanted to save Jake Marshall for her own selfish reasons. The result would be the same, but the thoughts motivating her actions scared her.

When they reached the shuttle bay, she took a deep breath. This time, she motioned the other two women to go in first while she and Vanian kept guard over their two charges. Bythan went in high, Moyra low. They disappeared into the bay, DEGs trained and sweeping. Long seconds passed in silence.

Leia's nerves stretched taut. She darted glances back over her shoulder to Vanian, toward the door, then back to focus on the corridor. Silence hovered over them for a long time. Then, to her relief, Moyra poked her head around the bay door. "It's clear."

They hurried to the shuttle ramp, she and the other two Guards sweeping the bay as they moved. Bythan was already powering up the ship. To her relief, neither Jake nor Matt balked at the small shuttle-craft, nor did they hesitate to climb in. She would try to explain all this later. Now, she thanked the saints they didn't cause any delays.

The shuttle hatch sealed the instant Leia's feet touched the deck. "Get us out now," she shouted up to Bythan. "Gentlemen," she said in English. She motioned them to seats lining one side of the shuttle. They sat without comment and the safety mesh closed over their bodies from chest to ankle. She saw them start to struggle. "No." She touched Jake's shoulder. "Don't struggle. It's just a…a type of seatbelt. But you have to relax. You'll be fine. I promise."

He met her gaze, held it for a searching heartbeat, then relaxed into the restraint. She smiled her gratitude for his trust. Quickly, she took her own seat, forcing herself to relax as the mesh closed around her. Struggling against the mesh made it tighten more to secure you in place. The sensors assumed your movements were the result of being tossed by the forces of the flight. What did a safety harness know about panic attacks and the fear of being encased with your ability to move arms and legs restricted? She'd never much liked the sensation either, and she understood what the mesh did and why it was necessary. That Jake Marshall could accept and submit even when he didn't completely understand, said a lot about his inner strength.

The rumbling of shuttle engines whined louder as the ship lifted up from the bay floor. Leia watched on a small console screen stationed in front of her seat as the bay doors pulled back, slowly revealing the black star-dotted vacuum of space beyond. "Emergency shields down," the computer voiced.

"Here we go," Bythan called back.

Leia felt her stomach lurch with the sensation of changing g-forces. They cleared the bay an instant later.

"There's one hell of a fight going on back there," Bythan said with a low whistle.

Leia vocally ordered the console to switch views so she could see the damage. Blue streaks of energy bolted into the cruiser from not one but three pirate ships. A smaller transport shuttle anchored to the side of the cruiser. From what she could see, it looked as if they'd punched through the hull and boarded the *Persephone* not far from the room where Jake and Matt had been kept. The thought made her dizzy. She'd been that close to losing him.

She closed her eyes an instant, overwhelmed by a sense of disaster narrowly avoided and a relief so strong it made her weak. When she opened her eyes, she forced herself to take in the rest of the scene. The cruiser floundered under the repeated hits from the pirate ships. Already two more boarding shuttles made their way through the cross-fire toward the cruiser. Very few shots were being fired from the cruiser now and as she watched one of the main guns exploded, leaving a sparkle of debris floating off into space.

She cursed, low and with feeling. She could only hope the crew and the rest of her Guard would be left to limp home when the pirates discovered the cargo had escaped. She waited for one of the ships to break off and follow. But the *Persephone* crew kept the pirates distracted despite the cruiser's handicaps, giving the escape shuttle precious time to get farther away. To her surprise, the cruiser got off a lucky shot, destroying one of the boarding shuttles. Leia let out a pent-up breath.

Bythan whooped in triumph.

Leia said a small prayer to Saint Flur, the saint of soldiers, for the crew and her Guard. She watched the battle until their shuttle moved out of range.

———

THEY TRAVELED AT SUB-DRIVE SPEED, NINETY-SEVEN PERCENT OF THE speed of light, until they were well beyond sensor range. The shuttle could only make short journeys through hyperspace, so Bythan took them through a series of jumps to hide their trail, moving away from Nas to avoid another ambush. They sketched out a rough plan before beginning the hyperspace jumps. If they could get to Dockland Depot in the Bentan system, Leia had a contact there who could arrange a better ship, one the pirates wouldn't be able to trace. Hopefully.

Once back on Nas, Leia would have to unravel the links leading to this disaster. She hated to think there might be a traitor among the *Persephone* crew or her Guard. But she couldn't imagine another way the pirates would know a Nasen distress code and enough information to guarantee the *Persephone* detoured to a specific location. An ambush would be nearly impossible to pull off unless they had someone inside passing on information. With a keen sense of frustration, she knew she couldn't do anything about hunting down the traitor until she returned to Nas. For the moment, she had to concentrate on keeping the two men alive.

She turned her head, not for the first time, to look at Jake Marshall. Sometime during the quiet journey, he'd fallen asleep. Leia's lips lifted in the barest of smiles. He looked very relaxed. Asleep, he lost some of the hard edge that sculpted his face, but not all.

Hoping the others would assume she'd fallen asleep, she studied him through eyes narrowed to slits. He'd shaved off the beard scruff. She was a little disappointed, but even shaving couldn't take away from his rough, menacing good looks. In fact, with his jaw clean, the jagged scar on his cheek jumped out into sharp relief. The face scar reminded her of the other scars running across his pectoral muscles. The sight of his hard body wrapped in nothing but a towel, displaying his obvious prowess as a warrior, had made her mouth water. Only the knowledge that the women who'd brought his food had been trying to tempt him kept her from launching herself at him the moment she saw those hard muscles and sexy scars.

The surge of jealousy and possessiveness that coursed through her when she'd seen the other women propositioning him had surprised her. She felt her righteous anger justified given her position as leader of the Guard sent to protect the two men. But her job wasn't the reason she'd launched into the skin-flaying lecture she'd given the women. The real reason slept next to her with the face of a warrior from ancient times.

She still couldn't believe she'd kissed him. She'd broken every rule, ignored her own ethics and given in to the temptation of a primitive male. And saints what a kiss! The feel of him hard against her had awakened a primal part of herself she barely recognized. All female and needy. Knowing he wanted her after he'd refused the others gave her a sense of satisfaction that mortified her now.

Her behavior was unforgivable. What had she been thinking? She knew better. Her stomach knotted. What if Vanian or the other Guards found out? She'd broken one of their biggest taboos. Her commander could have her stripped of her duty for the transgression. She was not allowed to take advantage of the primitive men brought forward in time to be sold as slaves. She was forbidden to seduce him. Period. She had to control herself around him. No matter how delicious he tasted, or how much she wanted him. She had a duty. Her honor was at stake.

She'd never reacted to a man like this before. Never wanted one so much she was willing to sacrifice her ethics to have him. Her lack of control frightened her. Jake's obvious attraction didn't help matters, either.

For the first time, she could understand why people paid such a phenomenal amount of money for primitive Earthmen. The lure was almost irresistible. She'd sworn to protect these men, yet she still wanted to keep one for herself. She squeezed her eyes shut, horrified by the thought. She couldn't allow this. She had to regain her professional distance. Sympathy for his plight was one thing. Falling for him quite another.

Because, unfortunately, she knew more than lust motivated her reaction to Jake Marshall. Oh, there was plenty of lust. And knowing he reacted to her made it worse. But more than any physical reaction, she admired Jake. He'd been swept into a situation he couldn't possibly understand, ripped from his home, his world. And he hadn't even balked at boarding a space shuttle the likes of which wouldn't exist in his world for another five hundred years. He had allowed her and her Guards to take the lead and followed orders meant to protect him without so much as a word of protest. Despite his primitive looks and build, he hadn't tried to dominate or take control of the situation. He had allowed her to do her job and taken in the mysteries of his surroundings with a stoicism she could only respect.

Her curiosity was piqued. More so than before. She wanted to know about him. Did he have a family? Wife and kids? Saints, she didn't want to think about that possibility. What did he do for a living? He looked like a warrior of some kind but her knowledge of early Earth culture was very basic. He seemed amazingly able to adapt and was obviously intelligent. What did he do in his spare time? Did he have spare time? Did he have hobbies? What kind of foods would he like?

When she started considering the sorts of meals she might cook, she groaned inwardly. She could *not* cook for him. She had to get both Jake and Matt home. There was no time for getting to know Jake, or engaging in any little, nearly acceptable intimacies like cooking. And if she went so far as to cook for him, she knew she'd only find it harder to resist him. Distance. She needed professional detachment and distance.

She let her eyes slit open again, taking in his strong face. She looked past him to the other man—Matthew Donnelly. Matt was by far too fair and pretty for her tastes, but she could see why Grettel chose him. While he wouldn't bring as high a price as Jake, he would suit the more perverse buyers—or anyone from Hrokwall.

Matt and Jake seemed to be close. They had probably been near each other when they were taken. She wondered about the relationship. They obviously knew each other, were comfortable with each other. They'd talked for a while after the escape, quietly just between themselves. She'd waited for the barrage of questions they no doubt had, but the questions never came. And when the two men finished talking, they relaxed into their seats and dozed off. Matt had made a half-hearted attempt to flirt with Vanian but exhaustion took its toll.

She found herself smiling again and had to control the expression. Matt was an amusing male. Almost comic in the way he flirted and teased as if he expected women to adore him. There was a charm in the false confidence that some might even find attractive. She'd have to be just as careful in protecting Matt as Jake. But she was less worried about Matt. If Grettel had been one of the pirates trying to recapture this cargo, Leia had no doubt the effort was made for Jake.

Matt wasn't worth the risk. Jake was.

She turned her head away, suppressing a sigh. Jake was worth a lot. How the hell was she supposed to maintain her distance when all she wanted to do was kiss him again? They couldn't get to Dockland Depot and home to Nas quick enough. The sooner Jake Marshall was out of her life, the better for her conscience and her heart.

JAKE WATCHED LEIA TURN HER HEAD AWAY FROM HIM, WATCHED THE rise and fall of her chest. She was probably the most stunning woman he'd ever encountered, so sexy she made him forget himself and his situation.

A situation that was far worse than he'd originally thought.

His gut worried at the things he and Matt had seen. Try as he might, he couldn't explain away the ship they'd boarded or the space battle he'd seen on Leia's computer screen. Either both he and Matt had gone insane at the exact same time and were living in each other delusions, or they were on a spaceship. *In a galaxy far, far away.* The thought edged on hysteria. Get a grip, Marshall. No need to assume you've stepped into *Star Wars* just because you're on a spaceship. The idea of meeting Darth Vader face-to-face made him want to laugh.

Just a little too hysterical. There, at the edge of his thoughts… If he weren't insane already, dropping into that pit and not having to worry about any of this would be very easy. He could just let the hysteria sweep over him, give in to it and go completely loo-la. His captain had been telling him he was headed that way at any rate. Maybe he'd already crossed over the line.

Matt's humor had turned a little hysterical, too. Despite his California tan, his face was pale. The situation was way beyond what their logical minds considered possible. Though somehow, knowing his partner was going through this with him made it easier to tolerate. They couldn't both be insane. So there was another explanation.

And Lieutenant Leia Ballore was their link to that explanation.

He studied the fall of her dark ponytail across her shoulders. She made it easier to deal with all this, too. He could think about that brief kiss and forget everything else in his life was currently a shambles. Maybe if he kissed her again. And again. All this would go away and he'd be back in L.A., closing up the Patterson murder, planning a late night dinner with Leia Ballore.

Or maybe she'd vanish with the rest of the nightmare.

That idea appealed to him less and less with each passing minute. She'd been amazing on the *Persephone*, managing to get them out and away without bloodshed. She'd put herself between them and danger without hesitation. She couldn't know he and Matt were well able to take care of themselves in a fight. And she'd defended them without a moment's consideration for herself. He didn't hesitate to follow her lead because her lead proved so sure and able. She displayed strength and courage.

She'd make a great cop.

She fascinated him and captured his curiosity. And since thinking about Leia was a lot more pleasant than trying to understand what had happened, he let his mind drift, wondering about her. Where was she from? How had she gotten to be a lieutenant? Did she have a boyfriend or was she married? God, he hoped not. What did she do for fun? What was she like as a child? Did she have a lot of friends? Was she close to her parents?

He couldn't help wondering if they'd have time to know more about each other. Then again, if he'd gone insane, he had all the time in the world to live out this fantasy. Involuntarily, his gaze drifted over the interior of the ship. They sat against one wall of a space roughly the size of a walk-in closet. The interior was more than tall enough to accommodate his height without bumping his head but was narrow like the corridor on the *Persephone*. The wall opposite was a series of panels with flashing lights and the hatch through which they'd boarded the shuttle. The flashing lights and symbols were similar to those on the panels in the *Persephone*. Now he was sure they weren't Arabic or some other Earth language.

Jesus, he wasn't anywhere near Earth anymore. The idea made his stomach twist tight. Like every kid he knew, he'd wanted to be an astronaut when he grew up, but the last time he'd had that ambition he'd been ten! He was a grown man now, with work to do, murderers to catch, crimes to solve.

But no real life.

The thought came unbidden. He hated admitting, even to himself, that he didn't have much in his life outside his work. He didn't actually think about it most of the time. He dated occasionally, hung out with Matt in his off time when Matt wasn't out with his latest conquest. But he lived and breathed his job and there was very little room for anything else in his life. His parents had passed away years earlier. His only brother lived on the opposite side of the country, and Tim had a life, a wife and four kids to keep him busy.

The idea of four kids always made Jake's skin crawl. Kids were fine for some time in the future, but never in his immediate plan. Now, at thirty-six years old, his immediate plan hadn't changed much.

He'd never considered himself lonely. He had the job. He helped people. What more did he need? Besides, being a cop's wife sucked. He wasn't in a hurry to put any woman through that. He'd watched too many cop marriages fall apart and the ones that lasted… Well, he wasn't prepared to take the risk he might have one of those rare marriages that stuck. Because if the marriage didn't stick, the fallout was brutal. So, he'd avoided commitment, marriage, the whole situation, and concentrated on his job.

He turned away from his inspection of the shuttle to look at Leia again. Did she put someone through that? Were the people in her life worried about her? Or did she live for the job like he did? He had an absurd feeling she would understand why he'd avoided long-term relationships or commitments.

And somehow, the idea that this stranger would understand something so vital as why he lived as he did helped settle him in the midst of his impossible reality. He was pretty sure he wasn't insane. Which meant he really was somewhere very far from Earth. But he could face the situation. He'd survive, and he'd find a way home. If he really had traveled to "a galaxy far, far away" he'd just learn to deal with it.

Since this faraway galaxy contained someone like Leia Ballore in it, he didn't think the job would be too hard.

4

———————

Dockland Depot was one of the cleanest, most sophisticated, most dangerous deep space stations in the galaxy. Leia had only been to Dockland three times. The memory of the last visit still left a bad taste in her mouth. Though this stop was unavoidable, she dreaded going back.

But Dockland was their best chance of getting back to Nas in one piece.

The station itself was an impressive mesh of advanced technologies. It was made up of a series of rings connected by spokes to a central core. From space, the station looked a bit like a planet with gaps at various longitudes, or different sized wheels stacked on top of each other to make a sphere. Each ring could rotate at a different speed around the central core, providing varying gravity bases in each ring. Moving between the rings was only possible through lifts lining the outside of the central core. But most of the traders in Dockland Depot came to a specific ring for a specific purpose and didn't move around much.

Leia and Vanian had debated the best story for being in Guard uniforms on the station. Guards or military from any system were considered fair game, and what there was of a local authority was as corrupt as the rest of the residents and traders.

Leia and her Guards didn't have a change of clothing. But being a Guard on Dockland without a good excuse would be suicide. The two men, in little more than tunics and loose trousers, would be fine so long as they displayed their bracers. Time-theft cargo were often bought and sold on Dockland.

The station also harbored those few men who escaped slavery on their own. As the bracers couldn't be removed, the time-displaced men were permanently marked as former slaves no matter where they lived. On Dockland, the label didn't matter. Here the rule was every being for itself and you either survived on your own brains and brawn or you died—whether you were a former slave or a former master. Those time-stolen individuals who managed to escape usually proved more than capable of taking care of themselves, even on Dockland. Leia had a feeling Jake and Matt fell into this category of former slave.

So the two men were easy to explain. The trick was in passing off herself and the other three women as something other than Guards escorting recovered cargo.

After a long discussion, they finally decided to play renegade Guards—those rare traitors who chose to take their recovered cargo and turn a personal profit instead of returning them. Guards didn't turn renegade often because if the authorities of a renegade's system captured the Guards, the lightest punishment was a death sentence. But since Guards did occasionally go renegade, it was a believable story. Just the sight of Jake should dispel any suspicion about their motives as renegade. Jake, by himself, would bring enough profit to keep four Guards in luxury for the rest of their lives. Add the profit gained from selling Matt to one of the more perverse buyers, and no one would wonder why she and the others had turned. Hopefully.

The problem with playing renegade well enough to be believed by the Dockland thugs was that any semi-legitimate Nasen on the station would spread word to Nas about the Guards turned traitor. They'd be risking a very unfriendly homecoming if they couldn't send word ahead of their return. But any other option would likely get them killed before they could get home. So, renegade it was.

As they approached the station, waiting for permission to dock, she outlined the plan for Jake and Matt while the others geared up. The women would triple the number of weapons they carried outwardly and add a number of concealed weapons for those just-in-case moments. Fortunately, Dockland didn't enforce elaborate security scans when boarding or leaving.

"You will have to play the part of kidnapped men—which you are," Leia said with a little frown. "The only chance of surviving long enough to reach my contact on the station is by playing this part. And some may still not truly believe we've gone renegade. Most cargo would be drugged, but I'd rather you were both awake. I cannot give you an obvious DEG, but…"

Jake held up a hand. "DEG?"

She frowned and concentrated on the translator chip, searching for the proper words to explain the term. Finally she said, "DEG stands for directed-energy gun. DEGs are analogous to your guns. They come in various sizes and strengths, but we use directed-energy, a type of… laser, instead of projectiles like your bullets."

"Laser guns?" Matt said. "Cool."

"Unfortunately, even the most compact DEG would be too large and obvious for you to carry." Leia reached out to Vanian who handed her two very small laser blades. "These will cut through most substances when activated. Don't accidentally turn them on inside your pockets." She showed them how the little devices worked and watched as they studied the weapons.

Taking a deep breath, she said, "We will have to have you restrained…handcuffed? But you'll have the code to disengage the cuffs if it becomes necessary. I must ask that you do not act, in any way, unless I give you permission or your lives are in danger." She met Jake's dark blue eyes. "I know this won't be easy. You will want to act. Don't. Please. Let me and the other Guards handle this. You do not fully understand your situation."

Matt raised a hand, stilling her words. "And there's the rub, Lieutenant. What exactly *is* our situation? We've pretty much decided between us that 'we're not in Kansas anymore, Toto'. So, where in the goddamned universe are we?"

She shook her head. "I don't have time to explain now and it wouldn't make sense to you anyway. You're in a system far from the system where Earth is located. In a different galaxy. But without a map it would be difficult to explain. The distances would mean little to you. And who is Toto?"

Jake grinned, quick and startling. The expression added a whole new dimension to his handsome face. "What, you don't have classic films here?" he said.

Films? She frowned as her translator struggled with the word. She gave up with a shrug.

"Don't worry, Dorothy, it's not important. And we'll deal with *where* we are when we have time. You've told us we were kidnapped, we're considered cargo on this station. We were to be sold, is that it?"

"Yes. Slaves. If you survived."

"Worth much?" Matt asked with a touch of humor and a quirked eyebrow.

She felt her cheeks inexplicably warming. "Jake would be worth a fortune in any system in the known galaxies."

"And me?" Matt's voice rose slightly.

"Well… There are those who would pay quite handsomely for an Earthman like you." It was the most diplomatic way she could think of telling him.

"Hmmm… How much?"

"In *Tracnas*—"

"How much in U.S. dollars?"

"There is no…translation. No way to compare the currencies. Let us just say you would be worth more than ten million *Tracnas* in open auction."

Matt grinned, slapped Jake on the arm. "You hear that. Ten million of anything's got to be a lot of money."

"Ten million Italian lire was worth about ten bucks before they switched to the Euro, so don't get too excited." Jake chuckled.

The sound went all the way to Leia's toes. She could listen to that chuckle all day. The deep vibrations of his voice stole her breath and, for an instant, she couldn't think of anything else but stripping off his loose tunic and trousers and indulging her every wicked fantasy. It took her a moment to blink away the erotic fantasy, a moment longer to realize Jake was speaking to her again. "Sorry?"

"How much would I be worth? In *Tracnas*?" He was still smiling but the look in his blue eyes made her stomach twist.

"At least a half…"

Matt started to laugh, punching Jake's arm this time.

"A half billion *Tracnas*," Leia finished "That is where the bidding would start."

Jake's dark brows rose, his only reaction.

Matt's mouth dropped open, and his face turned red. "Why the hell would he be worth so much more than me?"

Jake chuckled again, patted Matt on the knee. "Because they know a good thing when they see it."

Leia couldn't agree more.

"Yeah right," Matt spat. He slumped back in his chair, grumbling, "Ten lousy million."

Bythan signaled from the front of the shuttle. "They've given us a landing sequence, Lieutenant. We're approaching docking Area 20, Bay 5, Ring C2 now."

"Thank you." Leia touched her jaw again to reactivate the translation chip. "We'll be landing soon, gentlemen. Do you have any questions?"

"Why here?" Jake sat forward, serious and intent.

"Because I have an…acquaintance who will help us with a faster ship, a ship that can get us back to Nas without being waylaid by the pirates again."

"Can you trust this acquaintance?"

She laughed. She couldn't help it. "Not really. But my mother would kill him if he didn't help."

Jake's dark brows rose again in a sardonic gesture she was coming to recognize.

She smiled. "We won't stay on Dockland for longer than necessary. I will explain as much of your…situation as I can once we are away. For now, remember you are our prisoners and we intend to sell you, but we are not prepared to take bids yet. We're building up the anticipation to raise the price. You will do nothing without my permission. Some of what you see will surprise you. Some of the behaviors of the inhabitants of Docklands will scare you or seem aggressive. Do not attempt any aggression in return unless I tell you to. Do you understand? If you don't follow my instructions, you could get all of us killed."

Matt grumbled something under his breath that didn't sound very polite. She could swear she heard "ten lousy million" again but couldn't be sure. "Gentlemen, do you understand and do you agree?"

"You'll answer our questions?" Jake asked. "All of them."

She sighed. Tell them any more than they knew went against every protocol in the book. Even now, they knew much more than was supposed to be permitted. But she had little choice if she wanted their cooperation. "I will answer what I can."

Since the men didn't realize they'd traveled in time, there was still a chance of containing some of the damage. As far as they knew, they'd been kidnapped by aliens. Stories of such phenomenon abounded on Earth during their era. Some such stories probably arose from kidnappings and returns from this time period. Others were likely myths. But if the men believed they'd been kidnapped by aliens instead of plucked from their own time, there was less chance of them doing something that could upset the timeline.

Grettel's continued theft of men from early Earth history was a constant source of worry for the intergalactic council. Each kidnapping risked upsetting the delicate balance of time. And there was little they could do to correct the timeline if it changed because no one except maybe the Kyzits would notice the difference. Whether or not the Kyzits would tell anyone that the timeline had been changed was a much-debated topic. The Kyzits remained silent on the matter.

Thinking about the time paradox gave her a headache, so she didn't much. She just knew it was better to keep the cargo as ignorant as possible and to return them as close to the exact moment of their kidnapping as possible.

Jake and Matt exchanged a long look. "Okay," Jake said after a moment. "We'll follow your lead because this is your turf. But don't expect us to let some bug-eyed alien eat us because shooting it seemed rude."

She smiled and nodded. "Don't worry. I won't let anything eat you."

She strapped on her additional DEGs as they began the final run into their docking station. Leia took a deep breath as the shuttle settled onto the floor of the bay and Bythan started shutting down all flight systems. "Okay," Leia said in English. "Here we go."

THE HATCH LOWERED, GIVING JAKE AND MATT THEIR FIRST VIEW OF Dockland Depot. Jake wasn't sure what he'd been expecting but it wasn't the spotlessly clean bay they walked into. The walls were a dark metal and more panels with lights dotted the area. Behind the shuttle the bay doors sealed tight, for which he was grateful. The clear window looking out onto the vacuum of space beyond left him more than a little disoriented. It was like looking out onto a blue screen projection at a theme park. Even the passing ships beyond the bay doors didn't seem part of a real world but something created by clever special effects artists.

The air inside the bay was clean and easy to breathe, so clean it had a strange smell, almost antiseptic but not like a hospital. Maybe a little stale? At home, he had to cut his smog-thickened air to breathe it. This wasn't hard enough for his lungs. The gravity felt normal. Space stations always brought to mind images of astronauts floating through narrow tubes, connecting quarters crammed with equipment and wires. The room they stood in was easily the size of a sound studio or warehouse on one of the movie lots, and there wasn't a loose wire or a crowd of equipment anywhere.

In fact, the floor was spotless, not a single grease stain or oil spill, and looked ready to hold any number of huge cargo containers. Not that he expected them to use oil and grease in this advanced culture but, for some reason, he'd figured a docking bay on a dangerous space station would be…dirty. Tracks were set into the floor where he assumed wheels or some other advanced technology allowed crates and containers to be moved through the bay. Other than that there was no evidence that anyone used this area.

"Too clean," he muttered to Matt. "Gives me the creeps."

"That's because you're a slob," Matt said, but the wisecrack couldn't hide his awe. "This is one big space, man."

Leia turned to face them and touched her jaw.

Jake was pretty sure now that jaw touching thing had nothing to do with habit and everything to do with Leia being able to speak their language. A translation device maybe? If it was, he wanted one. He hated not being able to understand them when they spoke in their own language. He'd learned Spanish because he hated not being able to understand the Hispanics he'd dealt with frequently when he was in uniform. Most of the Asian languages were beyond his meager talents, but he had managed a few phrases so he could understand the gist of what people said. Here, he felt vulnerable not being able to understand anything. And he had a feeling that sense of vulnerability was going to get worse.

"This is an average-sized docking bay within the station," Leia told them. "There are bays to accommodate much larger ships as well. Those ships too big to dock inside the station are serviced by small transports from their docking spot beyond the station to the station itself. This is a very busy place. A lot of money passes through here." She paused, looked around the huge room, and lowered her voice. "There are places on this station that are neither this clean nor this secure. We are being monitored now."

She said this last with real regret, then took out one of her weapons and poked Jake in the ribs with it, moving him roughly forward. Vanian did the same with Matt. The other two Guards took positions in front of him and Matt, forming up around them like a phalanx. He suspected the formation was as much for their protection as for the show they were about to put on.

As they approached, a smaller door opposite the docking doors opened. The corridor beyond teamed with life, many forms of which he didn't recognize. But enough humans walked past, he didn't feel overly conspicuous. Until they moved into the midst of that throng and the staring started. Every human and alien they passed seemed to pause and stare. And not just at the gorgeous women surrounding them but at him and Matt. Some of those looks he could read and he didn't like what he saw. Many of the looks he couldn't read. He liked that even less.

The corridor before them cleared as they marched. He couldn't help craning his neck to get a look at everything at once. The place reminded him a little of a science fiction movie set, except fortunately he didn't see any Storm Troopers. But some of the other things he did catch glimpses of worried him more than Storm Troopers ever had. So caught up in gawking, he forgot he was supposed to be a prisoner until Leia poked him in the ribs with her weapon.

He dropped his head but darted a glance at Matt. His partner's gaze darted around, busy trying to see everything at once as well, the look on his face one of barely suppressed excitement. Matt was a big *Star Wars* fan. For him, this was probably like walking into the middle of a film session, being told he'd get to meet all his favorite characters and to ice the cake, would even have a bit part in the movie.

Jake's own excitement dimmed when he took the time to look at their Guards. All four women were tense and carried more than one weapon visibly. The two in front carried weapons that looked like machine guns. The contrast between their whip-thin bodies, artfully cut and styled hair, and the arsenal of weapons they wore was pronounced. They glared down anyone brave enough to look at the small group but that didn't seem to deter most of the crowd.

Jake had a hard time accepting that he and Matt were worth this much attention. Well, Matt maybe. Matt had always drawn attention. But he hadn't had to deal with this before. He felt like an insect under a microscope. Not a comfortable place to be if you were the insect. He tried to keep his head bowed, but the feel of so many gazes on him was an itch he couldn't scratch with his eyes averted. Unable to resist, he looked up.

In time to see a huge, scale-covered alien with a spiked dinosaur-like tail step into their path, forcing them to stop.

The dinosaur alien waved a weapon in the air, pointed it randomly around the corridor, and shouted in a guttural language in the direction of their group. It seemed to be trying to solicit a reaction from the crowd. Jake couldn't be sure, but he suspected whatever that thing was saying didn't bode well for them.

"This doesn't look good," Matt murmured, echoing Jake's gut reaction.

As he watched the shouting alien, Jake got the uncomfortable feeling Matt had underestimated the situation.

LEIA'S STOMACH TIGHTENED WHEN THE GORMALATH STEPPED IN FRONT of them. She kept the reaction from her face, but her heartbeat jumped and sweat trickled between her breasts. She grunted a single word in Nas and her Guard rearranged around the Earthmen so she could face the Gormalath.

"You stirring up unwanted trouble," she told him in his own language. This language she spoke without the help of a translator chip because her less-than-law-abiding cousin had drilled it into her. Gormal was a language full of nuance and subtlety that couldn't be accurately translated by a chip. And if you didn't get the nuance just right, you could end up with a Gormalath tail spike through your throat.

"You ain't Nas," the Gormalath said. "You're too short and fat. Who you?"

Short and fat was a compliment coming from a Gormalath. Leia took her cue from that. She cocked her hip to one side to accentuate her curves and tilted her head so her ponytail spilled over her shoulder. "I'm Belax, *palamna*." She let her eyelids droop to a sultry invitation as she used the Gormal word for superior male specimen. She supposed for a Gormalath he was handsome enough, and he had a great set of tail spikes. But she didn't do the interspecies thing. Still, it never hurt to keep things on a friendly note. "Name of Leia, clan name Ballore."

"Leia of Ballore. Name here Jaxin, clan of Deent. What you doing with Nas Guard, *devesa*?"

Sexy woman, huh? Well, things were definitely friendlier than they had been a moment ago. And Jaxin presented an unexpected opportunity to set up her story. No one argued with a Gormalath. If she could convince him, they had a chance. "Easier work, *palamna*," she purred. "Easy work." She nodded over her shoulder at Jake and Matt, let her half grin grow. "Not got a clue I've bolted yet. Took some good cargo with me, too."

"Others are Nas." The tone was a warning, easily missed if she didn't know the language well.

"Yeah, but they sound," she assured with just the right amount of edge to her voice. "They like profit, too."

"You get good profit off that cargo. Can see why you bolt. What that other one though?"

She shrugged, glad Matt couldn't understand this conversation. His ego would take an even harder hit than learning his selling price. "He get good money from certain kind."

Jaxin nodded in a knowing way, his wedge-shaped head bobbing on a long, slender neck. "You really bolt, *devesa*? I heard of you, even out this way. Ah ya, I know you now. The Belaxi on Nas. You hero in that place."

"You hear 'bout that out here?" She kept her growing panic carefully concealed behind a lazy smile. "Never hurt to fool the skinny, right. Got in good. Trusted me with expensive cargo."

Jaxin fell silent, his huge gray eyes flickered as his transparent second lids blinked.

She held her pose but swallowing around her dry throat took effort. She couldn't believe her reputation had traveled as far as Dockland Depot. Of all the rotten luck. She'd been hoping to be anonymous here. Being a known hero would make it more difficult to convince people she'd turned renegade.

She watched Jaxin consider her and her explanation. They needed him to believe, now more than ever. If she couldn't convince him she'd acted hero to fool a mark, she'd have a hell of a time convincing anyone else. Though, convincing anyone else would be a moot point if they didn't survived this standoff.

She let her gaze roam over Jaxin, taking in his gray and blue scales, the thickness of his tail, the way his leather vest fit tight over huge pectoral muscles and revealed long, strong arms. She hadn't played this game in years, distraction through seduction. She'd been too busy trying to get away from these games, too busy trying to get people to see her as something other than her looks. Nas had rid her of her over-confidence in her appearance, but she could tell Jaxin thought her an attractive human woman and that was all it took to fall back into the old ways.

Smiling up at him, she moving her DEG so it rested along her thigh. The gesture drew his gaze down and a lipless smile opened his mouth to reveal three rows of sharp teeth. Yet another reason she avoided interspecies romances. Too many parts that didn't quite fit. She didn't truly believe Jaxin was after a tumble either, just playing the game. At least, she hoped so. She intended to play this particular gambit only so far.

When he looked up again, he said, "You play your mark good, they give you that cargo to carry."

"I play good, *palamna.* Every time."

He chuckled, a deep rumble that vibrated through her bones.

"You need a trader, *devesa,* you give Jaxin of Deent a shout. I get you a good price. Even on the ugly one."

She grinned, nodded her head in companionable agreement.

Jaxin stepped aside.

She motioned the others on. "Jaxin, you know fixer named Telani, he work here?"

"Ya, Telani lodge in the lower ring, Belaxi refuge. Business run out of the Ulami."

At least Telani hadn't moved. "Ta, Jaxin. We catch you 'round."

She walked away with as much dignity as she could, pulling in all her willpower to keep her wobbly knees from buckling.

"That was close," Bythan whispered.

Her voice sounded about as steady as Leia's knees. "Very. Let's get to the Ulami before anyone else decides we're interesting enough to stop." She traded places with Moyra so she could explain the situation to Vanian. "They know who I am here," she told her second. "They've already heard about the bloody Governor General. The Gormalath will spread word I've gone renegade for the profit but that may not save us hassle now. We need to work fast."

"Moyra says they won't give us clearance to leave for a full cycle. We're gonna have to find a place to hole up while you're dealing."

Vanian's smooth rich voice sounded strained. She spoke quietly despite the noise in the corridor. Someone would have to have pretty sensitive equipment to overhear them, but Vanian had never been one for ignoring simple precautions. One of many reasons Leia was glad to have her here.

She glanced at her second. Vanian's short white hair curled artfully around a narrow, sharp-boned face. Her flawless skin, the color of mahogany, betrayed no hint of her anxiety. Even her deep jade gaze focused steadily forward, alert but not concerned. She played the part well, and Leia admired her skill.

She only hoped her own act held up so well.

"We'll get a safe hole from Telani," she said, hoping saying the words aloud would make them true. "He owes me. With a bit of luck, we'll be on and off Dockland Depot within a single cycle."

Vanian's mouth ticked up at one corner, her only outward sign of reaction. "Lieutenant," she murmured, "you better make sure that's good luck you're asking the universe for."

Leia repeated a plea to the universe and the saints for *good* luck all the way to the central core lifts.

JAKE STARED AT THE GROUND WHILE HE TRIED TO REIN IN HIS TEMPER.

Ridiculous to be jealous of a dinosaur alien, ridiculous to feel such anger. But he did. Jealousy seethed in his blood, making it damned hard to think straight. His hands actually ached from where he'd ground his fingernails into his palms to keep from reacting to Leia's play with the dinosaur.

There had been no mistaking the way she'd handled the situation, even if he couldn't understand the words spoken. Her body language changed from the solid, professional soldier to a sexy temptress in the blink of an eye. Equally obvious, she'd got them out of a potentially deadly situation. He should admire her actions. And he did, in the more rational parts of his brain. In fact, the part of him that could think logically was impressed with her style. But the part of him that wasn't thinking logically, the part he wanted buried inside Leia at the soonest possible moment, hated the way she'd flirted with that huge alien *thing*. He felt like an idiot. But he wanted the sexy temptress for himself, damn it.

She wasn't his. She didn't belong to him. Hell, she intended to get him home soon. Nothing was going to happen between them. He was a prisoner. He'd been kidnapped and nearly sold into slavery. He had bigger things to worry about right now than whether or not Leia flirted with weird creatures in her spare time.

A sharp pain made him wince. Slowly, he relaxed his fists, looked to see blood welling in the crescent nail shape in his left palm. Okay, he was acting stupid and illogical. And getting nowhere. He was in a space station, for Christ sake. The least he could do was look around.

The corridor they passed through, despite teeming with varied life, remained spotlessly clean as the bay. He scowled at the floor. Everything was so damned clean. Didn't feel natural. The air seemed so... empty, no taste, no smells...

That was what bothered him about this place—no smells! There had been smells in the bay, a clean scent, stale, but a scent nonetheless. He couldn't detect even that stale, clean scent in the corridor, despite any number of different species running around the place, including some pretty slimy-looking things. No body odor, no perfumes, no oils, no dirt, no nothing. The place smelled blank.

"You notice the smell," he murmured to Matt, wondering if he'd gone a little insane after all.

"What smell?"

"My point. There isn't one. Doesn't this seem like the kind of place that would stink?"

"Maybe. Maybe they just have good air circulation."

"No body odor, no perfumes?"

"I don't know," Matt hissed irritably. "I've never been on a space station before. You tell me, billion *Tracnas* boy."

The childishness in Matt's voice almost made Jake laugh. "That still bothering you?" he asked with a half smile. How could he be too nervous when his partner was acting like an ass?

Matt cast him a sideways smile. "Just don't let it go to your head, buddy. Soon as we're home things will return to normal, with me the good-looking one and you the scruffy worthless one."

Jake chuckled, hiding the laugh behind a cough. Leave it to Matt. The man had some talent for lightening even the worst situation. Matt stayed sane by injecting humor. Jake stayed sane by ignoring the worst of a case and allowing himself to appreciate Matt's humor. They both survived by catching the bad guys.

Though he wouldn't have wished this predicament on his partner, Jake was glad to know Matt was here to back him up. Their current situation would have been far worse if not for the measure of control Leia had given them by providing weapons and the code to the restraints they wore around their wrists. He felt more like he was working undercover than being held prisoner, and the illusion kept him from chafing.

He went back to contemplating the lack of smell as they turned down a corridor into a narrow, round tunnel. Forgetting to keep his head bowed, he glanced up. The top of the tunnel was made of some see-through material that gave a brilliant view of myriad spikes crossing from the outer rings to the inner core. Jake stared at the lines of lights above him and again thought of a special-effects screen. The view was awesome and yet unreal. His brain didn't really believe what his eyes saw just beyond that clear substance over his head.

"Bit like a ride at Disneyland," Matt murmured.

Jake nodded. That was exactly what it felt like. A ride. He glanced at a small, multiple-armed, green creature with hair that reminded him of snakes and a set of very sharp teeth in both mouths. Okay, maybe a dangerous ride.

He fought the temptation to glance back at Leia, just to be sure she was still there, to read her reaction to all this. With effort, he kept his gaze forward, taking in the passing scene with a sense of numbness. He just couldn't make his mind believe all this was real.

He remembered the feel of Leia in his arms, the touch of her lips against his. *That* had felt real. Everything about Leia felt real. Good, sexy, soft and lush. He could sink into fantasies of Leia with ease, putting all his other concerns on hold.

Another bizarre-looking creature walked past—this one with what looked like wings coated in scaly armor, a body spotted with patches of velvety feathers, and a wicked-looking beak. Given the world he'd walked into, he probably should pay attention to his surroundings and not fall into fantasizing about Leia. He was actually surprised his survival instincts left any room for fantasies. But there they were, teasing him. Good thing she was walking behind him. If he had to watch her move, he knew he could walk into a tunnel of flames without noticing.

They came to a round, iris-like door that spun open as they approached. Beyond was a clean gray chamber, the size of a walk-in closet. As they piled in, the guards turned to face the door. No one else got into the closet room with them. "An elevator?" he asked the back of Leia's head when the iris spun closed.

Leia touched her jaw but didn't look back.

He let out a relieved breath. Bad enough he had such a good view of her backside now. Worse if he had to look into her eyes.

"We have to travel to another ring," she said. "The gravity will be different to what you are accustomed to. It will feel like you are wearing…lead boots, difficult to pick up your feet. Walking will be an effort. But not so difficult that you can't move. Understand?"

"Uh-huh. Why?"

She glanced back then, a flash of dark eyes.

He swallowed, trying to think past his racing pulse.

She grinned, just a slight lifting of her lips. "The gravity is like that of my home world," she said. "Belax."

She faced forward again, denying him the view of her seductive profile but leaving him free to let his gaze, and mind, roam over her back, the curve of her hips, the length of her legs. She wasn't nearly as tall as the other women, but her curves were so much more interesting.

The iris whirred open again suddenly. He hadn't even felt the elevator move. Another special effect. They stepped into the room and the scenery on the other side, "off screen", changed. He felt the difference in gravity the instant they started to move. Walking into the elevator had been easy, normal. Taking a step out felt more like moving through thick mud. "See what you mean," he murmured to Leia's back.

"This is just the adjustment. You won't feel the ring's gravity until we've left the transfer tunnel."

He watched with some amusement as the other three women and Matt all moved gingerly out of the elevator, alternately dragging their feet then lifting them in exaggerated steps against the sucking pull of the gravity shift. He knew he moved with the same exaggerated motions.

Leia stepped high twice and then resumed a normal gait. She chuckled and said something to Vanian as they moved down the transfer tunnel toward the ring.

Her chuckle set his skin tingling. He wanted to ask what she'd said, but there were others in the tunnel now. He had to remind himself he was supposed to be her prisoner.

He glanced up at the lines of light above him, connecting the outer rings to the inner core. A glowing blue light illuminated this tunnel, subtler than the white glow of the first tunnel. The air was different, too. Still easy to breathe, light, clean… But there was something. An actual smell. He couldn't place it. A hint of spice? A tang of citrus? Very faint, but noticeable after the complete lack of smells in the first ring.

They stepped into the ring proper and were swept up into a carnival. The corridor was packed with a multitude of creatures, all shouting and yelling. A lower ceiling in this ring made the cacophony of sound more intense. From a nook in the corridor's main wall, a group dressed in strange costumes played what was probably supposed to be music. What he thought might be a food vendor pushed a cart down through the crowd, shouting in a lilt Jake could understand even without knowing the words. If they had hotdogs and popcorn in this place, that vendor was hawking them.

The smells hit him an instant after the noise. The vendor's cart let off a noxious odor that reminded him of burnt hair and melting plastic. The passing crowds left a mingling heavy scents in the air, too chaotic to identify, but it reminded him of walking into a department store when the women with the perfume samples were going crazy. Though the corridor was still spotlessly clean, a faint haze hung in the air, leaving him feeling a little dizzy.

"Whatever they're smoking in here should probably be illegal," Matt muttered sucking in a shallow breath.

As before, the crowd gave way before their little group. A murmur of interest followed them but no one stepped into their path. A long, slender, four-fingered hand reached out to touch Jake's sleeve as they passed. He jerked back from the caress.

One of the following Guards, Bythan, stepped forward with a raised weapon. She pointed her gun at the interloper until they were past, the threat obvious for all to see.

Jake resisted turning his head to get a better look. The slight touch had sent a shiver of revulsion through him for no reason he could explain. He didn't want to look too closely at a creature that could cause that instinctive reaction with a mere touch.

His head bowed again, he concentrated on studying the chambers they passed branching off from the packed corridor. Some were shops selling things he couldn't identify, others seemed to be warehouses or storage rooms and still others looked like bars and nightclubs. A large number of doorways looked in on what he could only guess were brothels—though some of what they pandered in those rooms obviously wasn't intended for humans. When he watched a human male walk into a brothel he'd been sure was for aliens, he shuddered.

Some things were better not to think about.

They passed one open door that drew his attention. The chamber inside seemed vast and dark, shadowed against the blue light of the corridor. He squinted into the blackness, wondering what had caught his notice. He couldn't see anything moving. The room looked empty. They moved past it before he could figure out what had disturbed him. Probably something else he didn't want to know about anyway.

A sound, quiet but distinct, pierced his thoughts. He startled, nearly stopping when he felt something unfamiliar brush over and through his mind. "What the hell is that?" He jerked around, trying to find the source. A faint whisper breathed through him, just beyond his ability to hear and understand. There was a pull to the whispers, a desire for… something. That nebulous desire made him retch.

"Jake," Leia said, her hands gripping his arms. "Jake, what is it?"

He forced a couple of deep breaths, pushing down his panic. The whispers faded to nothing. His head throbbed in their wake. He concentrated on the feel of Leia's sure grip on his biceps, the deep color of her eyes, the concern creasing her brow. The pain in his head eased. Another deep breath, and he said, "It felt like someone was whispering in my mind." He had to swallow before he could finish. "Trying to tell me something or make me do something. I couldn't tell." He shuddered so violently, Leia's hands dropped away.

He missed the contact and started to reach out to her before remembering the restraints on his wrists. He dropped his arms. The concern on her face didn't help calm his racing pulse. "That wasn't just my imagination, was it?" he asked.

She shook her head in a slight gesture of denial but her gaze was turned inward. Finally she looked up, her eyes so dark they were nearly black in the blue light. "If it happens again, tell me immediately." She turned to the other Guards, said something in their native language and they resumed their course.

He moved close enough so she would hear him over the noise. "You'll explain what happened to me later." He wasn't asking. This was one secret he would not allow her to keep. He'd thought he felt vulnerable before. His earlier feelings paled compared to how he felt now. Dirty. Invaded. How could he fight something he couldn't see or block? How was he supposed to shoot a voice in his head?

What if the voice had succeeded in persuading him to do its bidding? What would its command have been?

Leia didn't turn around, her step didn't change, but she nodded, a small gesture that let him know she understood.

5

Leia didn't let her fear show on her face, but it churned in her gut, leaving a sour taste in the back of her mouth. They had to get to a safe hiding place soon. They couldn't afford to parade the men through the corridors any longer.

She'd underestimated the interest the men would generate here, hadn't counted on someone trying to steal them away. She'd been more concerned with her own story, explaining herself and the other Guards. Their story was good, too—believable with Jake in tow. But if their story was believable because Jake was worth so much, then he was worth that much to anyone bold enough to take him. She hadn't taken the audacity of some thieves into consideration.

Not many would launch such a blatant attack against four armed, renegade Guards. And if the Gormalath on C2 had heard of her, then the throngs down here certainly knew about her. Only someone very cocky and sure of himself would risk trying to take what she'd claimed as her own.

To have someone like that stalking them scared her more than the attack itself.

She had to consider the attack could have been random. The Duster could simply have been playing a game. A very dangerous game, but a game nonetheless. But that wouldn't be typical of its kind. Too much risk for no immediate compensation. Dusters needed ready funds to pay for their habit. Without a financial incentive, what reason could there be for this one to act?

She'd grill Telani. He'd know if any Dusters on Dockland were aggressive enough to try stealing Jake on their own. If not, he'd know which thieves on the station were bold enough and had enough money to pay a Duster to steal Jake.

Because if this stunt wasn't just a Duster playing games, if someone *had* tried to take Jake, the station wouldn't be big enough for the thief to hide.

She breathed in the familiar, heavy scents of a Belaxian carnival and tried to calm her racing heartbeat. Not easy to do in the midst of the crowds. The push and pull of the throng left her even more edgy, her anger twisting tighter. Years ago, Telani's brothers had tried to scare her with stories of this Dockland ring. The atmosphere was always like this, a constant carnival, a never-ending party. A place where business was done in the midst of desperate revelry.

The celebrations felt forced and dirty. Frantic. There was none of the charm and joy she associated with Carnival on Belax. This party hid darker intentions, disguised lost souls and depraved motives, drew in the vulnerable like prey and allowed evil a free hand. She had to suppress a snarl of revulsion. This carnival was a perversion of her home world's custom. Everything about it sickened her.

Her disgust must have shown, or maybe the number of weapons she and the other women carried intimidated the crowds. Whatever the reason, the press of people cleared a narrow path for them as they made their way along the corridor to the Ulami.

A bar that catered to expatriate Belaxi, the Ulami, was their place. The constant carnival didn't intrude, the deals and business were kept amongst themselves. No outsiders allowed, no interlopers permitted. The Ulami was a haven to Belaxi and a death zone to anyone else.

She'd only ventured there once before. She'd been desperate, in trouble and in over her head.

Early in her career, before she'd moved to Nas and a position in the

Nas Guard, she'd worked as a mercenary to get the training she couldn't get legitimately on Belax. But the lifestyle hadn't been easy. She'd gotten in over her head more than once. She only worked freelance for two years before deciding to leave Belax for Nas.

A reveler stumbled too close to her group, and Leia raised her DEG in warning. The drunken Belaxi moved out of the way, holding up his hands in surrender. Leia snarled. Nothing changed here.

The assignment that had landed her on Dockland Depot all those years ago nearly cost her her life. She'd been sent by a very wealthy Belaxi farmer to return his runaway daughter. But the crowd of Nasen expats the girl fell in with wasn't prepared to give her up. They put a contract out on Leia when she proved impossible to bribe. Leia ran to the Ulami and the help of kin.

Since she'd saved Telani's butt more than once as kids, he returned the favor by giving her a safe place to hide until she managed to snatch the farmer's daughter from under the nose of her captors and get off the station. After that, they were even.

Until Telani had gotten himself in trouble on Nas.

Leia stopped her small group outside the door to the Ulami. "Wait here," she told Vanian. "Guard the men closely. This throng is dangerous."

Vanian nodded.

Leia watched for a moment as Vanian put the men close to the wall across from the Ulami's entrance and she and the other two formed up in front of them. Satisfied Jake was safe, Leia moved into the quiet, cool den of the bar.

The room was a large cavern made of the same gray metal as the corridor but softened by pink lighting. A window of one-way, darkly tinted glass looked out onto the corridor. No one in the corridor could see into the pub but the patrons of the pub could see the party outside. Tables scattered over the polished but scarred green floor. A long counter lined the back wall, behind which a Belaxi expat served drinks. The only other obvious door in the room was behind the bar, though she knew from experience hidden doors were located to the right near the entrance and to the left near the back. Otherwise, no decoration, ornaments, hidden corners or nooks broke up the monotony.

The Ulami was one big yawning space where secrets were kept out in the open.

Every patron in the bar turned to stare and the already quiet room fell silent. She stared back, cocking her hip to one side. Every man in the room came from Belax. And she was the image of femininity on Belax. She hadn't felt this much male attention focused on her in a long time. The usual annoyance she experienced was coated with a sense of relief. The fact she needed the reassurance meant she'd been on Nas for far too long.

She searched the faces until she spotted Telani.

He had his head ducked, his gaze averted. The only man in the room not looking at her.

She smiled and sauntered toward him. "Hey, cousin," she said with half the room still between them.

Telani looked up, grimaced. "I know I owe you. Does it have to be now?" He nodded at the distinguished-looking man across the table.

Leia's smile grew. So he was trying to do business, huh? Good news. He'd be much more cooperative if he wanted to get her out of his hair so he could finish his dealing. She strolled up to the table and settled her gaze on the man sitting with Telani. "My name's Ballore. Leia."

"Kahio Gasine. It's a distinct pleasure, Ms. Ballore." He held out his hand.

She shook his hand, not giving him the chance to kiss her palm as was traditional, and corrected his assumption. "It's Lieutenant Ballore."

"Lieutenant? In a Belax company?"

The man sounded so appalled, Leia almost laughed. "I'm in the Nas Guard," she said as she studied him. His hand was soft, his clothing impeccable, his beard and mustache a nice silver contrast to his brown skin. His eyes were as dark brown as Telani's. He had a single scar running from his right temple to his nose. He would be considered a good catch on Belax among the women looking for moneyed men.

"Leia's quite the hero," Telani spoke up.

The calculating look in his eyes warned her a second too late, giving her no chance to avoid his maneuvering.

"She'll make an excellent wife when she moves back to Belax."

Leia cursed silently.

"I imagine she will." Gasine looked her over slowly, his smile turning lecherous.

Leia remembered suddenly why she'd left Belax. She pulled her hand from Gasine's grip. "But since I won't be moving back for many years, it's not something to be worried about."

She turned to face Telani, letting him see her irritation.

His dark eyes widened as if asking, What?

"If Mr. Gasine can spare you a minute, cousin," she growled, "I need to talk to you."

Telani exchanged a look with the other man.

Gasine rose and left without comment, but he contrived to brush past her on his way, his hand sweeping across her butt in a caress so slight it could have been an accident.

She snarled but otherwise ignored the insult. She needed help here. Wouldn't do to start a bar brawl.

She dropped into the chair across from Telani, glaring until he lifted his shoulders and actually did say, "What? Your mother would have my head if I hadn't put in a good word for you with Gasine. He's worth a cool fortune."

"I don't give a flying *chook* how much he's worth, Telani. If you ever try to sell me to the highest bidder again, I'll cut off your nuts. We clear?" She'd been able to kick his ass since they were teenagers. He'd better remember who the hell he was messing with.

He raised his hands in defeat. "No worries, little sistah. Now, what can I do for you so I can get you out of my hair? I got business here."

"So I noticed. I need help. I need a ship, fast, unregistered. Something Grettel's gang can't track me in."

"Saints, Leia, what are you in?"

"I also need a place to stay tonight, big enough for six people. Just until we're cleared to leave."

"You don't ask no little favors, sistah. What're you carrying, and can I make a profit from it?"

"None of your business and no. I just need the ship and a place to stay. I saved your life, Telani. Don't get mercenary on me now."

He leaned back in his seat, taking her in with an almost brotherly expression. "Being a Nas Guard, it suits you, Leia. You always were a ball-breaker."

She grinned, leaned back in her own chair. "Come on, Tel. Don't mess me around. Can you get me the ship?"

"Yes. I'll need half a cycle to line it up."

"Genius. Got a place we can hide?"

"That's gonna be trickier. You're gonna have to tell me what you're hiding so I don't put you in the wrong spot."

Leia studied her cousin. He wore his long black hair pulled back in a high tail similar to her own. The hairstyle brought out the sharp cut of his cheekbones and gold color of his skin. He had two very distinct scars on his face. One ran across his right jaw, the other curled his top lip, giving him a permanent snarl. He kept his face clean-shaven to better display the scars. Telani was considered something of a catch himself on Belax.

She knew she couldn't trust him. He'd as soon sell her out as he would a stranger. And Jake was a fortune Telani would have a hard time passing up. Her cousin did not live on Belax anymore for a reason. Maybe if he didn't see Jake…

She leaned forward, resting her forearms on the table. "Okay, I'm on a run. I can't discuss the cargo. It's a retrieval and return." She watched his eyes widen, the avarice creep in despite his best efforts to keep his expression personable. "I've put out the story we're renegade," she continued, "to explain our uniforms. But I have every intention of returning this cargo, Telani. And I'll kill to make sure that happens. You understand?"

He nodded, but his dark eyes had hardened, his gaze narrowed. "Must be valuable goods."

"Aren't they always? They'd have sold well on Hrokwall."

Telani's eyebrows rose, his expression softened. "Hrokwall types, huh? I suppose we can find a place to hide them." He grimaced. "Don't fancy those types too much, little sistah. Hrokwalli have some strange taste in goods."

"Tell me about it." She straightened. If Telani insisted, she'd show him Matt. That should settle any greedy thoughts he might have. As long as she could keep Telani from seeing Jake, they should all be safe. "So we okay? You got a place?"

"I do indeed. Give me ten to close with Gasine. Then we'll move. You want to bring them in?"

She shook her head. "We'll keep them outside the fold." Given Telani's interest in her cargo, she didn't think the Ulami would be a safe place for them to lay low, even for ten minutes. She also had to figure out a way to keep Telani from getting a look at Jake. She stalked back outside, drawing the gazes of the men in the bar as she moved. But she was too tense and worried to appreciate the male attention now. She'd rather be invisible.

And if possible, she wanted Jake invisible, too.

JAKE WAS WATCHING THE DOOR TO THE BAR, SO HE SAW LEIA AS SOON as she walked out. He sighed out a breath he hadn't realized he'd been holding. She looked worried, but she wasn't hurt. Worried they could handle.

She insinuated herself into the group, talked quietly with Vanian for a few minutes. The suspense had him tapping his foot. He'd never been good at surveillance, didn't have the patience for it. This was worse because their lives were on the line. That brush over his mind still had him shaken. The sooner they got off this damned station, the better.

After a moment, Vanian moved off into the crowd.

Leia turned to face him and Matt. She pressed her jaw and said, "Telani is going to help us, but we have a problem. I don't want him to see you, Jake. He is too greedy. He'd give us away for a cut of what

Jake is worth. Vanian is going to acquire a couple of hoods. They're used sometimes for slaves."

"Hoods? We won't be able to see?" Jake was pretty sure he hated this plan.

"I hate that idea," Matt said. "I'd rather see an attack coming."

"I understand," Leia said. "I do. But I cannot let Telani see you." She sighed and glanced over her shoulder toward the front of the bar.

Her Guards were blocking Jake and Matt from view, but anyone determined to get a look could probably see glimpses through those dark windows.

She faced them again. "Please. It's the only way I can make sure you are safe. I won't seal the hoods. You will be able to remove them easily."

Jake sucked in a big gulp of smoky air. He looked at Matt. A wealth of misgivings were exchanged in that look. They had to decide, here and now, did they trust Leia Ballore? Jake turned back to her, taking in the concern in her dark eyes. She didn't fidget or show any other signs of nervousness. To someone not looking into her face, she appeared perfectly at ease. But he could see she was worried. Worried for him.

The thought warmed him to his toes. He turned to Matt. "Better than being dead."

"If you say so." Matt didn't look nearly as sure, but he nodded his agreement, trusting Jake's instincts.

Jake had lived for years on excellent instincts. "We'll agree to the hoods so long as we can remove them," Jake said.

Leia's eyes widened, and she let out a whoosh of air. "I won't let you down. I promise." She held Jake's gaze as she spoke.

He felt the look like a caress. His heart rate sped. He was getting just a little too caught up in Leia Ballore's dark eyes and sexy body. The woman had a way of distracting him, until nothing else mattered but her. He and Matt were in danger of being killed or sold into slavery, and all he could think about was getting Leia alone. *You've got some very screwed up priorities, Marshall. And somehow, that didn't seem to matter either.*

"How do you know this guy?" he asked, needing to talk so he could keep from doing something he was pretty sure she'd find embarrassing.

"He is a cousin. On my mother's side. We've managed to get each other out of a scrape or two in the past. He owes me now, but I'm sure he'll call this even when we're done."

"You think he'd sell you out."

"I know he would. For a piece of what you would bring at auction, he'd sell out his mother. Which is why he's living here and not on Belax."

Jake smiled, a crooked grin that was at complete odds with their predicament. He'd bet money her mother and her cousin's mother were forces to be reckoned with. "Why does he owe you?"

Her grin flashed. "I saved his sorry life on Nas, kept him from facing a potential death sentence when he was caught trying to smuggle restricted minerals off-planet. He owes me big for that."

"So you won't be even when this is over. He'll still owe you?"

"Oh no. We'll be even."

He frowned but before he could ask about her last comment he spied Vanian in the crowd. The tall woman trotted toward them, making her way easily through the throngs. Most hurried out of her way. She handed Leia a small black bundle then took up her post again, further blocking him and Matt from curious onlookers.

Leia murmured, "Bend please. I'll put them on."

Jake and Matt exchanged another worried glance, then Jake bent his head, putting himself, once again, into Leia's hands. She moved close enough that he breathed in her clean scent, a small space of fresh air in the smoke-filled corridor. He met her gaze as she lifted the black hood, held it while she pulled the hood over his head. When the stiff black material settled into place, blocking his sight, he felt her gentle grip on his shoulder.

She leaned in and whispered near his ear, "I'll guide you, Jake. Don't worry."

He tipped his head closer to hers. "I'm not worried." He could still smell her through the hood and the scent did funny things to him.

Without sight, he was acutely aware of the warmth of her hand on his shoulder, the brush of her hair against his arm, the scent of her, the huskiness in her voice. And her sincerity. Erotic images of dark sweaty nights filled his imagination. In his artificially black world, he could concentrate on those images, expand and develop them. He swallowed hard and stood up straight before he did something supremely stupid.

He strained to hear everything going on around him. With the noise in the corridor, he had difficulty focusing on any one thing. He concentrated on the sounds of Matt and Leia next to him.

Matt grunted when the hood was down and murmured something about S&M.

"Ignore him," Jake said. "He loves this. He just doesn't want to admit it."

"Keep it up, buddy, and I won't tell you when you can take off your hood," Matt said.

The tinge of fear Jake heard in Matt's voice earlier had intensified.

Jake hated having his sight restricted, but this would be much more uncomfortable for Matt. Matt's older sister and father had both succumbed to a sudden and irreversible blindness that the doctors couldn't explain. They blamed genetics, though they couldn't give any good explanations. The idea of going suddenly blind terrified Matt.

Jake reached over and grabbed Matt's wrist, squeezing. He couldn't tell if Matt felt much through the bracers, but he'd know Jake was with him. Someone understood.

They stood rigid and quiet until a new voice rose into the group. Jake listened to the new voice talking with Leia and wanted to curse. If he had one wish at the moment, he'd wish for one of Leia's translation thingies.

Leia watched Telani's face closely as he moved into their group, looking for any sign that he knew more than she wanted him to.

"Hoods? You need hoods for Hrokwall cargo?"

"Can't be too careful," she said, keeping her voice neutral. "Where're we going?"

He stared another minute at the two men.

Leia held her breath. She'd hate to cause a serious rift with Telani, but she'd do it to save Jake.

"Hrokwall buying 'em bigger now?"

Jake was much more muscled and heavy than Matt who had the slim, toned look she associated with adolescence, the build most popular on Hrokwall. Jake could never be mistaken for a teenager. She shrugged, hoping her growing panic didn't show. Her heart thumped so hard it hurt. "Once he loses a little weight, he'll be perfect. Has that kind of face."

Telani nodded, his scarred mouth pursed.

He didn't believe her. She could see it in his narrowed eyes.

He studied her closely.

Only extreme self-control kept Leia from fidgeting or looking away.

He lifted a shoulder in a casual shrug. "If you say so. Personally, I'm glad I wasn't born Hrokwalli."

Leia let out a slow, quiet breath. Telani might not believe her, but he wasn't going to push the situation, either. The less he knew, the better for both of them. She smiled at her cousin, glad that for once he let familial loyalty overcome his greed. Maybe he was more grateful for her last favor than she thought.

As Telani moved off down the corridor, Leia took hold of Jake's arm and led him forward. Vanian escorted Matt, falling in behind Leia and Jake. Moyra and Bythan took up the rear. Leia had to concentrate to keep her mind off the feel of Jake's biceps under her hand, the flex of hard muscle, the texture of his skin. Her senses filled with his musky scent. She had a nearly uncontrollable urge to pull him into the nearest dark room and keep him there for the rest of her life. She didn't dare look at him. Even with his head covered, his sheer maleness over-whelmed her.

A drop of sweat rolled down his thick biceps, landing on her hand. Without thinking, she rubbed his arm in a comforting gesture, sure the unseen dangers surrounding him caused his reaction. She was warm as well, but for a very different reason.

She forced herself to concentrate, to pay attention to their path.

Telani led them around the ring toward the residential area. Here, the doors sealed tight against intrusion and the partying crowds thinned, though they didn't completely vanish.

She took note of the few shops they passed, studying the route. It wasn't easy to get lost in one of the outer rings. They didn't branch off into different corridors except where the spikes led inward to the lifts between rings. Only the central rings were large enough to have more than one level. But a person could still get turned around even in the outer rings. Every section looked similar to every other section, the distinctive markers hard to tell apart if you didn't concentrate. A visitor to Dockland could be found wandering in never-ending circles, trying to find their way back to something familiar.

She counted the sealed doors between one marker and the next, making sure she could get back to the appropriate lift quickly. Every second would count when they left the station.

Telani stopped at a nondescript door, sealed closed like so many others. The crowd ebbed and flowed in gentle waves behind them as Telani keyed a code into the panel beside the gray door. It swished upward with the sound of escaping air. Thick dark shadows left the room's interior a mystery.

She hesitated outside, waited for Telani to go in first.

He smiled as he moved inside, acknowledging her caution. He wouldn't have walked into an unfamiliar room first either.

She remained in the hall, trying not to let the tension in her body travel into the hand holding Jake. He didn't need to know how nervous she was. He'd placed a great deal of trust in her. She wanted to deserve that trust.

The lights inside flickered on, a soft pink glow similar to the interior of Ulami. Telani poked his head back out the door, a grin stretching his scars. "Welcome to Chez Telani where all your hiding needs will be met."

Leia rolled her eyes as she moved past him, easing inside. She scanned first, checking for anything suspicious. The room was a huge open space. Pink lights soothed the cold white marble covering the floor. They were on the outer side of the ring and a huge floor-to-ceiling window gave a spectacular view of the star-speckled expanse of space beyond. The furniture, three large couches and a number of stuffed chairs, was plush and soft looking in shades of pink and orange.

She glanced up and gasped at the intricate mural painted on the ceiling. The scene came from Belaxian mythology with a beautiful woman held captive by a fire-breathing dragon. The knight facing the dragon wore silver armor that glowed orange from the dragon's flames. The colors of the mural blended with the color of the furnishings.

She noted the single door to the left and searched the right wall until she spotted the area she was sure had the hidden door. "Do I need a special code to get into the room to the right?"

Telani gave her a rueful half smile. "Should have known." He crossed to the gray wall, blank but for two narrow floor-to-ceiling tapestries. Just between the tapestries, he pressed a section of wall, midway up. The wall dented in and the door swung open. "Not too complicated. It'll respond to your hand." His grin widened. "Not much there of interest to you, though. It's empty."

"For the moment." She had no doubt he usually housed something in that room. He must be between jobs. "The other door leads to a bedroom?"

"No, that's the bathroom. But you'll love it. Could probably sleep another six people in there."

She glanced around the room again. "So, you're telling me I'm bedding down on a couch tonight?" There were only three in the room. Someone would be sleeping on chairs. The marble floor did not seem a reasonable option for a good night's rest.

"'Fraid so. Best I could do on short notice. Be grateful I got a space with a bathroom. And since it's empty, no one'll be nosing in here. At least not in the next cycle."

"We'll be gone as soon as you get us a ship and we get clearance. Get me the specs and I'll get Moyra to work on the leave clearance immediately."

"No problem, little sistah. I'll get it to you in a couple of hours.

And I don't want to know about it when you leave. I'll assume you're gone after a cycle."

Telani turned toward the door as Leia settled Jake into one of the chairs. "Telani," she called.

He paused in the doorway, glancing back at her with a raised brow.

"Thanks, brah. We're even now."

He nodded. "Yeah." He glanced at Jake. "I'd say we are."

When the door closed behind him, she let out an audible sigh and turned to remove Jake's hood.

He already had it off and was staring up at her, his blue eyes intense.

She tried to smile and failed miserably. She didn't know what to say. He knew she didn't trust Telani. No point in hiding her relief.

She glanced around to see if Matt still had his hood on, an excuse to look away from Jake before she embarrassed herself.

The other man stood rubbing his still cuffed hands over his face. His blond hair was mussed, his face red and sweat streaked. The hoods hadn't been that warm.

She frowned, pressed the translator. "Matthew? Are you well?"

He half smiled, half grimaced. "Fine. Great. Where's the bathroom?"

She motioned Vanian to remove the cuffs. "The door to the left." She pointed Matt in the right direction then turned back to Jake. He hadn't moved, hadn't taken his gaze off her. She knelt down next to the chair to remove his cuffs, keeping her gaze on her task so she wouldn't have to meet his.

"He's got a fear of going blind," Jake said quietly to the top of her head. "That was more of an ordeal than he wants to let on."

She looked up. "I'm sorry. I didn't realize."

"Didn't have much choice anyway. He'll get over it. Just needs a few minutes."

She leaned against the chair's thick arm, looking at the cuffs she held. She noticed Jake flexing his hands now that the restraints were off. He had large hands with long fingers. Capable hands. Strong hands. The idea of him touching her body with those hands sent a shiver down her spine.

"You okay?" he asked.

"Fine." She kept her head bowed so he wouldn't see the color rising in her cheeks. She could feel the telltale heat and wished her hair was down to hide her. "Are you okay?"

"As good as can be expected. I'm pretty damned hungry, though."

Her head snapped up. "I forgot. I'm sorry. Just a minute." She scrambled to her feet and motioned Bythan close. She gave instructions for food she thought Jake and Matt would be able to stomach and sent Bythan off. So much had happened, she'd completely forgotten about food. They'd all had to live off ration bars in the shuttle during the long journey to Dockland, but the last time they'd eaten was nearly half a cycle ago. Now that Jake mentioned it, she realized her stomach was growling.

She crossed back to him, tempted to sit at his feet again just so she could stay close. She resisted the urge. The floor was too damned hard anyway. "Bythan's bringing food now. I'm sorry I forgot. You should have said earlier."

"You were a little busy." He grinned, quick and wry.

Her heart jumped. Saints, he was sexy. She was going to hate watching him return. The idea jolted her hard, unexpectedly. She knew he'd be leaving. She'd been reminding herself of the fact since meeting him. But all at once, his departure seemed both real and unbearable. She wanted more time with him, time to really know him. There was something about him... The man was incredibly brave, and yet displayed a wry sense of humor that touched her. Her lips burned for another of his kisses. She wanted more than a single quick brush of lips. She wanted to keep him to herself for a very long time.

Looking away, she hoped he didn't see her sudden longing. Jake didn't need to know she was mooning over him. He had enough to worry about. "Make yourself comfortable," she said to his feet. "We'll be here a while. Sleep if you can."

She moved away to consult with Vanian, trying hard to ignore the pain in her chest.

6

Jake stared up at the ceiling mural without really seeing it. The room was quiet, the only sounds the soft snuffle of breath from those sleeping.

Moyra sat in a chair pulled up to one side of the door, taking her turn on watch. Her weapon rested on her lap, her gaze stayed focused on the door. In the dim light, her vibrant red hair looked a dark blood red and her pale white skin tinted pink.

Matt, Vanian and Bythan stretched out on the three couches, deeply asleep by the sounds of their breathing. The room's pink glow had been dimmed to make sleep easy without leaving the room in complete darkness.

He'd taken one of the huge chairs, assuring everyone he could sleep sitting up. He could most of the time. A knack he'd developed early in his career. But now, he had too much on his mind to sleep. He glanced toward the hidden doorway. Leia had disappeared into the room a while ago. He couldn't even guess at how much time had passed. There wasn't so much as a clock in the place. But it felt like she'd been in there for hours. Was she sleeping?

He rolled his head until he faced Moyra again then slowly got to his feet.

She glanced at him.

He nodded and moved toward the hidden door. When she didn't object, only turned back to stare at the outer door, he let his shoulders relax. He pressed several spots on the wall before he heard the distinctive click and hiss of the door cracking open. He eased inside, closing the door at his back.

Leia sat on the carpeted floor in the middle of a large, empty room. Nothing decorated the walls or ceiling here. There wasn't even a chair to sit on or window to look out. He took in the room in one sweeping glance then focused on Leia.

The first thing he noticed was her hair. She'd let it down. A cascade of thick dark silk hung around her. A few strands fell over her shoulder, drawing his gaze to the swell of her breasts beneath her uniform. He forced his gaze back to her face. With her hair down, her features were softened but still stunning. Her eyes were heavy lidded, giving her a just-crawled-out-of-bed look that made his palms sweat.

She stared up from her seat on the floor. Her legs were crossed, her hands resting on her knees. She appeared both relaxed and alert.

"Am I interrupting?" he asked.

She shook her head. "Are you okay? Do you need something?"

He needed her. Probably best not to blurt that out, though, Jakey boy. "You've been in here a while. I wanted to make sure you were okay."

She smiled, a quick charming grin that hit him right in the libido.

"I'm meditating," she said. "To prepare for tomorrow."

He nodded and edged back toward the door.

"I'm finished now. Would you like to sit?" Her gaze danced away when she offered but returned to his face, open and more vulnerable than he'd seen her before.

He couldn't resist that look. He sat near her, close enough he could feel the heat of her thigh near his.

She didn't move away.

This close, the temptation of her hair was too great. He reached out and smoothed his hand over the strands covering her shoulder. It was as soft as it looked. He twined a single strand around his finger, tempted beyond logic to tug that loop of hair until she moved close enough to kiss.

"This is the first time I've seen your hair down." His voice sounded husky even to his own ears.

She reached up with one hand and rubbed at her scalp. "It was getting sore, having it up for so long." Her grin was crooked, self-conscious.

He smiled back, utterly charmed. His fingers threaded through her hair, running the soft silk over his palm. "So, you meditate often?" he asked to distract himself.

"I try to, at least once a cycle. Part of the training."

"You must have been through a lot to reach your position."

She shrugged, a movement that pulled her hair through his fingers again. "What did you do…before…at home?"

"I'm a homicide detective for the Los Angeles Police Department." He watched a slight frown crease her brow as she thought.

"You investigate murders." She grinned as if she'd solved a mystery herself.

"That's it. I was in the middle of a pretty big case when all this happened."

She leaned forward, just a little. "Can you tell me about it?"

She was so close now his heart pounded in awareness. To keep his sanity, and distract himself, he nodded. "We have a man named Hugh Patterson under investigation for the murder of his wife. We haven't been able to break the case. There was no evidence, no direct link back to the husband. He's got very influential political connections and some powerful links to the less than law-abiding as well. Those connections have kept him out of interview, kept us from doing every-thing that needs to be done to catch him." He shrugged, reluctantly letting his hand drop from her hair. "Matt and I had just come up with a way to bring Patterson into questioning when we were…taken."

"What way?" Her eyes were wide, her attention riveted on his story.

His gaze traveled over her face, taking in each dip and shadow, each curve and peak. He tried to concentrate on the story, but the scent of her fogged his brain. "He has a known association with an individual who went to prison for tax fraud. That person was killed in jail. The person who killed this tax-evading associate of Patterson's was convicted of the murder the day before we were taken." He still found it strange to say that out loud. Taken. He'd never considered himself vulnerable to kidnapping.

"In exchange for a transfer to another prison," he continued, "the killer agreed to answer a few questions for Matt and me. Specifically about the stuff the man he killed had let slip before a contract was put out on him."

"The man who killed the…tax evader was a contract killer? Why would he talk to the authorities? How did he get caught? If he was a contract killer, wouldn't he be more careful?"

Jake smiled. She was as smart as she was sexy. That was saying something since she was too sexy for his peace of mind. "He wasn't the one contracted for the kill. We don't know who that was. We only know about the contract because this guy attempted to use it in his defense, saying it wasn't him but a contract killer who'd committed the murder. The tactic failed. He'd left behind too much physical evidence. Anyway, he and the dead man had had a fight over something—a book of all things. He knifed him as a warning. Hadn't actually meant to kill him."

"That's incredible. So did he give you anything against Patterson?"

"Enough to bring him in for questioning."

"You must be a brilliant detective."

He grinned. "I'm not bad. I've caught a few bad guys in my time. What about you? You must have had some interesting moments in your job."

She shrugged. "A few, I suppose." Her head dipped, a faint flush colored her cheeks. She glanced up through her lashes.

The look was so unconsciously sexy, he almost groaned out loud.

"I'm considered a hero on Nas," she said, shyly. "I saved one of the most important political figures on the planet, the Governor General, during an assassination attempt."

"Were you hurt?" His right hand clenched, automatically reaching for a gun that wasn't there. The idea of Leia being injured brought out every protective instinct he had.

"I was shot in the left shoulder. Not a bad injury. Just glanced off the muscle. I got the Governor General on the ground and a few shots off before the other Guards surrounded us. They tell me I hit the assassin in the heart. I can't take credit for the shot, though. I didn't even aim."

"Best way to shoot, they say. Fire then aim."

She shrugged, pride in her skill sneaking through the dismissive gesture. "I was only attempting cover fire so one of the other Guards could bring down the assassin. They told me later no one else even got off a shot. I'd killed him before they could."

"No wonder you're considered a hero. Very impressive work, Lieutenant."

She grinned, as if she couldn't help it, trying to hide her smile without much success. "You should probably know about my status since the people here have heard the story already. They know who I am on sight."

"Your cousin told you about the news spreading?"

"The Gormalath told me while we were talking."

"Gormalath?" He pronounced the word slowly, imitating her accent. "That was the dinosaur alien."

She chuckled. "I never thought of them that way before."

"He was hitting on you, wasn't he?" He couldn't seem to keep the growl out of his voice. He tried to remind himself being jealous of a dinosaur was stupid. He was the one alone with her in a quiet room, not the dinosaur. But he had to keep his hands fisted in his lap to keep from reaching for her.

"A little. That happens a lot off Nas," she said without vanity or even much interest, just a matter-of-fact statement. "On Nas, I'm considered ugly."

"You must be joking."

Her smile softened. "No. I'm considered short and fat and very plain."

"They're blind," he mumbled.

Her lashes swept down, concealing her thoughts, but a flush of color washed into her cheeks.

He couldn't resist touching her again. He reached out to reclaim the silk strands of her hair, twisting a thick band through his fingers. She was probably the bravest woman he'd ever met. So practical and strong and beautiful. She obviously knew men considered her attractive, yet she blushed at his compliment. She was a complex mixture of womanhood, a puzzle he could spend the rest of his life trying to solve.

He was so caught up in the look and feel of her hair, he lost track of the other questions he'd wanted to ask. He needed to know more about their situation, about where they were and why. But at that moment, nothing mattered beyond Leia.

She stared back, caught in the same silent spell.

He could have stayed that way for hours.

When she licked her lips, a quick flick of her tongue, his hand fisted convulsively in her hair. He relaxed his grip, smoothing out the crushed strands. But the need to pull her close was overpowering. Just one kiss. One more taste. If he could get past the need to take her into his arms and ravage her mouth, maybe he could remember what it was he wanted to ask.

He moved his hand to the back of her neck, his fingers tunneling up into her hair as he eased her closer. If she resisted, he'd stop. If she said no, he'd be able to pull back.

She didn't resist or say no. She leaned forward until her hot breath brushed his cheek.

The scent of her filled him. He stared into the depths of her eyes for a long minute, then gave in to temptation and took possession of her lips.

He felt no resistance from her, only the sweet taste of her hunger, the overwhelming softness of her mouth. His need turned greedy the instant her tongue touched his. He pulled her close, deepening the kiss, his hands moving to frame her face.

He'd never felt anything like this before, the sharp charge of electricity, the bone-deep need that made his hands tremble. He'd only known this woman a few days and already he wanted more from her than any other woman he'd met. Without lifting his mouth from hers, he dragged her onto his lap, desperate to be closer. His hands moved over her, caressing her arm and shoulder, her back and hips. When his hand closed over her breast, she arched into him with a soft moan.

Hunger burned through him in a flash fire of heat. His hand kneaded her soft curves through the barrier of her uniform and it wasn't enough. He wanted more. Skin to skin, heat against heat. He handled her more roughly than he intended, moved too fast, but her single moan of pleasure had pushed him beyond logic and control. He raked his mouth along the column of her throat, tasting her, teasing her with his tongue and lips. She clutched his shoulders, her head dropped back to give him better access. Her hair fell over his arm, the silk teasing his already sensitive skin until the touch was almost painful.

"Leia." He groaned her name against her throat, his voice rough as gravel. She responded to his every touch, every taste. Her hands clenched at him, shaping the muscles of his shoulders and chest. With each quiet whimper, each quivering response, she brought him closer to the brink of madness. He wanted, needed so much he couldn't think of anything else.

He moved his hand to the collar of her uniform, searching for a clasp or zipper. "I want this off," he growled. "Now. I want to feel your skin."

She trembled in his arms as she reached up to open her tunic.

His gaze burned into her, watched every move of her agile fingers in hungry anticipation.

She opened the high collar and the first button of the tunic then her hand stilled.

He struggled to hold his impatience in check, fought the raging need that left him hard and uncomfortable and more desperate than he could ever remember. He met her wide gaze, waiting, afraid to speak first, afraid he wouldn't be able to say anything reasonable.

She blinked rapidly and confusion creased her brow. "What am I doing? I can't do this," she murmured. "It's not fair to you. Oh saints." She launched off his lap, scrambling a few feet away. She turned to face him, kneeling on the floor, her eyes huge. "I can't believe I did that. I… You're… I'm supposed to be protecting you, returning you to your world, not seducing you."

His heart twisted at the guilty anguish in her voice. He sat very still, made sure she was looking into his eyes when he said, "I was doing most of the seducing. And you have no reason to feel bad about it."

"Yes, I do," she wailed. "Don't you understand? This isn't ethical. It goes against everything I believe. You were to be sold into slavery. That's why you were taken. To make you a sex slave to some rich woman. I'm supposed to be protecting you from that. Preventing it. If I can't keep my hands off you, I'm no better than they are. I'd be using you, too."

He edged closer, wanting desperately to ease the confusion in her gaze. He couldn't stand seeing her like this. His need to comfort was as strong as his need to possess. He'd probably be worried about that reaction later. "You wouldn't be using me, Leia." He knelt in front of her, raising a hand to still her protest. "A slave has no choice, right? They're forced to do whatever they're told or suffer consequences. They're denied choice."

She nodded and her frown deepened, but the panicked guilt was no longer stark on her face.

"If I choose something, of my own free will, then that action can't be considered a form of slavery, can it?"

"I…suppose not." She bit her bottom lip.

He eased closer, framing her face with his hands. The confused, pained look in her eyes dragged at him, pulled him deeper. "How long do we have? When we leave here, you'll send me home as soon as you can?"

"Yes. It's important to get you home quickly."

"Then this may be the last chance we're alone together? The only chance we're alone together?"

She gulped in a breath and nodded.

His voice dropped to a quiet whisper. "Do you want me, Leia? Would you regret being with me if there were no ethical dilemma between us?"

"I could never regret it."

"Even though I'll be gone soon?"

"Never." Her hands came up to clench his wrists. "I don't understand my reaction to you. I've never felt this before. It scares me. But I wouldn't regret being with you. I do want you, Jake. I have from the moment I first saw you."

He smiled slowly as the tension eased from his hands. "Then stop wasting what little time we have on worrying, Lieutenant."

Jake leaned in and kissed her, hard, demanding, leaving no question as to who was taking the lead. He chose this. Her. She melted into him. He rose on his knees, pulling her up with him so he could feel her body pressed to his, the pressure of her generous breasts molding to his chest, the soft cushion of her stomach against his erection.

She buried her fingers in his hair as he wrapped her in his arms. The intensity in her flexing grip drove him wild. He couldn't taste enough of her. His mouth raked down her throat, nuzzled at her half-open collar. His hands stroked down her back, gripped tight when she moaned. Every sound, every taste, every scent left him desperate for more. All he could think was more. He wanted more.

Now.

He pushed at the tunic again, let her take over when he still couldn't figure out the clasps. His hand followed her fingers as she deftly opened the tunic, caressing skin so soft it left him weak. Under the tunic, she wore a tight halter that cupped and supported her breasts. Generous mounds of soft flesh rounded over the scooped neck, too tempting to resist.

"You're so beautiful," he murmured as he dipped his head to taste more of her skin. His hand flexed on her breast through the halter, his thumb rubbing over her already peaked nipple. Her groan thrilled him, drove him. He rose to take her lips again, desperate to taste all of her at once. He pulled her tight. He needed to feel her, naked and hot and writhing beneath him, needed it so much he couldn't think. He pushed her tunic down her arms, exposing the smooth muscles of her shoulders, more soft skin he had to kiss, to taste.

Her hands flexed over his shoulders and back, fisted in his hair, tugging and pushing. She gripped his shirt. "Take this off, Jake. I need to feel you."

He moved back from her long enough to jerk the shirt over his head. Then she was in his arms again, driving him crazy.

Close, he thought, close but not enough. He wanted skin against skin with no barriers between them. She dropped her arms, letting her tunic fall onto her calves, and he wrapped her tight against him.

"God, you feel good, Leia." His hands squeezed her hips, sinking into soft flesh and muscle, forcing her tight against his hips, his need.

"Jake." Her voice was breathy, husky.

She sounded as desperate as he felt. Knowing she wanted him that much, hearing the desire in her pleas and moans, feeling the passion in her hands and trembling body, left him reeling with hunger and a deep, primitive satisfaction he didn't recognize in himself.

A satisfaction that growled, *His. His woman.*

Their wants were primal, their needs basic and universal. Their heat unquenchable. He wanted her and nothing else mattered. He had to bury himself in her or go crazy. And even then, he wasn't sure his sanity would hold.

He tugged the halter over her shoulders, down her arms, swallowing her moans. Her breasts sprung free, full and golden, her large nipples dark and peaked. He abandoned the halter, leaving her arms pinned, and cupped her fullness, savored the weight, teased the hard nub of her nipples with his thumbs. She was trembling, her breath rasping as he bent his head to indulge, taking one pert nipple into his mouth and savoring.

She was perfect, soft and swollen, pressing against him. He ran his tongue over the upper swell of her breast, kissed the underside, returned to her nipple. He shaped her narrow waist with his hands, reveled in the generous flare of her hips. She was all he wanted, everything he needed.

She murmured to him, panted words he couldn't understand, but the sound of her voice, desperate and hot, made him ache. He couldn't remember who removed what after that, only knew when he finally had her naked body pressed against his, he was as close as he ever thought he'd get to heaven.

She drove him wild with her stroking fingers, her curious tongue. She traced the lines of his scars with the tip of her tongue as she cupped him, already so thick and hard he felt like he was going to explode. The heat of her hand scorched him, dragged a desperate groan from deep in his throat. He thrust his hips against her, mindless and needy. "You're killing me," he said, straining to speak, struggling desperately for control.

She chuckled against his chest, moved her lips lower, over his abdomen. He knew he'd lose control if he let her go further. He wanted her mouth on him, hungered for it, but he wouldn't last if she moved any lower. He dragged her up, capturing her mouth, devouring her.

He couldn't seem to soften his touch, gentle his hands. He knew he was probably leaving bruises and he couldn't stop himself. He clutched and squeezed, desperate to get closer, to feel all of her. When he rolled her under him, lifted her legs so they wrapped around his waist, he struggled for control, struggled to move slow, savor the entry.

She was hot and wet against the tip of his erection as he pushed in, just a bit.

Her head rolled back, her eyes closed.

"Now?" he asked, shaking with his need to remain still. He watched her slumberous, sexy eyes, her flushed face as she pressed that point on her jaw. "Now?" he demanded, harsh and grating. He didn't even recognize his own voice.

"Yes. Please yes." Her nails dug into his shoulders, her hips thrust up, forcing him farther inside her heat.

And his control shattered. He rammed into her, too hard, too fast, too desperate. She was tight and wet and perfect.

She cried out against his mouth, muffling the sound in a kiss that anchored them both.

He wanted to move slowly, but he was no longer in control of his own needs. He thrust into her, again and again, harder, faster. His hands fisted in her hair, his lungs strained, his mouth raked over her face, devoured her mouth. He felt her straining, her body bowing under him, meeting him thrust for thrust. Her breathing was ragged, her skin slick with sweat. She was the sexiest, most stunning woman he'd ever seen. "Come," he demanded, framing her face with his hands. "I want to see you, feel you. Come, Leia."

He watched the sensations swim over her face, the rising flush in her cheeks. He moved harder, deeper, until her head bowed back, her body arched and she shattered around him. The feel of her inner muscles clenching tight around him broke the last of his control and he let himself go, burying his face in her hair as his world exploded.

He wasn't sure how much time passed before he could think again. When his breathing slowed and his body answered his commands, he lifted up onto his elbows so he could study her face. She looked sleepy-eyed and sated, her hair a mass of tangles around her face. She smiled up at him, and his heart twisted painfully in his chest. He smiled back, leaned down to press a gentle kiss to her lips, savoring the musky smell of her.

Now that his brain was working again, a realization slowly seeped in, making him frown.

"What's wrong?" she asked, her hand cupping his cheek, stroking his jaw.

"I just realized, I didn't stop to consider... Do you worry about...?" Jesus, how did he say this without sounding crude after what was, for him at least, one of the most earth-shattering experiences of his life? "If I were on Earth, I'd have thought to..."

She grinned, a sudden lightening of her expression that made him forget what he'd been trying to say.

"You're worried about pregnancy and disease," she said.

"Pregnancy anyway." His frown deepened when he realized he was only worried about it because he was leaving. The very idea that he wasn't *more* worried about getting her pregnant terrified the hell out him.

"Don't." She caressed his cheek again, lifted up to kiss his throat. "I would have to plan for it. We have a chip inserted beneath the skin to control fertility. Once removed, I would still have to wait a month before my body was able to conceive."

"Probably for the best." He kissed her, feathered his fingers over the soft skin of her cheeks, and wondered at the vague disappointment he felt, a reaction so out of character it was tantamount to having a split personality.

He watched emotions he couldn't read swim through the dark sea of her eyes. His heart turned over as he studied her. He wanted to memorize every line, every curve, every dip and hollow of her face, knowing those memories would have to carry him for a lifetime.

Getting home no longer held the same appeal as when he'd first regained consciousness in that dingy, dark little cell.

LEIA CURLED IN JAKE'S ARMS, RESTING HER HEAD ON HIS SHOULDER, unable to sleep despite her lethargy. She listened to his quiet, even breathing and savored the feel of his heat against her. She didn't want to sleep and miss any of this since this moment was all she would have. She could hardly believe she'd allowed this to happen, but she didn't regret a minute. He was perfect. Strong, rough, hard, so male he took her breath away. She fingered the scars on his chest, delighting in her freedom to touch him. She was ashamed to admit it, even to herself, but she could see why women across the galaxy would pay the price of a planet to have a man like Jake Marshall. He was worth far more.

She worried at her bottom lip as she breathed in his scent, all dark male and sex. She hated that he was considered a slave in her time. He was too proud, too strong, too independent to be a slave. She didn't want to think of him as cargo. He was more to her. Like it or not, he was much more. And she hated the idea that anyone else would think of him as cargo, either.

She couldn't put a finger on her own emotions, couldn't say why she was so bothered, wouldn't have been able to explain why her chest ached at the thought of someone thinking Jake a mere slave.

She had to send him home. She'd known that from the start. Going back was best for him, vital really. She couldn't risk the consequences if he stayed. Wouldn't risk his life and his future that way. He could never live normally here. He would always have to worry about the pirates and slavers. He needed to be in his own time, with his own people.

But saints, she wanted him to stay. She didn't want to spend the rest of her life pining for a man who had been dead for three thousand years. And she knew she would now. She had let things go too far, had given in to a dark temptation that scorched her and branded her for life.

What other man would ever compare to Jake Marshall?

She nestled closer, wishing for more time. She wanted to ask him more about his life, about his work. The details of his investigations fascinated her. She was thrilled by the idea of a far away time and place. Los Angeles, an ancient Earth city of legend and myth. She wondered what it was really like to live in such a time, so primitive, yet on the cusp of growth. Brutal and beautiful and capable of creating men like Jake. The thought of his work being so similar and yet so different from her own, gave her a shiver of intimacy completely at odds with the time they'd known each other.

As she stroked a hand over his chest, through the hair covering hard muscle, she sighed. She wanted more. More time. More talk. More familiarity. More intimacy. More Jake.

She stretched out until her spine popped, then rolled away to get dressed. She pulled on her uniform trousers and felt her face heating at the memory of getting out of them. They were just lucky no one walked in. She hadn't even thought to lock the door.

Her hands stilled on the final catch on her trousers. Saints, how was she going to face the others? They knew, they understood what it meant to have Jake and Matt here, even if Jake didn't. Had she just thrown away whatever respect they'd had for her by seducing Jake?

She sucked in a deep breath and let it out slowly. He'd done the seducing, she reminded herself. She smiled a little. He'd been very clear on that point. He was the one doing the seducing, not her. His choice.

His choice.

The thought staggered her. He'd chosen her. Of all the women he could have in this time, he wanted her. She leaned down and swept her halter off the floor, absently pulling it over her head as she let herself savor the feeling of being wanted by someone like Jake. So what if her squad had a lower opinion of her now? She'd been bucking social approval and opinion her whole life. What could a little more scandal possibly do? Jake Marshall wanted her. And life didn't get much better than that.

Scanning the floor for her uniform tunic and boots, she turned a circle. She noticed her jacket a second before she noticed Jake. He was awake, propped up on one elbow, studying her with such intensity her heart hammered. She wanted to say something but sound stuck in her throat. He was so gorgeous, so male. He left her breathless just by sitting there staring at her. He was still naked and she couldn't stop her gaze from wandering over the hard planes of muscles, the strong length of his legs, the thickness of his already growing erection.

Her eyebrows twitched up and she forced her gaze back to his face.

His eyes were still intense, but a smile played around his delectable mouth.

"I didn't mean to wake you," she muttered because she had to say something or she'd start staring at the thick, hard, very male part of him again.

"I like watching you move," he said. "I like watching you get dressed, so I can imagine undressing you all over again."

Her head went light and her body went liquid. Only years of discipline kept her knees from giving out and dropping her to the floor. Her heartbeat sounded loud in the empty room. Could he hear it?

With his gaze still locked on hers, he rose to his feet, agile as a wild *henta-cat*, and stalked toward her.

She couldn't have moved if she wanted to. She stood helpless against the pure, unadulterated masculinity of him. Her breath caught in her throat when he pulled her into his arms.

"You're very strong," she said, then nearly cringed at how dumb that sounded. Of course, he was strong. He wouldn't be here if he wasn't. But he moved in the heavier gravity with relative ease now. He was too tall to be from Belax, most of the men were her height or shorter, but he had the thickly muscular build of a Belaxi male. Did that make it easier for him to adjust to the gravity? Maybe his easy adjustment was just a sign of his natural strength.

His kissable mouth twitched, but the smile dropped away and his grip on her waist eased. "I was too rough before. I'm sorry. I didn't mean to hurt you."

"You weren't! You didn't. You were perfect." She watched his lips twitch again. This time the smile formed. And she thought, Perfect.

His grip tightened as he lowered his head to hers, kissed her with such gentle care her heart ached. Just a minute more, she thought, pressing into him, soaking up his heat and need. Just one minute more alone with him. Then she could face the world. And do her job.

When he lifted his head, she was breathless and more than a minute had passed.

"We'll have to go soon?"

She nodded. "I need to check on things outside, too." She didn't move away and his hold on her didn't slacken.

He kissed her again, this time a little deeper, a little hotter. "Do you have to check this minute?" he said against her mouth, possessing her lips again before she could answer.

She rose onto her toes, rubbing against him, wondering what he was talking about because she'd stopped thinking the minute his lips touched hers. His hands dropped to her bottom, ground her against his hips. The groan that rumbled in his throat thrilled every feminine cell in her body. She tasted him, her tongue sweeping up the thick column of his neck, tasting salt and Jake. She didn't know a man could taste this good, feel this good.

He shaped her curves, his hands flexing over her skin as if he couldn't get enough of her in one handful and wanted more.

And she felt deliciously female. She'd used her femininity before, in the games so common to Belaxian relationships. Then she'd run away from those games to pursue her dream. But she'd never wallowed in her sex appeal, never allowed herself the simple luxury of being a woman with a man. Knowing he wanted her brought out her cravings, her desire to please. She ran her hands over his thick shoulders, into his hair, pressing close to try and ease the pressure building low in her.

A sharp rap on the door jolted her backward. She sprung away as if he'd burned her. In one quick glance, she took in his naked and still very aroused body and the tenuous state of her own clothing and knew she didn't want the other women to walk in. She stalked to the door, surprised to realize it wasn't embarrassment but possessiveness that urged her to keep the others from seeing Jake in all his male glory. Just the night before, she'd been worried about breaking the taboo of seducing Jake and losing the respect of her soldiers. Now, her protectiveness toward Jake far outweighed the implications of her social breach.

She pulled her hair together and twisted it into loose tail. The tail wouldn't hold without a fastener but she hoped it would disguise the tousled knots. She opened the door a bare inch, aware of Jake moving around the room behind her to collect his clothes. She nearly sighed. What a sin he had to get dressed. She wanted to keep him just as he was for a very long time.

Vanian looked in, her face carefully blank. "Message has come from Telani. The ship's in dock Area 54, Bay 10 Ring C1, registered to Ilana Timone."

At Vanian's frankly curious expression, Leia actually smiled and said, "My mother's maiden name and my grandmother's first name."

Her second nodded, a slight grin tugging up her lips. The grin dropped as her gaze flicked to the room at Leia's back. Leia knew she couldn't see Jake, but she still had to fight the urge to block the door further.

"Everything okay, Lieutenant?"

"Fine. We'll leave as soon as Moyra gets the clearance for the new ship and arrangements have been made for the escape shuttle. Organize some food. They'll need to eat before we move out."

Vanian nodded sharply and walked away.

Leia closed the door, frowning. Telani had them leaving from C1, one of the two central and largest rings of Dockland. They weren't going to be able to sneak through the crowds unnoticed, not with

Jake and Matt. And there'd be trouble if anyone discovered they were leaving without making a sale. No telling who was watching them.

She wouldn't put it past anyone on this station, Telani included, to want to steal Jake and Matt. Most of the seasoned vets of the slave trade had enough sense not to mess with renegade Guards. But the ones willing to take the chance, the ones so desperate or greedy or arrogant they'd risk death for a score, those were the ones she had to worry about. The dangerous ones.

She sucked in a breath and turned to face Jake, still frowning. He had pulled on his trousers but not his shirt. He looked like a gladiator, she thought for a dizzying minute. With the bracers and the thick muscles of his arms and chest glistening with a light sheen of sweat, he looked dangerous, primitive and altogether too sexy. He didn't move closer, and she was grateful for his restraint. She found it almost impossible to think straight now. If he got any closer, she'd forget everything and jump him.

She pressed the translator chip in her jaw. "The new ship is ready. We're just waiting on clearance and arrangements for the shuttle we arrived in to be taken care of after we leave."

He nodded, studying her face. "Something's bothering you."

She almost smiled. He was very perceptive for a primitive Earthman. "The ship is in a docking bay in one of the central rings. We'll have to walk a gantlet to reach it. I was hoping for something closer."

"You're worried about another attack?" He lifted his hand to his temple, pressed then raked his fingers back into his hair.

She couldn't lie to him, but she desperately wanted to ease the tension edging into his body. "Yes. I didn't get a chance to question Telani about the Duster yesterday." She'd avoided the topic in the end because she didn't want her cousin to know too much about Jake. Telani would know if someone had hired a Duster to lure Jake, then Jake was worth more than a Hrokwall sale. "We'll avoid the dark rooms… The rooms where the Dusters have to stay—"

"Dusters?" he interrupted, resting his hands on his hips. "Is that what got into my head yesterday? That was one of the many questions

I meant to ask you last night." His blue eyes darkened. "You distracted me."

"I distracted you? You kissed me first."

"Because you're so kissable, I couldn't possibly resist." He dropped his hands from his hips and took a single step closer. Then stopped himself and shook his head. "Tell me about these Dusters," he said on a loud exhale. "What the hell are they?"

Her stomach danced with a mixture of delight and anticipation, but she tried to force down the feeling, to concentrate on his question. "Dusters are…dangerous. They are humans with psychic abilities who've amplified the ability with a mineral called Dust. Dust is addictive. It makes them extremely photosensitive and slows their metabolisms so they tend to get very fat no matter how little they eat. But there's a lot of money available to a powerful psychic. So many with even a spark are willing to risk the effects of Dust to get a share of the fortune. The problem is the Dust takes over."

"I've seen that with heroin and crack."

She had to think a minute before she remembered the drugs common to his time then she nodded. "There comes a point when some of the weaker-willed psychics will do anything for their next hit. They're the most dangerous. They'll take risks others won't. Deal with clients…sponsors, others would not touch. I'm not sure if the psychic who touched you yesterday was really trying to steal you for someone or just…seeing if he could pull you in. If the Duster was playing at luring you, he or she isn't a threat. If this psychic was working for someone, someone bent on having you or Matt, then he's very dangerous."

"Is there a defense? Some way to fight or block them?"

She sucked in her bottom lip, shook her head. "No way to block an attack. But to lure someone with a strong will costs a Duster a lot of energy. And they can only enter the mind of one person at a time. We have an advantage there. Though they tend to live together in small clutches, most Dusters refuse to actually work with others. They're jealous of their talent. And there's a myth that one psychic can steal the talents of another if they work together toward the same task. Dust also seems to inspire superstition and paranoia," she added wryly. "Something most of us are grateful for. If they ever learned to cooperate, we'd be in trouble."

He settled his hands on his hips, nodding slowly as he thought through what she'd told him. "So as long as six of them don't hit us at once, we can look out for each other, make sure no one goes wandering off toward any dark rooms."

"Right. But Jake, they're not the only danger. I'm sure word has spread. Even if Telani didn't see you, others on the station did. Some will consider the trade-off between the staggering fortune you'd bring at auction and the danger of taking on four highly trained renegade Guards worth the risk."

"Matt and I can take care of ourselves. You've given us weapons and free hands so we've got an element of surprise. We won't let someone drug us and cart us off this time. Anyone who tries to take us will have a fight on their hands." His grin was quick and feral, the glint in his eyes deadly.

Suddenly, Leia felt sorry for anyone who tried to kidnap Jake. If she didn't kill them first for threatening him, Jake would probably rip off their arms. The idea both terrified and excited her. There was something intoxicating about being with a man prepared to fight for himself and prepared to fight alongside her while he was doing it. She shivered.

Jake's gaze sharpened. "You okay? Are you cold?"

"No."

"Worried?"

"Not now." She crossed to him before reality forced her to change her mind. She fisted her hands in his hair, pulled his face to her and kissed him.

7

Jake's arms banded around her, strong and hard and fast. His muscles flexed, his tongue tangled with hers. He pulled her flush to his body, forcing a low moan from deep in her throat.

Leia wanted more. "Skin to skin," she murmured, easing back enough to slip her halter over her head. Her breasts ached, her nipples so sensitive even the brush of air made her dizzy. She flattened against him, rubbing her sensitive skin against the abrasive feel of his chest hair. His mouth ground down against hers, desperate, hungry. She reveled in it, fed his hunger, encouraged his demands. She wanted him out of control, fast and hard. And now. She reached for his trousers.

He stilled her hands. "I promised myself I'd take more time with you."

"Next time." She twisted her hands out of his grip and pushed down his trousers over the hard muscles of his butt. "I don't want slow now. I want fast. I want you hard inside me. Now. I can't wait." She kissed his throat, his shoulder, his chest, her hand cupped him between his spread thighs, massaged. His head dropped back with a groan and his grip flexed tighter. "Please, Jake," she said, her mouth racing over his face. "Please. Now. Don't make me wait."

He looked back into her eyes, his a blazing blue that took her breath away. He growled, a sound so primitive a shiver danced up her spine.

With barely contained violence, he jerked down her pants then lifted her with his hands cupping her bottom.

She wrapped her legs around his waist and devoured his mouth.

He turned, pressed her against the wall and plunged into her in one long, hard thrust.

She clenched her teeth to hold back her scream of satisfaction, let the exclamation out in a tensely controlled moan. He filled her completely, deep and thick. His thrusts were wild, his breathing rough. The scrape of beard stubble against her shoulder and neck where he nuzzled her throat was almost more than her sensitive skin could take.

"Hold on to me," he said.

She wrapped her arms around his neck, locked her legs around his waist. He moved one arm to hold her around the waist and braced his other hand against the wall.

Then he was moving harder, deeper, faster.

"Leia." He groaned her name, his voice rough and harsh. "Jesus, you feel good. So hot and tight."

She slipped into her own language, unable to concentrate on the translator. She whispered of her need, telling him how good he felt, how he filled her, how he made her desperate and hungry, how she never wanted him to stop. She felt her body trembling, buried her face in his neck as the pressure spun tighter and tighter, winding her up until she thought she'd break.

And when she peaked, the explosion was sharp and sudden and overwhelming, shaking her soul with the intensity. Her orgasm went on, longer than she thought possible, wave after wave of painful pleasure rippling through her as he continued to thrust. She clenched around him, drawing out the sensation, willing him to fall with her.

He groaned, pounded into her hard, once, twice then his body stiffened and his back arched as he came.

She ran her fingers through his hair, over his shoulders as her breathing slowed. His heart pounded strong and wild against her breast. When she felt she could speak again, she reactivated the translation chip and eased back to look into his face. And words failed her. She touched his stubble-roughened cheek with her fingertips, traced the scar on his jaw. He was beautiful. Too stunning to be real.

His arms circled her waist, gentle and strong, holding her in place even though she could feel the fine tremor running through his body.

She smiled. "You should probably put me down now. I'm no skinny Nasen."

"I could hold you like this for hours," he said.

His words stole her breath yet again. "You say things like that and I can't think straight anymore."

"Good." He brushed his lips over hers in a tender caress then buried his face against her neck, into the mass of hair hanging over her shoulders, and hugged her.

In that single instant, she felt her heart give. Tears burned her eyes, but she blinked them back. She couldn't have fallen in love. There was so much she didn't know about him still. Love should take longer. They needed more time. Time they didn't have. So, she couldn't really be in love with him. But an unfamiliar emotion twisted through her, and she knew whether she called this feeling love or not, it was going to break her heart.

WHEN THEY LEFT THE LITTLE SUITE LATER THAT MORNING, TENSION hung over the group as heavily as L.A. air when the smog was thick and the breeze dead. Jake flexed his hands inside the restraints, willing himself to accept that they were a necessary camouflage. He glanced at Matt, noted the circles under his eyes, the harsh set of his mouth.

"You okay?" he muttered as they walked down the corridor, through the din of desperate celebrations.

"Yeah."

Matt didn't say more but Jake saw the way his arms flexed.

"I don't like the things either," he said "Not after yesterday. I'm still reeling from that psychic attack."

Matt slanted him a glance, his mouth lifting in what would have been a wry grin if he'd finished letting the expression form. He nodded, understanding moved between them.

They'd been partners long enough that few words were ever needed.

He'd told Matt about the psychics, their addiction to Dust, the danger they posed, the danger others on this station might be, and that they might have to fight their way to the ship. Matt had taken it all with a stoic nod, and a feral gleam in his green eyes. Matt might look all flash designer clothing and pampered-Hollywood lifestyle, but he had a core of steel. Jake always felt covered with Matt at his back.

The women formed a close guard around them, tighter than the day before. Even the few hands that reached toward them didn't dare move past the stern faces of their protectors. If he could relax, Jake was pretty sure he'd be enjoying the situation, being guarded by four gorgeous women. But he was worried. Worried about those damned psychics. Worried about having to fight his way off a station filled with creatures he could barely comprehend. Worried about Leia.

He didn't want her stepping in to take fire meant for him. He knew she would. She was strong and had stepped in front of weapons fire before. She wouldn't hesitate. And that terrified him. He'd rather take the shot himself than see her hurt.

Last night, and this morning for that matter, had left him shaken. His need to protect her overwhelmed him. If they got off this station, he had every intention of talking her into letting him stay longer. Someone else could take care of the damned Patterson murder. He wasn't ready to go home and leave her yet.

He still didn't understand his situation fully. He needed answers. Not the least of which was why he had to keep on these damned bracers. They were comfortable enough. He'd stopped noticing them sometime in the last day. But then he would reach to scratch his wrist or move his hand and he'd remember. He had no doubt they marked him and Matt as slave fodder. It was damned hard to blend in with these things strapped to his wrists.

And he wanted to blend in so he could stay with Leia a little while longer. Just a few more days, a week maybe. Like a holiday. He hadn't taken a holiday in…well, so long he couldn't remember the last one. He hadn't even visited his brother since the birth of his youngest kid. That kid was five years old now. He'd earned a holiday. Matt could go back and fix the Patterson interview. Jake only wanted a week. Was that too much to ask? Just a short holiday with a gorgeous and sexy woman.

Then he'd be ready to get back to work. He needed to see the Patterson case finished. But a little more time away from his job wouldn't hurt anyone. And if he could just get one more week with Leia, one brief holiday, he knew he'd be able to leave.

Leave Leia.

He frowned, resisting an urge to scrub at his beard stubble. Even with that hoped-for week, he wasn't sure he could leave her easily. Already the idea tore at him. But he didn't belong here. He had to go back eventually. He had a life, a family…even if he never saw them and even if that life was all work. There were too many cases he hadn't closed. They were his responsibility. He couldn't just leave them. People, the families of victims, depended on him for justice.

So he had to leave. But the idea actually hurt. Physically. Like tearing out a piece of him. And the pain didn't come from leaving behind all the fascination of traveling through space, seeing aliens, exploring a space station and new planets.

It came from the thought of never seeing Leia again.

He watched the swing of her hair, the sway of her hips, and had to fist his hands to keep from reaching out.

Groaning silently, he looked away. They didn't live in different parts of the world. They lived in different galaxies. He couldn't just get on a plane and go visit her or pick up the phone and call her. Once he left, he'd likely never see her again. His hands twitched with the need to scrub at his face, to scrub away the frustration. Maybe he'd be better off not staying while he could still picture his future without her.

Unfortunately, the picture of his life without Leia was a long and lonely stretch of emptiness. Not a picture he much liked.

They headed into one of the corridors connecting to the inner core. Nothing had changed from the day before. The lighting in the corridor, the noise and smoke, the strips of light over his head in the connecting tube. Everything was the same. Space beyond the station still loomed dark and star-filled. Outside of the lights from the station and a few of the ships holding in space, there was no other source of light. No sun, no moon, no change to tell him the time of day. He only considered it morning now and yesterday as yesterday because Leia called the time they arrived yesterday. Disconcerting. But he'd lost all track of time the moment he was kidnapped, so it hardly mattered now.

When they reached the elevator, the iris spun open, and immediately, Jake felt the easing on his muscles and bones. He felt lighter, like he could move several steps forward in one bounce. He cast Matt a half grin.

"Easiest weight I ever lost," Matt said, answering his grin.

Leia looked over her shoulder as the iris spun shut, trying to hide the smile that tugged at her lips. "Nas' gravity is a little bit lighter than this. It is a strange sensation to go from Belax gravity to Nas." When the elevator opened again, her face rearranged into stern lines as she turned back to face the tunnel.

Jake resisted the urge to draw her into further conversation. The crowds were filling out again. Wouldn't do to be caught having a friendly chat with the woman ready to sell him into slavery.

His shoulders tensed as they plunged into the crowded corridor of the ring. As before, the masses left a clear swath for them to walk through. He noticed the subtle change in both Leia and Vanian. Their backs straightened, their hands rested on their weapons. When they scanned the area, he caught glimpses of their hard, cold expressions. Without firsthand knowledge of just how warm Leia could be, her demeanor would have warned him off.

Anyone who messed with them was an idiot.

As they walked, he kept expecting someone to block their path, to stop them in some way. He scanned the area, watching for attack. Several times someone shouted at them from the crowd. Leia or Vanian answered the calls without stopping. Their voices were sharp and businesslike but not threatening. A few chuckles, the shouting of what he guessed were offers from buyers followed them.

Leia deflected all comments with a casualness that looked authentic to someone not used to watching her. But he'd made a hobby of watching her and knew she was more nervous than she let on.

He glanced at Matt. He had his head down, but his gaze moved restlessly over the crowd, taking in everyone who passed within arm's length of their small group. His hands twitched, a gesture that made Jake realize his own fists were clenched. He hated being in the damned restraints, too.

"Almost there," Leia said over her shoulder, barking the comment in a hard voice.

But her words were a comfort. He could feel his shoulders relaxing, even as his stomach danced. Almost there. He itched to get out of the crowd. He wondered if Leia would be embarrassed if he pulled her in for a kiss the minute they were on this new ship. He bit back a smile. He liked seeing her cheeks flushed. If this new ship proved big enough, he intended to make sure they had more time alone. Already he missed being able to touch her. He didn't want to think how he'd feel once he got home.

A noise like weapons fire sounded behind them with a shout so loud the crowd fell quiet. Jake looked over his shoulder as the four Guards turned as one to face the noise.

Behind them, three very tall men stood with weapons pointed in the air. The shortest, still a few inches taller than Jake, stood in the middle of the three. He was slender and fair with a thick, ugly scar crossing his face from right temple to left jaw. His right eye was nothing but a white marble. His nose looked split and barely healed. He smiled but the expression wasn't pleasant. All three were dressed in similar tunic and trousers, all a pale tan color. The other two men were only a little heavier than the man in the middle, their faces not distorted by scars, but the hard look in their eyes matched the shortest man's expression.

To Jake's surprise, when the shorter man spoke, he spoke in English. "Leia. Good to see you again. I hear it's Lieutenant Ballore now."

"Pakker." Leia's voice was neutral, soft. She moved around to stand in front of Jake while Moyra moved to guard their backs. "Long time."

Pakker fingered his scar and smiled. "They're saying you went renegade." His gaze flicked to Jake and Matt. "Suppose I could see why. Once a mercenary, always a mercenary."

Leia shrugged, didn't move her hand from the weapon now resting against her thigh. "What can I do for you, Pakker? And why are we talking in this language?"

"Thought your cargo might want to hear their new fate. You cost me quite a small fortune last time we met, Leia. That farm girl would have sold well. Time you paid me back."

Her eyebrows rose, a look just condescending enough to make Pakker snarl.

Jake had to fight back his own feral growl. His hands twitched. Pakker threatened Leia. Using Leia and Bythan as cover, Jake loosened his restraints so they would fall away with one jerk if he needed his weapon. From the corner of his eye, he saw Matt do the same.

"You picked a poor time to ask for an ass-kicking, Pakker. I've got places to be."

Jake almost smiled at Leia's quick answer. She didn't sound the least bit worried. He kept his gaze on the three men. Noticed when they shifted to a firmer stance, tightened their grip on their weapons.

"I wouldn't do that, Pakker," Leia said and raised her weapon. Next to her, Bythan also took aim.

"You owe me," Pakker snarled. "Kelana was worth a lot. And I've waited a long time to pay you back."

"Not now. Not these." Leia's voice dropped, turned deadly. More dangerous than Jake had heard before. "I'm not the same green merc as when we first met, Pakker. These two are mine and I'm not letting them go without a fight. You don't want to fight me. Not here and not like this."

"You think I'm afraid of some Nas Guard." He spit on the ground. "I don't believe for a minute you've gone renegade. You didn't have the stomach for merc work. You'd never give up that cushy number on Nas."

Leia nodded over her shoulder. "Who wouldn't turn renegade for the price these two will bring? And I'm not giving that up, Pakker. Do not underestimate how much we want this."

He laughed, an ugly snorting sound. "Like I said, I owe you. And I haven't underestimated you."

A third voice, deep and too familiar as far as Jake was concerned, shouted into the now-quiet corridor. The Gormalath Leia had spoken to the day before stood with two other dinosaur aliens, blocking the direction to their ship. The Gormalath's mouth hung wide open, his sharp teeth white in the gleaming lights. The Nas Guards were hemmed in now, no room for escape. And the dinosaur alien sounded like he meant business. Not for the first time, Jake cursed his inability to understand.

Leia switched languages with ease, slipping into the same mix of guttural noises interspersed with higher pitched clicks and trills that the Gormalath used. He watched the slight, flirty smile dance over her mouth and had to clench his teeth together. He kept his eye on Pakker and the other two humans. Their weapons were aimed now, keeping both the Nas Guards and the three dinosaurs in their line of sight.

Jake's fingers itched to take out his laser knife, but he held his patience. Waiting and watching. From the corner of his eye, he noticed Leia watching both of the groups bracketing them. She was still talking with the Gormalath but Pakker had joined in. His voice sounded strange, the language not so easy or fluent for him. He was smiling, though. And Jake was pretty sure that smile meant bad news.

Then suddenly an arc of light lanced through the air from a Gormalath and hit Pakker in the chest. As he toppled to the ground, all hell broke loose. Shots fired from all directions, making it impossible to see who was firing on whom.

Moyra and Vanian, braced back-to-back, shot in opposite directions into the mêlée while Bythan and Leia pushed he and Matt toward the scant cover of a docking bay doorway.

"What the hell happened?" he shouted as he let the restraints drop and pulled the laser knife from the pocket of his trousers.

Leia tapped her jaw in-between firing into the crowd. "Don't use those," she said without looking at him. "This isn't close enough quarters for them to be useful."

"Hey, isn't firing weapons in a space station dangerous?" Matt shouted above the noise. He had out his laser knife as well, his hands free.

"Only if someone slices through the hull. But they'd have to get through the outer walls first." She fired again and scanned the crowd. "Unless they hit the ceiling or floor."

"What?" Matt's voice rose a level.

"Don't worry," Leia said as she took aim and fired. "Emergency shields on Dockland are the best in the known galaxies."

"Comforting," Matt grumbled. "Very comforting."

Jake ducked as a shot hit the docking bay door just above his head. He cursed under his breath, wishing for a weapon he could use. Then he remembered Leia had more than one. "Give us something to shoot with," he said.

She paused for a heartbeat, then reached into the holster on her hip and pulled out a weapon similar to hers—a DEG, he remembered. She clicked a button on the forearm-sized tube, glanced down at it once, fired her own weapon, then handed the gun to him. "Hit the orange button, one tap for each shot. Don't hold down your finger or it'll burn out. Don't hit any other button or it might explode in your hand." She motioned Bythan to hand Matt one of her spare weapons and returned her attention to the chaos in the corridor.

Jake studied the tube in his hand, then picked a target and fired. A lance of red light arced into the corridor, punched into the chest of an alien and knocked it on its back. The weapon had no kickback and the aim was perfect. Jake smiled grimly.

As he fired into the crowd, he asked Leia again, "What happened back there? After the dinosaurs showed up?"

"Pakker accidentally insulted Jaxin." She barked out a harsh laugh. "Didn't speak Gormal as good as he thought. Idiot."

"What did Jaxin want before he was insulted?"

"He wanted you. Decided he'd help me for a piece of your sale price. Pakker was trying to negotiate, offering him a higher percentage than I was willing to give. Might have worked if Pakker hadn't told Jaxin his mother was a…a very bad word."

Jake laughed outright then, still firing past her shoulder into the crowd. A chaos of screams and shouts filled the corridor, but the weapon he used didn't make any noise, which surprised him. "And once one shot was fired…"

"Everyone had to start shooting."

"Now what?"

"We get to the ship before the station authorities decide this is bad for business and come in with sweep stunners."

Jake studied the corridor. Most had taken cover in rooms and doorways, leaving the corridor itself a no-man's-land. "If we inch along the wall under covering fire, we could make the next bay. How much farther do we have to go?"

"Four doors."

Damn, they'd almost been safe. Too bad Pakker was already dead. Otherwise, he'd personally kill the stupid bastard.

To Matt, he said, "Covering fire. We'll leapfrog. You and Bythan first." He looked around the hall, spotted Vanian and Moyra farther down the corridor, closer to their destination. "Will Vanian and Moyra figure out what we're doing?" he asked Leia.

A shot blew a panel just beside Leia's head.

Jake jerked her back against his chest, firing in the direction the shot had come from. He had the satisfaction of hearing a high-pitched scream. "You okay?" he said into her hair. His heart slammed painfully in his chest. That shot had come entirely too close. Without thinking, he shoved her farther into the doorway and blocked her with his body.

"I'm fine," she said, leaning around him to fire, covering his exposed side. "I'm supposed to be protecting you, though."

A touch of humor colored her voice, with none of the rancor he might have expected after his he-man attempt to shield her.

"You're something else, Leia Ballore. Let's move. This fight is getting old." He glanced at Matt and nodded once.

Matt and Bythan moved into the corridor, backs to the wall, firing in opposite directions.

Jake and Leia started firing as soon as the other two had moved, covering them with sweeping bursts. "Do these things run out of power, or whatever?"

"The power cells have a limit." She squatted low, still sending cover fire into the corridor, and pulled a second, smaller weapon from a leg holster. "If you run out, this works in the same way." She touched his left biceps with the weapon.

He reached up and took it without taking his gaze off Matt and Bythan's progress. When the other two reached the relative safety of the next doorway, he motioned to Leia and they moved out.

Seconds after they'd abandoned cover, Jake saw one of Pakker's men step into the corridor and point something that looked like a rocket launcher right at them.

8

Jake grabbed Leia by the arm and dove for cover, back to the doorway they'd just left. An explosion behind him knocked him another few feet, throwing them both to the ground just beyond the cover of the door.

Screams rang down the corridor. Jake covered Leia with his body and his own head with his arm as another explosion sounded nearby. The already manic weapons fire crossing the corridor tripled as cover was abandoned for retreat. Alarms that had been silent during the original battle now clanged loudly, competing with the noise of the crowd. Red lights flashed, throwing the bright corridor into dim madness.

And he thought the original fight was bad.

In the chaos, Jake hauled Leia to her feet and ran, using the escaping crowd for cover. A man next to him screamed and fell under the feet of the others. Jake glanced over his shoulder but with the flashing red lights and smoke, the tangle of people, he couldn't see Matt or any of the three Nas Guards. Keeping a hand on Leia's arm, he bullied his way through the crowd until he reached a door far enough away that he thought they'd be safe. He pulled her out of the crowd and checked behind them again.

"What the hell was that? And why did it cause this reaction?"

"Matter jumbler," she shouted over the claxons. "Powerful enough to cut through the hull like soft fruit."

"No wonder the panic."

"Jake, we can't go back. The shield will be up but the authorities are going to come down on that area like hungry *cheenas*. They might be prepared for hull breach, but they get really pissed off when it happens. They'll be sweeping the area with stunners."

"Matt?"

"The others will take care of him." She put a hand on his arm, squeezed. "We have to find another transport. We have to leave now. Too many witnesses. If they can find us, they'll haul us into questioning and probably lock us up for starting the fight. We don't have much time before the station freezes clearance and prevents all ships from leaving. Vanian will be getting Matt to the original bay. She'll get him out. We'll rendezvous on Nas."

He hesitated. His every instinct rebelled against leaving Matt. They were partners. You didn't abandon your partner in an alien galaxy in the middle of a gunfight on a space station. His body tensed, ready to charge back to find Matt.

Leia's hand moved up his arm, drawing his attention. "We have to go. He'll be all right. I promise. The others will make sure he's safe."

Frowning, he studied her face. Concern and anxiety filled her eyes but also a sincerity that urged him to believe her. To believe *in* her. He nodded and motioned her to take the lead.

She flashed him a brief smile then turned to study the corridor. "Follow me." She edged into the slowly thinning crowd.

They passed several bay doors, Leia stopping briefly by the panel outside each before moving on. Outside one, she shouted in triumph and punched the panel. The doors hissed open. They ducked inside, sealed the door behind them, and she keyed something into the inner console panel. "Delaying lock," she said as she worked.

He studied the small, sleek-looking ship in the bay. It was larger than their shuttle but obviously smaller than the first ship they'd been on. "Our new transport?"

She smiled without humor. "This ship was scheduled to leave five…minutes ago so it'll have clearance."

"How'd you know it was still here?"

"It belongs to Pakker."

He raised his eyebrows in appreciation. "How did you know it'd be here?"

"I didn't. Got lucky. I was looking for something scheduled to leave within the next few minutes, hoping I could bribe or bully our way onboard. The authorities won't be able to shut down the leaving clearance for another few minutes." She turned from the panel beside the sealed door to study the ship. "Now I'll just have to override the drive codes on that thing and hope no one has mentioned Pakker's name to the authorities yet."

"Will they come after us if they know?"

"No. They'll fire on us and blow us to vapor."

He glanced back at the ship. "Sure this is a good idea?"

"Better than getting stuck on the station when all ships and shuttles are grounded. We don't have time to find anything else before that happens." She stalked across the bay to the ship.

He enjoyed watching her move for a heartbeat then hurried to follow.

Leia studied the controls of Pakker's B-60. Pakker had been too clever for his own good, leaving the access hatch open and landing ramp down. He'd obviously intended a fast getaway after stealing Jake and Matt. She cursed under her breath, vivid Belaxian curses that would have scorched the ears of her Nas commander, Jolene. She almost wished she'd been the one to kill Pakker for his audacity, thinking he could take Jake from her. She would have strangled the wretched man barehanded.

She blew out a breath, reining in her temper to concentrate on the controls. Pakker hadn't left his ship completely defenseless from theft, and she didn't have time to daydream about getting revenge on a dead man. The controls required an access code and voice ID or they would short out, leaving the ship useless. She couldn't swing the voice ID even if she could override the access code. Her only chance was bypassing the security measures altogether using a coded bypass hack. One of the few things Telani had taught her without charge when they were kids.

She set to work, her fingers nimble on the keyboard as she hacked into the drive system. It took her thirty seconds longer than her best time, but within a scant two minutes she had the engine running, the hyperdrive systems coming online, and the navigation system readying to accept their destination coordinates. She manually transferred the clearance code that would initiate the opening of the docking bay doors and let out a pent-up breath when the doors started to pull back.

"Ready or not," Jake murmured from his seat in the copilot's chair.

She edged up the ship, inched it forward until the bay doors were just wide enough to squeeze through, then accelerated fast enough to slam them back in their seats. They cleared the bay doors just as the red emergency lights began to spin and the doors reversed direction. "Close," she muttered, studying the visual display console to the right of her seat.

Jake grunted.

She glanced over at him, saw how pale he'd gone and grimaced. "Sorry, Jake. That wasn't the softest liftoff."

"The only soft liftoff I've experienced so far was when I thought I was on some high-class boat or submarine." He smiled, his color returning. "Don't worry, Lieutenant. I'll get over it. Are we being followed?"

She studied the display screen again, punching up a visual of Dockland. "No. Hopefully, they've got their hands full. We're not the only ones making a run for it." She switched the display to holo so Jake could see the green images of other ships, their specs displayed under their image, hurrying away from the station. "None of those are pursuit ships. And the Depot itself hasn't fired on anyone. Yet."

She entered a series of numbers into the drive controls, studied the arc of readouts, adjusted their current course and put the ship into auto-drive so she could start the nav-system calculations for the jump to hyperspace. She moved from the cockpit to the little room just behind it that held the navigation system.

Jake followed, standing behind her as she studied the floor-to-ceiling console without touching it. His hands landed gently on her shoulders and squeezed. "Problem?"

"Where to go." She sighed and turned to face him. Before she could explain, he pulled her close and kissed her. The kiss was a melding of controlled passion and tenderness that nearly brought tears to her eyes. She melted into the strength of his embrace. Only in that moment did she realize how close she'd come to losing him. Her fingers tangled in his hair to hold him, keep him. She might have lost him. Just like that he could have been gone, and she wasn't ready to let him go yet.

Her kiss heated, her tongue plunged, tangled, danced against his. She needed to feel him, to know he was real. His arms wrapped tighter, pulled her closer, one hand moving to cup the nape of her neck. For just a minute, she allowed herself the indulgence of holding him, meeting his hunger, answering with her own. Her hands shaped the thick, broad muscles of his shoulders, tunneled back into his hair. "Were you hurt?" she asked against his mouth, plunging in again before he answered.

"No," he said as he moved to kiss her neck.

She dropped her head to one side to give him better access.

"You?" His voice was muffled against her skin.

She still heard the gruffness. "No. We were lucky." She brought his face back to hers, captured his lips, desperate to drag in his scent, his taste, his feel. It would never be enough.

He pulled back to look into her face, one hand coming up to caress her cheek. "I nearly had a heart attack when that shot hit so close to your head. I'm not sure I'll get over that fear any time soon."

"I thought Pakker would talk Jaxin into dealing. I was so afraid. I could have lost you." She could feel tears stinging the back of her eyes and blinked to hold them in.

"Never. We would have fought our way out." And he kissed her again.

She clung to his lips, his body, his words. *They* would have fought their way out. Together. Her heart twisted tight, an ache so deep and new she couldn't name it. Didn't try. Jake was strong and safe in her arms. That was all she needed to know.

With great reluctance, she eased back. "I need to program in a destination or we're not going to get anywhere."

He nodded but his gaze raked over her face as if memorizing. "I need to make sure Matt got out, too. So, where are we going? Nas?"

She frowned, her brow creasing. "Not directly. Not in Pakker's ship. He's Nasen. He's wanted for so many crimes they'll fire on a ship registered to him before asking questions. And at the moment, my name will be under suspicion. News about what happened on Dockland will reach Nas before we can. I'd rather not add the sin of arriving in a known criminal's ship to my list of transgressions." She couldn't meet his gaze when she said the last sentence.

"Is there somewhere else we could go, somewhere we could stay for a while, until things were ironed out?" He grinned. "Someplace isolated. We could take a little vacation, just the two of us. I'm overdue for a vacation anyway."

She was so tempted by the idea, she almost forgot to breathe. Time stolen for just the two of them. Would she be able to let him go then? If they had a little more time together, could she send him home without feeling lost? Maybe.

Or maybe spending more time with him would make sending him back harder.

What would delaying his return do to the timeline, to Jake? She knew some time-stolen men managed to live out their lives here. Dockland was a haven for them. But what disasters had this caused, changes in the timeline they wouldn't even know about? What of the families and friends of those men? And those escapees were rare cases, she reminded herself. Most couldn't stay sane in this new time.

She stared into Jake's deep blue eyes. He seemed to be adjusting, but would she be risking his sanity just to keep him to herself for a little while longer? It would be a crime to destroy such a fine, sharp mind. Because she couldn't resist, she reached up to run her fingers over his cheek, rubbing over the rough texture of beard stubble. He didn't know he was in a different time, in what to him was the far-flung future. Would that make it easier or more difficult for him to adjust?

He must assume his time spent here was time moving on at home. He had to think his family, his work colleagues would be missing him. Yet he wanted to stay, to be with her. He might find it easier to stay if he knew the truth.

Then again, the truth could make things worse.

"I…" She had to swallow, take a deep breath. "I would love to take a holiday with you. But there are some things we should talk about. You need to understand your situation before you commit to spending more time here than necessary." She watched his frown, ran her fingers over his lips to sooth it. "We can go to Belax to dump Pakker's ship and get a message to Nas. We can check on Matt, make sure returning to Nas won't get us shot. My family will help. From there… Well, we can decide what to do after I've explained a few things." She smiled faintly. "I was just thinking recently that I needed to visit home."

He answered her with a soft smile and placed a gentle kiss on her brow. "I doubt you'll tell me anything that changes my mind about wanting to stay. As long as I can make sure Matt is okay and on his way home. He can handle our backlog for a week."

He brushed his lips across her cheek, over her mouth. "I'd like to see your home," he murmured. "I'd like to meet your family." Now he grinned, a devilish glint sparking in his eyes. "If you're any indication, I imagine your mother is a force to be reckoned with."

The statement surprised a chuckle out of her even as his desire to meet her family made her heart hammer. Part of her wanted to introduce Jake to her family. Her mother would no doubt adore him—and probably start feeding him the minute they walked through the front door. But another part of her, the part that was aware of the bracers on his wrists pressing into her back, wanted to keep him to herself, somewhere private. Someplace where no one would comment or judge.

"Belax it is then," she said, allowing one last lingering kiss before pulling out of his arms. She turned back to the navigation computer to program in the destination. Her hands trembled and she had to re-key the coordinates twice. She was so aware of Jake standing just behind her she could practically feel his touch. When she finally got the nav-system programmed, she blew out a breath. "Okay, it'll take the system a few minutes to calculate the route. Then we'll jump."

"How long will the journey take?" He stepped back so she could precede him into the cockpit.

She sat in the pilot's chair and keyed up the hyperdrive unit. "From here, a little over a cycle."

"Interstellar travel in a day. Pretty amazing to a hick from Earth." He settled into the copilot's chair. "Will this jolt?"

"It may feel a bit strange at first. Once we're traveling through hyperspace, you won't notice any movement."

"Okay. Ready when you are, Lieutenant."

She smiled, then as gently as she could, took them through the jump.

Once she was sure they were safe, she turned to face Jake. His eyes were wide, his face filled with quiet wonder. She grinned. "You look like you're having fun now."

"Now that I'm not immediately worried about getting shot or sold at an auction or some strange alien eating me…? Yeah, I'm kind of enjoying this." His grin was quick and full of wicked charm. "Can this thing fly itself?"

"I have to check on it every so often, but yes, it will fly itself now."

"Good." He rose, took her hand and pulled her to her feet.

The look in his eyes made her pulse race.

He walked her backward, out of the cockpit. "I don't suppose this ship has beds?"

Her heart kicked over as heat moved through her, pooling low. "There should be two bunks down the back."

He smiled, a slow sexy grin that she felt to her toes. "Good." He wrapped his arms around her but continued to walk her backward, through the corridor to the larger open space at the center of the ship. He dipped his head, touching her lips with a brief, tempting kiss that only whet her appetite for more. "Further back?" His hands roamed up and down her spine, sending tingles racing over her skin.

She nodded, her hands fisted in the material of his shirt. She couldn't speak around the lump clogging her throat.

He stared intently down at her, barely glancing away to guide them through the ship. She could drown in that deep blue. His erection pressed against her belly. Knowing he wanted her sent heat licking over her skin, boiling through her blood. Her stomach clenched in anticipation of his touch. Suddenly, her clothes felt too tight and hot, the barrier between their bare skin intolerable.

He edged them back to the small room with its two bunks bolted to the wall, one above the other. He flicked a look at the beds, with their thin, utilitarian mattresses, and grinned. "This probably won't be any softer than the floor last night."

She chuckled. And because she couldn't resist any longer, she rose up on her toes to kiss him. Heat and need exploded as their lips touched, scorching her. Desperation moved through her. He was alive. He was still with her. And she wanted him so much she could barely breathe.

His mouth was hard, his hands rough, rushing over her, possessive and demanding. "I need you, Leia. Need to know you're not hurt. I have to get inside you now or I'll go crazy."

"Yes. Please. Now." She met him demand for demand, gripping and squeezing, rubbing and caressing, trying to feel and taste all of him at once. She toed off her boots as he worked the clasp on her pants. She pulled back to jerk off her uniform jacket, then tugged his shirt over his head. They were a tangle of hands and arms, working frantically to remove the obstruction of clothing.

When they were finally skin to skin, Leia groaned her satisfaction. She rubbed against the hard planes of male muscle, reveled in the harsh brush of his chest hair against her sensitive breasts. "You feel so good," she breathed, tasting the skin on his neck, over his pounding pulse. "I don't know what I would have done if you'd been hurt."

"Me neither." His hands tunneled into her hair, loosening the tail. "God, Leia," he said with a harsh groan. He eased her back, carried her down to the lower bunk. His mouth moved over her throat, down to her breasts, savoring and teasing.

She was helpless against the feel of his rough hands running over her sensitive skin. His lips moved lower, his tongue teasing a trail over her stomach. She shivered in reaction. The contrast of his warm wet tongue and his rough beard stubble sent her reeling, the sensation so intense she thought she might scream. She tried to urge his head up, bring his mouth back to hers.

He resisted. "I have to taste you," he growled against her belly. His gaze burned into hers with primal intensity. His hands dug into her hips and he moved lower, his mouth hot enough to brand her.

When his tongue slid across her moist heat, delved into her, her head rolled back and her body bowed. All thought fled in the face of sensation. She strained helplessly against the tension, the building pressure that grew more unbearable with each lap of his tongue. The hungry heat of his mouth feeding on her, tasting her, drove her already screaming body over the edge, ripping a harsh cry from her dry throat.

Her body trembled, her heart slammed in her chest. She struggled for breath as he moved back up her body, covering her. The weight of him filled her with such satisfaction and longing.

He held her gaze, his face tense with his own longings, and thrust into her. He filled her, fast and hard.

She arched up to meet him, pulling him deeper, needing him inside her.

He held her for a long moment, remaining still, squeezing her tight. "Leia," he whispered her name against her neck, into her hair. His heart thudded against her breast. A fine tremor ran through his muscles.

She clung to him, kissed his shoulder, his rough cheek, and thought, Nothing could feel better than this.

Then he began to move.

He started slow with long sure strokes that urged her up again. She was so sensitive she felt every thick inch of him pushing in, easing out, creating a rippling friction of sensation.

He captured her lips, his tongue slipping in to taste and tease as his hips moved in a steady, maddening, excruciatingly slow pace that drove her wild. Her body tightened, squeezed him.

He groaned into her mouth but didn't increase his pace.

He eased her closer, stroke by slow stroke. She matched his thrusts, pulling him deeper, wanting him to move faster. Never wanting him to stop. The slow tension became an ache, the ache a spiraling need. The need stunned them both by winding back into tight desperation.

"Jake." Her voice rose as the pressure built. His strokes sped, pounding into her. The sound of skin slapping against skin drove her tighter, higher, faster. She held him, pressing her face into his shoulder as her body broke, arched, shattered around him. He followed her over, pulsing deep inside her.

Leia held him close and wanted nothing more than to stay in that moment forever.

———

THEY SLEPT, SHOWERED, MADE LOVE AGAIN AND AGAIN. SOMETIME during the long day, they uncovered a handful of ration bars and a bootleg bottle of Tamarian *declah* juice in a storage hatch. Once Jake got used to the odd bitterness of the *declah* juice, he enjoyed the rough-and-ready meal.

"Better than my cooking," he told her with a wink.

"I like to cook," she admitted a touch shyly. "I just don't have much time for it."

They talked for a long time about family and friends, work and their normal daily lives. Neither one brought up the current situation. By silent, mutual consent, they ignored the outside world and concentrated on one another. It was the most intense day Jake had ever spent with a woman.

He could barely keep his hands off her. Even when they were just sitting and talking, he had to touch her hand, her hair, her skin. He marveled at her eager, uninhibited response. When he couldn't control himself, when he handled her roughly, she reveled in it, meeting his passions with an unquenchable wildness. When his need to be tender, to give as well as take, overcame his more primitive instincts, she melted beneath his touch, soft and pliant and warm. He was surprised by his need to be tender and gentle. He'd never been with a woman whose pleasure was more important to him than his own.

She was a constant surprise. She mixed tough, strong intelligence and quirky, wry humor. She enjoyed cooking and got shy when she talked about her accomplishments. She listened intently to the tales of his misspent youth, never once condemning him for his earlier mistakes. And she delighted in his stories of his early days in the academy. He could hardly believe she'd worked as a mercenary for two years, yet the career fit her in a strange way. From what he could tell, she'd always taken on jobs that involved protecting or rescuing someone or something. Not too different from her job as a Nas Guard.

The reason behind her leaving her home world was still something of a mystery. She hedged around the question whenever he asked, simply saying she had better opportunities with the Nas Guard. Why the Belax military or law enforcement wouldn't take her baffled him. But he figured it was Belax's loss and Nas' gain.

During one of their quiet conversations in the lazy aftermath of sex, he asked about her reaction to his pushing her behind him during the fight on Dockland. "If I'd done that to one of the policewomen I work with, they'd have stripped the skin from my bones."

She laughed, snuggling closer in a way that made his heart turn over and his pulse thump.

"I suppose it was something I would have expected," she said "I can hardly take offense if a man acts on his instincts. Besides, just because I can take care of myself and fight my own battles, doesn't mean I don't like the idea of a strong man wanting to defend me. It's a nice feeling. And you didn't try to stop me from fighting. You let me take the lead when I was the one best qualified, and you followed willingly. You never tried to stop me from doing what needed to be done, what I do well. But when I was nearly shot, your first reaction was to protect me." She shrugged and met his gaze. "I don't know. I liked it. You made me feel…cared for."

He couldn't talk around the lump in his throat. Instead, he'd pulled her close, kissed her long and slow, letting his lips and body tell her what he couldn't put into words.

She amazed him, in so many ways, he could spend the rest of his life on that little ship getting to know her.

But all too soon they reached the Belax star system and their perfect time alone came to an end. As they maneuvered through the system toward the purple-blue and green planet, Jake felt the real world intruding. The need to ask questions pressed him again. He wanted to stay longer, to spend more time with Leia. He knew she would only let him once she'd told him what she had to. Whatever she had to say wouldn't matter, wouldn't make a difference. He wanted more time with her. And he intended to have it.

She sent ahead, requesting clearance codes, stating her name and rank with confidence.

"Leia!" a voice from the other end of the connection exploded into the small cockpit. "Good to have you back. We've been hearing quite a few stories about you. Can't wait to hear which are true." Genuine humor colored the female voice.

Leia smiled. "Hi, Pehili. Would you mind messaging my mom, let her know I'll be dropping in with a guest? She'll kill me if I don't give her some warning."

"I'm sure she'll have the sauce pot boiling by the time you get there."

Leia laughed and disconnected. "Prepare for the finest, largest meal of your life," she told Jake with a grin. "My mother will be convinced we're both too skinny."

"I could use a good meal after those ration bars." He reached across and squeezed her knee because he had to touch her. He was excited about seeing this new planet. He still found it hard to think of himself traveling through outer space. Maybe walking on alien soil would make his situation feel real.

"Hey," he said, straightening in his seat, "how could I understand the controller or whoever she was? You use some sort of device, don't you? When you press your jaw."

"The translation chip. Where it's placed in my jaw, it can feed me both the translation of spoken foreign languages as well as give me the ability to speak—in any language it's programmed for. There's a translator chip in the communications console here."

She pointed to a spot on the console in front of her that looked just like any other spot of colored lights and indecipherable symbols to Jake.

"I set it to translate to English so you'd understand as we came in." She shrugged. "I thought you might enjoy hearing what was happening."

"I did. Thanks." He grinned when a faint touch of pink crept across her cheeks. "Don't suppose I could get a translator chip?"

"I'm afraid not. That wouldn't be…advisable." She shifted in her seat and concentrated intently on the console in front of her.

He had a brief flash of annoyance before he stopped to consider. There was probably some stricture against passing on technology to Earthlings or something. Like the *Star Trek* prime directive, maybe? Not being able to understand irritated him. But he didn't want Leia to get into trouble on his account, so he let the subject go. Instead he said, "Your English has gotten better, more natural. Does the translator make you more fluent as you use a language?"

Her answering smile was huge and full of relief, and he was immediately glad he hadn't tried to push her.

"It actually uses the sounds generated by a native speaker to enhance the linguistic skills of the user," she said. "So by talking to you as much as I have, the chip is adapting, feeding me a more…colloquial form of English."

"The colloquial form of the language suits you," he said, and lifted her hand to brush his lips across her knuckles. That charming pink he loved crept into her cheeks again, making him grin. He sat back and watched with avid fascination as they began to land.

Leia hit buttons, punched keys on the board in front of her, and murmured into the console. "Shields optimal. Telemetry on target. Altitude 300 kilometers. Attitude adjusted."

She handled the craft deftly, angling into the upper atmosphere with no more difficultly than parking a car.

He watched out of the front window as fire licked the outer hull.

The ship shook a little, but not the bone-jarring tremors he expected. And without so much as a sound, they moved into the inner atmosphere and the fire cleared away.

Leia pulled the ship around for landing.

"Our astronauts would be jealous of that reentry," he told her, loosening his grip on the sides of his seat. "Always looks a lot more traumatic in movies and on TV."

She opened her mouth, looked as if about to speak, then closed her mouth and concentrated on the controls. After a moment, she said, "Most of that was the ship and the planetary landing control unit. I'm only a sometime pilot, not professional grade by any means. My own manual reentries aren't nearly so smooth."

He frowned as he turned to look out the front screen. He could have sworn she wanted to say something else. He shook off his curiosity, too overwhelmed by the scene as they landed to worry about what she'd left unsaid.

The planet from this altitude was a patchwork landscape of white and green islands amidst oceans of pale purple-blue water. The largest continent didn't look much bigger than Australia. No landmasses as large as Earth continents were in view. What land there was looked more like strings of islands stretching across the ocean. Archipelagos? Was that the word? White and gray clouds drifted through a sky that was blue, but a slightly different shade of blue than he was used to. Maybe with a hint of purple?

They angled toward the largest continent, the one that looked the size of Australia. Here, great stretches of red and black disrupted the flow of white and green. "Volcanic?" he asked without looking away.

"Yes. Many still active. The volcanoes underwater are still creating islands all over the planet."

"It's beautiful," he murmured, glancing at her in time to see her quick smile. She was watching the scene with a kind of melancholy satisfaction. Her expression reminded him of the way he looked down on the smog-thickened skies of L.A. when coming in for a landing at LAX—a combination of happy to be home and dreading the return. "You're not entirely looking forward to this, are you?"

Her grin flashed quick and wry. "I haven't been back since I moved to Nas. I'm going to be grilled mercilessly by my mother, given a guilt complex by my sister for putting my father through this, pestered for military details by my brothers, and questioned about my future plans by aunts and uncles alike. Cousins will harass me, neighbors will stop in to visit just to see if I've turned into a grizzled old crone, and anyone who's heard of the events on Nas will want to talk to me just so they can tell their neighbors they did."

"And if news from Dockland Depot has made it this far?"

"Then I'll be in even more demand! And my aunt will want to know how Telani is doing."

He grinned. "Sounds like fun." He didn't even know his neighbors, except the old lady who lived in the apartment across the hall. Most of his family was gone or lived in another part of the country. The only other person who might miss him and demand to know his where-abouts for the last week besides the Commander, would be Matt. And Matt knew where he was... At least, he had known before they were separated. "Will we be able to check on Matt soon?"

She glanced over, nodded. "I'll have to contact Nas Command immediately. We'll do that before we leave for my parents' house."

The understanding in her gaze made him smile. "Thanks."

They landed as smoothly as they'd reentered, on an open landing pad, dropping onto the smooth surface like a helicopter instead of sliding along a runway. They landed in a row of other ships of roughly the same size. As soon as they'd settled onto the ground, Leia began shutting down the ship. She studied the quiet console a moment, blew out a breath and said, "Here we go."

He felt the heavier gravity even before they started down the ramp. He adjusted easier after the time on Dockland but still found himself lifting his feet higher in an attempt to resist the stronger gravitational pull. The air was warm and moist, hinting of late spring tropical heat, and scented with a disturbing contrast of exotic flowers and overheated tar. At least, he thought the under-smell was tar. But would an advanced culture use tar? The sun glowed brightly in a sky spotted with a few white clouds.

The minute they stepped out onto the landing pad, a flock of official-looking men descended. All the men wore matching trousers and brightly colored shirts with short sleeves in deference to the heat. The officials stomped forward and lined up in front of them with one man moving just ahead of the others.

He was short and stocky with long thick black hair, a brown complexion and three long scars cutting a diagonal across his face from right to left. The man growled and gestured at Leia as soon as he stopped walking, his hands slicing the air in sharp, quick movements.

Leia stood with legs braced, hands on hips, her head tilted down so her long ponytail fell across one shoulder. She looked resigned, irritated, but patient. She even rolled her eyes at the shouting man, which only made him shout more.

When the official stalked toward Leia, his shoulders stiff and his fists clenched, Jake took one step forward, putting his body just in front and to the left of hers. The move put him in a position to stop the man from physically attacking her but didn't disrupt Leia's line of sight or fire.

The man glanced up, did a double take, and staggered back a step with his mouth hanging open. He fell against the other officials who had finally looked up and noticed Jake. The man started shouting and gesturing again, but his voice was an octave higher and he didn't step away from the safety of the group.

When Jake heard Leia's throaty chuckle, he glanced back. The sound made his gut clench in pleasant anticipation.

She shook her head and said something to the still-shouting man.

He fell quiet, looked between her and Jake, his brown eyes wide. Then he started mumbling, holding up his hands, gesturing at them to precede him back toward the building the group had come from. The entire group of officials changed from angry to obsequious in the blink of an eye.

Jake raised an eyebrow at Leia.

She grinned, pressed her jaw and said, "They invite us to use whatever facilities we need. They'll be happy to accommodate us for as long as we're docked here."

"That wasn't what they were saying at first."

"No. Mr. Hanyoh was actually lecturing me on bringing a stolen vehicle belonging to a Nas criminal into his jurisdiction. He said he would fine me more than I made in a year, if not get me jail time."

"Could he do that?"

She shrugged. "If I didn't want to pull rank, maybe. But as I'm on a recovery-and-return mission, which is an intergalactic concern, and because I'm a Nas Guard, and," she grinned again, "because you look like you eat lava rock for a snack, he's decided he doesn't need an explanation. Anything I've done must have been in the name of performing my duties so no offense intended."

Jake laughed, unable to resist her cocky grin and waggling eyebrows. He was tempted to pull her into his arms and kiss her senseless just to shock the officials but was afraid once he got started, he wouldn't want to stop. He let her lead, following behind like a good bodyguard. The officials scurried after them, surrounding them with questions and concerns he couldn't understand so he tried to ignore them.

One bold young man actually grabbed his arm. Jake glanced down, scowling at the boy. The boy snatched back his hand and asked a question. "What's he saying?" Jake asked.

Leia said, "He wants to know if you'd like…more appropriate clothing."

"What's wrong with what I'm wearing?" He glanced down at the loose tan trousers and short-sleeved tan tunic he'd been given on the *Persephone*. Boring but serviceable. Not uncomfortable and scratchy like the pajamas he'd woken up in inside the rusted-out medical cell. Inappropriate seemed a bit harsh.

"Nothing's wrong with your clothes," Leia said. "But he seems to think you'd be more comfortable with long sleeves."

"In this heat?"

She nodded down at the bracers so obviously displayed on his wrists. "Those make it very obvious who and what you are. He's actually trying to make walking around easier without drawing too much attention."

Jake raised a brow and looked at the surrounding group of men. The tallest still stood several inches shorter than Leia. And Jake had a good five inches on her. "Are all the men on Belax this size?"

She grinned and nodded.

"Then it won't matter what I wear, I'm gonna stand out."

"True. But you might just look like an off-worlder and not a…a man kidnapped and nearly sold into slavery." She finished in a quiet murmur, her lips turning down in a frown. "You might be more comfortable with long sleeves. The material will be light enough for the heat."

He studied her face. He couldn't decipher the emotion he saw in her eyes. Confusion. Worry? He took a step closer, reached out to touch her shoulder, but she sidestepped him, avoiding his touch. He frowned and dropped his hand. "Something wrong?"

"No." She continued on toward the white and tan building that was their destination. "It's up to you, Jake. If you'd like a change of clothes, accept the offer. Belaxi don't usually give away things." She smiled back at him again.

Something unreadable still hovered in her eyes. He followed silently, letting the groveling ramble of the officials flow over him. He glanced down at the bracers, wondering for the first time in two days what the damned things *really* meant.

9

Vanian, Matt and the others hadn't reported in to Nas yet. Leia stared at the now-blank messaging screen and nibbled a nonexistent fingernail. Nothing to worry about, she assured herself. Traveling to Nas from Dockland Depot took longer than traveling to Belax. They had to be in transit still and hadn't wanted to drop out of hyperspace to send a message. Vanian would know they'd be vulnerable to attack just beyond the edge of the Nas star system. Pirates brave or desperate enough could lay a trap there if they knew a ship carrying a recovered cargo was due at a particular time.

Then again, Nas command could have arranged the usual military escort at the edge of the system to guarantee their safety if Vanian had messaged ahead. An escort was standard procedure. If pirates hadn't waylaid the *Persephone*, there would have been a military convoy waiting to follow her to the planet.

Vanian was smart, Leia assured herself. She'd employ the necessary measures to get Matt to Nas unharmed. Leia continued to frown. There'd been a definite bite to the General's voice when she'd messaged to explain why they hadn't delivered the cargo yet.

"Why did you go to Belax instead of returning directly to Nas from Dockland?"

"Sir, I felt it safer to move away from expected behavior and message ahead with my report." While General Adimar didn't admit over the link they knew what happened at Dockland, Leia got the impression he still suspected her of turning renegade.

"This incident will have to be investigated upon your return, Lieutenant."

"Yes, sir."

"We will contact you at your family home as soon as word of the others has reached us. You will return within a week, Lieutenant. With the cargo." He'd cut transmission before she could argue or defend herself.

With a sigh, she pushed up from the console. The one bit of good news she'd received was that the crew of the *Persephone* and the rest of her team had escaped the pirates. Two soldiers were killed and almost everyone onboard sustained some injury, but they'd defended well against the attack. When the pirates discovered the cargo had escaped, they abandoned the *Persephone* to her fate. A passing Gormal cruiser stopped to help the stranded ship and the surviving crewmembers returned to Nas.

Leia walked out of the communications room still uncertain of her future. She glanced up, absently waved away Mr. Hanyoh when she saw Jake. He leaned against a wall, arms crossed over his massive chest, the image of masculine beauty. He took her breath away and made her heart bound with one look from those intense blue eyes. Every woman in the room kept stealing glances at him, longing and lust plain on most of their faces. She could practically feel the heat in the room rising with each passing minute.

She glowered, irritated other women stared at him, thought about him in that way. Okay, he was gorgeous. How could they not want him? But the reactions still bothered her. Did he notice their furtive gazes, their obvious desire? Did he enjoy the attention?

She made the mistake of looking into his eyes and for a moment forgot everything but him. She could live in the depth of that blue.

He was studying her, his face wary. The same wary expression had been in his eyes since she'd avoided his touch in front of the officials.

How could she explain the reaction? She hadn't actually meant to move away, would never have considered flinching from his touch. She loved his touch, craved the feel of his big hands on her body. But in that instant, some unconscious social survival instinct she'd thought long dead reared its ugly head. She'd reacted without conscious thought.

Jake was considered cargo here. The only women who slept with men stolen from the past were labeled depraved, overindulged slavers. The worst sort of sexual deviants. They were looked down on by those who considered themselves civilized.

Leia glanced around again. The women in that room might have fantasies about Jake, might consider him a perfect, primitive male specimen. And they sure as hell wanted him. But none would risk social condemnation by having sex with him.

And she'd done more than just sleep with Jake. She'd fallen in love with him.

The realization made her lightheaded. She blinked and widened her stance so she wouldn't list. Her parents had thought it a scandal when she wanted to join the military. They were going to disown her for this.

She let out a careful breath before crossing the gantlet of the room to reach Jake.

He never took his gaze off her and continued to study her as she got closer.

She reminded herself *he* had seduced her. He'd *chosen* her. She hadn't bought or sold him. She hadn't taken advantage of her position as part of his Guard escort to seduce him. And come the end of the universe, she was not going to be embarrassed by their relationship.

No matter what her parents said.

She stopped within arm's length, close enough to touch if she wanted to. Was she brave enough, strong enough to be so forward in public? She sucked in a breath, but her hands remained at her sides. Maybe not just yet. "Nas command hasn't heard from Vanian and the others yet. No word on Matt."

Jake straightened away from the wall, concern washing away wariness. "Something's gone wrong. What can we do? Can we track them?"

"The best thing we can do is stay here and wait for word. I've been ordered to return you to Nas in a week. If we haven't heard anything in the next two cycles, we'll decide what to do then." The concern, the fear, and more than anything the guilt in his expression eroded her awareness of breaching social taboos. She reached out and touched his forearm, just above the bracer. The contact brought his gaze to hers. Her need to comfort overwhelmed other thought. "The journey is longer to reach Nas than Belax from Dockland, Jake. Vanian is very good. She'll keep Matt safe."

His gaze stayed locked to hers for a long moment, then he dragged in a deep breath, let it out slowly and nodded. "You know the way things work here better than I do. I'll trust what you say."

She swallowed around a lump in her throat and squeezed his arm, to thank as much as to reassure. She only hoped her assurances deserved his trust. She tried a smile but was afraid her heart showed in her eyes. "My mother will have the house scrubbed and her famous red sauce boiling by now. Nas Command will contact us at my parent's home if there's any word. Shall we get out of here?"

For the first time since she'd jumped from his touch, he smiled. His slow, sexy smile, the one that made her pulse jump and her insides go liquid. She had to smile back.

He reached up, slow and careful, his gaze locked on hers. When she didn't flinch, he ran one finger down her cheek in a gentle caress.

She heard the gasps behind her, the sudden undercurrent of specu-lation filling the room like smoke. Without turning to acknowledge the gossip, she led him from the room, back into the main concourse.

Mr. Hanyoh hurried after them, following on her elbow as she and Jake headed for the transport the Wialiki Ground Control Executive had already arranged. "Are you sure your…gentleman friend wouldn't like another shirt?" he asked. He was still fawning over her and keeping a safe distance from Jake.

But when she turned, she saw the flash of something in his eyes… Condemnation? Or just cunning slyness? Hard to tell whether her awareness of the taboo she'd just flouted was interfering with her judgment, or whether Mr. Hanyoh's look really did criticize her actions with Jake. Either way, he still seemed in a hurry to do as she ordered so she let the look go.

She expected worse from her mother.

"Mr. Hanyoh wants to make sure you wouldn't like another shirt," she said to Jake. "Don't bother if it will make you uncomfortable." She met his gaze, willing him to understand she meant what she said. She regretted flinching and wanted desperately to make it up to him.

"Will you be embarrassed to introduce me to your family if these things aren't covered?"

The starkness in his voice tore at her. He knew why she'd flinched. He didn't fully understand. How could he? But he knew the bracers on his arms were the cause of her discomfort. "No," she answered firmly, willing it to be true. Her parents would just have to deal with how Jake got to be in her life. She gnawed the inside of her cheek, trying not to worry.

When his hand dropped onto her shoulder, she let out a relieved sigh. She hadn't flinched.

"I'll take the long sleeve shirt," he murmured, squeezing her shoulder. "But you're going to explain all this as soon as the preliminaries of meeting your family are over. I want to know what these things on my wrists really mean."

"I'll explain everything," she promised. She switched to Bel, and to the still hovering Mr. Hanyoh said, "Arrange a week's change of clothing for Mr. Marshall, including long sleeved shirts suitable to the heat."

Mr. Hanyoh practically fell over himself in his hurry to follow her orders.

Definite relief in his eyes now, but was that still censure?

<hr>

MR. HANYOH ARRANGED A SMALL, PERSONAL TRANSPORT FOR THEM, automated so Leia didn't have to drive. "Ballore residence, Mahana

Way," she instructed. The little silver bullet launched into the air, skimming over the treetops on its route.

Jake sucked in a sharp breath.

When she turned, he was gripping the door handle, looking out the window. "Are you all right?" she asked, noting his white knuckles.

He glanced at her with a self-mocking grin. "I wasn't expecting this thing to go airborne."

"It's easier than ground travel. You can't even access some areas from the ground because the jungle is too thick."

"Nice to know you don't just bulldoze the jungle to build roads."

"Well, they do where they can. It's just that Belax has some jungles very resistant to development." She sighed, looked down at the leafy canopy beneath them as they rushed past. "I'm glad they haven't been able to destroy much. The jungle and the sea. They're the two best things about Wialiki—this continent."

"Do you swim? In the sea?"

"I was a fish as a child. My mother couldn't drag me out of the sea except by bribery with food." She laughed. "I haven't been swimming in years." She turned from the view to face him, still grinning. "Maybe we can make some time for a quick dip in the ocean?"

"I'd like that. I don't get down to the ocean very often at home. I work too much. But I like to swim."

She reached for his hand, twining her fingers through his. If she could have any wish at all, at that moment, she'd wish to run away with Jake to an uninhabited island in the southern archipelagos, just the two of them, leaving the rest of the universe to fend for itself.

By the time they reached her family home, Leia felt just about ready to face her parents. But when the transport landed outside the front door of the sprawling, single story villa, her gut clenched. Okay, maybe not as ready as she thought.

The house looked the same as the day she'd left. So familiar she'd almost forgotten the details. The large, wooden front door and blue window shutters, thrown wide to let the breeze carry through the house. The plants hanging from the arch-tiled roof or spilling out of pots on the flat-tiled floor of the porch. All her mother's carefully tended spices and flowers scenting the air, mixing with the tangy scent of the orchard to her left and the sweeter scent of the jungle to her right.

The smell of home, Leia thought, and smiled despite her anxiety.

Sun heated the packed tan earth of the landing area, glistening with a near-blinding glare. Leia shaded her eyes, watched the dark arched doorway and waited. She didn't have to wait long.

"Leia! You're home! You've lost so much weight. You're wasting away. What man will look at you like that, with nothing to you but bones? Haven't you been eating the food I send you? Oh, it's been so long." And with a wail of joy, Malini Ballore pulled her daughter into a bone-crushing hug.

Leia wrapped her arms around her mother and sighed. Now, this was home. She grinned, laughed, hugged back, trying to hold in unexpected tears. She turned her openly weeping mother to face Jake. In Bel, she said, "Mom, this is Jake Marshall. A friend." She gave her mother a stern look that warned against saying anything.

"What? What's with this look?" Malini said, then turned to Jake. "Young man, you're so big and handsome. But someone is starving you. You need to eat! Come in. I have a sauce on and some *bucho* meat to tide you over."

Leia translated, adding an introduction to her mother for Jake. "Her name is Malini, and if you want to make sure she likes you, eat everything she offers and only stop when you can't possibly eat any more. She won't accept anything less."

With a huge grin that would have charmed the hardest of women, Jake nodded a greeting to Malini and said, "It's a pleasure to meet you. I'm starving. Thanks for feeding me. I'll be forever in your debt."

When Leia translated, Malini giggled. Her mother actually giggled. Had to be his grin, Leia decided as her mother scooted Jake toward the house, chattering nonstop even though he couldn't understand a word.

Leia let out a pent-up breath. That went a lot better than she'd expected. She didn't look forward to hearing what her mother had to say about the bracers when she finally saw them. For the moment,

Jake's new long sleeve shirt hid them. But her parents would have to know soon.

A confrontation she wasn't looking forward to.

She followed as her mother ushered Jake through the front door, still talking as fast as a *tiki* bird. Probably for the best that Jake couldn't understand Malini. She was already rambling on about marriage.

The inside of the house was cool and dark, despite the white walls. Leia sighed, taking in the familiar sights of home. She honestly hadn't realized how much she missed this house. Or the people in it, she thought as she heard her father's booming voice from the corridor to her right.

"Leia! It's been too long." He stalked toward her, intercepting her on her way to the kitchen. "Your mother worries. You should come home more often. How is the Nas Guard? You look good. Too skinny. Your mother will feed you, though. We hear you're a hero." He wrapped her in a gentle hug with arms as thick as her thigh. "My daughter, the hero."

Her father was her height but easily another person wider. She rested her head against his big shoulder, breathed in the scent of his much-loved tobacco. The pride in his voice nearly brought her to tears again. That had to stop. She couldn't just burst into tears every time she reunited with another member of her family.

She pulled back, holding her father's shoulders as she studied his face. He had her dark hair and tan skin, but his eyes were a deep purple, unique and beautiful. Her brown eyes came from her mother. Her father's hair was now streaked with silver and his face more lined than she remembered. But his eyes sparkled happily.

"You look good too, Dad. Mom's been feeding you well."

"She's a good cook, your mother. She does good by me."

"How's the farm?" She put her arm around her father's waist as his arm fell across her shoulders and they wandered back toward the kitchen where she could still hear Malini chattering at Jake.

"Fine. Fine. Good crop this year. The olives will turn us a tidy profit, too."

"Any news from Aunt Ilika? I met Telani recently. I should let her know how he's doing."

"That boy! A bane to his family. Not a hero like my daughter." His arm tightened around her shoulders.

Leia started to squirm under her father's praise. A moment ago, his approval had felt like basking in the sun. Now she feared watching that pride turn to shame when he learned the full truth about Jake. She held her breath a moment then said, "You know, I've brought someone with me."

"Your mother told me. A young man."

Leia ducked her head, avoiding his gaze as she prepared to tell him everything.

But he squeezed her shoulders before she could speak and said, "I already know he's a Recovery."

Her gaze jumped to his. His big brown eyes were calm and full of understanding.

"You've been trying to get him back to Nas for some time now, yes?"

"He and his partner, Matthew Donnelly. They were taken from the turn of the twenty-first century Earth. But there's more, Dad."

He smiled, but the look was tinged with sadness. "You have feelings for him. I know. Pohala Nee couldn't wait to ring and spread the gossip our hero daughter had been seen cavorting with a recovery at the terminal." His smile brightened then. "Your mother gave her an earful and reminded Pohala about her own daughter's disgraceful behavior at the last Carnival."

If she hadn't been so stunned, Leia would have laughed. "You know…everything? Mom knows?"

"We have a good idea." His brows bunched together over his eyes, and he frowned. "I will have to meet this young man before I pass judgment, though." One corner of his mouth ticked up then settled into the frown again.

She could tell he was trying to put on a stern expression but he failed miserably.

Leia could barely talk around the lump in her throat. She'd

somehow forgotten all this, the unity, the love. She'd somehow convinced herself her parents wouldn't understand, when deep down, she knew they would. "Thanks, Poppa." She hugged him again, quick and hard, then scrubbed the tears from her face so she wouldn't have to explain them to her mother.

When they stepped into the huge, bright kitchen that was her mother's domain, Leia felt lighter and happier than she had in months.

JAKE WAITED UNTIL HE COULDN'T EAT ANOTHER BITE BEFORE HE ASKED Leia if they could go somewhere to talk privately. They'd spent several companionable hours in the Ballore kitchen, talking, with the help of Leia to translate, and eating like a famine was on the way. Jake couldn't have said what half the dishes were, but he loved almost everything. The one or two things that tasted too much like fish for his liking, he'd swallowed politely anyway because he would have cut off his own hand before insulting Momma Ballore's cooking.

They sat around a huge stone table, on long wooden benches and traded the food around while talking.

Malini stood the entire time, puttering over a huge number of pots and pans on the longest stove Jake had ever seen outside a restaurant. She punctuated comments with her ladle or a knife and laughed as often as she scolded.

Apani, Leia's father, sat at the head of the table, eating whatever was put in front of him and holding court over the conversation—when he could get a word in around his wife. He smiled and laughed with such enthusiasm, Jake worried he might fall off his bench. The man was short but huge, all thick, corded muscle despite his obvious love of food. Matt would be appalled at the thick red meats and artery-clogging concoctions they ate. He'd be even more disgusted to see the food had no effect on Apani's health or fitness.

The thought of his partner gave Jake a twinge of guilt. He could do nothing but wait for word and hope for the best. But he wanted to do something, felt like he should spend more time worrying about Matt and less time enjoying the Ballore family. Yet, he couldn't keep from getting sucked into the atmosphere. Even without understanding the language.

They laughed a lot, Jake noted. His parents had been kind people but there hadn't been a lot of noise and laughter in his home growing up. They'd been a small family, too. Only himself and his brother. His parents' families lived in other parts of the country and rarely visited. And while he got along all right with his younger brother, living a continent apart wasn't much of a hardship on either of them.

Leia, on the other hand, had three brothers lurking out in the fields, tending the family farm, and a sister with her own home and family on another island—all of whom were on their way for a visit. Leia had cringed when she told him that come nightfall, half the Ballore and Timone family would descend on the house. And despite the shudder that moved over her shoulders, humor and happiness danced in her eyes.

She loved her family. She fit here.

A hope he hadn't even acknowledged before died in that kitchen. Leia wouldn't come to Earth with him. She wouldn't leave her family behind.

And he could never ask her.

Leia nodded at his request for a private chat outside, gave excuses to her parents then rose gracefully from the bench.

Despite not having to lift his feet while walking, the gravity still made his body feel heavy and sluggish, like he'd put on all the weight Matt warned him he would if he didn't start eating better. He admired her smooth, easy movements in the heavier gravity.

He followed Leia through the open wall that made up one side of the kitchen, out onto a tiled patio and beyond into an orchard of fruit trees. The scent of the place was heady and spiced, a mix of fruit and herbs and something tangy he couldn't place. Pervasive, but not over-whelming. Drawing a deep breath brought a buffet of wonderful scents that changed subtly with each breeze.

He waited until they were out of sight of the house before he pulled

Leia into his arms. He had to kiss her, the need primal and impossible to resist.

She took a deep breath when he pulled back and smiled up at him. "What was that for?"

"I haven't kissed you in a while. I missed you."

"You've completely charmed my mother, you know. She's in love with you now. I'll have to sneak you out of the house to get you back to Nas."

He chuckled, pulled her close so he could rest his chin on her head. "Always wise to get in good with the mother. Smooths the way for most things in life."

Her hands rubbed up and down his back, and a soft sigh escaped her. "They know about the bracers," she murmured so quietly he almost missed it. "They know you're a recovery I have to return."

He nodded. "And this means?"

"It means they're a lot more understanding than I ever gave them credit for." She pulled out of his arms, took his hand and led him further into the orchard. "You've been asking about the bracers. You know they mark you as a slave here. And because I'm a Guard, everyone knows my duty is to return you. I'm not supposed to be involved with you. It's a…taboo. Like… Like walking around in public completely naked is taboo in your world. No, worse than that." She stopped near a wooden bench, pulled him down onto the seat with her. "It's considered a bit like molestation."

"That's why you flinched from my touch? Everyone here would think you were…using me?"

"Exactly. Little better than the people who would buy you at auction. And they won't consider that you seduced me."

She smiled when she said it, and some of the tightness in Jake's chest eased.

"All they'll see," she said with a sigh, "is a woman in a position of power taking advantage of a kidnapped primitive."

His eyebrows shot up. "Primitive? We might not be flying between planets yet, but I'd hardly call us primitive."

She nibbled on her lower lip, looked out into the fields of lush green and purple trees. "I'm not sure if I should tell you this. You're adjusting so well ..." She fell silent, still staring into the distance.

When she didn't speak again, he reached up to take her chin in his fingertips, turning her face. "Tell me. I'd rather know everything."

"Yes, you would." She took a deep breath. "Jake, you weren't just kidnapped from Earth. You were kidnapped from early twenty-first century Earth."

He frowned, his brow creased. She made it sound like... "What are you telling me?"

"You have been taken more than 3000 years into your future. This isn't just another galaxy. This is another era." She touched the bracer on his arm. "These are the only things keeping you here. If they're removed, you'll either be sucked back to your own time—a shock that could do much damage psychologically and physically—or you'll die. Not a nice death either. It's like being ripped apart from the inside out. Not only do those bracers mark you as someone to be sold as a slave, they can't be removed until you return to your own time."

Jake sat back and shook his head. This couldn't be true. Three thousand years into the future? Impossible. Time travel was impossible except in fiction. Wasn't it? Starships and intergalactic travel he could believe. He had to believe, he'd been experiencing it. But time travel?

"There's more," she said reluctantly. "Your bracers were tampered with by the pirates before you were recovered. The metal on the leather... It's called zanathim. As far as anyone knows, it can only be found on one planet. The configuration on the leather is specific and tampering with it means a special effort is required to get you and Matt back. That's why you were being brought to Nas for the return."

He shook his head again, struggling to deny her story. No. Not possible. He stood abruptly, walked several paces from the bench. Why was time travel any more difficult to believe than space travel? Because it was, damn it! Because space travel was scientifically feasible. Even Einstein had trouble with time travel. Three thousand years. He clenched his fists. "Christ."

"Jake?" Leia's voice was soft, hesitant, full of concern.

He turned to face her. "So, if I take off these things, I'm dead one way or the other. If I leave them on, I'm considered a slave here. Right?"

She nodded. "I'm sorry, Jake. I know—"

"When you return me," he interrupted, "when I'm sent back to my own…time, will I go back to the moment I was taken? Does anybody there even know I'm gone?"

"It's relative. If we don't return you ever, then they'll notice. And all kinds of time paradoxes could result. We'll try to return you to as near the time as you were first taken. To preserve the timeline."

"And you can do that? Get me back close to the time I was kidnapped?"

"We can. If the damage to the bracers can be overcome."

"How does it work?"

She turned up her hands and shook her head. "I'm not even supposed to tell you you're in a different time. Do you realize the damage I've caused just by telling you this?"

"What am I gonna do, corner the California lottery numbers for the next fifty years? You've got me three thousand years in the future. Even if I did tell anyone about this, they'd just lock me up for being crazy." His voice rose with each sentence until he was almost shouting. He closed his eyes, tried to rein in his temper and panic. "How does it work?" he murmured without opening his eyes.

"There's a species, the Kyzits."

Her voice drifted to him, gentle and quiet as the breeze.

"They move through time and space," she said, "without the help of machines or technology. They won't explain how. Some think they don't know how. They just do it, like we just breathe, naturally. Their hair is woven into a type of leather that makes the bracers. And the zanathim patterns on the bracers are designed by the Kyzits. Both the leather and the designs are needed to make the bracers work. They've never explained why. Only that if the designs are tampered with, a whole family is required to return a recovery."

"And there are a lot of these families?" He opened his eyes.

"Families of Kyzits live on most of the main trade planets. They help return recoveries, and they trade in the relics and precious minerals collected from different times and worlds."

"Not altruists, then," he said. "They use their skills for profit."

"They're a rich species, yes, but an honorable one. They don't corrupt the timelines with what they take or carry other species on joy rides through time. Kyzits have some…sense, I suppose, about what will and won't corrupt the timeline. They seem to know things, how events should go."

"Wait." He held up a hand. "This sounds more like magic than science. I thought you were a technologically advanced…time."

"We are, compared to twenty-first century Earth. But don't discount magic, Jake. Sometimes magic is just something in nature we haven't figured out the mechanics for yet. The Kyzits are what they are and do what they do. We don't know how. And if they do, they aren't telling."

"So…" He took a deep breath, his head reeling with the story she told him. "If they're so honorable and won't corrupt timelines, why are Matt and I here?"

"One family of Kyzits have aligned themselves with a pirate named Grettel. She runs the largest group of slavers in the known galaxies. Her Kyzits don't have the same ethical stance as the rest of the species. Either that or she's found a way to hold and use them. If so, she's the only one. Others have tried and failed."

She shifted on the bench, frowning a little. "One story tells of a wealthy man from Vesna Prime who tried to capture a family of Kyzits using Dusters. The Kyzits didn't take too well to the ploy. They can pull out of psychic lures easier than most other species, but they're still susceptible. The story says they took this wealthy merchant into some hellish time and left him with bracers designed to crumble after five years. He was never heard of again."

"So, you'll have these Kyzits send me back…"

She nodded, but her gaze dropped and her fingers wrapped around the edge of the bench.

He watched her knuckles turn white as she clenched the stone. "And then what?"

She blinked up at him. "What do you mean?"

"Are you going to erase my memory or something? Or am I just stuck knowing everything I know now?" His jaw tightened and suddenly he found it hard to breathe.

Leia shrugged and looked away. "We normally avoid the level of contamination you've been exposed to. We can usually convince a recovery of a story that keeps them happy enough once returned. In the end, most think it's some sort of dream."

"Contamination? That's what you call this?" Jake laughed. He couldn't help it. And if the laugh sounded a bit hysterical, even to him, well so what? He was three thousand fucking years in the future. He had a right to be hysterical.

"Jake." Leia rose from the bench and reached out to touch his shoulder.

He jerked away. "I need to be alone for a few minutes. I need to think." He turned and moved off blindly into the orchard.

His heart thumped too hard. His brain reeled against the story. It wasn't possible. Couldn't be true. Kyzits? Who'd ever heard of a time-traveling alien species called Kyzits? Leia was making up the time travel part of this story. Had to be.

Because if she weren't, he'd never see her again after he went home.

Until that moment, he hadn't realized he held the small, secret speck of hope in his heart. He did, though. A part of him hoped if he could travel through space to meet her once, then he'd come back one day to see her again. They wouldn't have to say goodbye forever. He could hope for something beyond that.

After watching her with her parents, he knew she'd never cross the galaxies to be with him. And he wouldn't ask her to give up her family, even if she were willing. But he could probably give up his world to stay with her. If she wanted him, if he could remove the bracers, if…

But the fucking bracers couldn't be removed.

He let out a harsh breath. If he stayed, he'd be screwing up some timeline he found it hard to give a damn about. But what if by staying, this world ceased to exist? Hell, he had no idea the implications of his being here. Maybe he was supposed to solve some important case on Earth that only he could solve. Kids? What if he was supposed to have kids in his own time?

He couldn't imagine having a family with anyone but Leia. Scary enough he was considering a family at all. Knowing he couldn't hope for that family with Leia because they were separated by millennia cut deep.

Had they already screwed up the timeline with their affair?

Did he care?

Not really. He couldn't care about some nebulous timeline when his chest and gut felt like they were being ripped out with meat hooks. He couldn't think past the lonely stretch of life in front of him without Leia. He knew now, without excuse, he couldn't stay. No matter what, he was going to lose her. Forever. The idea hurt so much he thought getting shot would be easier. He only had one choice. He had to pull back, salvage what was left of his heart. He needed distance and time. Before he got any crazy ideas about staying. He needed to leave as soon as possible. He doubted he'd hurt less by ending their affair now, but he wouldn't make the leaving worse by spending more time with her, knowing they had no future together.

He dropped his head, staring at the tan soil beneath his feet without really seeing it. Around him, the air hung thick with a spicy fruit scent he couldn't place. The trees moved in the breeze, creating a gentle rustling chorus. The only other sound was that of his breathing and his too-loud heartbeat. He raised his head, let the late evening sun wash over his face. He sighed, opened his eyes to look at the purple leaves of the trees surrounding him.

He might already be too late to save his heart.

He caught her scent, heard the soft shuffle of her feet before she cleared her throat. He kept his back to her, waited until he felt more in control of his reaction to her presence. If he had to look at her now, he'd probably do something stupid like pull her into his arms and kiss her until all his aching loneliness went away.

"I shouldn't have told you," she murmured. "It's driven other men insane to find this out. I hated not telling you. But the situation might be easier if you didn't know…"

"I'm not losing my mind," he said, not at all sure he spoke the truth.

"I know you're stronger than that. That's why I told you. But I shouldn't have. I should have let you think you were in a different place but the same time. The illusion would have made your return easier."

"Maybe not. It might have been harder." He pulled in a deep breath. "I asked for the truth. You were honest and I appreciate that."

"It doesn't change things really," she said, sounding hesitant.

He felt her move up close behind him. When her hand gripped his shoulder, he shuddered. Step away from her warmth, from the flood of heat and comfort coming from her touch. But he couldn't.

"Now you know why the bracers are so important." She moved closer, pressing against his back and wrapping her arms around his chest.

The imprint of her breasts, soft and full, made his breath hitch.

"But nothing else is different," she said. "You'll go home soon."

"Things are different now." He eased out of the temptation of her arms. "When I leave, I can't even hope to see you again. Knowing we had a galaxy between us was hard enough. Three thousand years is a lot more formidable barrier."

"What are you saying?"

"I need to go home. Soon. I can't stay here another week, another couple of days. I have to leave as soon as possible." He forced the words through clenched teeth. When he heard her sharp intake of breath, he fought every instinct to remain in place, to keep from turning and pulling her into his arms. He couldn't look at her and say what he had to say. "Can we leave for Nas tomorrow?"

She was silent for so long, he wasn't sure she'd answer. He turned his head, just enough to make sure she was still there.

"I'll arrange things tonight," she said, her voice hollow. "We should be able to leave by tomorrow morning."

The slight catch in her breathing tore at his heart. He nodded. Then because he couldn't resist any longer, he turned. In time to see her running back toward the house. He took two steps toward her, intending to follow, before he stopped. This was the only way either would be able to say goodbye. Maybe if she were angry, she wouldn't hurt so much. His own pain would be with him for a very long time.

1 0

Leia avoided the kitchen, making her way directly to her old bedroom suite at the far end of the house. She didn't want to face her parents and have to explain her tears. Explaining their sudden departure would be hard enough. She couldn't tell her parents she'd fallen in love with a recovery and was now heartbroken because he didn't want anything to do with her anymore.

She wasn't sure what she'd expected once he found out the whole truth. A part of her had hoped nothing would change and he'd still want their week together. She'd already built up a little fantasy of running away to an isolated island where they could make love for days and not have to think about the outside world. She supposed the time they'd spent alone on the ship was all the "isolated island" fantasy she would ever get.

She pushed open the slatted wooden patio doors of her bedroom and crossed the tiles to her bed. The room was cool and dark, the white sheets on the bed soft and inviting. She flung herself onto the mattress and buried her face in a pillow, letting the tears flow. Her breathing came in short, stuttering gasps around the tightness in her chest. She tried to console herself. Jake had every right to be angry and upset. Why should he want to stay in this time any longer than necessary?

157

Because she wanted him to, she thought, barely holding in a wail as she gripped the pillow harder. She'd believed he cared enough to want to stay, even for a short time. She'd hoped… She'd hoped in vain, she admitted.

Slowly, her sobbing eased. She hiccupped once and released her death-grip on the pillow. Turning over, she stared through sore, blurry eyes out the now-open patio doors to the orchard trees beyond. Above the trees were hills covered in the ever-encroaching jungle. The sky beyond was bright and cloudless, turning soft shades of orange, pink and deeper purple as the sun set. A gentle breeze drifted in past the wooden slats of the patio doors, cooling her already cool room.

She couldn't count the number of times she'd woken to that view. For years, she'd wanted out of this room, this house. She'd wanted her own life. Well, Leia, look what your own life has gotten you? A broken heart. She sighed and rubbed at her damp eyes. She wasn't being fair to herself. She loved her life, loved being a Guard and didn't even mind being a hero. She was just a little homesick.

And she didn't want to face the future without Jake in her life.

The console on the nightstand beside her bed rattled, announcing an incoming message. Leaving the visual screen black, she hit a button and opened the call. "Yes," she said, proud to hear her voice didn't sound as tear choked as she felt.

"Lieutenant Ballore?" The voice at the other end of the call sounded hesitant without a visual to confirm her identity. "This is Wialiki command. A message has just been received from Nas for you. Priority One."

She sat up, dropping her legs over the side of the bed. "Transmit." She waited until the console beeped its acceptance of the prerecorded message then played it. The face of a Nas General filled the screen. Not General Adimar. But General Nemays, a hero in her own right on Nas.

"Pirates have recaptured the recovery Matthew Donnelly," the General said without preamble. "You must return with the other immediately." She frowned, her smooth white skin creasing on her brow as she glanced away from the screen. When she turned back, her eyes looked troubled. "Your position has been compromised, Lieutenant. Take what precautions you can." Her frown deepened, her eyes narrowed. "The pirates caught the others just at the edge of the Nas system."

The transmission cut out abruptly. Leia tweaked a few buttons trying to recover the rest, then realized there was no more. That was the message. Get back soon. The pirates had Matt.

She launched off her bed and ran back into the orchard. She found Jake where she'd left him.

He looked up when he heard her approach.

The look in his eyes passed through a series of emotions she couldn't read. Then he must have recognized her anxiety because his shoulders straightened and his gaze sharpened.

"What is it?"

She sucked in air. "The pirates have Matt. I've been ordered to get you to Nas as quickly as possible."

"Matt? We have to help him. Get him back. How do we—"

"I've been ordered to get you to Nas, Jake," she interrupted. "Two of us can't go after Grettel alone. I don't even know if it was Grettel."

"I can't just leave him to be sold into slavery," Jake growled. "I won't. Will you help me or not?"

"I would if it were possible. But Jake, I wouldn't know where to start. If we reach Nas without getting caught ourselves, we'll access whatever information they have and we can go from there." Because she needed to, she closed the distance and cupped his cheek in her palm. "I'll help you find him. I promise. I won't let them send you back before we've recovered Matt."

He pulled in a deep, trembling breath and nodded. "Fine. We leave tonight?"

"Tonight."

ARRANGING PROPER TRANSPORT AND GETTING OFF-PLANET TOOK longer than Leia liked thanks to Belaxian bureaucracy, but she knew the paperwork could have been worse. Her parents had been so understanding about the sudden departure, her touch of homesickness intensified, and she'd found it hard to leave them. She promised she'd take time to visit soon. And she meant to keep that promise. But first she had another to keep.

If she couldn't have Jake, the least she could do was make sure he and Matt went back to their own time together, as they were meant to. She'd help him find Matt. And then she'd let him go.

She ignored the pain in her chest as she directed the ship toward the outer system for the jump to hyperspace. "The trip to Nas, planet to planet, takes about two cycles," she told Jake when they were well underway. She tried hard not to think about how they'd spent their last voyage.

"How long is the journey from Dockland to Nas?"

"Three to four cycles, depending on the route and the ship."

"How did Matt and the others get caught by pirates so soon then? They should still be traveling, shouldn't they? Only, what, two cycles have passed since we left Docklands?"

"A little over actually, more like two and a quarter. But you're right. They should have been in hyperspace when we were contacted." She frowned and went over the General's message. "I was told they were caught outside the Nas system. They wouldn't have had time to get that far. I didn't stop to think..." She paused with her hand hovering over the controls. He was right. She should have noticed, should have realized.

Leia sat back and frowned at the console as she thought through Nasen emergency procedures. Vanian had three choices. She could come out of hyperspace somewhere along the way to Nas and send a message ahead to announce their return. She could avoid coming out of hyperspace and go straight to Nas. Or she could do what Leia had done —find a neutral base and message Nas from there.

None of those options would place Vanian and the others at the edge of the Nas system when pirates captured them. So how, and where, were they really taken? And why did General Nemays say Vanian had been captured near the Nas system?

She thought back to the first attack, the fact that they'd been lured away from the recovery station, farther away from Nas, by the Nasen distress call they'd picked up.

So much had happened, she'd forgotten about the suspicion over a spy she had at the time. Maybe the traitor hadn't been in her squad or even the *Persephone* crew. Maybe the traitor was in Nas Command. General Nemays? That didn't seem likely given her record. Possibly, the General had been deceived or passed a false story. But what if she was the traitor?

Was the General's message intended as a trap?

Leia's head spun with implications and possibilities. Now what? She'd been given a direct order from a General in the Command to return to Nas. She couldn't disobey. Not if she wanted to keep her position in the Guard. But if this was a trap, could she afford to follow the order? She could message Command but that would give away her position, plans and suspicions to anyone monitoring subspace transmissions.

"Damn," she murmured out loud, using English unconsciously after so much time with Jake.

"What is it?"

She startled at his voice, quiet in the mechanical humming of the ship. "I'm not sure what to do," she admitted, turning to face him. "You're right. The message I received said they were captured just outside the Nas system. Given the delays in transmissions, they couldn't have been near the system for another cycle. If they'd dropped out of hyperspace to send a message to Nas, they'd have been vulnerable to detection by pirates. But the pirates would have to know where to find them and be near enough to reach them before they jumped again. Not an easy accomplishment."

Jake frowned. "You can't send a message from hyperspace?"

"No. You can't send or receive during a jump. The *Persephone* was caught because we picked up a subspace distress message before the jump, and we were the only ship close enough to lend aid. They lured us away from Nas, but that was obviously planned in advance, knowing our location and our destination."

"And it would be almost impossible for anyone to know Vanian's route unless she sent a message ahead?"

"Right." Leia shrugged. "Well, unless there was a tracking device attached to the ship Telani gave us. But Vanian would have checked for that, disabled it before making the jump. She's too good to blindly trust Telani. Even if he is my cousin."

Jake's brow creased as he worked out the problem. "Once we reached Belax, though, someone would have known her route. Whoever you talked to on Nas."

"That's what I'm worried about," Leia admitted. "I was afraid a traitor in my squad, or in the *Persephone* crew, gave us away to the pirates the first time we were attacked. Someone gave them the Nasen code used in the distress message. But the traitor could have as easily been in Nas Command. And if they were, they'd have learned our route and Vanian's when I called in. They may or may not have been able to waylay Vanian. If she never dropped out of hyperspace, they wouldn't be able to track her until she entered the Nas system. But they'd know where to find us."

"They'd also know the exact information that would send us running back to Nas without thinking," Jake said.

She nodded. "So, what do we do now? We can't go back to Belax. If we're wrong, I'll have disobeyed a direct order from my Command. Losing my commission will be the least of my worries."

"Then we go on. And hope to avoid pirates along the way. They can't take us while we're in hyperspace?"

"No. We have to drop out ourselves."

"Then we don't. We just keep going."

"And if there's an ambush at the system's edge? General Nemays didn't say whether or not we'd have an escort waiting. I assumed we would but if this is really a trap..."

"If we don't have an escort, we'll be vulnerable to ambush?"

"Very."

"Then we'll deal with that when we arrive. Unless you have any other ideas."

"I don't." Short of running away to some far-flung system and keeping him safe and all to herself forever. She stared down at her hands in her lap for a long moment, then said, "I'll try to improve our chances by shooting us past the system and bringing us in from the direction opposite the Belax reentry point. If there's an ambush, we may be able to avoid it that way. The trip will take a little longer, but the ploy may give us an element of surprise."

"Okay. Whatever you think is best."

She smiled, just a little. "I'm sorry. I've put your life in jeopardy because I didn't analyze the message closely. I was too... Well, I'm sorry."

"Don't." He reached out and gripped her hand. "From the start, you've done your best to keep me alive and get me home. You've got nothing to apologize for."

The feel of his warm hand on hers made her heart ache. She swallowed around the lump in her throat. "Once we make the jump, we'll be safe."

"I know. How long to the edge of the system?"

"Less than a quarter cycle now. Time enough to get some rest if you like." She should pull her hand away, but the sad, needy part of her that loved him didn't want to lose the contact. She wanted to fall into his arms and stay there for the rest of the journey.

She couldn't, but she wanted to.

He'd remained distant even after they'd gotten news about Matt. He hadn't touched her, not even in passing. He'd done what needed to be done to get underway, but he hadn't tried to get close or spend any more time in her company than necessary. His withdrawal hurt. It was too sudden and she wasn't ready for him to be gone, especially when he was still sitting right next to her.

"Maybe I will," he said after a quiet moment. He pulled his hand from hers and left the cockpit.

She stifled a sigh, sniffed, then scolded herself for being a ninny. Time to get ready for the jump. Later, she could brood about Jake, during the long, lonely journey ahead.

Her throat closed again and she had to press her hand to her mouth to keep from crying aloud. With tears tracing over her cheek, she left the pilot seat to program the nav-system. Once they made the jump, she'd go lie down herself. She was so tired and emotionally battered. Maybe she'd just sleep for the rest of the trip. When she woke up, Jake would go home and she could try to convince herself the whole thing had been a dream.

She punched coordinates into the nav-system, concentrating so she wouldn't have to reenter the sequence. The last thing she wanted was to accidentally jump them to some strange system farther away from Nas because she'd been too emotional to enter the correct coordinates. Navigation mistakes could be more than inconvenient, too. They could be deadly.

Unlike Pakker's ship, the Belax vessel had two rooms to accommodate travelers, a larger cockpit and nav-system, but a smaller communal area and less storage capacity. This ship was designed to be fast and comfortable without being luxurious. They had a better stock of food onboard, too—including some of her mother's red sauce and *bucho* beef. They wouldn't have to live off ration bars.

Leia turned from her final programming of the nav-system and took a deep breath. She didn't want to think about their last trip. It had been perfect. One perfect, beautiful cycle. She'd been hoping for more. Hoping even after he discovered the truth, he'd want to spend what little time they had together. Now, she had to face the fact he didn't want anything to do with her anymore.

She couldn't blame him. She'd lied to him, or at least omitted the truth. He was angry, confused. And out of his time. But seeing him and not being allowed to touch him hurt, to know he would jerk away from her touch if she tried. She couldn't believe how much her heart ached.

He deserved to know the truth. She couldn't regret telling him. Her only regret was that she hadn't told him she loved him. She didn't believe the admission would change anything. If she let herself believe his excuse, then he wanted to leave because he cared too much already to risk more. She wasn't sure she believed that excuse though. She'd known from the start they'd be separated permanently, but she still wanted to spend every second possible with him.

More likely, he was just angry with her, maybe even hated her now.

So telling him she loved him wouldn't have changed his mind about going home. But he'd know. He'd carry the knowledge to his own time. And knowing, maybe he'd be able to forgive her one day.

She debated checking on him but knew she'd only be torturing herself. She needed to remain at the helm in case anything unexpected happened on the journey out of the system. Scrubbing her hands over her face to wipe away the tears, she settled back into the cockpit, starring out as they neared the second to last planet in the system. Not long now and they could make the jump. Then they'd be safe until dropping out in the Nas system. And she had two full cycles to worry about that part of their journey.

The sudden lurch of the ship threw her forward against the helm console. With a grunt of pain, she pushed back into her seat and studied the screen in front of her. They were still moving forward, but their course had altered. She punched in a few commands to correct, couldn't, and tried to slow down the ship. When that failed, she cursed under her breath and started scanning the space directly in front of them. She spotted the distant silvery hull of the ship where it had obviously just emerged from behind an asteroid.

Jake dropped into the seat beside her. "What the hell happened?"

"We're caught in a tractor beam. Damn it. I didn't think the pirates could get all the way to Belax so quickly. I should have been scanning." She tried reversing thrusters but knew her action was futile. This ship had a weapons system, she'd made sure of that when making arrangements with Wialiki command. But she couldn't fire while they were in the other ship's tractor—too much chance of backfire. If she could break the lock, she might get off a few shots, create a distraction so they could make a run for it.

"Can we pull free?"

"I'm trying." Her hands flew over the helm, shunting power to the reverse thrusters, hoping for one little break. They were still too far into the system to make a jump, but if they could break the tractor, they could run. "We need to send a message back to Belax." She pulled up a screen, turned it to face Jake. "Talk. It'll record and translate. Tell them we're under attack."

As she continued trying to maneuver out of the beam, even as it pulled them closer to the other ship, she heard Jake record a Mayday. When he finished, she said, "The panel beneath, enter 648, 710, 10, 1. Then hit the blue button with the double triangle. You see the one?" She pointed but didn't take her gaze off the other ship or her helm controls.

"Got it."

She heard the distinctive beeping to indicate a message being sent and almost smiled. Jake did catch on quickly. The ship lurched again, forcing a grunt from her. She studied the readouts before her and started some serious cursing in Bel. She poked the translator and said, "Two ships. I can't fight both tractors. Damn it." She shut off power and sat back in her seat, running through possibilities. They didn't have many. "There're weapons in the back. We might stall them. Until help from Belax arrives."

"They'll board us?"

She nodded, one quick jerk of her head. "Those ships aren't big enough to carry this one. They're probably shuttles from a larger ship. They'll have to dock with this ship and try to take us out. We can make that a damned difficult task."

"Will it work?"

She locked gazes with him. "No."

"But we may take some of them with us?"

"Exactly."

"Then point me to the DEGs, Lieutenant."

She smiled without humor and led him back toward the weapons locker.

11

Jake blinked against the bright light overhead, squinting to block the glare. His brain felt fuzzy and thick. He was so groggy he had trouble keeping his eyes open against the lights. It would be easy to drift back into oblivion. He clenched his jaw, forced his brain to concentrate, think, remember.

Their desperate stand against the pirates hadn't lasted long. They held off the first group boarding through a hole the pirates had cut in the hull. They took refuge in a corridor, with Leia squatting and firing low, while he stood over her, firing high. They drove back the first group, wounding and killing a few pirates before the rest retreated through the air-seal connecting the two ships.

The second group wielded a weapon that knocked out him and Leia before they could fire another shot. A vague memory of Leia mentioning a sweep stunner surfaced. That must have been what hit them.

His head hurt like hell. He tried sitting up and found he couldn't move. He tensed his arms and felt straps tighten. One of those damned harnesses like they'd worn in the first escape shuttle held him pinned to a steel table. Okay. This was bad. He lifted his head, the only part of his body he could move. A shape appeared over him, blocking the light. When the shape resolved itself, he sucked in a sharp breath. He cursed and pressed back against the table, struggling to get away.

The alien standing over him was the classic image of aliens on Earth—long neck, large round head with a pointed chin, huge eyes, a tiny mouth, hairless. And the damn thing was green! Thin hands reached out and a long finger moved close to his face. He struggled harder in the bindings, tossing his head away from that reaching finger.

A very feminine laugh stopped him mid-struggle. He looked back at the alien as it straightened. The creature touched something on its belt and suddenly a very human-looking woman stood in its place. And she was laughing.

"Sorry, hon, I couldn't resist. Americans always fall for that trick." The woman's voice was deep and husky. She was tall and well built. With blond braids running down either side of her face, she reminded him of a Valkyrie. Except she wore the clothing of a classic Hollywood pirate. Tight black pants tucked into thigh-high boots, a thick red sash around her waist holding a weapon that looked a lot deadlier than a sword, a white blousy shirt and a black vest fitted tight to generous curves.

"What trick?" he asked around a dry throat. "And why the hell does my head hurt so much?"

"Stunners'll do that. The headache. The trick was my handy holo-imager. You thought I was one of those aliens that performs strange experiments on humans, didn't you? The ones filling the pages of your tabloids." She laughed again, shaking her head. "I just love that. Funny as hell."

Her English was better than Leia's. "Who are you? Where's Leia?"

The woman's grin turned sly. "Your lady friend is right there next to you. Just hasn't recovered from the stun yet."

Jake turned his head and relief washed over him when he saw Leia looking uninjured, even if she was still unconscious.

"As for who I am."

The woman's voice brought his attention reluctantly back to her.

"The name's Grettel. I'm sure you've heard of me." She winked.

His fists flexed inside the restraint and the belts tightened. "You're the one responsible for kidnapping me and Matt." He didn't try to hide the growl in his voice.

"Relax, hon. You keep flexing like that and the restraint will tighten so much, you'll have trouble breathing." Her blue eyes twinkled, bright with amusement.

The cocky expression only made Jake angrier, but he forced his body to relax. He'd had these stupid restraints clamping around him before. Since he wasn't sure he could control his anger, he simply stared, waiting. In his experience, most criminals liked to gloat when they got the drop on you. He had a feeling Grettel would be big into gloating.

After a silent minute, she chuckled. "You are one hell of a handsome man. You know that? You're gonna make me a lot of money."

"Not if I have any say in the matter."

Jake's head snapped around at the sound of Leia's voice. Her eyes blazed as she glared up at Grettel. His heart thumped hard in his chest. She looked beautiful when she was angry. "Are you hurt?" he asked, ignoring Grettel's laughter.

"No. I can't even feel the shoulder wound."

Jake's jaw clenched. He'd forgotten the wound she'd received in the first volley of fire. He'd nearly had a heart attack seeing her take the hit. His first instinct had been to pull her aside and block her, keep her safe while he took on the entire pirate fleet if he had to. But the wound had barely slowed her down. She continued firing, despite the pain she must have felt. Her bravery humbled him. She knew, even better than he, their fight was hopeless. Yet she'd fought on. To defend him.

"Are you hurt?" she asked, finally looking away from Grettel.

"The restraints are a bit snug."

"Such a sweet reunion," Grettel said, sarcasm thick in her voice. "Let me just draw you back to your situation, shall I? You," she nodded at Leia, "took something that belongs to me." She nodded at Jake. "He owes me a good sale."

"What I owe you is a—"

"No need to get aggressive, big boy," she said, interrupting Jake's outburst. "Now, we'll get your friend back before some misguided fool tries to send him back without you. Then we're going to the nearest auction hall." She glanced at Leia.

Jake was positive he didn't like her assessing look.

"And you, Lieutenant Leia Ballore... We'll have to see what to do about you."

The pirate turned, walking away. Over her shoulder, she shouted something in another strange language, then she was gone.

A moment later, a ragged-looking bunch of humans swarmed over them. The restraints were removed and they were lifted to their feet. Cuffs, similar to the ones Leia had made him and Matt wear on Dockland Depot, were snapped around his wrists. At Leia's hissed curse, he looked to see her hands being pulled behind her back as the cuffs clicked into place. The wound on her shoulder oozed blood.

"Watch it," he growled at the pirate manhandling Leia, jerking against his own captors to get closer.

She dipped her head, pressed her shoulder to her jaw then said, "Don't struggle, Jake. I'm fine. The movement just started the bleeding again."

"They need to get you a bandage for that."

"A bandage is the least of our worries right now." She sounded grim.

"You're not giving up on me, are you, Lieutenant?"

She met his gaze, her eyes hard and determined. "Never."

"Good. Then tell me what Grettel said before she left."

Their guards pushed them none too gently out into a long, narrow corridor. The ship was darker than the others he'd been on so far, the lighting dimmed, the walls and floors made of dark metal. Even the panels covered with multicolored lights along the way seemed dim and subdued. He couldn't feel the ship moving, not even the fine vibration through the soles of his feet he'd experienced before. So, they'd probably made the jump into hyperspace.

"We've been ordered taken to holding cells," Leia said. She stumbled, falling into him.

He turned, catching her as best he could with the cuffs on his wrists. The pirate behind her growled something Jake couldn't understand. When Leia got her balance, she straightened away from him. Jake glared at the man behind her, the one who'd commented, and got a loutish laugh in response.

"Jake."

Leia's voice brought his gaze down to her upturned face. They were pushed forward, set in motion again.

But Leia stayed as close as their captors would allow. "We're to be cleaned up then brought before what Grettel called the Council. Where I think our fates will be decided."

"She's already decided my fate." Jake's voice shook with suppressed fury.

"I think…" Leia hesitated.

He looked down to study her profile.

She was nibbling her bottom lip, glancing around the pirates, assessing the situation. "I think there's something… I don't know."

"What?"

"Just a feeling. I can't explain it. We'll see." She went back to nibbling her lip.

Her silence annoyed him. He wanted to hear what she thought, but he understood. Some of the pirates probably had a translator that allowed them to understand English. She wouldn't want to give away a possible advantage.

They passed an open room in which several pirates hunched over a holographic image, placing bets on whatever was happening in the holo. Another room had smoke pouring out to fill the corridor.

Jake choked on the thick stink as he passed through the cloud. It left him slightly queasy and lightheaded.

"What the hell are they smoking in there?" he asked Leia.

She coughed and cleared her throat. "*Opeeti* beans. Strong drug."

"Grettel runs a pretty loose ship," Jake said.

A pirate hit Jake in the back with something hard and curved. Jake grunted at the pain punched into his shoulder. He looked back to see the pirate glaring. So he was right, some did speak English. He grinned at the pirate, just to annoy him, and faced forward again.

They were taken down a level in a lift and led to a set of solid doors. A pirate opened one and pushed Leia inside, still cuffed. She fell against the opposite wall on her bad shoulder, hissing a curse at the pain.

Jake lunged forward, trying to get to her, but was held back. The solid metal door slid down in his face. The pirates holding him pushed him to the next door and tossed him into a room similar to Leia's.

He spun. "She needs medical attention," he said to the pirates hovering in the door. "Get her something for that shoulder wound."

One particularly large, ugly pirate stared in. He had long, ragged hair, wore a tattered jumpsuit covered by a very expensive looking orange and red jacket decorated with gold filigree, and his face was covered by a heavy beard and mustache that left his expression unreadable. "Why should we help her?" the pirate said after a minute.

"Because she's hurt."

"She killed my cousin. I don't care if she's hurt." The door slid down in front of the pirate, sealing Jake in. He cursed, long and eloquently until his already dry throat turned his voice into a croak. He tried to work up enough spit to swallow while he paced the small cell. It was dark but cleaner than he'd expected. A small, thin cot sat snug against one wall and a sink and toilet took up another corner. Better than the first cell he'd been in, he thought. At least, he could take a piss here.

The cell was too small to pace but he paced anyway. Four steps to the door, turn, four steps back. He paused and studied the cuffs. Like those he'd worn on Dockland, they had a panel on them where the code was entered to open them. He wondered what would happen if he punched in the wrong code. Tempting to try, but if the cuffs sent a shock through him or knocked him out again, he'd be at the pirates' mercy. Better not risk it.

He moved to the wall closest to Leia's cell and pounded. "Leia, can you hear me?"

No response. He sighed and sat on the cot, leaning against the wall that separated him from Leia. Helplessness swamped him. He needed to tend to her wound, to make sure she was okay. His fists clenched on his lap, tightening the cuffs. He forced his hands to relax, rested his head back against the wall. Not much he could do now but sit and wait.

He must have drifted off because the sound of the door hissing opened jolted him awake. He launched off the bed to face the pirates while standing.

A woman walked in with a bundle of clothes under one arm and an electric razor in the other hand. She was one of the smallest women he'd seen so far. She had short black hair, smooth pale skin, and the brightest green eyes he'd ever seen. She would have been pretty but one side of her face was puckered with burn scars, giving her a permanent snarl. Dressed similarly to Grettel, her clothes emphasizing her petite but curvy shape.

She tossed the clothes onto the foot of the bed, keeping her distance even in the small space. She motioned with the razor and said, "It'll take that scruff off your face but won't cut anything else."

"You're telling me it's not a weapon."

"Not even close." She dropped the razor on the bed then motioned to his arms. "Raise your hands." When he did as she ordered, she punched a sequence of numbers into the cuffs and released them.

"Your English is good," he said, rubbing his now-freed wrists at the edge of the bracers.

"Grettel taught me." She pulled something that looked like a baton out of her belt.

From the way she held it, Jake assumed it was a weapon.

She stared a moment. "Shave," she finally said and backed to the door. "Change. You'll be collected shortly."

"Wait. Leia, the lieutenant, how is she? Has someone seen to her wound?"

The small pirate stopped in the doorway, tilted her head as she studied him. "She's being treated."

His shoulders relaxed and he let out a long breath. "Thanks."

She frowned, brows lowering over narrowed eyes. Then she nodded. "Hurry. You don't have much time." The door whooshed shut as she turned out of the cell.

He cleaned and shaved as best he could in the little sink. With no mirror, the task proved tricky but not impossible. He hadn't shaved since that first day on the *Persephone* so scraping the scratchy hair off his face felt good. He would have preferred a wet shave, but he didn't think they'd trust him with a razor. He did test the shaver just to be sure it couldn't be used as a weapon. Short of throwing it, the oval chunk of plastic wasn't good for anything but scraping off facial hair.

He frowned as he studied the clothes. Not something he would have chosen for himself. The pants were a soft black material, a little like velvet, stretching and shiny—way too glam-rock for his style. They fit him well, showing off the muscles in his legs and probably his ass by the way they clung. There was no shirt, only a black leather vest designed to draw attention to his chest rather than cover it. Polished black boots came up to his thighs and folded back to leave a cuff around his knees.

The thought of rebelling against the outfit obviously designed to sell him at auction was tempting. He was more comfortable in the loose tan trousers he'd been wearing for days and the long sleeved shirt he'd been given on Belax. But if he didn't show up to this Council wearing Grettel's chosen attire, he'd be forced into it anyway. And he didn't want to piss off Grettel over something as small as clothing. He wanted her to think of him as a nice easy captive.

When he finished dressing, he looked down at the outfit. With the vest and leather bracers, he could pass for a pirate himself. Probably better he didn't have a mirror. He didn't really want to know how he looked in the getup.

The door to the cell hissed open not long after he'd finished dressing.

The little pirate and two larger male pirates filled the door. "Raise your arms," the little pirate said.

He did as ordered though he had to force himself not to jerk away from the cuffs as they snapped into place. He sighed when they clicked closed and couldn't stop from twisting his wrists to test the security of the cuffs.

"Come on." The woman motioned him into the hallway. She held the sticklike weapon against her thigh.

In the corridor, Jake immediately turned to look for Leia. She eased out of her room, her arms cuffed behind her again. Much to his relief, he noticed her wound had been bandaged.

Then he noticed her outfit.

She wore a long red skirt made of some sheer material with a slit up the front through which her long legs were temptingly displayed. At the top of the skirt, a sash of gold mesh covered her hips and whatever underwear she might have on—but only barely. The sash skimmed the top of her thighs, the slit in the front of the skirt running up under the mesh, drawing attention to the apex of her legs.

He had to suppress a groan.

The shirt was little more than a bikini top, barely covering her ample breasts and showing off her small waist. With her arms pulled behind her back, her breasts thrust out in a way that made his mouth water. Her hair hung loose, creating a silky veil over her shoulders. On her feet, she wore strappy, flat sandals that showed off her small ankles and firm calves.

She looked sexy as hell. For a minute, he forgot about the pirates, the slave auction and everything else but her. "Jesus," he murmured, not realizing he spoke out loud.

She was staring too, her eyes wide and sparkling with heat. A moment later, her eyes narrowed into a glare. "*She* picked that, didn't she?"

For some perverse reason, the scowl on her face both surprised and pleased him. "She picked something pretty sexy for you, too," he pointed out.

A flush of pink crept into her cheeks but the scowl stayed in place as she glanced down at herself. "It's undignified. If I have to do more than walk in this, I'm going to fall out."

He allowed a moment to be intrigued by the idea then shook his head to clear the fantasy. "Probably the reason you're wearing that getup," he said. "Couldn't really hide a weapon anywhere."

She snorted.

"If you two are finished lusting over each other," the little pirate said, her voice frosty, "Grettel is waiting." She nudged Jake forward with her stick.

He fell into step beside Leia. "I don't think the little pirate likes me very much," he said conversationally.

"Probably likes you too much," Leia grumbled so quietly he almost missed it.

Leia jealous? The idea sent a completely inappropriate wash of pleasure through him. He shouldn't want her to be jealous. He wanted her to hate him so she wouldn't hurt when he left. But knowing she didn't like other women looking at him any more than he liked watching the male pirates drool over her left him feeling almost chipper.

If not for the pirates and their leers, he would have felt downright good. He glanced over his shoulder and caught one of the pirates watching Leia's butt as she walked. The pirate licked his lips and Jake felt his blood pressure rise. He growled, low in his throat, a sound that drew the pirate's attention. He wasn't sure what the pirate saw in his face, but the man actually stumbled a step and raised his weapon defensively. Jake glowered a moment more then purposefully turned his back.

When he glanced down at Leia, her mouth curved slightly, a smug little smile he really wanted to kiss away. Get a grip, Jake. He was in serious danger here, his life, his freedom on the line. Leia's life was on the line. A very bad time to get caught up in his hormones. Especially since he'd promised himself he'd pull away, to make his leaving easier on both of them.

Deep down, he knew leaving her would never be easy, no matter what he did. He'd be dreaming about this woman for the rest of his life. He ground his teeth together. If he had any brains, and they managed to get out of this alive and free, he wouldn't waste any of the time they had left together.

He glanced around at the pirates circling them. That was *if* they got out alive.

To get his mind off Leia's body and back onto their situation, Jake said, "Why are your arms cuffed behind you when mine are cuffed in front?"

"I could eventually break out of these if my hands were in front where I could study the cuffs. And my…" She paused and color tinted her cheeks again before she said, "My hips are too big for me to get my arms around them and under my butt so I can get the cuffs in front."

This wasn't taking his mind off her body. Instead, her words drew his attention to the generous curve of her hips, the sexy swish of them as she walked in that barely-there skirt. He swallowed and looked away. Concentrate, Jake. She could break out of the cuffs, given the opportunity. Something to keep in mind. They just needed the opportunity.

They were led back down the corridor, into a lift and up two levels. They stepped off the lift into a huge room dominated by a central pit. A balustrade of miniature seating surrounded the pit, and beyond the banister, filling in the rest of the room stood what looked to be the entire pirate crew. The pit itself remained empty. Just in front of the lift, a break in the banister allowed entrance.

Opposite the break, Grettel sat in a huge swivel chair, one leg thrown over one arm of the seat. She smiled and motioned to their guard. A moment later, he and Leia were shoved into the pit and the banister behind them sealed over.

Grettel grinned. "You both look good. I could probably get a fortune for you, too, Ballore. Has to be a client somewhere who likes feisty types." She shrugged. "Decisions. Decisions."

Jake and Leia stood side by side, facing the pirate, silent as they waited for more.

Grettel gestured and the lights in the room dimmed so only the pit remained lit.

Jake squinted. The glare made seeing the surrounding pirates nearly impossible.

Another gesture from Grettel and a hush fell over the crowd. A moment later, small figures started to appear along the banister. One by one they hopped up onto the small seats, settling as the next shape jumped up. Only when one of these shapes jumped onto Grettel's shoulder did Jake get a good look at it.

The creature had a body roughly the size of a cat, with the face of a terrier and the huge dark eyes of a lemur. Its tail was as long as a monkey's, curling around Grettel's neck and under one of her arms. The creature's rear legs were similar to a cat, with paws and retractable claws, but its forelegs had small, six-fingered hands that gripped Grettel's shoulder comfortably. The creature was covered in a soft-looking, white and brown fur. It swiveled its head to look at Grettel then continued the turn taking in the entire area, moving its head nearly 360 degrees on its thin, short neck.

"Kyzits," Leia breathed. "Family Hamain."

So, this was the creature capable of carrying him into the future and returning him to the past. It didn't look like much. Didn't look like its small body could be very strong. And he had trouble thinking of something that looked that much like a cat-dog cross as being intelligent.

"The family is here to help me decide your fate," Grettel said. "They're quite interested in you, Ballore. They've heard about your heroic rescue of the Nas Governor General."

"Has everyone in the known worlds heard about that?" Leia's voice sounded pained.

"And some of the unknown ones," Grettel chuckled. "You're the real sticking point, you see." She leaned back and the Kyzit on her shoulder settled against her neck. "Jake here is worth an awful lot of money and we invested a fortune to bring him here. He has to be sold so our investment isn't wasted."

Leia took a single step toward Grettel before she stopped herself.

Grettel raised a brow, her crooked smile goading. "Don't like that, do you, Ballore?"

"Of course not."

"Is it because your duty says you have to return him, or because you want him yourself?"

Jake risked a glance at Leia. If looks could cause damage, Grettel would be writhing on the ground in agony about now.

"Human slaving is wrong and immoral," Leia ground out. She didn't directly answer the pirate's question.

"For two years before Nas, you were a mercenary." Grettel change the subject without a blink.

"How did you know that?"

"Public record. Made a point of getting to know you."

"Why?"

"Because you had something I wanted back. What made you quit the merc work? Pay is better."

"I wanted *legitimate* work in the military or police service. I always did. I had no intention of staying a mercenary."

"You might want to rethink that position," Grettel said. She leaned in close when the Kyzit bent to her ear, nodded absently as if the creature had spoken, and turned her attention back to Leia and Jake. She stared silently, then motioned to someone behind them.

Jake turned to see the barrier drop away long enough for three pirates to move into the pit.

Two were big men, brawny and muscled. But the third was absolutely huge. He wasn't tall, but he was wide and so muscled he made Leia's father look lean. In his meaty fists, he held two sets of long knives.

Jake's gut clenched.

"How much do you want to protect him?" Grettel said as the three men circled the interior of the pit. Her gaze settled on Jake, assessing. "How much do you want to protect *her*?"

Before Jake could answer, the two smaller pirates grabbed his still-cuffed arms and pulled him back against one side of the pit.

A roar rose up among the watching pirates, and the Kyzits started chattering in deep rumbling voices.

The huge pirate approached a wary Leia.

She backed away, keeping her gaze trained on the large man.

"Shit. Leia!" Jake struggled against the two men holding him and tried to pull out of their grasp. He yanked one arm free before they captured him in a bruising grip and jerked him back. A sharp pain along the back of his legs brought him to his knees. The two holding him clamped down on his shoulders, keeping him on the hard metal ground despite his struggles.

"Let him take off your cuffs, Ballore," Grettel said, her voice relaxed and amused. "Or you're not going to last long."

"I won't last long with one of those knives in my back either," Leia muttered, continuing to back away from the huge man.

Grettel sighed to the crowd. "There's just no trust anymore."

A moment later, a section of the banister lowered and the little pirate with the scarred face came into the pit. "Take off her damned cuffs so we can get the entertainment underway, will you, Polly?"

Polly the pirate? Jake would have laughed if he weren't watching Leia face down a man twice her size holding four dangerous-looking blades.

Polly stalked up to Leia, whispered something as she released the cuffs then left the pit with a brief glimpse at Jake.

Leia rubbed her wrists, never taking her gaze from the man with the knives, but she snarled something over her shoulder at Polly.

Grettel laughed. "Well, well." She motioned to the big man.

He tossed two of the four knives to Leia, handles first.

She snatched them out of the air.

"Jesus," Jake muttered. "Grettel, at least give her a chance. Knife fighting is a specialized skill."

"Yes," Leia said, raising her voice to the crowd. She flipped the knives so the blades lay along her forearms. "It is a specialized skill." And she began stalking around the huge pirate.

———

LEIA FOCUSED ALL HER ATTENTION ON THE PIRATE IN FRONT OF HER. She couldn't afford to look at Jake, being held down by the other two, or to scan the crowd. Her back itched under the scrutiny of her audience, but she couldn't stop to think about all the weapons just outside the pit. First, she had to keep the big pirate from sticking one of his knives in her. She'd worry about the other weapons later.

She watched the man move and studied his steps. He was huge but graceful and light on his feet. People probably assumed he couldn't move fast because of his size. She wouldn't make that mistake. From the scars on his face, the dark coloring and gold eyes, he was Belaxi. Used to heavier gravity, he would feel lighter and move like he weighed less.

But then, so would she.

She drew him in, circling and watching. Waiting for him to strike first. Wanting to gauge his skills without giving away her own. Telani had cut her enough to guarantee she got good. The feel of the fighting blades in her hands brought back that training, the touch and movements. But she wasn't about to underestimate her opponent.

The big pirate finally broke, lunging close with a slashing stroke she barely escaped. Yeah, he was fast. The collective gasp that followed his slash left little doubt how close he'd come to cutting her.

Jake roared her name.

She had to block out his voice or risk diverting her focus. She circled more, then suddenly spun, lunged, and danced away. Her blade left a shallow cut on the pirate's biceps. She resumed her circling.

So did the pirate. He hadn't made a sound when she cut him.

Thanks to the front slit in her skirt, her movements were relatively free. She would have felt better in trousers, but the skirt could have been worse. The material was so flimsy it wisped away when she spun instead of tangling in her legs. She just had to make sure the pirate didn't use the skirt to stop her. She danced away from his slash, ducked under a quick follow-up from his second blade and spun from another jab that whispered close enough to her waist to make her skin crawl.

She moved inside his guard while he was overextended on the jab and lay open a shallow line along his chest. He slashed down, faster than she expected, and she had to take the full force of his blow on one of her own blades where it partially guarded her forearm. The strength of the blow sent her reeling backward, stumbling to regain her balance.

The large pirate pressed his advantage and was on her too fast.

She tripped, fell to the hard metal floor of the pit and rolled away from a quick downward slash of his blade.

With her heart pounding hard in her chest, she twisted up and met his next attack on her feet. Sweat slicked her skin and dripped down her temples. She ignored it. Her hair clung to her shoulders, under her arms. She'd stuffed it behind her ears to keep it out of her face, but she wished desperately they'd left it up. Each spin twisted locks around her neck, into her face and she wasted precious seconds disentangling herself.

"Grettel," Jake roared.

His voice sounded so raw and deep Leia barely recognized it.

"Call this off. Now."

"Why?" Grettel laughed. "She's holding her own."

"I swear to god, if you don't stop this, I'll kill you."

Grettel didn't answer.

Leia couldn't risk a glance at her expression. But the noise of the other pirates watching the fight quieted to near silence.

The Belaxi pirate used the silence, lunging again. She spun but felt the blade slice over her shoulder blade. She hissed against the pain, finished her spin and brought her knife down across the pirate's face, slicing across an old scar in his cheek and laying open his skin. She lurched back.

The pirate touched his cheek with the side of his hand and looked at the blood that came away. For the first time since the fight began, he changed expressions. He smiled. In Bel, he said, "Now I'll be even better looking, *bella*. Maybe even good enough for you, eh? Ta." He started circling again.

Leia ignored the shallow gashes she was accumulating, ignored the blood soaking the pirate's face and the silence of the surrounding crowd. She watched, waited, and lunged in under the big man's guard, going for another chest hit. She sliced across his pectoral muscle, but he caught her on the back of the head with a knife handle. She hadn't expected the hit. The power in the man's blow sent her skidding to the floor. She hit, shoulder first against the edge of the pit, and felt her wound from the firefight break open again.

Black spots danced in her vision. She blinked but couldn't control her limbs. Before she could shake off the stun of the blow, the big man stood over her, lifting her to her feet.

He held her by the neck with one hand, pressing her against the banister, and positioned a knife against her throat just above his hand.

"Leia!" Jake's voice echoed in the quiet room.

But she couldn't take her gaze from the pirate.

The big man chuckled, leaned his face close, and stopped as his eyes bulged. He stumbled away, a hand cupping his groin.

She pressed a hand to the stinging line on her neck and shook her head as she picked up the knife he dropped. "Oldest trick in the book, *chook*. You should know better."

He growled and charged.

Leia raised the knife to continue the fight.

"Enough!" Grettel's voice rang out into the silence.

The pirate stopped but he glared at Leia, his chest heaving as he gulped in air.

Leia risked a glance around.

Jake sprawled on the ground at the feet of the other two pirates, not moving.

She choked, terror swamping her, and charged across the pit to kneel beside him. Panic made her breath hitch. She reached out to touch him, feel for a pulse and almost cried when she heard him groan.

He lifted his head, shook it then groaned again.

"Jake? Jake, are you okay?"

"Leia? Jesus, I feel like I was hit with a sledge hammer." He sat up suddenly, paling as he did so, but he reached out with his still-cuffed hands. "Leia." He touched her face, her shoulder, his fingers hovered over the thin line of red on her neck. "You're okay? Does this hurt?" He looked at her shoulder. "You're bleeding again. What happened?"

"She kicked his ass, or more to the point, his balls, that's what happened," Grettel said, clapping. The sound boomed in the silence. "Jiips had to hit your man with a stun, Ballore, when he got out of their grip. Didn't like seeing you with a knife to your throat."

"Enough of the games, Grettel," Jake hissed. With Leia's help, he climbed to his feet.

"That wasn't a game, big boy, that was a test. And she passed. Now she has a decision to make." Grettel dropped her leg and leaned forward so her forearms rested on her thighs. The Kyzit on her shoulder shifted to accommodate the move. "As I see it, you've got two choices here, Ballore. The first is the one most of my people would prefer, I think. Death. Your second choice is to join us."

Leia's brow rose. "What?"

Grettel spread her hands. "Join us. You'd make a fine pirate. Wouldn't be the only Belaxi in my crew, as you've noticed. You've been mercenary before. This is just another step along that ladder."

She couldn't quite believe what the pirate was saying. "My options are death or become a pirate? That's it? You don't leave me a lot of choice."

"Think about it carefully, Ballore. I'd hate to kill you. You've got something I think we could use." The sparkle of amusement in her eyes went flat. "But I won't hesitate to kill you myself. You're a threat. I can't let you go. And I doubt if I offered, you'd abide my conditions anyway."

"Conditions?"

"Forget about Jake. Don't try to follow or find him. Leave this situation alone, go back to Nas and continue your nice cushy job with the Executive family, listening to the horny one having sex all night while the others sleep."

"How do you know all of this?" Leia felt like she'd taken a blow to the stomach. She had to concentrate on breathing.

"Good information is invaluable to one in my profession. And I pay well. I know all there is to know about you. Which is why I know, even without that stubborn glare on your face, you wouldn't accept my conditions. You'd try to find him, to rescue him. It's what you do. And I can't allow that. So, you can't be turned free." She shrugged.

"Why ask me to join you? You don't trust me. Why would you risk it?"

Grettel grinned. "Better to keep your friends close and your enemies closer, right? I could keep an eye on you here. Loose, you could get up to all kinds of mischief. Here, at least I'd know what you were about all the time. And if you tried anything, I have plenty of loyal people who'd kill you as soon as look at you."

"No matter what I decide, you'll still sell Jake, though." She made it a statement. Her hand clenched involuntarily on his arm.

"'Fraid I have to. He's cost me a fortune already. I need to recoup my losses. Not a lot of choice. My Kyzit family would never forgive me if I let this kind of profit get away." Her look turned sly as she said, "And what happens to him after that… If his owner can't keep him… Well, that's not really my business, is it?" She eased back in her seat.

Leia's gaze narrowed. "Then why don't you want me going after him?"

"Now, how would that look?" Grettel cocked her head to one side and raised a brow. "I let a Guard go and she recovers a slave after he's sold? The client would blame me and demand their money back. I can't be blamed if he escapes on his own, can I?"

"You're not leaving me a lot of options, Grettel."

"Those are the only options I have."

Leia cursed under her breath in Bel. Joining the pirates went against everything she believed in. But she sure as hell didn't want to die. She wouldn't be helping either herself or Jake if she got herself killed in the name of her ideals.

Could she fake it? Her jaw clenched. They'd know. They wouldn't trust her enough to give her room to escape. So she'd either live up to being a pirate or get killed anyway. And in the meantime, they were going to sell Jake. The thought sent a sharp pain of anxiety through her gut. The helplessness was so frustrating, she cursed again.

Jake took hold of her arm and squeezed. "Don't get yourself killed," he murmured. "I can survive anything if I know you're okay."

She pressed the translator chip and whispered, "I won't let them sell you."

"You heard Grettel. I'll figure out an escape. You don't have a choice if you want to stay alive."

"Jake." Pain leaked into her voice, making it sound thick, almost as desperate as she felt.

He reached up and touched her cheek. "I want you to stay alive, Leia. I won't survive otherwise."

She bit the inside of her cheek to keep from crying. She wouldn't give the gawking pirates the satisfaction. All the emotion churning inside her must have shown on her face, though, especially when she looked up into Jake's solid blue eyes. She hated the pirates witnessing this moment between her and Jake. "I thought you hated me," she murmured. "For not telling you about the time travel."

"Never. I wanted you to hate me. But I could never hate you." He leaned close and kissed her, despite the audience.

Her breath caught.

"Isn't this just precious," Grettel said, her voice heavy with sarcasm. "Well, hell."

The last was said with enough genuine frustration that Leia looked up.

The pirate slouched back in her chair, the Kyzit on her shoulder leaning close to her ear. She nodded as she listened, rolled her eyes once and shook her head. "You know I can't do that," she told the Kyzit.

The creature kept talking, too quiet to be heard by any but Grettel.

And everyone waited silently.

After another few minutes, she barked out a laugh. "You're joking? I don't believe you."

As Leia listened to one side of the conversation, she noticed Grettel's English was very good. She used it even though she didn't need Jake to understand what she said. She wasn't using a translator chip. The pirate had learned to speak English. Why? To talk to her captives? Why bother when she could just use a chip? Leia couldn't imagine Grettel talked much to her captives anyway. So, why would she go to the trouble of learning English?

"Who'd have guessed it?" Grettel said to no one in particular, her voice filled with quiet awe. She turned to face the Kyzit, who leaned back to make eye contact with Grettel. "You're serious?"

The creature shook its head, a gesture Leia knew meant yes to a Kyzit.

"That's one expensive whim, Brybel."

The Kyzit's little cat shoulders shrugged.

"Okay. You know about this stuff better than I do. And I'd hate to see it, too."

Grettel sounded amused now, and resigned. Leia wasn't sure the resigned part was good for either her or Jake.

"Well," Grettel said, facing them. "Seems my family here has made a decision. I think they're too practical for their own good. But what can I say? If I want to stay in business, they have the final word on time slaves. Not much I can do for you now." She shook her head. "Shame really. I was enjoying the show."

1 2

L eia met the pirate's gaze and waited for the decree.

Grettel smiled, just a little. "See we, Brybel and I, we just couldn't face ourselves in the mirror if we let you go now. Either of you. It's funny. Brybel was just accusing me the other day of being too romantic. Now I see I'm not the only one."

Leia frowned and her heart kicked up a beat. This didn't sound like the death sentence she expected. But Grettel had been playing with them from the beginning, so she didn't trust the grin on the pirate's face.

One of the surrounding pirates, that little one, Polly, moved close behind Grettel and whispered something.

Leia glared. The petite woman was officially one of her least favorite people on the ship, second only to Grettel. Even the Belaxi hulk that had cut her ranked higher on her likeable list than Polly.

Grettel's eyebrows rose as Polly talked. Then she let out a laugh. "True, Polly. Very true. We could do that, but Brybel has spoken."

"What the hell's going on?" Jake murmured. "I'm not sure I like this."

"Oh no, you'll love this," Grettel said. "Polly suggested we sell you both, as a breeding pair. We could get an obscene amount of money for you. More even than for Jake alone. There's this group in the Galore system, looking to breed their own…product. You two would make a good addition to their breeding herd. But…" She raised her hand to stall their comments. "Brybel has his own suggestion and to be honest, I have to agree. Besides," Grettel's gaze turned sly, "I'm not sure it won't be more fun Brybel's way."

Polly cursed and snarled at Leia.

Leia snarled back. She had no idea what the little pirate had against her and she didn't care. If Polly wanted Jake for herself, she probably wouldn't suggest selling them both. But Leia wasn't so sure Polly didn't have ulterior motives with the suggestion. Maybe to provoke Leia into getting herself killed? Either way, if that little witch thought she could seduce Jake, she was going to have to get through Leia to do it.

"What's the problem with you and Polly?" Jake asked under his breath. "I don't think she likes you any more than me."

Leia made a humming noise, not sure if she could answer without embarrassing herself.

"What did she say to you?" he prompted. "When she was taking off the cuffs."

"She asked me if I really thought I was woman enough to win you," Leia said.

"And you said?"

Leia scowled up at him. Was that amusement? Better not be. "I told her to watch and learn."

Jake struggled against a smile but lost in the end. "Is that all you said? She seems pretty pissed off."

"I might have called her…a less than polite name."

Jake didn't even bother to cover his chuckle. "God, I love you, Leia."

Leia felt her entire body still, every molecule, every atom paused. Then her heart started to hammer. "You do?"

He looked down with the barest of smiles curving his lips and nodded.

"This is better than a soap," Grettel shouted, laughing. "Such surprise on her face. Ballore, hon, you really need to pay closer attention."

The need to tell Grettel to shut up tingled on the tip of her tongue, but she thought better of the rash words at the last minute. Jake loved her. She wanted to savor the thought for a while more before they killed her.

Grettel shook her head. "He loves you, you love him. Everyone else but the two of you get it. Now, would you like to hear what Brybel's decided or do you want to keep making moon eyes at each other in front of the entire ship?"

Leia felt heat wash over her face. And she'd thought the outfit was embarrassing. Having her private life played out in front of the pirates was infinitely worse. She squirmed a little under the now-perceived scrutiny of the surrounding crowd.

"I'd hate to split up true love," Grettel said, sounding surprisingly sincere. "Problem is all that money we've invested in you. Polly's suggestion would have worked. At least, you'd be together. But Brybel wants something else. He thinks it's important you join us. Both of you. You can stay together. And you won't be running loose in the galaxy like a couple of potential bombs waiting to go off."

"Jake has to be returned, Grettel." Even as Leia said it, the idea cut through her heart. She'd be willing to turn pirate if it meant keeping Jake. But she couldn't forget her duty. Keeping Jake in this time was wrong. And dangerous. "The damage you'll cause the timeline by keeping him here is—"

"Stop!" Grettel's voice lashed out, cutting off her sentence. She dropped her forehead to her hand, rubbed. "I can't believe you people are still living under that assumption. Don't you get it? Are you all so damned stupid you haven't figured this out yet?"

Leia's muscles tightened. "Figured what out? What the hell are you talking about?"

"He was a dead man, Ballore!" Grettel's bellow echoed in the room. As the echo died, she murmured, "He was a dead man."

Jake took a step back from the pirate as if he'd been hit and looked around the crowd still mostly hidden in darkness. His face paled.

Leia felt her heart stop. "What do you mean?" she said, reaching out to grab Jake's hand.

Grettel ran a hand over her hair and tugged at one of the braids. "Shit," she muttered and turned to talk to Brybel. This time both sides of the conversation were too quiet to hear. After a few minutes, Grettel turned back and said, "You want to stay alive, you want to be together? You join us. Now. Today. I'd rather not have a lovesick Belaxi ex-Nas Guard haunting the halls of my ship. So it's either you both join us, or you both get sold. Or you can both die now."

"Can we think about it?" Jake said into the silence.

His voice sounded strong, stronger than Leia felt.

"You've got a few hours. We'll be stopping to pick up supplies. After that… Where we go depends on what you decide. You've got four hours." She rose from her chair.

The Kyzit stayed on her shoulder, its tail flexing to keep it balanced.

"I might suggest accepting our offer to join our ranks. We don't make the proposition lightly. Or often."

Grettel turned away, disappearing into the crowd. The barrier behind them vanished and four pirates moved into the pit to surround them.

Leia's hands were cuffed again, behind her back. Then she and Jake were led from the room. Around her, she heard a quiet murmur start. The murmur turned into a loud debate before the lift doors closed.

They were led back to the brig. But instead of being separated, the pirates shoved them into the same cell with barely enough room to maneuver. One of the pirates in the doorway murmured something rude that Leia didn't care to translate and the door hissed shut.

She opened her mouth to speak but Jake's lips dropped to hers and silenced her. Her world tipped sideways as relief and need overwhelmed all other emotions. She chafed against the restraints, wanting her hands free so she could wrap them around his neck, bury her fingers in his hair.

He inched her backward to the wall and pressed closer. He angled his head to deepen the kiss and his hands flattened against her stomach, hot against her bare skin. The restraints were awkward, she had to press her hands to the wall and the cuffs still cut into her back, but she barely noticed. Jake was kissing her. Nothing else mattered.

He made a sound deep in his throat and moved his arms over her head, pulling her closer. Her breasts molded against the solid muscles of his chest, and she moaned. She couldn't get close enough. His vest gaped so she was pressed against the warmth of his chest, only the stupid little top she wore separating their bare skin. He felt so good and solid and hot. His fingers twined with hers as best they could. For that moment, all was right in Leia's world.

When the kiss ended, Leia sighed.

He dropped his forehead against hers, still holding her close. "I missed that."

"Me, too."

"I'm sorry I was going to waste our last days together. I didn't want to hurt so much, and I didn't want to hurt you."

She pulled back to look into his eyes, that deep blue so sincere and loving it stole her breath, and smiled a little. "I'm glad you changed your mind."

He smiled, slow and devastating. "Me, too."

She snuggled close, tucking her head under his chin. She loved the size of him, tall like a Nasen yet broad and strong like a Belaxi male. She felt safe in his arms, had never felt so safe with a man before. In the past, she'd always had something to prove, to herself, as well as others. She was *strong* enough to survive on her own, she was *good* enough to be a guard, she was *independent* enough she didn't need to play on her looks to get a man.

Jake accepted these things. Even when he worried about her, she knew he accepted her strength and independence. And because he did, she could relax with him.

"Was Grettel right?" he asked, kissing the top of her head.

"About what?"

"You loving me."

Her heart thumped hard, and her throat closed. "Yes."

He sighed, a sound both happy and resigned.

She looked up. A slight smile touched his lips, but his eyes were sad.

"No matter what, we're going to hurt when I have to go back. If we survive long enough for me to go back. I hoped at least you wouldn't have to suffer. But I'm not sorry to hear you love me. Say it again."

She smiled. "I love you, Jake."

"I love you."

He leaned down to touch her lips with his, his touch so gentle and tender her heart squeezed tight.

"So, what are we going to do to survive this, Lieutenant?"

His voice held only confidence but worry shifted through his eyes.

"Short of joining the pirates," she shook her head, "I'm not sure we have a lot of choices. But..."

"But you'd be sacrificing everything you've worked for, compromising everything just to stay alive."

She sighed and nodded. "I don't want to die. I don't want you killed. I really don't want to be sold as part of a breeding pair." She shuddered, not because having children with Jake upset her, but because she'd be damned if she'd let anyone take their children to sell as slaves.

"We could take our chance as slaves, then try to escape."

He didn't sound any more confident about that idea than she felt. "Or," she said, "we can play pirate for as long as it takes to get away. Eventually, they'd have to trust us, to give us an opportunity to escape."

"You'd never be able to go back to the Nas Guard," he cautioned. "It could take us awhile to earn the trust needed to escape."

"I could always go back to mercenary work," she said without enthusiasm. "The Belaxian military may take me now that I've proven myself on Nas. They aren't as stringent about past...enterprises as the Nas command."

She hesitated a beat, then said, "But Jake, keeping you here for a long time could be very dangerous. And Matt's return home will be delayed. Nasen policy is to send you both back together, if at all possible. If you or he died, some other arrangement would be made to send the surviving one back, but that's a last resort. Until they know you're irrecoverable, Nas Command will keep Matt in this time."

"How will that affect him?"

"He's adjusting as well as you. I doubt he knows he's in a different time though. If he continues to think he's simply in another galaxy, his mind may hold out for as long as necessary. But time passes for him here. He'd notice differences when he returned home. He'll have a hard time resolving the amount of time that's passed here to the time he's returned. The situation could be dangerous."

Jake took a deep breath. "There's not much I can do about that now. If we're sold, he'll be delayed here too. If we're killed, they'll send him back right away." His expression turned wry. "But I'd rather avoid dying."

She nodded, in total agreement. The thought of Jake dying made her chest so tight she could barely breathe.

"What do you suppose Grettel meant when she said I was a dead man?" He shifted positions so he could lean against the wall while she relaxed against him.

"I'm not sure."

"Have you, the Nas Command, anyone who returns people like me, have you ever checked historical records to see what happens to them…after?"

"Well, the Kyzits let us know if everything has balanced. They sometimes make a report regarding a recovery but only if sending them back proves difficult—like you and Matt with your damaged bracers. I assumed others outside the Kyzits actually did check historical records when a recovery was made but…"

"But?"

"Well as soon as you're kidnapped, any historical data could change. And we don't know who the kidnapped are until after they've been recovered."

"So how do you know history hasn't been changed?"

"We don't. The Kyzits are supposed to tell us, but they don't actually tell us a lot, only that the timeline has been maintained. This isn't my field. Maybe there are other ways to check. I've always assumed the intergalactic governments knew what they were doing."

Jake laughed but it wasn't a happy sound. "In my experience, not all the bureaucrats who are supposed to know what they're doing actually *do* know what they're doing."

"That's not a pleasant thought." She took a deep breath, tried not to be distracted by the feel of her breasts rubbing against his bare skin. Her hormones flew out of control around Jake. "So, what do you think Grettel meant?"

Jake blinked, pulled his gaze up from an inspection of her mouth. He shook his head. "Is there historical data on everyone? I'd like to look at whatever historical data exists on me."

"There's data on most. The Kyzits get it for us if we don't have enough information."

"The Kyzits… Could they be pretending to return people?"

"No. That I'm sure of. I actually saw the record of one man after he was returned."

Jake frowned. "But couldn't the Kyzits be providing falsified historical data? How would you check?"

Leia had never thought about that before. Everyone considered the Kyzits a moral and upstanding species. They might not reveal their secrets about space and time, but they always worked to keep the time-line intact. The only family to go against this species-wide code was the Hamain family.

At least, that's what everyone in the known worlds thought. What if the Kyzits did falsify records? What if they weren't as moral as believed?

"You wouldn't know," Grettel said.

Leia's head jerked up at the sound of the new voice in the room. She hadn't even heard the door open. She looked over her shoulder to see Grettel leaning against the doorframe with her arms crossed beneath her breasts.

Jake lifted his arms so Leia could step out of his embrace and turn to face the pirate. His hissed intake of breath brought her attention back to him. "What?"

"Your shoulder. I forgot." He looked at Grettel. "Do you have bandages?"

Grettel's sardonic half smile turned into a full-blown grin. She uncrossed her arms and revealed a wad of bandages in one hand and a medical skimmer in the other. When she stepped into the room, the door closed behind her.

Leia got a brief glimpse of a couple of pirates standing guard beyond the door and then just the three of them remained in the too-small cell.

Grettel passed the bandages to Jake, but she turned Leia and ran the skimmer over the shallow knife wounds herself. "This cleanses and disinfects," she said as she worked.

Her touch was surprisingly gentle. The cuts tingled a little as they were treated, but Leia didn't feel any of the stinging bite she expected.

When Grettel finished, she settled a hand on Leia's shoulder and turned her back to Jake. "Go ahead and bandage her."

Leia frowned as she faced the pirate again. She hadn't expected any tenderness in a woman who kidnapped and sold men into slavery for a living. "What do you want?" she asked the pirate, knowing her voice was too harsh but unable to soften it.

Grettel raised a brow. "To pass on the supplies to heal your wounds. And to find out what you're thinking. What have you decided?"

"We still have a few hours," Jake said.

He carefully covered the slices on her shoulder blade and arm, but she could feel the tension in his body.

Grettel flopped down on the cot and stared up at them for a silent moment. "You have questions."

"Yes," Leia said.

"Ask. It'll save some time."

"Why did you say I was a dead man?" Jake said.

He asked the very question Leia wanted answered first. She watched the pirate closely, gauging her reaction.

Grettel grimaced and faced the wall opposite her spot on the cot.

"Figures," she muttered. "You would ask the one question I'd rather not answer." She rolled her head against the wall to look up at them.

The pirate's position appeared vulnerable, Leia realized with a start. If she and Jake wanted to take Grettel hostage, even with the cuffs they could overpower her. Knowing Grettel would never leave herself so open to attack, Leia looked closer. The pirate wasn't as comfortably slouched as she seemed. Her right hand hovered near a weapon in her utility belt, her left rested on her stomach just at the edge of her red sash. Leia would lay a bet with Telani that Grettel had another weapon hidden there.

No, the pirate wasn't nearly as relaxed in their company as she wanted them to believe.

After a long, silent moment, Grettel heaved a sigh. "Okay, here's the thing. You," she nodded at Leia, "and all your little Guards have been told I mess up the timeline by kidnapping the men I take. What no one wants to publicize is that I only take men who are going to die. And I usually take them within a day of their imminent death. Closer if we can manage it."

Leia felt like she'd taken a punch to the stomach. Behind her Jake stilled, one hand pressed against her shoulder.

Grettel nodded at whatever she saw in their faces. "Now, you get it. I don't mess up the timeline. We insure the records of their deaths are close to what would actually have happened."

"How?" Jake's voice sounded rough and quiet.

"How do we arrange all this, or how were you going to die?"

"How do I die?"

"You and Matt would have been executed in a dark alley in Hollywood. It's later discovered a man named Patterson arranged the execution."

Jake sucked in a breath.

Leia whirled to face him.

All the color had drained from his face. He leaned back against the wall, his eyes dulled by shock. When he looked up and met her gaze, he looked so lost.

Leia wanted to touch him, but her hands were still cuffed behind her back.

He held her gaze as he asked Grettel, "Was he convicted? For the murders?"

"Yeah. He goes down for conspiracy to kill two police officers, for the murder of his wife, and for a number of other major felonies. Life sentence. No parole. He was knifed in prison after serving only fourteen months of his sentence. Dead by the time he hit the floor. Getting convicted displeased his other associates."

Jake nodded, his gaze still locked with Leia's.

Leia stepped closer, wanting to comfort and not sure how.

"So, you see, big guy. There's no reason for you and Matt to go back. And if you do, you'll be killed," Grettel said, matter-of-factly. "You're stuck in this time or you're dead. No matter what happens here and now. But hey, there are worse things, right? At least, you've got the lieutenant here. So you had to cross three thousand years to find real love. Most people never find it."

The pirate sounded wistful, an emotion so at odds with her attitude up to now, Leia almost turned to study her. But Jake's expression kept her focus firmly on him.

His brow creased. He nodded and shifted his gaze to stare at the empty space next to Leia's shoulder.

Worry edged into her stomach, cold and oily. Jake had adjusted to everything so far without going crazy. He'd eventually accepted the time change, the space travel, the need to go home. Watching his pale face, the hollow look in his eyes, she was afraid this latest bit of news would be too much for his mind.

"Jake?" She stepped closer, brushed against his arm with her body, her action the closest she could get to offering comfort.

His gaze returned to her face.

She watched emotions she couldn't read churn in the blue depths.

"If I go back, I'll be killed."

He didn't ask, he stated, a strange note in his voice.

"Matt and I have to stay."

"They won't let you," Leia murmured. "Nas Command will send you back anyway. They always do. Even if they knew about this…"

Her voice trailed off. Suddenly, the last thing she wanted was to get Jake back to Nas. She hadn't wanted to let him go before. Now, she knew sending him home would be a death sentence. "Saints," she breathed. "We can't go back to Nas."

"I thought that bit of news might affect your decision," Grettel said, her usual humor creeping back into her voice. "I hate telling people, though. It can screw you up pretty bad. I've had a few go nuts when they found out how close they'd been to the Reaper."

"Some go crazy without knowing this much," Leia said. A little of her fear for Jake crept out in her voice. She swallowed and tried to concentrate, to think rationally beyond the anxiety.

"True," Grettel said. "And some die here anyway. Three thousand years is a long way to go, but if the Reaper follows you this far, there's very little you can do. Some manage to avoid him for a few years. It's more time than they would have had otherwise."

"But you sell them into slavery," Leia said. "They spend what little time you win for them as slaves."

"Hey, don't get me wrong. I don't do this to be altruistic." Grettel chuckled when Leia turned to face her. "I do this for the money. Good money. But if I give some poor slob a chance…?" She shrugged.

"Where did you learn English?" Jake asked. "You're not using a translator chip, are you?"

His question startled Leia. So, he'd noticed, too.

Grettel grinned and shook her head. "This here's my native tongue." Her accent thickened, drawling out with a twang. "Born and bred in southern Texas, USA." She flicked back the long cuffs of her blousy shirt to reveal two thin leather straps circling her wrists. Strange designs were cut into the leather, decorated with blue stones highlighting parts of the design. They looked more like jewelry than the bracers worn by Jake and the other recovered men.

"But there's no zanathim," Leia said, staring at the thin straps.

"The stones are the only other material that can be used with Kyzit leather to keep a time-displaced human stable. The Kyzits don't like knowledge of the stones to get out. They're rare, but not as rare as zanathim." She shifted her gaze to Jake. "Zanathim can only be found on the Kyzits' home planet, which is extremely well guarded against attack. This stone—which I'm not gonna name, just in case—can be found on more than one planet. But either will work with the Kyzit hair leather so long as the leather stays over pulse points. The bracelets are less conspicuous, smaller and not as annoying as a thick leather collar—the other option for a stabilizing brace."

The pirate smiled faintly, her gaze turning inward. "I was six when the Hamain found me, nearly dead, and brought me here. Took a long time to recover, then to accept. But hell, I was young. The young adapt easier."

"What happened to you?" Leia whispered. She couldn't take her gaze off the bracelets circling Grettel's wrists.

"Had a sonofabitch for a father and an even worse mother. When he beat me near to death one night, she drove me out to the middle of nowhere and dumped me. Left me to die. Brybel won't tell me what he and the Hamain were doing in the middle of nowhere Texas when they found me. All I know is they did and they brought me here."

"What year? What year were you born?" Jake's voice was firm and steady.

Leia let out a quiet breath.

"This is gonna blow your mind, handsome." The pirate grinned and waggled her eyebrows. "I was born in 1995. They picked me up only a couple of years before I came back as an adult for you."

"That's just…weird."

She chuckled. "Yeah, I know. I would have died that night if the Hamain hadn't taken me forward in time."

"Why don't they do that for every abused person, every child nearly killed?" A thread of bitterness tinged Jake's question.

Leia could only imagine how many broken children a Los Angeles policeman would have seen on Earth in the early twenty-first century. His touch of anger didn't surprise her.

Grettel shrugged. "I have no idea. They don't tell me their motives any more than they tell anyone else. Probably this all makes sense in the grand scheme of things, if you can actually figure out the grand scheme. Me, I'm just happy to be alive and living well in any time period."

"Why am I wearing these huge clunky bracers when you can get away with only those little straps?" Jake had pulled away from the wall and now stood just at Leia's shoulder.

He sounded better. She looked up and was relieved to see the color back in his face.

"Actually, not much is required to hold you here. Especially if the pulse points in the wrists are used. We designed the bracers to appeal to our clients. Gives you a good primitive aura, makes you look a little scary, a little dangerous. Like a gladiator. Ups the selling price by nearly twenty percent."

"Does that mean I can get a set like yours? Something not quite so obviously made for a slave?"

Grettel grinned. "Does this mean you've made up your mind to stay? Work with me? 'Cause if your choice is to be sold, I'd rather leave you in those bracers."

Leia turned to face Jake. Waiting. She didn't know how to feel in that moment, what she wanted him to say. But she definitely didn't want him to die—in any time. If he was reconciled to staying, at least he'd have a chance at survival.

He looked down, his brow creased. "I can't go back," he said. "And if I go to Nas, they'll send me back. Short of dying, I'm not sure what else to do."

Leia nodded. There was just one problem. Now, she wasn't sure she could stay. To keep Jake alive, to stay alive herself with the intentions of one day escaping, she could face being a pirate, even if it meant giving up the career she'd worked so hard for.

But if he voluntarily stayed with the pirates, if he had no intention of escaping one day because escaping might mean being sent back to a death sentence, then he was safe. With or without her here.

Staying with the pirates now would mean giving up any hope of her former life. She might never see her family again, and if she did, they might not want her around. She could end up outcast like Telani, only worse. Telani had always been an outcast. She still had the strength and support of her family to depend on. Could she do this to them, to herself, just to stay with Jake?

Jake watched her closely. Could he see her conflict? Did he realize if he stayed of his own free will, her presence was no longer needed? "I…" She swallowed, not sure what she wanted to say.

"We'll need more time, Grettel," Jake said, his voice quiet, his gaze still intent on Leia. "But I have one more question."

"Ask away."

"If I stay and join you willingly, would you let Leia go? She won't try to rescue me if I choose to stay. She won't try to send me back, not now, knowing what we do. I'd earn enough for you to make up the expense of bringing me here. You won't need to keep Leia anymore."

Grettel was silent for a long time.

Leia couldn't look away. He was trying to give her back her life. He understood. She felt a tear slid down her cheek. In that moment, she loved him so much her chest hurt with the pressure. Knowing he would do this for her made the decision to return to her own life even more difficult. How could she leave a man she loved this much?

Finally, Grettel said, "I might be able to arrange that. If you're willing to work to pay off your debt, I'm sure the Hamain won't mind letting her go. And if Ballore isn't gunning for us once she leaves, she's no longer a threat. So I can afford to risk it. Are you sure you want me to send her away?"

"If I knew she was safe and doing what she was meant to do? Yeah, I'm sure I'd want you to let her go."

"Huh… Well. Never thought I'd see it."

There was an emotion in Grettel's voice Leia couldn't identify, and she didn't try. She could do nothing but look into Jake's eyes. Knowing he understood her made her heart soar and an ache deep in her soul.

Grettel stood, motioned Leia to turn around.

With narrowed eyes, Leia turned her back to the pirate, but she held herself ready for anything. She was surprised to feel Grettel working the lock on the cuffs.

"I'm leaving these mostly open," Grettel said. "I'll do the same with Jake." She moved to Jake and he raised his arms so she could punch in the release code on his cuffs. "When the door closes behind me, you can finish unlocking them. If you release these before the door hits the ground, I'll kill you both. No matter how much I like you." She showed them the final bit of the code on both the restraints, then said, "Don't waste the time I'm giving you. I'll expect your final decision when I come back." She grinned. "But first, you'll have a few hours of privacy."

Leia turned to watch the door slide down.

As soon as it hit the floor, Jake punched in the last of the code and released her cuffs.

She sighed and rubbed at her wrists, then returned the favor.

His cuffs hit the ground with a clang and he pulled her into his arms. His muscles were like bands of steel, hard and immovable.

Then he kissed her, so tenderly another tear slid past her eyelid, to trickle down her cheek. She buried her fingers in his hair and sank against him. He tasted so good, like the last meal she would ever eat, and she fed hungrily. But she matched the tenderness in his touch, knowing this might be her last chance to show him just how much she loved him.

"We'll be in the same galaxy," he said against her mouth. His lips moved over her jaw to her throat. "We'll be in the same time." He pushed one strap of her top down her arm, tasted the skin at the curve between her neck and shoulder. "I'll earn my way free of Grettel eventually." His lips moved to the curve of her breast above the precariously perched material of her top. "You'll stay a Guard."

"Jake," she said his name as a plea.

He pushed down the other strap of her top, peeled the material lower so her arms were trapped at her sides but her breasts spilled into the warmth of his palms. Her breath caught as his thumbs teased her nipples into hard peaks.

"We'll have a chance at being together someday," he murmured. "If you'll wait for me."

He kissed one nipple gently, a mere brush of lips that made her gasp. "Forever. I'll wait forever. As long as it takes." She knew she would, too. There would never be another man for her. Only Jake.

He suckled at her breast, drawing a moan from her. She had to touch him. The straps holding her arms at her sides were intolerable. She wiggled her arms free while Jake lavished attention on first one then the other breast, nearly bringing her to her knees with longing. When her arms were free, she buried her fingers in his thick hair, her fists clenching. His lips moved back to hers, his kiss still so gentle it was almost painful. She traced the width of his shoulders, the muscles of his arms, the hard lines of his biceps, the scars across his pectoral muscles. She wanted to memorize everything about him, every touch, every taste. She pushed his vest off his shoulders, down his arms so it dropped to the ground. Then her mouth followed her fingers.

His groan, the feel of his hands clenching in her hair, the taste of his skin on her tongue filled her with delight and need. She pushed his trousers down his hips and dropped to her knees in front of him. She had to taste all of him, feel every part of him.

He whispered her name, his voice a harsh echo in the small room.

She kissed his lower abdomen and smiled when his muscles clenched. Then she took him in her mouth. She savored him, the taste, the feel. He was silk over steel and she knew she'd never have enough, no matter how long they had together.

His hands fisted in her hair, his head dropped back on his shoulders.

She watched him as she moved her mouth over him, the straining muscles in his arms and neck, the fierce heat of his eyes when he looked down. He made her feel feminine and sexy. Not like Belaxi men, not as if she were little more than the sum of her looks, a piece of decoration to boost some man's status. Jake made her feel as if she were the only woman he would ever want, the only woman that could satisfy him, the only woman that could fill his needs. He gave her a power no man had before, and he made her feel the need to give in return, to let him have anything he wanted. If he asked, she would give.

He growled, a dangerous sound that made her blood sing, then he forced her away.

She released his pulsing erection with a whimper of protest, but the heat in his eyes was enough to make her comply with his every command.

He shifted to sit on the little cot, swiftly removed his boots and trousers. "Come here," he ordered.

She obeyed willingly.

He pulled her onto the bed and settled her beneath him. His touch was no longer so gentle as he impatiently pushed her top back up and over her head. When he'd discarded the garment, he kept her wrists pinned above her head with one large hand and moved his free hand to her breast. "I'll never get tired of the feel of you, Leia," he said. "Or the taste." He bent his head to her breast.

She cried out at the hot, wet feel of his mouth.

"There's a chance for a future for us," he said. He swirled his tongue over her nipple and blew gently.

She arched up against him, groaning at the pleasure-pain of his lips so near, hovering just above her straining nipple.

"I want that future," he murmured. "I want you. I'll do whatever I can to be with you again."

She cried his name as his lips dipped lower, moving over the quivering muscles of her stomach.

He released her wrists and ran both hands down the side of her waist, clenched at her hips.

Her hands gripped his shoulders. Anticipation thrummed through her blood.

He nuzzled the top of her skirt where it dipped low on her abdomen. "What's under this?" he said as he fingered the edge of the golden mesh shawl around her hips.

"Not much," she breathed, smiling and feeling sexy as hell in the stupid outfit.

He moved lower on the cot, kissed the inside of her thigh and slid his hands up the outside of her legs, under the skirt. He fingered the little scrap of material that Grettel gave her for underwear and a grin curved his lips. "You're right. Not much to these." His hands flexed, pulling the thin line of silk over each of her hips, and the material tore.

Her eyes widened at the sound of ripping silk and her heartbeat pumped harder. Her already shaky breathing turned into a pant. That show of strength shouldn't have turned her on so much. But she was too stunned and too excited to care.

He raised a brow, his grin almost embarrassed. "Sorry." He pulled the panties out from under her skirt. He gave the remains of red silk a cursory glance then dropped them onto the floor, turning his full attention to the apex of her thighs. "How do you remove this chain mail?"

She showed him the clasp at one hip and would have removed the offending scarf for him, but he pushed her hands aside, taking his time unlatching the mesh. His breath brushed hot against her thighs, his face hovered so close she thought she'd go insane if he didn't put his mouth on her soon. His touch had turned from desperate to taunting and she loved it, but she wanted him desperate again.

She lifted her hips to allow him to slide off the mesh scarf. Instead of moving farther away as she'd feared, he ran his tongue over her inner thigh in a slow caress. She couldn't speak now, her body too hot and needy. Sounds escaped her tight throat but she barely recognized them as coming from her.

The rest of the skirt was held in place by a single string tied low on her stomach. The red material pulled away from the string in a V-shape that displayed the tight dark curls between her legs.

Jake groaned and his lips finally settled against her.

She arched up on the cot, overwhelmed by the wet heat of his tongue on her most sensitive skin. Her climax hit her like a punch, ripping through her with such force it stole her breath. She collapsed back against the cot, her body trembling and clenching with the aftershock.

Jake kissed his way back up her body, covered her with his heat. He framed her face with his hands, kissed her gently, and thrust inside her with one long powerful stroke.

Her body, still so sensitive from her first orgasm, shattered again. The feeling swept over her, through her, surprising her with its sudden force. She clutched at Jake to keep from blowing apart.

He held still until she settled, then he began to move. The feel of him inside her, moving deep was more perfect than anything she'd ever experienced. She rocked with him, held him, and savored each stroke. She urged him faster when she knew he held back, whispered in his ear, told him how good he felt, how much she loved him. She spoke in English until she couldn't concentrate anymore then switched to Bel. And when she could no longer speak because the sensations were too much, she told him with her body how much she needed him. As he climaxed, she rode the wave, down into pure sensation.

13

Jake rolled to his side, pulling Leia with him. They were still joined. He couldn't let her go just yet. But he was too heavy to stay on top any longer. He touched her face, traced her cheek, her lips. He wasn't sure how he would face being without her for any length of time. But a part of him rejoiced. He wasn't going back to his own time. He would remain in her time, in her galaxy. And that was more than they'd had before.

Even though they weren't particularly close, he'd miss his brother and his family. He'd probably miss his own world, too, one day. At the moment, staring into Leia's dark eyes, he couldn't imagine anything he'd miss more than her, even the familiarity of his own world.

He didn't like the idea of being a pirate. It went against the very instincts that had driven him to become a cop. Could he disregard laws, even laws he didn't know, and do the job Grettel would demand? He'd spent his lifetime hunting down people who broke the law. He'd stood for something. Now, in this strange place and stranger time, he had to become the very thing he'd fought against. Would he have to steal? To kill? Killing to defend or in self-defense, well he'd done that already. But to kill for no other reason than profit? He'd have trouble with that.

And he knew he'd have a problem kidnapping men from the past the way he'd been kidnapped. Grettel might not demand it, given his background. But she might, as a test of his conviction and loyalty. And he'd either have to follow her orders or die. Being a pirate would require becoming a different man. He hadn't had much before, but he'd had his honor, his ethics. He wasn't sure he could live with the man he'd become working for Grettel.

But if being a pirate meant he'd live and Leia would get back her life, then he'd find a way to live with what he had to do. A choice between his conscience and her happiness wasn't much of a choice.

He pushed aside the worry he might never pay back Grettel. He'd find a way. And he and Leia would be together again. No other option existed now. They had a chance and he intended to take it. Just one last thing he needed to settle.

"If Grettel agrees to let you leave," he said, cupping her cheek, "will you find Matt? Will you make sure they don't send him home? Help him get somewhere safe, where he can live out the life he's been given."

"If he wants to return?"

"Tell him about the executions. Tell him what Grettel told us."

She wet her lips and studied his face. "I'll try. As long as you're alive, they won't want to send him back. Getting him off Nas won't be easy, but I can make sure he won't be sent home."

"That's all I ask." He leaned in and kissed her. "What kind of trouble will losing me cause you? How will you explain the pirates letting you go?"

She heaved out a heavy breath. "If she lets me go, I imagine she'll leave me off wherever she's stopping to resupply. I'll tell Nas Command the pirates knocked me out and left me behind, taking you. It's pretty serious business, killing a Guard. Not that I think Grettel wouldn't do it. But maybe Nas Command will think she didn't want to take the risk."

"Will this affect your status, your career?" If he let her go, the last thing he wanted was to send her back in disgrace.

"Maybe." She shrugged. "If I weren't already a hero on Nas, I might be demoted. Given my status, though, they'll probably just stick me back with the Executive Family and leave me there. I won't be trusted with recoveries anymore."

"And the traitor in Nas Command?"

She made a little humming noise and rolled her eyes to the ceiling. "That will depend on how much of my story is believed. I'll need to investigate, to uncover the traitor. That person has been selling information to Grettel. While Grettel may be giving us our lives, I can't stand by and let all of Nas Command be compromised."

Jake smiled. He couldn't help it. She was such a police officer. He tried to ignore the anxiety trickling into his stomach at the thought of her going after this inside person. Whoever they were, they were probably highly placed and sure to resent being discovered. They might even get wind of Leia's investigation and try to stop it before she could uncover anything useful. He didn't know what the sentence was for a traitor on Nas, but he was sure it wouldn't be pleasant.

And by taking away Grettel's connection inside Nas Command, Leia might again make herself a target. He might not be able to help Leia once she returned to Nas, but he'd die before he let Grettel hurt her any more.

He gently touched the bandage on her shoulder blade. It seemed to have survived their lovemaking, but he'd forgotten about the injuries on her back. "I didn't hurt you, did I?" he asked, still fingering the edge of the bandage.

Her eyes widened. "Of course not." She snuggled closer, tucking her head under his chin.

His heart sped at the intimate gesture. Her wiggling movements brought a part of him awake he thought well sated. Her sharp intake of breath let him know she felt him hardening inside her. He rubbed his palm down her back and across her bottom. The red skirt still covered her backside. He pushed it aside so he could caress her skin.

She clenched around his growing erection, and he knew he had to have her again. They had so little time. They needed to talk but if his body was eager enough for a second round he wasn't about to let his brain override the urge. He could make love to her for the next hundred years and never tire of her. His chest tightened.

They didn't have a hundred years. They only had a few precious hours.

He made love slowly, gently, savoring every inch of her, taking his time, memorizing. He wanted memories to keep him company on the lonely nights ahead. Just knowing there would be an end to those nights, that someday they would be together again, made what could have been a bittersweet encounter into a loving moment to be cherished.

After, they lay tangled together, talking quietly of the future. They could have a future now. Since they couldn't guess how long he'd remain with Grettel, they made vague plans. Lazy days on a beach on Belax, a little cottage at the edge of the sand, looking out onto the blue oceans and white-capped waves, the thick jungle whispering in the background, making love in the sun with nothing but the sound of trees and water. If he had to work until he was a gray old man to have those experiences with Leia, he would still consider his life a success.

"Will you miss Earth?" she asked.

"Eventually. But there's too much here to keep me interested." He cupped her breast, squeezed gently. He loved the way her eyes flickered almost closed when he touched her, the soft moan that trembled from her lips.

"I'm going to miss you," she said, arching into his hand.

"Not for long."

With a resigned sigh, she pulled away and sat up. "I don't want to get caught naked and in the middle of something when Grettel comes back." She grinned over her shoulder then turned to search the ground for her clothes. She plucked up the tattered remains of her panties, laughed as she waved them in front of his face. "I'm going to get an awful draft now. I hope Grettel doesn't want to see me fight again. I'll end up flashing the entire ship."

He chuckled but a possessive streak truly hated the idea of her flashing the ship. He reached over the back of the bed and plucked up her top. Shame to have her cover up again, but he didn't like the idea of Grettel and her band of men walking in while Leia was naked either.

He slid off the cot and pulled on his own clothing, wondering if he'd be stuck with the leather vest. At least the ship wasn't cold. He turned to see Leia fastening the gold scarf around her hips, settling it into place so it covered her. He frowned. "That only barely covers your butt."

"I know." She laughed. "It only barely covered my butt before, too."

"Yeah, but you had something under it before."

"And whose fault is it that I don't now?"

His frown deepened. "Grettel's not resupplying somewhere like Dockland, is she?"

"I imagine the location is someplace less conspicuous. Why?"

"Because we'll be leaving you alone, and I don't like the idea of you stuck on some cesspit in that outfit."

She grinned and sauntered toward him to drape her arms around his neck. "I'm sure Grettel will give me something to defend myself with. She might even give me more respectable clothes." Her grin faded around the edges. "She hasn't said for sure she'll let me go."

"If she doesn't, we'll think of something. We'll go back to the original plan of looking for an escape." He kissed her and pulled her tight.

They were still standing in each other's arms when the door hissed open and Grettel walked in.

"We're nearing Byzanum," Grettel said as she strolled into the room with an armful of clothes. "Have you made your decision?"

"I'll stay willingly if you let Leia go," Jake said before Leia could say anything else. "I'll do what it takes to repay you. Just let her go free." The decision was an easy one when finally made. And if Grettel agreed and Leia went free, Jake knew this was a decision he could live with.

"So be it. She stays on Byzanum." Grettel's voice was matter-of-fact.

For a split second, Jake wasn't sure he'd heard her right.

"Really? You're going to let her go?"

"Yes. Now, you're gonna need a shirt to hide those bracers." She tossed a blousy white shirt at Jake. "You'll get less conspicuous bracelets when you prove you're not gonna run. And you..." She grinned at Leia, eyeing the outrageous red outfit. "You will need some-thing less provocative."

"Yes, she will," Jake said as the male pirates behind Grettel vied for a glimpse into the room.

Grettel chuckled and motioned the others back.

To Jake's surprise, they moved without hesitation. Whatever Grettel might be, she did command respect from her crew.

She handed Leia a pile of clothes. "Those'll have to do. I can't set you down on Byzanum in your uniform. Not if you want to survive."

"I understand." Leia fingered the red blouse on the top of the pile.

The material looked suspiciously see-through. This is what Grettel termed *less* provocative? Jake thought. There looked to be as much leather and lace in Leia's outfit as Grettel's but everything was red.

"You got a thing for me in red?" Leia asked, still studying the clothes.

Grettel laughed. "Polly picked the outfit. She calls red a harlot's color."

"What the hell does that woman have against me?"

Jake stepped closer and pulled a red leather bustier out of the pile, eyeing it speculatively. Leia did look good in red, but this was going a bit far.

"A woman who looked very much like you stole a man from Polly when Polly was pregnant with his child," Grettel said. "The man bore a vague resemblance to Jake, but wasn't as good looking."

"Gee, thanks," Jake said.

Grettel winked. "The woman was responsible for the scars on Polly's face."

"I'm not that woman," Leia said.

"Yeah well, Polly is good at holding a grudge and doesn't fuss much with the logic." Grettel shrugged. "Doesn't matter, you'll be free of her fashion sense soon."

"But dressed like this won't she be a target?" A part of Jake still didn't believe Grettel would let Leia go so easily. There had to be a catch. He lifted the material of the shirt which was so sheer Leia might as well walk around naked. He scowled.

"Yeah, she'll be a target. But you want her released. I'm sure she can take care of herself."

"I can."

Leia's voice was quiet and monotone. She didn't look at him while they talked to Grettel, wouldn't meet his gaze. She didn't try to touch him or move any closer than the small cell necessitated. In fact, she'd remained aloof since Grettel entered and Jake announced his decision to stay willingly in exchange for Leia's freedom. And it shouldn't have bothered him that she held herself away. Maybe she needed the distance she was building to be able to leave him behind. But he didn't have to like it.

"You're really going to do this?" he asked Grettel because he had to be sure. "Just let her go and let me work off my debt to earn my freedom?"

"I told you I would and I am. Stop asking me the same damned questions or I might change my mind. Most of my crew already thinks this is a sign I'm going soft. If I were smarter, I'd kill her to get my crew to stop speculating."

"But you're not going to kill her. Why?"

Grettel sighed and flicked him an unreadable glance. "Didn't I just tell you to stop asking questions? I'm doing this because I feel like it, all right. Leave it alone, Jake. Or I'll kill you both to put you out of my misery."

Jake closed his mouth. He wasn't happy with Grettel's response. He didn't trust her. She had to be getting something out of this. But for now, he'd remain quiet.

"Byzanum, huh?" Leia said.

"I do believe that's what I said."

Leia nodded, her eyebrows raised slightly and her mouth pursed.

"What is that look about, Ballore?"

"Byzanum's a rough moon. People get killed for singing a song the wrong way in the wrong place. So down and desperate, they wouldn't know the difference between a pirate and a guard. They'd sell their own limbs if they could get enough. And not a single being on

Byzanum will notice whether you're walking or dead on the street unless you get in their way."

With each image Leia painted, Jake's scowl deepened. "This is the kind of place you're leaving her, Grettel?"

"That's Captain now. Don't forget it." Grettel's voice dropped to a low warning.

"Don't worry," Leia said.

Those were the first soft-toned words she'd spoken since Grettel walked in.

"They'll ignore me there, and I'll buy my way onto a freighter heading toward Nas."

Jake turned her, held her by the shoulders and made her look into his eyes. "Are you sure? I don't want anything to happen to you."

She smiled, just a little, a sad expression that tore at him. "I'll be able to bribe my way home." She turned, looked at Grettel, her eyes narrowed with a speculative glint. "You couldn't have picked a better place to leave me. The inhabitants of Byzanum are so unconcerned with whatever is going on in the outer galaxy, no one would be bothered by me, even if they recognized my face."

"And your point here would be?" Grettel said, her gaze traveling the little cell.

"You really are letting me go. And giving me the best chance possible to get home."

"You say that like you're surprised."

"I am."

"There's just no trust in the universe anymore," Grettel said, shaking her head. "Besides, if I left you someplace you'd get killed, then I'd have to sell Jake because he wouldn't be much use after he found out you were dead, would he?"

"That's what you were going to do to begin with."

"Yeah, well, I changed my mind about wanting to, didn't I? Jesus, the two of you. Haven't you heard the old story about not looking a gift horse in the mouth? Just take advantage of the chances I'm giving you both and deal with it." Grettel cursed under her breath and moved to the door, issued an order to the guards outside.

The guards moved off, leaving the corridor outside the cell empty. She stood with her back to them for a heartbeat. When she faced them again, she stared back with hard blue eyes. But her frown was more confused than aggressive. "I don't get it, either," she said after a few minutes. "And I don't care to think about it this hard. You two are just asking to get shot, you know that?"

Jake couldn't help the crooked grin he flashed Grettel. For all she looked like a Valkyrie, she seemed more like a confused and lost young woman at the moment. A frustrated woman, no longer sure of her own motives. "I don't suppose you'd just let us both go?" he asked because he couldn't help himself.

"Don't press your luck, handsome. Even if Brybel would let me get away with it, my crew would know for sure I'd gone soft then. I wouldn't be able to hold them anymore." She threw her hands in the air and stalked out the door. "I'm tired of this talk. You two are too much of a pain in the butt."

She swiveled in the corridor, her hand on the weapon in her belt. "Change quick. I want you up on the bridge when we enter orbit around Byzanum. The guards will collect you in two minutes. If you're not ready by then, you're either coming up to the bridge naked or they'll kill you and drag your bleeding bodies up on deck so my crew will stop whispering." Her face held no humor or confusion. Instead, she looked serious and dangerous.

When the cell door closed behind Grettel, Leia let out a breath. She shimmied out of the sheer skirt and top and hurried into the new red outfit.

The shirt was as see-through as Jake had feared. He watched with a mixture of anger and lust as he pulled his own shirt over his head. He wouldn't mind her in that outfit if he were the only man to see her. The leather trousers fit tight over her hips and butt. The bustier hugged her waist and pushed up her already-generous cleavage, barely covering her nipples. With the sheer material of the shirt above the bustier, she wouldn't have much room to move without the risk of her curves popping out and flashing any onlookers.

His scowl deepened when she bent to pull on the thigh-high red boots. "Polly is gonna answer for that outfit," he growled.

Leia glanced up, giving him a tempting view of her cleavage and a genuine smile lit her face. "Nice to know my modesty is in good hands."

He watched her finish dressing, unable to look away from her graceful movements. They would be in orbit soon. He would have to say his final goodbyes. He swallowed hard and rubbed a hand over his chest to ease the ache. He didn't want to say goodbye. He wanted to run away with her, even if they were on the run for the rest of their lives. When she straightened, Jake pulled her into his arms and rested his forehead against hers.

No. He wanted more for them, a real life. Not running and hiding forever. They had a chance for more, for whatever reason Grettel choose to give them that chance. They'd take advantage of it.

Leia glanced up at him and the longing and love in her eyes broke his heart. He pulled her close, hugging her so tight he was afraid he was hurting her. He never wanted to let her go. "I love you, Leia. Remember that."

"I love you, Jake."

He took her chin in gentle fingers, lifted her face up to his and kissed her, tasting the salt of her tears. In that moment, with the taste of her love and heartache in his mouth, he didn't care if Grettel returned and killed them. All he cared about was the woman in his arms and memorizing this moment. He lifted his mouth from hers reluctantly, wiped a tear from her cheek with his thumb. "Get Matt somewhere safe. I'll get messages to you whenever I can." He kissed her again and felt the sting of tears behind his own eyes.

When the cell door opened again, he dropped his arms and turned away before he changed his mind. They had a chance, he kept reminding himself. He could let her go now if it meant they would be together again. Without looking, he took her hand and followed the waiting pirates to the bridge.

Leia only released Jake's hand when they stepped through the arched doors leading onto the bridge. A handful of pirates worked at various stations, maneuvering the ship toward the distant moon of Byzanum where it circled a gas giant called Lothos. She'd barely felt the drop out of hyperspace, a tribute to the quality of Grettel's ship.

You could buy a lot with the blood of slaves.

She couldn't censor the bitter opinion. Grettel claimed the men she kidnapped were dead men anyway. For Jake's sake, Leia had to believe the pirate. She couldn't risk sending him back if Grettel was telling the truth. But what Grettel did wasn't right.

Her feelings for the pirate were mixed now that Grettel had granted her freedom and given Jake a chance to earn his. She didn't trust the woman. And she knew Grettel would kill them if she thought it necessary. But Grettel was giving them a chance, and it was more than Leia had hoped for.

The bridge crew worked fluidly, moving about in a choreographed dance that got the business of running the ship done without fuss. Little unnecessary conversation sounded, which surprised Leia. She'd always imagined pirate crews to be constantly boisterous and rude, angry and hard to handle. Grettel obviously expected more from her crew and they gave it. She was sure Grettel paid them well. But Leia couldn't help wondering if the crews' allegiance came solely from the money, or if their support of Grettel came from something more.

Grettel sat in the captain's seat, studying a screen raised from a chair armrest to perch in front of her. She frowned at the readings on the screen, giving the occasional order to the pilots, her brow creased with concentration. She didn't even acknowledge the new people on the bridge.

Leia glanced around the crew and spotted Polly, with her smug little smile, standing near a console to the left. When Polly looked up, Leia fingered the blouse and raised her brows.

Polly grinned, shrugged.

Leia mouthed the words "thank you" in a language Jake wouldn't know, and received a touch of mean satisfaction when Polly snarled and turned back to her console.

"What's so funny?" Jake asked quietly, tilting his head closer as he spoke.

She poked her translator. "Nothing." She wiped the grin from her face as best she could and didn't look up at Jake for fear she'd laugh out loud.

Jake turned his head in Polly's direction then turned back to stare straight ahead. "Ah," he said.

At the humor evident in his voice, a warm wash of emotion flowed through her veins. Saints, but she loved him.

She was still struggling with her grin when the deck pitched violently, hurling her to the ground.

14

Leia pressed a hand to her head as she blinked up into the chaos on the bridge.

Jake knelt beside her, bracing her shoulders. "You okay?" he asked, his hand gently fingering the lump on her head.

"I will be. What happened?"

Jake glanced over to where Grettel stood cursing and shouting orders at the crew. "Don't know. Can't understand her now." He helped Leia to her feet while the crew dodged around them. Their guard escort had abandoned them to help the bridge crew, leaving Leia and Jake to sort themselves out. "I think we took a shot, though," Jake said.

"Weapons fire?"

"Got that impression from the first curses Grettel spewed out. Then she switched languages."

Leia tried to catch the various shouted comments flying across the bridge, but they were using at least three different languages simultaneously and her translator chip wasn't advanced enough to keep up. She concentrated instead on Grettel and focused on one of the languages Grettel used. She caught only a few words, but enough to make her draw in a sharp breath.

"Sounds like we've taken a hit to something vital." She concentrated. "Another pirate ship… Rivals." She hissed. "Quinup."

"Who's Quinup?"

"Goddamnsonofabitch," Grettel shouted.

"I take it she doesn't like this Quinup?" Jake asked.

He took most of Leia's weight when she leaned into him. "No. And she has good reason. Rumor has it Quinup is after the Hamain, Grettel's Kyzit family. There's been hostilities between them for a while now." Leia frowned, listening as Grettel switched back to commanding her crew. "He's only got one ship… Hit a power cell… They've both got weapons targeted." The ship bounced under them.

"Was that from Quinup or Grettel?"

"Another hit from Quinup, but Grettel's knocked out one of his more powerful weapons so her shields will hold." She paused. "I think they're at a standoff. He's got heavier weapons, but she's got better shields."

When the forward screen blanked and a face swam into view, Leia sucked in a breath. The man facing them could have been a relative of Grettel's. As blond and bronzed and big as Grettel, his form was the chiseled masculine perfection to her female perfection.

"Been a long time, Grettel sweetie," he said in English.

Grettel growled at Quinup's sneer. "Quinup."

Leia watched Grettel as the pirate stared at her rival. Grettel remained silent so Leia assumed she was waiting for Quinup to make the first move. Leia flicked a quick glance at the crew behind Quinup but only a few were in view. They didn't look outwardly different from Grettel's crew. She glanced around the deck at Grettel's pirates. They stood at their stations but their attention centered on Quinup. Her gaze swept the control panels that flashed warnings of the damage around the ship. But no one paid any attention.

Leia frowned and inched to another panel.

Jake followed, his gaze shifting constantly over the now-silent crew. They moved so as not to draw attention to themselves, careful and slow.

Leia studied the console they reached, careful to stay quiet. The bridge was silent, both sides waiting for the other to crack. When Quinup broke first, Leia had to hide a smile.

He huffed out a breath. "Grettel, honey, really. This is ridiculous. I've got you outgunned. Two other ships are due here within an hour. Your closest backup is at least a quarter cycle away. You don't want to die."

"You don't want me to die," Grettel said, and a touch of her usual humor crept into her voice, a hint of the cocky pride. "You need me alive. Which means you can't destroy my ship. That would mean killing the Kyzits. And that wouldn't accomplish much, would it?"

"It would get you out of my hair," he purred.

A couple of the pirates behind him laughed.

"Oh, but Quinnie, you like when I'm in your hair." Grettel matched his purr. "Now, I suggest we start negotiating. You're not going to get the Kyzits. We both know that. And you can't blow up my ship because, in the end, you wouldn't sacrifice the Kyzits any more than I would."

"I'm not that attached. If I can't control them, why would I want anyone else to?"

Grettel's face closed up, her humor dried away leaving steel and granite and a temper Leia was surprised Quinup would tempt.

"You. Won't. Get. Them." Grettel leaned back slightly in her seat. "And I'd rather we all die than see them fall to you."

Leia raised a brow and looked around at the other pirates. All stayed firm, not a flicker of fear or doubt on any face—save one. She frowned. There was one man, a pirate she hadn't seen before, thin and haggard looking.

His eyes widened and he glanced around at the others on the deck, then he looked down quickly, hiding the fear in his eyes.

Leia narrowed her gaze. She watched from the corner of her eye as the man reached out to the panel in front of him, hit a few keys and snapped his hand back, glancing around nervously before dropping his gaze again.

So... Not all Grettel's crew were willing to die for the Kyzits.

As if thinking of them drew them out, the Hamain family flowed onto the bridge, circling Grettel like cats, rubbing against her before they settled in a half-moon around the captain's chair facing the screen. One Kyzit jumped up onto Grettel's shoulder, wrapped its tail around her arm and leaned in close to her ear.

"You see, Quinup, my family here is prepared to die with me. You won't take them. They won't allow it." Grettel leaned forward and her voice dropped to ice. "I won't allow it."

The quietly spoken threat startled Leia because she recognized the tone. She would have used it if someone had threatened her parents or one of her siblings. Grettel consider the Kyzits family. Her family. And she was fully prepared to fight, and if necessary, to die for them.

Some of Leia's distrust of the pirate eased. Not that she actually trusted her. More like she felt some empathy for Grettel where she hadn't before. Suddenly, Grettel seemed more human. Leia could understand a woman trying to protect her family.

But Leia didn't want to die to protect Grettel's family. She stared at Quinup, gauging his reaction to the Kyzits. He stared with greedy, hungry eyes. He wanted them. He wanted them enough to do whatever it took. And there was a spark of something deep in the depths of his blue eyes. Triumph.

Leia frowned, her gaze flicking instinctively to the suspicious pirate she'd spotted earlier. He fingered the control panel in front of him again. From the general layout of the bridge, she had a sick feeling he stood over the defensive array.

Beside her, Jake touched her shoulder.

She glanced at him quickly, not wanting to take her gaze off the thin pirate.

He nodded down at the board in front of them.

She flicked a look over it, almost dismissed it, until she noticed the flutter of the lights. She froze and stared. The lights on the panel flashed, stopped, flashed again, a pattern of some kind, something she didn't understand but there was definitely a pattern. Her gaze snapped back to the thin pirate, but he stared at Quinup's face on the screen.

Jake leaned close and whispered, "That's Morse code."

"Morris who?"

"Morse code. A signaling system of dots and dashes. You don't use that in this time?"

"I've never heard of it." She glanced at all the consoles within her view. Many flashed the same repeating pattern, but those panels controlled nonessential systems. Nothing controlling weapons fire or scans flashed. "It's something from Earth?"

"Yeah. It's an SOS signal. If you've never heard of it, I'd guess it's coming from Matt."

"Matt? Where? How?"

Jake shrugged. "Any way to answer this?"

"I don't know." She glanced around the room. Everyone was still focused on the increasingly hostile conversation between Grettel and Quinup. Even the thin pirate was paying more attention to their debate than the others on the bridge. Could he have caused the flashing lights instead of Matt? He didn't look like an Earthman, but maybe Grettel had taught him this Morse code. Only one way to find out.

"Let me see if I can track the signal," she murmured to Jake. "Keep an eye on that pirate to my left, the thin one with the sunken eyes. He's up to something. I think that's the defensive array he's standing over."

"I'll watch him, you track that message. Could they be in a shuttle nearby?"

She didn't waste time answering but set to the console, running a quiet trace. The signal was harder to follow than she would have thought, but when she pinpointed the origin she let out an involuntary gasp. The thin pirate wasn't responsible for the signal.

The slight noise drew Jake's attention. "What is it?" He leaned in close, but kept his gaze on the pirate.

"The signal is coming from Quinup's ship."

"Damn it," Jake hissed under his breath. "If Grettel launches full out against Quinup, she may end up killing Matt."

"I can answer this, but it'll take a minute."

"Hurry. This pirate over here has just punched something else into the panel. And Quinup's voice just turned smug."

Leia's gaze darted up to the screen. Quinup's expression had gone from secretly triumphant to outwardly gloating. He had something to use against Grettel, Leia could see it in his face. She glanced at Grettel who was listening to the Kyzit on her shoulder. From the look on Grettel's face, she knew Quinup had something, too.

"I think we're finished throwing threats now, Grettel honey. Time you hand over the Kyzits."

"Why don't they just…leave?" Jake asked, leaning close to Leia's ear to be heard. "They can jump through space and time. Why don't they just get out of range of Quinup?"

"It's not that easy. It takes time for the family to build up to the transfer. They can't just snap into a new time and space. It's a bit like warming up a ship's engine and getting its speed up before making a jump. You can't just go from a standstill to a jump. Without speed and the correct coordinates, you either don't get anywhere or you reenter in an asteroid. Neither are good options."

Jake grunted. "Point taken. How's that message going?"

"Give me another minute."

"You think you've got something," Grettel said to Quinup.

He laughed. "I know I've got something, honey. I've got something good."

Grettel smiled, a taunting expression that was almost indulgent as if she were dealing with an imaginative child. "Of course you do, Quinnie baby. Something that'll make me give up the Kyzits?"

"Something that'll give you no choice."

Leia looked up from the panel in time to see Quinup raise his hand. A second later, the ship bucked in a dizzying jolt, throwing Leia against the console. Power lines crackled, sparks erupted, equipment flew across the bridge, consoles flashed with multiple failures.

The captain's chair buckled and rolled forward, sending Grettel careening across the deck. Screams and curses cut the air, vying with the alarm claxons.

"What the hell just happened?" Grettel shouted into the din.

"He's got past our shields," a pirate shouted. "I don't know how…"

Leia looked to where the thin pirate had been standing. He was running toward the door that would take him off the bridge.

Jake intercepted the pirate. A single punch to the jaw sent the smaller man to the floor. "I think this one might explain it," he said to Grettel, lifting the man off the ground by the collar of his shirt.

The ship rocked again under another shot from Quinup's ship. "Damn it, get our shields up again," Grettel ordered. She stalked over to the man in Jake's grip. "What did you do?"

Her voice was so low, Leia just heard her over the noise. Then she saw Grettel move in close, her voice dropping so low, Leia could no longer hear what she said.

The thin man squeaked and struggled in Jake's grip.

Jake shook him hard, once.

The man stopped struggling, but his sunken eyes widened with terror.

Grettel continued to whisper to the pirate while the crew shouted to each other, and another shot made the ship buck.

As Leia watched, the thin man began to babble to Grettel. She listened, snarled, then moved to the panel he'd abandoned. "Polly, Quinup's got access to our defensive grid. Block the sono-fabitch."

The sound had been cut to Quinup's communication link, but Leia could see him laughing from the corner of her eye as she watched Grettel's crew struggling to regain control of their ship. Quinup's laugh made Leia's palms damp.

"Fire on his fucking ship," Grettel shouted, still working feverishly at the thin man's control panel.

Leia watched the pirates at the weapons array start firing. She turned back to her own console. She was close to being able to answer the signal. She needed to finish. If Matt sent the SOS, and she was sure the signal came from him now, she had to warn him. She worked quickly, watching the chaos from the corners of her eyes. No one seemed to pay attention to her as they frantically fought Quinup's attack.

Jake joined her after a minute.

"Where's the traitor?" she asked without looking up.

"Grettel's boys have taken him below. Not sure I want to know what they're doing. I think he'll consider whatever it is a blessing compared to what Grettel threatened him with." Jake's big shoulders shuddered.

"Tell me later. I'm almost through." A moment later, she shouted her success just as Grettel and Polly erupted into a roar of triumph.

"Now then." Grettel crossed back to the spot where her captain's chair had been. "Give me sound." When she knew Quinup could hear her, she said, "That was pretty good, Quinnie honey. Getting a spy into my crew. Very sneaky. Too bad he isn't as good as I am at this sort of thing." Her grin was lazy and cocky.

Quinup's laughter turned to a scowl.

"Any more tricks? No? Well then. I suppose we're back to negotiating. And you've just lost your ace."

Quinup's scowl creased with a brief flicker of confusion, but he recovered quickly.

As they exchanged a few more insults and taunts, Leia motioned to Jake, leaned in to him. "Can you do this Morse code?"

"Yeah."

"Okay, use that part of the screen there. Tap it to send your message. That should send a light signal like the one we're receiving back to the source of this signal. They can use our signal to help them fine-tune theirs so it's not hitting the entire bridge. Actually, from what I can tell this is hitting the entire ship, anywhere there's a console that connects to nonessential systems. But anyone who's noticed it probably thinks it's a side effect of the attack. Better if we're the only ones who can see it, though."

Jake nodded and set to work, tapping a pattern on the part of the screen she'd indicated.

While he worked, Leia looked up to where Grettel and Quinup still exchanged insults. Quinup's gaze swept the ship as Grettel commented on his less-than-superior equipment. Leia was pretty sure she wasn't referring to his ship.

Quinup's traveling gaze settled on Leia and a dangerous light flickered in his gaze. Her eyes narrowed as she watched him. Damn Polly and this stupid red outfit, she thought just as Quinup said, "You've got a few new additions I see." He nodded at Leia. "I've always loved women in red. Especially if the woman fills out the red like that."

Leia flicked a hard look at Polly, who shrugged, smirked, and turned back to the screen. Leia rolled her eyes. Great. Just perfect. Polly couldn't have known about Quinup's arrival unless she was also a traitor to Grettel. From the way the little pirate had worked during the attacks, despite Leia's own dislike of the woman, she couldn't fault her support of her captain. Unfortunately. She would have loved to have punched Polly the way Jake had punched the pirate who'd dropped their shields. But like her or not, Polly couldn't have set her up to be noticed by Quinup. The little bitch sure as hell seemed pleased it had happened, though.

Leia glanced back at Quinup's leer.

"Maybe we could make an exchange after all, Grettel honey," he said without looking away from Leia. "I get her, you get one of my crew."

Beside her, Jake growled, low in his throat.

From the corner of her eye, she saw him staring up at Quinup even as he continued to tap out a message on the screen. His hand moved subtly, calling little attention to his movements. But his blue gaze locked onto Quinup's face and his expression was not friendly. Fortunately for them both, the pirate wasn't paying Jake any attention.

Grettel flicked a glance over her shoulder at Leia, then back to Quinup. "I like her. She's valuable to me. Why would I want to trade her?"

Quinup smiled and for the first time since noticing Leia, his gaze shifted back to Grettel. "I might have something you'd like in exchange." He shot a hand out to the side and pulled someone into view of the screen.

Leia couldn't control her reaction. She gasped and took a step closer to the screen. "Moyra?"

The Nas Guard who had fled with them from the *Persephone* and stood by Leia on Dockland Depot looked like the other pirates on Quinup's ship.

Moyra's vibrantly red hair spiked around her pale face, matching the red blouse she wore with a white vest and trousers. She looked as shocked as Leia felt to be face-to-face.

Leia's gaze ran over the woman, looking for injuries. She didn't look hurt but a tear streaked over her cheek and her liquid silver eyes shimmered with what looked like pain.

Quinup's gaze came back to Leia now, his eyes narrowed then widened. "Well as the space dogs eat, it's the infamous Lieutenant Leia Ballore. Didn't recognize you without your uniform and with your hair down, Lieutenant. Looks good down, makes your eyes look even sexier. Moyra, darling, you didn't tell me she was such a fine-looking thing. And that figure. Yum."

Leia ignored Quinup. She couldn't look away from Moyra's tortured gaze.

"I'm sorry," Moyra mouthed to Leia in Nas.

"Why? What have you done?" Leia asked in the same language. Moyra wasn't a captive of Quinup's. Not the way his hand settled comfortably on her shoulder, or the way Moyra unconsciously leaned into his embrace, a gesture that looked natural and unfeigned even as another tear rolled over her pale cheek. Moyra wasn't afraid of Quinup. She wasn't playing a part. She looked like a woman used to his touch. Leia's heart hurt with the shock.

She winced from the implications of Moyra's appearance on Quin-up's ship, where Matt was obviously being held. She and Jake probably looked like any other pirate on Grettel's bridge, too, so maybe Moyra was playing the same game with Quinup. But she fit herself to his side like she belonged there, not like she was pretending to fit.

"Vanian? Bythan?" she mouthed the words, took another step closer to the screen before Jake's hand shot out and stopped her.

"They're alive—" Moyra started.

"They're in my brig for future sale and profit," Quinup interrupted in Nas. "My sweetie Moyra here was kind enough to give them to me."

Moyra's gaze dropped and she turned into the curve of Quinup's arm, hiding behind the long spikes of her hair.

"Why?" Leia breathed, hardly able to believe. Moyra had turned Vanian, Bythan and Matt over to Quinup? Moyra had betrayed them?

Moyra glanced through the cover of her hair and whispered, "I love him, Leia. I'm sorry."

Leia felt like she'd taken a punch to the stomach, stepping back as if she'd really taken a physical blow.

"Leia," Jake murmured. He stood against her back, his hands steady on her shoulders.

She was too shocked to feel the anger she knew would be there later. She leaned into Jake's strength, stared up at Moyra and tried hard not to scream.

Quinup chuckled, patted Moyra's arm. "This is very entertaining," he switched back to English from Nas. "We should have started with this, Grettel. What's the delectable lieutenant to you now? Don't tell me this hero of Nas has actually joined your crew?"

"That's really between me and the lieutenant, Quinnie. Let's just say she's valuable to me. As for trade…" Grettel flicked another look back at them. "See the big brute at her back?" She was grinning when she faced Quinup again. "She belongs to him. And if you don't recognize the danger you're in at the moment, then you've got no survival instincts at all, honey."

One of the Kyzits jumped up onto Grettel's shoulder again and leaned in close to her ear.

Grettel laughed loudly and patted the Kyzit's tail where it had curled around her shoulder and under her arm. "Brybel thinks you might not be smart enough to know when you're in danger. What do you think?"

Quinup's scowl shot to Grettel and the Kyzit on her shoulder.

Grettel took a deep breath, settled on her braced legs and crossed her arms over her chest, the look on her face smug. "Now what?" she said. "No more ways past my shield. No bargaining chips. No more firepower than I've got…"

"But you're seriously damaged now, baby," Quinup said, his voice gloating again. "We knocked out your hyperdrive, damaged some major systems, and punched through your hull in at least three places. You're not going anywhere fast, and I've got two more ships almost here. No one in this sector will come and help you. Hell, no one here is going to interfere. You're stuck. It's just a matter of time now."

"Not if I blow you out of space," Grettel murmured, her temper showing.

"You could try. But my shields will hold up to the weapons you have left and we both know it. You're barely better than space debris. If you try firing on me now, you'll just waste away to a floating rock. We'll walk onto your ship."

"You won't get us alive, Quinup. I'll self-destruct first."

Leia's stomach clenched. Grettel would do it. To protect the Kyzits, she'd willingly destroy her ship and everyone on it. And not a single pirate now on the bridge would say a word against it. In fact, they'd go down shouting her name and cheering the bold move. A glance around the bridge was all it took to confirm that truth.

Leia didn't want Quinup to have the Kyzits either. She had a feeling Quinup wouldn't be as restrained as Grettel, if Grettel could be considered restrained. At least, according to Grettel, she only took men about to die. Would Quinup be so circumspect? Would he even bother to worry about the timeline? Would the Kyzits work for him if he could get them? Either way, Grettel and her crew were willing to die before giving up the Kyzits.

But Leia didn't want to die. She didn't want Jake to die. She sure as hell didn't want Quinup to win.

"Jake," she murmured, leaning against the solid strength of his chest. "Matt?"

"He's safe," he said near her ear.

His breath was distractingly warm against her cheek.

"He, Vanian and Bythan are in a shuttle, working to get past Quinup's shields so they can escape to Byzanum." He squeezed her shoulders when he said, "Moyra helped them escape, gave them access codes to a shuttle, a way of accessing the nonessential ship systems they're using to communicate with us. No one knows they're gone yet, but they don't have much time before they're discovered."

She remained silent a minute, considering. "How close are they to disrupting the shield?"

"Matt says close."

"Can you find out which bay they're in?"

"Yeah. Why?"

"Because if we take advantage of that single shield breach, firing into the bay while the shield is down, we can do some serious damage to Quinup's ship." She murmured the idea so quietly no one but Jake would have heard her voice.

He gave her shoulders a squeeze and together they moved back the two steps to the console where Jake could signal Matt.

As he did, she kept her gaze on the screen, watching Quinup continue to exchange taunts and insults and ultimatums with Grettel. She watched Moyra closely, waiting. When the woman finally looked up, Leia made a hand gesture.

Moyra's gaze flicked to her, then to her hands and her gaze widened a fraction.

Leia made another hand gesture using a secret finger language the Nas Guard trained in.

Moyra subtly replied.

:*Are you willing to help us?*: Leia asked. :*I know you've tried to help Vanian and the others.*:

:*I love him,*: Moyra responded. :*But he's a bastard. He used me.*: Her gaze dropped before she met Leia's eyes again. :*He had Vanian and Bythan beaten…and worse. Bythan was nearly killed. That wasn't part of our arrangement.*: Moyra trailed off, her fingers fell motionless.

Leia glanced at Jake. "Anything?"

"Maybe."

"I'm trying to get Moyra to help. A distraction maybe?"

"Is that a good idea?" He didn't glance up as he asked. His gaze focused on the blinking light coming back to him.

"She tried to help Vanian and the others escape. She's sorry about all this. But she's in love with him."

Jake's gaze did flick up to the screen then. "That's a shame. Moyra seemed like a nice woman."

"I may or may not be able to get her to help, Jake. Can they do this without her?"

"They're gonna need a distraction so the shield isn't flooded closed again just as they leave."

Leia heaved out a quiet breath. Fortunately, Grettel and Quinup could exchange insults and taunts for hours without running out, so they had some distraction. She tried Moyra again. :*We need a distraction. To get Vanian and the others out. Can you help?*:

Moyra's expression looked hollow, lost.

For a long minute, Leia wasn't sure she'd answer.

Then she made a quick hand motion, a simple twist of her fingers.

Leia nodded, thanked her in gesture as well as with her eyes. "Where are they?" she asked Jake, leaning into him casually.

"Stern, port bay. Twenty meters from the…rear thrusters? Does that make sense? I'm not sure Matt knows what he's talking about."

"Close enough." She sucked in a breath. Adrenaline flooded her system, sharpening the edges of her world. They had one chance. "You stay here. We need to time the fire just right. Signal me when they're ready."

"Polly's on the weapons array now."

She wasn't sure if that was humor or warning in his voice. She ignored both and walked across the bridge to Polly.

Quinup's gaze followed her. "Where you going, Red? I'm looking forward to getting you over here. I've got plans for that outfit."

She stopped next to Polly and shifted into the seductress her mother had taught her to be. She smiled and let her lids droop to a lazy, sexy expression. "Plans already? You're assuming a lot. I'm not easy to please," she spoke in Nas so Jake didn't have to understand the conversation. He would recognize what she was doing, but she didn't want him to hear word for word. She'd never felt self-conscious playing this game before. Those feelings didn't arise because the game itself made her uncomfortable. She was uneasy now because the man she loved was listening to her play. "You think you're enough for me?"

His gaze flicked to Jake and back. "More than him, I'd bet. He looks a bit…primitive. Leia Ballore, not the upstanding member of society we all thought," he fairly purred, making the comment both compliment and insult. "Fucking slaves. Bet he's got some pretty scars."

She studied his face, working hard to hide her annoyance. "I notice you don't have any. Shame. Ruins a perfectly good face. How does a man in your position survive so long without scars?" She smiled slightly. "Doesn't speak well of your prowess, a pirate with not a single scar. Too scared to take the shots yourself?" She set her mouth in a pout. "Not strong enough to stomach a little damage to your pretty face?"

Grettel burst out laughing, clapping her hands in a slow appreciative rhythm. "She's too much woman, Quinnie. Just like me. And from the look on Jake's face, I'd say you're a dead man now. You just don't know it yet." She laughed again, and she and Quinup launched into another round of insults and taunts.

Leia took advantage of the distraction to whisper to Polly, "I know you don't like me, but I've got a plan to get us out of this mess. You willing to help?"

Polly didn't glance at her. Her jaw tightened, her hands clenched.

"Polly, I'm not the woman who hurt you. And Jake isn't the man."

A muscle in Polly's jaw twitched. She snarled, kept her gaze forward.

Leia's stomach knotted. If Polly didn't help, Vanian and Matt and Bythan might still escape. But they'd lose the chance to disable Quinup's ship. With that chance gone, there were only two outcomes to this standoff. Quinup would take the ship, or Grettel would set it to self-destruct. Neither option much appealed to Leia.

She glanced at Jake, telling him with a look she didn't think this would work.

Then Polly spoke. "What's your idea?"

"The shields at the stern port-side bay will drop in a minute so a shuttle can break out. If we time a shot to hit into the bay and the storage cells behind it, we can disable some of his weapons, maybe even his hyperdrive."

Polly finally turned her head to stare at Leia. She didn't say anything, just stared.

Leia kept her gaze forward, watching Quinup and studying Moyra still held under his arm.

Finally, Polly said, "I'll do more than that. Just let me know when."

"Jake will signal. I don't want to move again and call attention to myself."

Polly turned back to the screen without another word, but her fingers danced over the console in front of her and her gaze flicked between the console and Jake.

When Leia felt sure Polly would take care of the hit on Quinup's ship, she gestured to Moyra. :*Now would be a good time for that distraction.*:

Moyra nodded shallowly. In a move both sudden and shocking, she pushed out of Quinup's arm and pointed a weapon. "You bastard," she hissed. "You'd leave me for her, wouldn't you? That slave user, that whore! I'm no longer useful? Is that it? I can't go back to Nas Command, so I'm not good enough for you anymore." Her voice rose with each sentence nearing a shrill screech. Her hands shook and tears streamed over her cheeks.

For a heartbeat, Leia couldn't tell if Moyra was acting or if she would really shoot the pirate. If she did, Leia couldn't find it in her to care. Killing Quinup would certainly be a distraction.

The bridge of Grettel's ship fell silent, all watching the scene in frozen fascination. On Quinup's bridge, the crew had pulled weapons of their own, all pointed toward Moyra, all focused on the threat to their captain. Not a single person on Quinup's bridge looked at their station consoles.

Moyra cursed Quinup even as he held up his hands and tried to pacify her. "Baby. Moyra. What's gotten into you? You know I love you. You're my heart."

"You liar," Moyra screamed. "You never loved me."

Leia couldn't stop watching the scene, terrified Moyra would get herself killed. But at the same time, the fight was an unbelievably effective distraction.

From the corner of her eye, she saw Jake raise a finger. Not a big gesture, could have just been a hand twitch, but that slight motion was all Polly needed. The rest of the crew, even Grettel, were too fascinated by the lovers' spat to notice the subtle movements. Leia watched Quinup's crew carefully, waiting for the first sign they knew something was wrong. Her stomach clenched.

With the screen focused on the rival pirate's bridge, she couldn't see what was happening at the bay. She glanced down at the screen in front of Polly where she could see the targeting coordinates and watched as the laser cannons fired. She held her breath.

The first pirate to notice the shield breach shouted at Quinup seconds before the ship was hit.

Quinup's bridge erupted into chaos, alarms blaring, people shouting and screaming—not unlike, Leia noted with a touch of satisfaction, Grettel's bridge had been earlier in this fight.

As far as Leia knew, firing in through the bay at the stern of the ship would cause considerable damage, but it wouldn't do any more damage than had been done to Grettel's ship. So she was as surprised as everyone else when the screams turned to desperate curses and the crew started streaming off the bridge.

Leia caught Polly's smirk out of the corner of her eye. She turned to the little pirate and raised her brows.

Polly grinned outright. "Quinup's not the only one with spies."

Leia's eyes widened, then she started to laugh. "You hit something more than the storage cells, didn't you?"

Polly just grinned and turned back to the chaos on the screen.

Quinup's voice snapped out over the noise. "Grettel, I'm gonna kill you for this."

Grettel laughed.

To her credit, she took the whole situation in stride, never letting on that she had no idea what just happened.

"I'd get to a shuttle, Quinnie. My readings show your ship's gonna blow in less than five minutes." Over her shoulder, she said, "Move us out of range."

"Grettel!" Quinup screamed.

"Don't worry, Quinnie. We'll pick you up." Her smile turned

vicious. "Unless, you want to go down with your ship. I won't argue with a captain's prerogative."

Quinup snarled at the screen, then charged off the bridge.

Leia watched the pirates streaming from the ship, looking for a flash of white and red. She sucked in a breath when she saw Moyra stumble to her feet and head to the door. The bridge was crumbling around her as she staggered out, the last person to leave. Leia's stomach clutched so tight she thought she might be sick. "Did Vanian and the others get out?" she asked Polly.

"They're shuttling toward Byzanum as we speak."

"Message them," Grettel said as she swung around. "Let them know we'll pick them up. Wouldn't do to have our co-conspirators receive less hospitality than our enemies."

"You're not going to take them prisoner?" Leia said, outraged. "After what they just did, what we just did?"

She took a step toward Grettel but stopped when a hand squeezed her arm. Polly was stronger than she looked, but Leia was prepared to shake off the warning grip to get to Grettel.

Grettel forestalled the fight by nodding Polly off. "And what exactly did you all just do?" Grettel asked, her brows cocked.

Jake stepped forward. "Moyra helped Matt, Vanian and Bythan escape the brig and get to a shuttle. They lowered a portion of the shields to get the shuttle out. We timed it so that a shot was fired into the bay when it opened."

"Polly was the one to hit the vital spot to destroy the ship," Leia put in. She saw Polly's jolt and turned to see the pirate staring with huge eyes. "You think I would take credit for your information?" she asked Polly quietly.

"I didn't expect…" She looked away but her eyes were still wide.

"Is this true, Polly? You plotting things behind my back," Grettel murmured.

Polly snapped to attention. "They had a good plan and there wasn't time to tell you without alerting Quinup. Ballore arranged the bridge distraction." She tossed Leia a "now we're even" smirk and faced

Grettel again. "I don't know how, but I know she got that Nas Guard to start the fight."

Grettel's only response was raised eyebrows. The bridge was silent, the atmosphere thick with anticipation and wariness.

"So," Grettel said after a minute, "somehow Matt and the other two Nas Guards got a message onto my bridge without me knowing—"

"It was Morse code," Jake added.

Grettel nodded. "Okay. They got a Morse code message to my bridge, without me knowing, and they managed to shut down part of Quinup's shields without him knowing—"

"That was why Moyra started the fight. To distract the crew so they wouldn't notice," Leia said.

"They got out of the ship and an instant later you fired into the bay while the shields were still down? Am I right so far?"

Leia nodded, saw Jake and Polly doing the same.

"And because Polly knows something about Quinup's ship, the shot actually set the *Yerkin* on its way toward destruction." As she spoke, the floor pitched under their feet like a sailboat rolling over an ocean wave.

Leia reached out to brace herself against the console.

Grettel rode the wave on braced legs without so much as taking a step to steady her balance. The way she moved, she looked like a part of the ship. She pursed her lips when the wave passed and the ship settled. "Make that, the shot destroyed the *Yerkin*."

There was no outward emotion in Grettel's voice, only a matter-of-fact tone that could mean anything. "Are we pulling in the escape pods and the shuttle?" she asked over her shoulder, in English. One of her pirates answered with a sharp, "Yes, Cap'n," in English.

"So… Jake stopped the spy who gave Quinup a way past our shields—nice punch by the way. Ballore, Jake and Polly managed to destroy Quinup's ship with the help of more escaped prisoners and a traitor Nas Guard. And I'm about to collect a hefty ransom from Quinup's crew for his sorry ass. Is that the whole of it? Anything else I should know?"

Leia glanced around. The crew all looked nervous, shifting from foot to foot, staring at Grettel as if their lives depended on it. Leia took a deep breath and prepared to meet whatever Grettel had to say. And if she had to fight for Matt, Vanian and Bythan's freedom, she'd do it with whatever weapon Grettel chose. If Moyra survived the destruction of the ship, she'd fight for her, too. Leia had promised Jake she'd keep Matt safe. She had a duty to protect the Guards in her squadron. She'd do both, no matter what.

She felt Jake's gaze and turned to face him. His look was steady, his body relaxed in a coiled, waiting way, prepared to fight, too. She smiled, a faint expression she hoped Grettel wouldn't take the wrong way. She let his return smile fill her with warmth. They were strong and could do anything together.

She turned to face Grettel and straightened her shoulders. Let the pirate do her worst.

1 5

J ake flexed his hands and waited. He didn't know what Grettel would do, but he told himself he was prepared for anything.

Grettel smiled slowly, her face opening by increments. "I am about to be a very, very rich woman." She chuckled and patted the tail of the Kyzit who still rode her shoulder. She murmured something to it and her smile spread.

Jake's gut clenched. She was going to sell Matt and the other Nas Guards. She might not release Leia now, either. He felt his muscles bunch, his body coiling tight to move.

"So I guess this means you've earned your freedom, Jake old boy," Grettel said, her grin growing with each word.

Jake's breath whooshed out in a rush. "What?"

Grettel laughed, loud enough it echoed in the utterly silent bridge. "Quinup is worth a small fortune in ransom, to his own crew, as well as other…parties. I can hold an auction and get close to what I would have gotten for you. Add to that the fact I will have a good portion of his crew to either ransom, sell or take on to my own crew, you've also earned back whatever Matt would have made at auction. So, my dear, dear man, your days as a pirate are officially over. A short, but illustrious career."

Jake was so stunned he mumbled, "Thank you," without thinking.

That earned another belly laugh from Grettel as she turned back to Leia. "And you, Ballore. I still stand by my first assessment. You'd make a damned fine pirate. If you ever consider giving up legitimate work," she edged the words with distaste, "you get in touch with me. I've always got room for a good hand."

Polly's snort was audible even to Jake.

Leia simply shook her head, looking as stunned as he felt. They were free? Both of them. Free to go and do…whatever they wanted. A bubble of excitement started in his gut, swirling and building until he felt himself about to burst. He let go a wild whoop, crossed the bridge in two long strides and swung Leia up in his arms. He kissed her soundly, ignoring the jeers and catcalls of the pirates surrounding them.

Leia laughed against his mouth, braced her hands on his shoulders.

When he set her back on her feet, her face was flushed a pretty pink, but her eyes sparkled up at him.

"If I'd known all we had to do was blow up another pirate's ship, I would have suggested it sooner," she said.

He laughed and swung her into the air again, hugging her tight. "Matt! We have to go see if Matt and the others are okay." He spun to face Grettel, keeping Leia firmly in his arms. "Has their shuttle been brought aboard?"

"They'll be there when you get to the bay." Grettel grinned, a crooked and self-satisfied expression. The Kyzit on her shoulder made a low, humming noise that sounded suspiciously like a purr, but the kind of sound a dog might make if it could purr. "Polly, show them the way, please."

Polly nodded, turned and headed off the bridge without a backward glance.

Jake moved to follow her but Leia stopped him with a hand on his stomach.

She faced Grettel and met her gaze for a long minute. "Thank you."

Grettel raised a brow. "Thank you. You helped save my family." The pirate's hand stroked over the Kyzit's tail as she spoke and the cockiness leaked from her expression, leaving a genuine gratitude behind. "There's not much I could do to repay that."

Leia nodded as if she understood then allowed him to usher her off the bridge. They trotted to catch up to the little pirate. Jake could have run the length of the ship on the energy buzzing through his system. He stopped long enough to pull Leia into his arms again and give her a solid, deep kiss.

"What was that for?"

Her sleepy, sexy voice made his heart hammer. "I love you," he murmured against her mouth, kissing her again. He felt drunk on the thrill of freedom.

Polly cleared her throat, shot them a disgusted look and carried on at her ground-eating pace.

Jake chuckled, took Leia's hand and followed.

When they stepped into the bay, Matt, Vanian and Bythan stood just outside the shuttle's lowered ramp, a ring of armed pirates surrounding them. At a word from Polly, the pirates backed off and left the bay. "We're going to see to our other…guests," she said and followed the other pirates.

Jake sucked in a breath at the sight of Vanian and Bythan. Both women sported black eyes and bruised faces. Vanian's lip was split and had started to bleed. Their clothes were torn, and both women moved like their bodies hurt. Sweat coated Bythan's face and standing looked like too much effort. She had a gash across her forehead that had bled down over her left eye and her right jaw looked swollen. She leaned heavily on Vanian, but she held a weapon in her free hand.

Matt looked a little better. He had a bandage on his cheek that had blood seeping through it, and he moved stiff and slow. But he didn't sport nearly as much damage as the two Guards.

For a quiet moment, they all stared at each other. Then Vanian said something and Leia nodded. Vanian's expression relaxed into a grin.

Leia crossed to her, taking her into a soft hug. She pulled Bythan gently into the embrace and all three women started to cry.

Grinning, Jake took Matt in a rough hug. At Matt's grunt of protest,

Jake loosened his grip and pushed him back to look at his face. "More than your face hurt?"

"Yeah, the back's a bit sore. Nothing I won't get over. Looks like I'll be as scarred as you now. But I didn't get the worst."

The venom in Matt's voice and the anger in his expression when he glanced at the women hit a chord with Jake. He was pretty pissed off at Quinup's treatment, too. But a selfish part of him couldn't help feeling grateful it hadn't been Leia. To see her like that would have killed him.

"You look better than I expected," Matt said, looking him over from head to toe. "God, I'm glad to see you again. I was afraid you'd been killed on Dockland. What the hell are you wearing?"

"I'm relieved to see you, too. And don't ask about the outfit. I blame Grettel." Jake's grin fell away. He pulled Matt a little farther from the women. Despite his excitement at seeing his partner again, Jake didn't want to put off telling him the bad news about their situation. He'd had time to adjust. Matt was in for a shock.

He stared at Matt for a moment, wanting to soften the blow. When he couldn't think of a way to make the news easier, he shrugged and just said it. "We can't go home."

"Is Grettel gonna try and sell us? We can get away again..."

"No, it's not that. Grettel is letting us go. Long story which I'll explain later. But we still can't go home. Ever."

Matt stepped away from Jake. "What the hell are you talking about?"

Jake took a deep breath and told him everything, the Kyzits, the time travel, and, most of all, that they would have died within hours of when they were kidnapped.

Matt's face paled until he finally had to sit on the floor of the docking bay with his head between his knees. "So, if we go back, we'll be killed. Definitely? No chance it could be a mistake?"

"We can check, I suppose. I don't figure Grettel had much reason to lie. You want to take the chance?"

"We know now, can't we change it?" He didn't look up as he spoke.

"We might screw up the entire timeline if we tried to change anything."

"But... They can send us back after the time we would have been killed... No, same problem. I... Jesus." He tunneled his fingers into his hair and tugged. "Time travel? I thought that was impossible.

Jake squatted next to Matt, put a hand on his shoulder. "I felt the same way when Leia told me. But the story seems to be true. Explains a lot. These bracers are the only things keeping us here. Removing them could kill us, or worse."

Matt shook his head, raised it and dropped his hands to his lap. "So..." He swallowed. "So, we have to stay here. If we go back, we'll be assassinated. But here, with these things, we're slaves. How the hell are we supposed to live?"

Jake let out a breath, not sure himself how they'd make a living. He glanced over at Leia where she stood talking quietly with the other two women. He didn't realize he was smiling until Matt punched him in the leg.

"Hey, get your brain out of your pants, Jake. We've got a serious problem here."

"We'll figure it out. I've got a few ideas. Besides, this way you can still be my best man."

"Your best..." Matt's eyes widened. "You're not serious? Marriage? Last I heard, you were dead set against marriage."

Jake shrugged. "I've changed my mind." He ran a hand over his chin. "I'm not even sure they do marriages here, or if she'll accept. But I'm not as unhappy about staying in this time as I would have been if I hadn't met her. In fact, I'm damn well delirious with the idea of staying."

Matt laughed. "I never thought to see the day. Jake Marshall in love."

Jake grinned self-consciously. "Yeah, came as a shock to me, too. So, what do you think? We can figure out a way to make this work. It's a pretty amazing time to be stuck in."

Matt nodded but his gaze was distant. "Our families? My parents are going to be devastated. My sister..."

"They would have had to live with your assassination anyway, Matt," Jake said quietly. "Unless you want to die, there's no going back."

"You're sure?" He looked up, his eyes bleak. "Yeah, you would be. I just don't like it. I would have liked to have said goodbye."

"Maybe Grettel will let us send a message somehow."

"Grettel! How the hell did you end up on this ship? Moyra gave us a way to access Grettel's unsecured systems, so we could send the SOS She said you'd be onboard, but she wasn't sure where. I assume she knew because Quinup knew, but… What the hell happened?"

"It's a long story." He frowned. "Quinup wasn't expecting to see Leia, but he knew Grettel had found me? He must have assumed Leia was killed or dealt with the way he dealt with Vanian and Bythan." His voice hardened and his fists clenched. He shook his head, trying to clear away the horrifying image of Leia suffering at Quinup's hands. Too easy to picture and too terrifying to think about.

He cleared his throat and relaxed his fists. "We're gonna need somewhere more comfortable to talk about all this. You've got some telling to do, too."

He rose and helped Matt climb to his feet then crossed to the three women. He couldn't resist touching Leia so he took her into a gentle embrace. "Can we go somewhere to catch up? Someplace with seats and maybe some alcohol? I think Matt could use a shot of something strong."

"You told him about…everything?"

"The time travel, the fact that we can't go back so we can't return to Nas, either. Yeah. There's more to talk about."

"There is." She nodded to Vanian and Bythan. "We've got a lot of catching up to do, too. But Bythan is hurt. She needs medical help." She switched to what he recognized now as Nas and spoke with the two women. After a brief conversation, she said, "They'd prefer to sit in the shuttle. In case we have to leave quickly. There's a medical kit in there."

"Won't be necessary," Grettel said from the door.

Vanian and Bythan both stepped back and took fighting stances, raising the only two weapons they had. Despite her injuries, Bythan stood steady. Her hand barely trembled.

Leia motioned them to ease down, but they followed the order reluctantly. He couldn't blame them.

Grettel smiled. "Thanks to you three, I've managed to blow the lead ship of my most-hated rival to pieces. You're safe on this ship. Hell, you're heroes."

Leia quietly translated.

"Your most-hated enemy is dead?" Vanian said.

Her clipped, accented English surprised Jake. He'd assumed none of the other Guards had translator chips because they'd never used English.

"No." Grettel's grin grew. "Quinup's on his way to my brig now. He's worth a tidy profit. And I have you to thank for that."

"I would have seen him dead," Vanian said.

Grettel's eyes narrowed. "Yeah, I guess you would have." Her gaze flicked to Bythan who swayed on her feet, despite her efforts to remain upright.

Vanian stepped closer and took Bythan's weight, supporting her without blocking her weapon hand.

Grettel tilted her head as she studied the two injured Guards. "Quinup's worth more to me alive than dead and since he's come to me breathing, I intend to keep him that way."

Vanian nodded in acknowledgement but didn't look happy.

"As for that other Nas Guard, Moyra, was it? She didn't make any of the escape pods we picked up. I don't know the whole of it, but sounds like she tried to fix things in the end. She gave you time to escape. You have my sympathies."

Bythan hissed out something that didn't sound like grief, but Vanian's face softened just a touch.

Leia lowered her head and whispered something he couldn't hear. When she raised her head, her eyes shimmered wetly but no tears fell.

"You'll have accommodation with us," Grettel said, "until you decide what you want to do next. I think you do have some decisions to make. We're going to be here for a while, until my other ships arrive and I can arrange repairs to this ship. Quinup's other two ships are due soon, but I suspect they'll be more than willing to keep from killing us when they hear the *Yerkin* was destroyed and Quinup's in my brig."

"Thank you, Grettel," Jake said.

"Now I've given you your freedom, I suppose it's back to first names. Shame. I liked hearing you call me Captain." She chuckled. "Follow me, boys and girls, and I'll show you where you can get that drink. And some medical attention. You ladies look like you could use both." After a beat, Grettel said, "Quinup do that to you himself?"

Vanian shook her head. "Ordered it, then watched. They didn't ask for information. It wasn't torture. They just beat us for enjoyment."

"Only a beating?"

Vanian didn't answer, but her hard stare was enough to make Jake's stomach roll. He'd been a cop long enough to understand that look, that anger. Unconsciously, his hands tightened on Leia.

Grettel pursed her lips and nodded. "Well. I suppose we should extend the same hospitality to our new guest. This way."

Jake's brows rose. Quietly to Leia, he said, "She's ticked off because Quinup had Vanian and Bythan beaten and…? Okay, I can understand why she'd be angry about the rape. Though given her chosen profession that seems pretty hypocritical. She's been selling men into a life not very different. And she put you in a knife fight with that goon."

Leia leaned in to him. "I think she chooses men who have a chance at escape." She shrugged. "Still hypocritical. But as far as my fight was concerned, I had the chance to defend myself, even win. Vanian and Bythan weren't given the option."

"No. No, they weren't," he murmured into Leia's hair, savoring her scent as he did. He could only thank whatever higher power looked after him Leia hadn't suffered the same fate. He kissed the top of her head. "I need to be alone with you. Soon."

She slanted him a sideways look out of her amazing dark eyes, a sultry grin lifted her perfect mouth. "Soon," she murmured and they followed the others from the bay.

Both Matt and Vanian supported Bythan as they stepped into the corridor.

Grettel motioned to a passing pirate and sent him scurrying toward the medical center. "We'd better tend your injuries before you settle in for that drink."

They were nearing the edge of the holding cells, almost to the medical center, when they saw Quinup. Two burly pirates held him with his arms cranked behind his back. His brow was bleeding and he looked angry enough to eat metal. His captors jerked him to a stop when they saw Grettel, giving way to their captain.

Quinup cursed at them, in English. The guard said something to him and Quinup snarled in response.

Jake couldn't help himself. He met the pirate's gaze and smiled.

"You want to try me, slave?" Quinup said, his voice low and gravelly.

"Love to. But Grettel wants you alive."

Quinup snarled. His gaze locked on Leia then, where she stood braced next to Jake. "You had something to do with this, didn't you? You and that bitch Moyra."

Jake risked a quick glance down at her. Her only response to Quinup's insult was a raised brow.

"You're gonna die for this, Ballore. My crew will buy me back. And when they do, I'm coming after you. You're a dead woman." His snarl turned to a leer. "But not too soon. I'm gonna enjoy watching you suffer before you die. See how long it takes you to break. You think you'll last longer than those two?" He flicked a nod at Vanian and Bythan.

Vanian took a step toward Quinup, stopped only because she still supported Bythan. She said something under her breath.

And Jake thought if Quinup had any brains at all, he'd realize he'd just issued himself a death sentence.

Quinup barely spared them a glance. His full fury rested on Leia.

"You have a death wish," Grettel said, chuckling into the tension. She shook her head and sighed. "Quinnie. Baby. You never were very smart. If I didn't need you alive, I'd be tempted to turn you over to them."

He spit at Grettel, missed her completely, but was jerked back by his two captors for his effort. "I'll be back for you, too, Grettel. We're not finished. I'm going to make you pay."

"Why do they always say that?" she asked the corridor in general, letting loose a gusty sigh. "You'd think three thousand years later, the bad guys would come up with something more original to say." She shook her head, turned her back on the rival pirate.

Jake raised his eyebrows, couldn't help but wonder if Grettel actually considered herself the "good guy". Probably better not to ask until he'd put half the galaxy between himself and Grettel.

He turned to follow her, had taken two steps when he heard a savage roar erupt behind them. He spun, taking in the scene in a spit second. Everything slowed and sharpened. Quinup freed from his captors. Two pirate guards crumpled on the floor.

The pirate's eyes were wide, anger pumping from him like sweat, a giant hunting knife clenched in one raised hand. He charged toward Leia, the closest one to him. All his attention, his fury centered on her.

She swung around to face his attack but was weaponless.

And Quinup was moving fast.

Jake absorbed the situation in a blink and acted without thought.

Quinup swung the knife down toward Leia.

Leia threw herself backward, away from the stroke.

Jake moved in, silent and fast. In that instant, when instinct and reflex took over, he wanted Quinup dead. He didn't think of consequences. He couldn't think of anything beyond keeping the madman away from Leia.

He plowed his fist into the center of Quinup's face and heard a sickening crunch. Jake's momentum lifted the pirate off his feet and sent him flying backward.

Quinup hit the floor hard. And didn't move.

The corridor echoed with silence. Quinup's face was a bloody mass. His arm twisted under him at an odd angle.

At the feel of a soft hand on his arm, Jake jerked. He looked down at Leia's upturned face. Her eyes were wide.

"Are you okay?" he asked, his voice gruff and hard.

"Yes." She touched the red leather vest Grettel had given her. "This thing's stronger than it looks. Your hand?"

He flexed his still clenched fist. "Better than his nose."

Bythan started to laugh, a bitter, almost hysterical sound in the otherwise quiet corridor.

"Well hell." Grettel stood with hands on hips, her gaze on Quinup's unmoving form. "Is he dead?"

A fallen pirate guard edged closer, felt for a pulse. He shook his head, spoke to Grettel in that language they'd been using on the bridge.

"Too close," Grettel muttered. "I warned him. Idiot."

Vanian stepped away from Bythan and Matt, stalked closer to Quinup. She stared at him for a moment, the weapon in her hand rested like a promise against her thigh.

"Vanian," Leia said quietly.

Vanian didn't look at Leia. But she raised her head, took a deep breath, and spit on Quinup's face. She turned her back on him and returned to Bythan and Matt without another glance.

"Take him to a cell and send Tevin to look after his face." Grettel shook her head. "Jake. That could have been a very expensive punch. If you'd put his nose into his brain, I'd be out a lot of money."

Jake said nothing. He met the pirate's gaze without emotion. He'd do it again. They both knew it. And if he had killed the man, he didn't have it in him to regret or care.

When Grettel raised her brows and hands, Jake finally said, "He threatened Leia."

"That he did. And I did warn him about doing that." She shrugged. "Well, I just need him alive. Never said I'd be sending him back pretty. Come on. I need that drink now."

Jake waited until the others had started down the corridor again. Then he pulled Leia close and kissed her. "He'll never get near you again," he murmured against her mouth.

She smiled. "I was never worried." She touched his cheek then ran her fingers over his lips. "I love you, Jake."

For the first time since hearing Quinup's roar, his body relaxed. He rested his head on top of hers and held her close, knowing he'd go to hell and back for the woman in his arms. His beloved Guard.

EPILOGUE

Leia launched up out of the blue salt water with a loud exhale. The ocean was glorious and cool, the perfect temperature on such a warm afternoon. The white sandy beach of the private islet sparkled in the sun. Overhead, the sky was clear and cloudless. Just inside the thick canopy of the jungle, she could glimpse the simple, open sided wooden hut that was their shelter. The huge bed and small kitchen that took up most of the shelter's space had seen a lot of use in the last week.

Smiling, she turned, easily treading water as she searched the gentle rolling whitecaps. He caught her from behind, startling a gasp from her that turned to a giggle when he wrapped his arms around her waist. "Jake, you're going to drown me."

"You swim like a fish. Hard to drown a fish." His lips were warm against her shoulder. "You look good wet."

Her heart hammered at the huskiness in his voice. Leia couldn't remember a more wonderful holiday, couldn't remember the last time she was this relaxed. She felt well loved and nearly delirious with pleasure.

She leaned back, dropping her head to one side so he could lick salt from her neck. "I thought we were supposed to be cooling off," she murmured.

"That was just an excuse to get you wet again."

"You didn't need water for that."

His hands flexed on her skin as he groaned. He turned her in his arms and captured her mouth. Their legs worked gently to keep them above the water as their lips and hands played. They let the current push them toward shore until Jake's feet touched the ground, then he lifted her and she wrapped her legs around his waist.

Since they had the islet to themselves, they hadn't bothered dressing for most of the week. So she was open and ready when he slid into her. She let her head drop back on her shoulders, savoring the feel of him, his heat a sharp contrast to the cool lick of the water. After a week of doing little more than eating, swimming and making love, she still wasn't tired of the feel of him inside her. They'd only been separated a month before this holiday, long enough to know she never wanted to be separated that long again.

She used the swell of the water, rising and lowering herself in long languid strokes. She watched his face, the heat in his blue eyes, the intensity, an equal desire to savor every stroke. She could look into his face forever.

The building pressure urged her to move faster, but he took her hips and slowed the rhythm again. His beat moved through her, edged her up steadily until her peak washed over her in an air-stealing flood of sensation. When she could breathe again, he held her close, his hands moving in a warm caress up and down her spine.

"You'd think we'd have worked that out of our system by now," she murmured against his neck.

"We have a month to make up for."

"You know, we've made love everywhere but on the actual beach. Think we should try that next?"

"Nah. Not as much fun as you might think."

"Oh?" She pulled back, her brow raised.

"So I've been told. Sand gets everywhere, they say. More painful than pleasant."

"Hmm… And you know this because *others* have told you?"

He chuckled. "Of course."

"I'm going to believe you only because I'm too tired and well satisfied to argue."

"Good. I aim to please." He kissed her then leaned back a little so he could study her face. "I haven't wanted to bring this up but… Are you sure?" he asked.

They were still joined and the intimacy made it impossible to hide from him, even if she'd wanted to. "About leaving Nas Command? Yes. That month was harder than I expected. I would have gone insane if I'd had to leave you with Grettel. And since you can't be on Nas with me if I stayed with Command, it would amount to the same thing. I don't want to go through what I went through this last month ever again."

"I don't either. I missed you more than I can say. But you've worked so hard to become a Nas Guard. I don't want you giving that up just for me."

"I'm giving it up for me. And I resigned with full honors, several special merits, a hefty financial bonus, and a very quiet slap on the wrist that won't even make it into my records."

He frowned. "For losing me and Matt."

"Well, I couldn't tell them I'd smuggled you onto Belax with a couple of Grettel's holo-imagers and the help of my family, could I? As far as they're concerned, you two were killed in the battle between Grettel and Quinup, along with Moyra. They looked at the historical records. History says you and Matt vanished under mysterious circumstances, then your bodies were discovered a week later. Patterson was convicted of arranging your deaths. So Command couldn't really complain about the fact that I'd lost you." She shook her head. "They didn't want to hear that Grettel was only taking men who were about to die. They'll continue to send recoveries home."

"Yeah, I thought they might. I wonder whose bodies Grettel used to pass for my and Matt's corpses?" He murmured the last sentence, then shook his head as if to dispel the morbid thought. He ran a hand through the wet strands of his hair, slicking it back against his skull.

"I'm sorry I couldn't say goodbye to my brother, but if I'd been bumped off, I wouldn't have had the chance at goodbyes either." He squeezed her, a quick rough hug. "At least this way, I got to go to heaven."

She laughed, leaned forward to kiss him. "That makes two of us."

"What did you tell Nas Command about Moyra?"

"The truth. She'd sold information, and Matt, Vanian and Bythan to Quinup. Vanian told me Moyra explained she was in love with the pirate, and she tried only to give him information that wouldn't hurt anyone. She handed over Matt and the others because she was angry with me for seducing you." She glanced down, studying the strong muscles of his chest rather than look him in the eyes.

"Don't you dare blame yourself for her actions." He lifted her chin.

She sighed and nodded. "I don't. Not for what she did to Vanian and Bythan and Matt. But I'm still sad she acted as she did because she thought I'd betrayed my oath. She helped us in the end, and it cost her her life. Because of that, her treason is being kept quiet. At least, her family won't live with the shame. The situation started an internal investigation, which can only be good for Command. They'll probably track down Grettel's insider soon enough."

"She won't thank you for that."

"She'll just find someone else to bribe. Do you think she won't?"

"You're right. But I'd like to avoid her for the next few years, just in case."

She grinned, wiggled closer so she could wrap her arms around his neck. He still looked so serious. "What's bothering you now?"

"This plan of yours."

"I thought you liked the idea." She straightened a little. "You won't be able to sit by and do nothing for the rest of your life. And you'd hate having to wear that holo-imager every time you left the Ballore estate. So would Matt. You're already investigators. We're just going to make a private business out of investigating. Legitimate mercenary work." She smiled at what she used to think of as an oxymoron. "Between the four of us, we'll be able to really help people."

"But I hate that you put all your hard-earned money into the business."

"We'll be making enough money to pay back my investment soon enough. Besides, it's not all my money. Some is Vanian's compensation for resigning from Nas command."

"Matt's not any happier about taking Vanian's money than I am about taking yours."

"He'll get over it. Just like you will. I'm sure Vanian is even now talking him out of his misgivings." She grinned and waggled her eyebrows.

Vanian had been both embarrassed and amazed at her feelings for Matt. At the going-away party Jolene threw, over a bottle of Nas wine, Vanian had admitted to Leia she never considered herself the type of woman to be attracted to Matt's sort. She asked if Leia considered her perverted.

Leia laughed, toasted the happy couple and told her she thought Matt was a very good choice. The new scars he had along his back and down his cheek went a long way toward improving his looks, too.

She was doubly glad of Matt's presence in Vanian's life now, as he helped her deal with her own new scars. Bythan was finding it harder. She took a leave of absence but intended to return to the Guard. She needed to work. At Jolene's urgings, Bythan had given in and quietly gone into counseling.

Leia studied Jake's still too-serious expression and pushed away worry for her friend to deal with his worries. "The business will be great. You'll see. And you and Matt bring a perspective to the business no one else will have."

He grimaced. "Yeah, a three-thousand-year-old perspective."

"We'll use that in our advertising." She chuckled. "We are all good at what we do. We'll make it work. And Ilio is just far enough away from the main trading routes no one is likely to think twice about you and Matt." She reached under the water to where his hands rested against her lower back and traced the leather on his wrists. "Especially since Grettel was feeling generous enough to give you and Matt these smaller bracelets."

The bracelets were two-centimeter thick straps of Kyzit leather carved with intricate designs and accented with the same blue stones that decorated Grettel's bracelets. They would be hard to confuse with the bracers since most people didn't know the stones worked the same way the zanathim metal worked. The new straps suited Jake, in Leia's opinion, and added to his primitive masculinity. And she was relieved to have him wearing bracelets that weren't damaged.

"Won't people realize what they are? Anyone who sees us often will notice Matt and I never take the things off."

She shrugged then lifted her arms to circle his neck again. "They might suspect. But very few will risk confronting you. You're too mean-looking."

"Mean-looking?" He raised a brow. "Is that what you think?"

"I think you're gorgeous," she said. "The most spectacularly handsome man I've ever met."

His smile was warm and sexy, sending a tingle of amazement through her. She still found it hard to believe, even now, even with their bodies joined beneath the water, that of all the women in the universe, Jake Marshall had chosen her. He loved her. The idea made her heart clench.

"You're pretty gorgeous yourself," he murmured, kissing her in that slow drugging way that left her lightheaded. "You're beautiful, sexy, talented, smart, brave, generous, loving, amazing. And after some serious persuasion, I hope to talk you into spending the rest of your life with me."

Her eyes widened. She leaned back to meet his gaze.

He grinned. "I even asked your father's permission. That's old-fashioned even for my time. He gave me his blessing, after checking with your mother first. So what do you say, Leia Ballore? Will you marry a man three thousand years older than you and make him the happiest human to ever live?"

"Second happiest," she murmured. "I think I have you beat there."

"That's a yes?"

"That's a yes."

"Good." He kissed her, long and slow and deep.

And Leia let herself float free on the warm currents of his love.

THANK YOU

Thank you for reading Marshall's Guard! I hope you enjoyed Leia and Jake's story.

If you're interested in more of my science fiction romance, please continue reading for an excerpt from Promise (The Naravan Chronicles 1).

EXCERPT: PROMISE

THE NARAVAN CHRONICLES 1

CHAPTER ONE

"Kira?"

"Hush," Kira hissed over her shoulder, never taking her eyes from the roadblock ahead. "Keep your heads about you," she told the four women in the back of the van. "They can't know if you don't give us away."

Kira studied the stiff navy uniforms of the Guards, her practiced eye hunting for the familiar face. He was there. She knew he would be there somewhere. This blockade had his mark.

Convulsively her hands clenched the rough steering wheel. By force of will, she relaxed both her grip and her shoulders. He wouldn't break her. Not now. And he wouldn't find her out.

They inched forward in the long line of vehicles, most the latest in synthesized transport—clean, efficient, small and cheap—toward the handful of Guards at the roadside. The day was bright with late autumn sun reflecting off the cars and the tarmac paving of the road, glittering in the rust sand that peeked between the long, low buildings edging this side of the city. Beyond the buildings, the land was covered with a mix of palms, succulent shrubs and sparse, patchy salt grass. At this southern edge, the faintest hint of sea scent wafted in the breeze.

This was the kind of day Kira loved as a child. Warm, but with a hint of winter to come. Days for playing in the backyard or running on the beach with her father. Now, she barely noted the sparse clouds scuttling across the azure sky or the late autumn flowers that still purpled the white salt grass. Her attention was focused entirely on the roadblock ahead, searching the Guards for that too-familiar face.

Seemingly at random, the Guard on the left signaled and sent vehicles off to a side area, near a hastily erected portable office, for closer inspection. Kira watched as the passengers exited their vehicles at a hand gesture from one Guard and stepped over to a second group of Guards who were obviously asking questions. Although she couldn't hear the interrogations, she'd been subjected to such "standard inquiries" before and knew exactly what was happening.

Kira felt her lip curl in a snarl. All very efficient. All very organized and outwardly by the book. She forced her mouth back to a straight, expressionless line.

Ten years ago, she wouldn't have been bothered by this scene. It was routine. The Guards were free to randomly inspect the citizens of Narava for contraband, drugs, illegal goods, interplanetary imports, immigrants trying to avoid taxes and fees, aliens. The Shifters.

No. Ten years ago, she wouldn't have been bothered. Because ten years ago there was so much she didn't know.

They reached the forward Guard, and Kira prepared for the inevitable questions. She didn't bother to smile or flirt. The Guard, a man in his late fifties, wore the familiar signet on his uniform. He already knew who she was.

"Farseaker," he greeted without inflection. His gaze traveled over her face, then into the back of the van, taking in the four other women.

"Officer Herot," Kira returned. She didn't know the man, not well, but she'd seen him before, dealt with him before.

"You know the drill, Farseaker. Contraband? Illegals?"

She couldn't help the cynical smile that answered his questions. He already knew her answers. "What do you think, Officer?"

"I think you've been skirting the law for too long now, Farseaker. He knows you're involved with them."

"If he had any proof that I was involved in something illegal," she said evenly, "he'd have had me locked away in a hole a very long time ago, Herot. And he would relish putting me there."

The Guard's thick dark brows drew together over a prominent nose. His thin lips pursed for an instant, then flattened. "Pull the van over to the side," he said, gesturing to the second set of Guards. "They'll have to be questioned further." He nodded to the four in the back. "And the van will be inspected."

"Of course." Kira didn't argue. She pulled the van to the side, hissing another silencing order as a nervous chatter started behind her. "Remember," she said under her breath, "they don't know anything. Can't know anything. Just keep your heads and we'll be all right."

"Kira?"

She looked over her shoulder at the sound of the timid voice. Vettine was only nineteen years old. Her cropped blonde hair and heart-shaped face gave her an ethereal beauty, but her deep jade eyes were wide with fear, making her appear every year of her youth. "You'll be okay," Kira assured her with a firm voice. "Don't panic on me now."

The girl took a long, shaky breath, straightened her shoulders and nodded.

"Good girl," Kira murmured as a Guard walked up to the passenger side of the van. This Guard was a man she'd never seen before. He was young, but not too young. Mid-thirties, she guessed at a glance. Handsome, but far from pretty. A faint scar along his right jaw and the first few wrinkles of his age saw to that. His short, brown hair held just a touch of wave. His black-coffee eyes were hard and efficient. But there was something…

Something in his eyes. Something familiar, that she couldn't name. Maybe it was an underlying quality of pain, or the hint of humanity she so rarely found in the Guard. Whatever it was, it was absent from the firm line of his mouth, the set of his jaw, the sharp movement of his arm as he gestured the four women behind her out of the van's side door. Whatever it was, he hid it well.

When Kira turned to open her door, he stopped her. "You're to wait in the car, ma'am."

And she almost smiled. He had a beautiful, husky voice. A voice she wouldn't mind hearing more. Her stomach twisted just a little, pleasantly reminding her that she was still a woman. Her gaze dropped to his chest, a rather nice, broad one she thought before noticing the signet above his left breast.

Her self-control snapped back into place.

She faced forward, watching through the front windshield of the van as a half-dozen fully armed soldiers led her four friends a short distance away. She tried to relax against the seat, tried to ignore the inconvenient tear in the imitation leather that poked her in the back. This could take hours if Ennoren saw fit to detain them.

The sound of the passenger door opening startled her. She turned to see the Guard settle himself onto the floorboard, shifting so that he wasn't visible above the dash. Kira cocked her head to one side, raising her eyebrows, and the man flashed the most charming smile she'd ever seen. The grin was just a touch guilty and would have made him seem like a mischievous boy if it hadn't stretched the scar and deepened the wrinkles around his eyes.

He plucked a pack of cigarettes from a pocket inside his uniform jacket and showed them to her.

"Not allowed to smoke on duty." He tapped one cigarette free, stuck it in his mouth, then returned the rest to his pocket and pulled out a small lighter. Before he lit up, he extended a hand. "David."

"Kira." She shook his hand, quick and firm, and pulled back before she had time to notice how nice his grip felt.

He lit the cigarette, took a long drag, then offered the end to her. She stared at the thing for a moment before helping herself to a puff. Through the cloud of tobacco-scented smoke she exhaled, she studied him. "You been with the Guard long?" she asked, handing the cigarette back.

"Twelve years now." He took another drag, never taking his gaze from her face.

"You're one of Ennoren's." She wasn't asking. She knew the signet on his uniform too well.

He nodded, his dark eyes still locked to hers. "For about three years."

She half-smiled, chuckled and shook her head. "Too bad, really." She turned to see how her friends were doing.

All four seemed to be holding up under the scrutiny of the men questioning them. Vettine's shoulders were straight, her posture unwavering. Grainne's stance was relaxed and cocky as she tossed her waist-length red hair over one shoulder. Breeanne had her arms crossed over her chest, her legs braced slightly apart. Her pale skin was flushed, but her expression controlled. And Jo, with her stylishly braided black hair brushing her shoulders in the breeze, had her hands on her hips, a slight smile on her full mouth and a sexy glint in her violet eyes. Kira couldn't help smiling. Her second would flirt with the Devil himself if she were standing at the gates of Hell.

"Why too bad?"

The husky voice brought her attention back to the man sitting on the floorboard of her van. He offered her the cigarette again, and she took a long drag before answering. "I would have liked to get to know you. Under better circumstances. I think I could have liked you," she answered without guile, a slight, sad smile tugging at her mouth.

"'Could have'?"

She shrugged. "You're one of Ennoren's men." She faced forward again because there was really no need for further explanation.

"You're jumping to conclusions. Judging me based on the commander I work under. You don't know me."

Kira snorted and met his gaze. "It doesn't matter whether I know you or not. You work for Ennoren."

A movement to her left caught her attention, and she turned away from David's narrowed eyes. She reached down for the cigarette without taking her eyes off the man walking toward the van. When she'd taken another drag, she said, "Your boss is on his way over. Better let me finish this."

David slid out of the van, unhooked a thin, foot-long cylindrical device from his belt and began running it over the interior of the van without another word. Her gaze flicked to the device, then back to the approaching commander. The steady beep of the detector echoed in Kira's pulse as she watched Ennoren step up to her open window.

He was tall and thin, with a face Kira had once found interesting, if not attractive. All lines and angles, sharp nose, hard mouth, heavy-lidded blue eyes; his face was imposing, commanding and often intimidating. But Kira had long since stopped being intimidated by Ennoren.

He looked at the cigarette in her hand, then into her eyes. "I thought you didn't smoke."

She set the cigarette against her lips, inhaled deeply and blew smoke in his face. "I don't."

He waved the smoke away, a sneer forming in place of a smile. For a long moment he studied her, his gaze running over her faded, ripped jeans and cotton flannel shirt. Then he turned to study her van, point-edly staring at the cracked dash, battered steering wheel and worn imitation leather upholstery. "New van?"

Kira nodded.

"I didn't think you'd be into this late twentieth-century Earth fad." He frowned. "But then, you always were a fashionable socialite, weren't you? And since you have the money to afford this mock-up of an Earth car…" He let the sentence trail off as he held her gaze. "You're looking good, Kira."

She returned his stare, taking another pull on the cigarette so she didn't have to answer.

When she remained silent, Ennoren shifted his attention to David. "Find anything, Officer Cario?"

David snapped to attention. "No, sir. Appears clean."

"Well," Ennoren said, turning a contemptuous glare on Kira, "appearances can lie."

"Was that a dig, Eain?" Kira kept her tone mild, even as she used his first name in front of another Guard—something she did only to annoy him. His mother had been a poet and fond of alliteration. Ennoren went out of his way to keep his full name, Eain Edward Evander Ennoren, from his subordinates.

He covered his indignation well, but the slight narrowing of his eyes and the flare of his nostrils gave him away. "Take from it what you will." He paused, studying her again. When he spoke, his voice was low. "The ring will collapse out from under you, Kira. It won't be long now. Do you know what will happen to you when you're found guilty of treason and conspiracy to commit treason against the planetary government?"

"They'll throw me into a hole?"

"They'll throw you into space without a suit," he hissed. Dropping his voice again, he leaned into the car, putting his face only inches from hers. "End this now, Kira. End it. Tell me where they hide. I'll make sure you get off with a light sentence." A slight smile curled his lips. "I might even arrange to serve as your paroler. Just like old times, eh?"

Kira turned her head to take one final puff off the cigarette, giving herself time to gain control over both her revulsion and her anger, before confronting his leer. "There's a reason those times are old, Eain. I wouldn't have gone to all the trouble of divorcing you if I'd wanted to end up right back under your thumb. Besides—" she half-smiled, half-snarled at him, "—how would I know where they hide?"

She watched with satisfaction as his leer transformed into a lip-trembling scowl. Flicking the cigarette past his shoulder, she turned back to David. He was standing at attention, a silent, emotionless witness to the scene. "Forgive my ex. He seems to think I'm some sort of underground anti-government terrorist leader."

David raised an eyebrow. "Are you?"

She smiled. Then she laughed.

The side door to the van opened and her friends climbed up to the padded bench along the side of the van. Kira kept her gaze on David, enjoying the twinkle of amusement in his eyes that didn't filter into any other part of his expression. When the side door slammed into place, she leaned across the passenger seat and pulled that door shut.

"It really is too bad we didn't meet under different circumstances, officer," she said when David leaned into the open window.

His crooked grin made his scar jump. His knowing stare set her pulse dancing. She chuckled and moved back behind the wheel. Without another glance at her ex-husband, she put the van into gear and returned to the line of traffic hurrying away from the blockade.

David watched her go, feeling like he'd been kicked in the gut and strangely liking the sensation. Kira was interesting. Beautiful, yes. Enough so that his pulse sped just remembering her golden brown eyes and the sound of her sultry chuckle. But there was something else about her, under that smile and sharp attitude, that he wanted to get to know better. Something that was almost familiar.

He couldn't remember the last time a woman had caught his attention, or his lust, this way. He wasn't even sure if another woman had before, and that was pretty damned terrifying. But anyone who could make Commander Ennoren lose control was worth getting to know. Whether she scared David or not, Ennoren's ex-wife could prove to be quite valuable.

His heart stopped for a single beat when the commander cleared his throat from right beside him. Out of the corner of his eye, David saw Ennoren staring after the rapidly retreating van too.

"Don't let her pretty face fool you, Officer Cario," Ennoren said, his voice low, almost a whisper. "She's not as sweet as she appears. A viper lives beneath that silky skin."

Knowing it best to keep his opinions to himself, David studied his commander's profile. His nostrils flared, but other than that, his sharp features were now composed and emotionless. Before David could look away, Ennoren turned, catching and holding his gaze.

"You don't believe me?"

"I have no opinion on the matter, Commander."

Ennoren smiled. "Yes, you do."

He cocked his head to one side, watching David with a sharp, perceptive gaze. The stare was disconcerting, but David had hidden from it before.

"Doesn't matter," the commander finally said. "Because I think I can use this situation to our benefit." He turned toward the temporary command post. "In my office, Cario," Ennoren ordered. "We've got a few things to discuss."

Kira pulled past the front of her house and into a narrow lane at the edge of her property. The paved road was flanked by thick stone walls covered in ivy and overhung by rows of dense, leafy trees. The entrance was so overgrown by foliage, it was almost impossible to see unless you knew where to look. The driveway led to the family garage, and only Kira used it now. Visitors used the front drive. Friends had other ways to get in.

As a child, she'd thought the lane, with its cover and solitude, a silly addition to the estate. But her father had liked his privacy, coveting it more and more as the years went by. She hadn't understood that need. Why should people want to hide behind walls? But then, she'd been an open and curious child who'd grown into a guileless adult.

Until her father's death.

She stopped the van halfway up the drive, puffing out a breath. She didn't have time to dwell on all the changes in her life. There was still too much to do. She opened her door and followed the others to stand a few paces in front of the van.

The transformation never ceased to amaze Kira. One moment, a perfectly ordinary van sat in the lane. The next, a beautiful, iridescent, hairless creature stood staring at them. Its huge, multifaceted eyes whirled through purple to blue to green as it tilted its otherwise featureless head to one side. The long lines of neck and limbs made the creature appear taller and far thinner than it actually was, but since it could shift to most any shape, its body dimensions were relative.

"That was close."

Kira smiled at its whispery voice floating through her mind. No matter their emotional state, the Shifters' voices always sounded quiet to her. *"Not as close as that, Xep. He never suspected."*

A human-like mouth formed in the iridescent gold skin of Xep's face. The mouth turned up in a mocking smile. Though they did have a form of external hearing, Shifters had no natural mouths or vocal cords. They could only speak using telepathy when in their natural state. And only a very few humans could hear and speak back in the same manner. But Xep was fond of shifting just enough to convey all too human facial expressions.

"He suspects, Kira," the Shifter said as the mouth melted away.

"But he doesn't suspect this. He doesn't have a clue Shifters like you exist."

Jo reached behind a thick clump of ivy and tapped a code into a hidden panel, opening a disguised passage in the stone wall leading to the interior of Kira's estate. The group ducked through the overhanging ivy and the door closed silently behind them. They walked over short, spongy green grass to a second secret hatch in the ground. This time, using her foot, Vettine tapped out the code that opened the door. After a short pause, a section of grass slid over with a hiss of escaping air. All six dropped down the ladder into a steel-lined tunnel, and Kira punched in the code at a command panel to seal the hatch again.

They turned and walked down the tunnel, lights overhead flicking on as they approached, flicking off once they passed.

"Kira." Xep's quiet voice touched her mind. *"It will not be long before he discovers. Ennoren is a smart man. A cunning human. And he is vicious."*

She nodded, silently considering Xep's words. She knew Ennoren was vicious, had seen it firsthand. Had run away from it in disgust and anger. And she knew he was clever. But she was clever, too.

"We're almost ready, Xep. We can hide from him until then." She glanced at the Shifter walking beside her, hoping to catch some sign of emotion in a face she couldn't read unless it allowed her. *"This won't be easy."*

"Nothing has been easy since the humans first came here."

Though no emotion came across in its mind-speak, Kira imagined the bitterness associated with that statement, and it made her heart hurt. She closed off her emotional response forcefully and turned her attention to the tunnel. She couldn't change what had been done to the Shifters in the past, and she couldn't save all of them now. But she could sure as hell try to save some of them.

"He seemed very nice."

Xep's quick subject change caught Kira so by surprise, she stopped for an instant. The odd looks the other women gave her started her moving again with an embarrassed grimace.

"Ennoren?" she asked.

"Officer David Cario. He seemed very nice."

The mention of the handsome officer's name brought with it an image of coffee-colored eyes, thick, dark hair and a dancing scar. Her stomach clenched and a tingle spread over her thighs at the memory of his smile. It had been much too long since she'd last been with a man, she thought ruefully.

"He's one of Ennoren's," she told Xep, forcing her mind-speak to sound stern. *"It doesn't matter if he's the nicest man on Narava."*

"He was quite taken with you. And you with him."

"And you're an expert on the subject, are you, Xep?" Her irritation leaked through with the comment. *"How would you know, anyway?"*

She glanced at the Shifter. The mouth that had formed in its face was grinning. She snorted and turned away, hoping Xep hadn't seen her blush.

"Stuff it," she muttered aloud at it. If she hadn't known better, she would have sworn the Shifter laughed.

Look for Promise (The Naravan Chronicles 1) out now!

BOOKS BY ISABO KELLY

THE NARAVAN CHRONICLES

Promise

Interface

Secret

Paradise

Flight

NEW YORK EMPIRES ANTHOLOGIES

Going All In

Icing The Puck

FIRE AND TEARS SERIES

Brightarrow Burning

Darkness Singed

Dawn Ignited

FATE'S HAND SERIES

Thief's Desire

Destiny's Seduction

Kellyn's Sacrifice

The Last Guardian

Bonfire Night

ABOUT THE AUTHOR

Isabo Kelly is the award-winning author of numerous science fiction, fantasy, and paranormal romances. She also writes best-selling paranormal romance under the name Kat Simons. Her life has taken her from Las Vegas to Hawaii, where she got her BA in Zoology, back to Vegas where she looked after sharks, then on to Germany and Ireland where she got her Ph.D. in Animal Behavior. Now Isabo focuses on writing. She lives in New York with her Irish husband and two beautiful boys, working as a full time writer and stay-at-home mom.

Don't miss out on new releases from Isabo! Sign up for her Newsletter here: http://eepurl.com/caxHa9

For more on Isabo and her books:
Website: http://www.isabokelly.com
Twitter: https://www.twitter.com/IsaboKelly